To Thine Own Self

Book Four
of the Souls of
the Saintlands

Tonya Adolfson

Published by Fantastic Journeys Publishing,
Boise, Idaho
PUBLISHING HISTORY
E-Book released through Kindle
Soft Cover trial edition June 2014
Mass market edition/ XXXXXX

Cover art: Photo of fabric by John Farmer
Created in Gimp 2.6 by John Farmer
Cover Art copyright by Fantastic Journeys Publishing
Interior Art by Suzette Snyder
Edited by Brady Sparks and Julia Stidolph
Content copyright ©Nov 2013 Tonya Adolfson.

Published in the United States of America.

ISBN: 978-1-941276-90-7

The characters and events portrayed in this book are fictitious. Any similarity to real persons, living or dead, common or deific, is coincidental and not intended by the author, unless, of course, I know them.
No Augustinians were harmed in the making of this book, though a few folks were roughed up a bit.

Reviews for the Souls of the Saintlands Series

Thine Enemy's Eyes

"I loved it I stayed up late several nights because I had to know what happened! It's a great read with excellent pacing and such entertaining and rich characters. I loved the rich world she created and the details used to make it stand out. I cannot wait to read the second book to learn more about the characters and places mentioned! I highly suggest this book."
Maryanne Durant, Amazon Review

"I cannot wait for the next book, and hopefully, subsequent books to follow."
Steve Nunez, Dragonfleet Studios

"Tonya Adolfson's debut novel is incredible! Full of intrigue, wildly imaginative characters and set in a medieval fantasy world of such authenticity it blew me away. I would heartily recommend this to anyone, and can't wait until the second novel comes out!"
I. J. Smethurst, author of the *E.D.F Chronicles*

"The plot has interesting twists and turns to keep you going straight through the book. When it ends, it leaves you wanting more."
Shelley Wolf, Amazon Review

"…good political intrigue… good action scenes… Not to mention one of the heaviest cliff hangers I've seen in a while."
The William Jones Review

An Unpolished Gem

"In a perfect follow through to Thine Enemy's Eyes, Ms. Adolfson continues to illustrate just how sticky the politics and personalities of her world really can be. She never lets go of you, even after the book is done. Just when I think I have a character figured out, they surprise me; I can't even tell how many sides to this story there are. I can't wait for book three!"
Julien McBain, author *Ghosts of the Past*

"It is difficult for second books in a series to have the same weight as the first. This is the rarer case of the second book surpassing the first."
Christopher Garcia, editor of *the Drink Tank*

"This book is just as captivating as the first book in the series. Again I was so enthralled with the characters, plot twists, and story line that I literally couldn't put it down and finished reading it in one day..."
Chalyse Padigimus, Amazon Review

"I love her writing style. She creates this world that becomes real to its readers. Oh and then there are these great characters with such richness and depth you cannot help but to love and in some cases hate them! She has written it in such a way you have no idea where or who, if anyone, the main character will end up with. There is such a depth in the story you just cannot put it down. I read it in a matter of hours. I know these are books I am going to read again and again throughout the years. It has to be a great book for it to have that kind of status on my bookshelf."
Maryanne Durant, Amazon Review

"Love the way the characters grow and mature. Can't wait for the next book!"
Shelley Wolf, Amazon Review

An Open Enemy

"I have flown through these books. I totally love the tangled story with so many twists ans turns. These are written by someone who knows how to keep their audience captive and I cannot wait for the 4th book!!! I have been dying to know what happens! This is definitely and awesome read every true fantasy buff should have on their shelf."
Maryanne Durant, Amazon Review

Also by Tonya Adolfson

The Souls of the Saintlands Series
Thine Enemy's Eyes
An Unpolished Gem
An Open Enemy
To Thine Own Self
Full of Sound and Fury*

Other Books
Surviving Your Own Creativity
Filling Up on 500 (With Todd Adolfson)

*Coming 2015

For John, who has been my partner, my rock, my
whip-cracker and my mule. This endeavor would
never have happened without his belief in me.
Words exist on these pages because he wanted to
read them,
I love you, man.

Acknowledgments:

First and foremost, I'd like to thank all the people who were inspirations for this book:

Gwen for Gwen, John for Raven and Giovanni, Dartanian for Alexander, Jeff for James, Misha for Emmy, Morgan for Alan, Rod for Xeno, Shanna for Fierah, Stephanie for Belladonna, Jennifer for Ce'Nedra, Daddy for Thessius, Kim for Ysabel, Joe for Nicaise, Jenn for Flora, Aggie for Aggie, David for Henri and all the hundreds of friends and family that have been contributors to this book. Your work has been amazing and your lives inspiring.

A very special thanks to Brady Sparks and Julia Proulx Stidolph, the best editors a gal could have!

The Wisdom of Stone was written during the peaceful time after the Soulless War. With so much destruction in such recent memory, the Dûcesa Serene, who ruled after the war, felt it was important to record all she had learned from the Land. Guided by her Stâpân, Raven Grasshair, she put to paper the tales and sayings of her people. This is her legacy.

Book One

Though you may be false to others, in
all things be true to yourself.
-The Wisdom of Stone

People who try hard to do the right
thing always seem mad.
-Stephen King

One

The wearer knows best where the shoe pinches.
-The Wisdom of Stone

"I want it to burn. No survivors."

Entivia Malatesta, known to the underground as "Boots", turned her back upon the flames consuming the pirate haven of Portabella. The bay was treacherous, sunken ships just under the surface designed to destroy hulls and trap vessels. The guns of the city could volley chain shot the width of the lagoon, stopping anything that penetrated the hidden cove. Surrounding the rest of it was a five hundred foot high cliff with stairs cut into it that could be defended by an old woman with a broom and a small dog, yet was within range of any of the guns. It was upon this cliff that Entivia looked upon the devastation she had wrought.

They never even saw it coming.

Portabella had been prepared for assault by land and sea, by ship and army, but had not been ready for a single woman slipping between shadows. She had run through anyone she met when doing her work, then used the amulet at her neck to drop her fire everywhere, but only from this vantage could one truly see every execution of her will. The ships hulls were sabotaged, as were the doors on every building. People were trapped, regardless of age or gender, in the fiery judgment of her employer's client.

She waited until she could no longer hear the peoples' screams barely climbing up the stone wall, and she couldn't hear the flames at all. This place truly was protected. She wondered if a Dirt Worshipper had convinced the cliff face to keep the sound from the world. She had heard stories that this was possible. At this point, though, it didn't matter. The deed was done.

She looked at the woodlands before her. Myrgen de Sablonierres had gone that way. She hoped he carried her salvation along with him.

Well, well. What have we here?

Dominic D'Medici picked up the amulet from the catacomb floor. Dim light filtered through his shadow from the torches flickering in the hands of the guards puttering around, looking for intruders in the labyrinth under the Patrasian royal palace. The shimmering amulet had called to his accountant's nature as well as his Mandian heritage being glittering gold. He glanced around the encroaching darkness, looking for movement, and then brought the amulet into his room. The stone door slid silently closed behind him, leaving the guards to find another way out.

In the firelight of his desk candles, the symbols raised even more beautifully from the surface. The gold was Mandian, from near the capital city of Vincenzia. The Fingers of Mande went their deepest here, a geological buffer against raiders from the sea. It was the best defended and also had the luxury of a strong vein of gold ore running nearly the width of the country. According to legend, a great quake thrust mountainous cliffs skyward, cutting off the country of Caratia from Mande hundreds of years ago. The result brought the vein to the surface and gold aplenty to the kingdom.

He turned the amulet over in his hand, and then brought the metal to his tongue. The ancient metal from the Risen Vein had a particular flavor to the trained palate, based upon the surrounding water and soil from which it was smelt. The method of casting also varied from city to city, each making its unique mark upon the gold, giving it a dialect, a telltale accent. The goldsmiths took a pride akin to arrogance in their casting. It would have been easy for him to identify the maker's mark.

Had the maker marked it.

The flavor claimed it as foreign, but the color was clearly Mandian. He knew his gold, regardless of the origin country. He learned the trade while in the company of his family in Florentine but had it put to work in the halls of the Tanglwyst Trading Company. Dominic's chief job as Chancellor for the company was finding the most economical route for trading the money. It honed his skills to a supernatural sense. He believed he could find gold under water.

A knock at the door called him from his investigations and the Grand Guard, Gomez de Santander, called to him from the hall.

"Your Lordship, are you in there?"

Dominic didn't get up. "Yes, Gomez. What do you want?"

"A large group of guards seem to be missing. Someone said you requested them?"

Dominic looked back at the amulet. "Haven't seen them."

He heard someone run down the hall and talk low to Gomez, but by the time they were walking away, Dominic was back in the gold amulet. The markings on the face were odd, but… *familiar*. He had seen them before. He turned to the book shelf near his desk and grabbed a tome on goldsmithing.

"If this doesn't have it, then what I'm holding doesn't exist." His voice echoed in the empty room and he looked around.

I've got to stop doing that.

Duncan walked to the Records Hall where Henri had gone and entered the small building. Piles of parchment bound into books lined the walls on shelves and there were ink stains on every horizontal surface. Not that they were dirty or cluttered, but simply well used. Ce'Nedra had obviously been there because he recognized her dining basket on the table behind which Henri was sitting.

Duncan cleared his throat when Henri didn't acknowledge him after a few seconds. When the official still didn't look up, Duncan stepped over and put his hands on the table. Henri started upon the sight and dropped his pen, splashing dots of ink across the parchment. He pulled wool from his ears and stood up.

"Hello. Sorry. Didn't, well," he held up the wool, "hear you come in." Henri squinted at the bald sailor almost a head taller. "You were with the king earlier."

Duncan nodded.

Henri glanced past Duncan to the door. "I thought he left. Was there a delay?"

Duncan shook his head and leaned forward. "No, he's gone, but he left me here to handle some unfinished business." Duncan straightened up and pulled a chair from another table.

"You mean the mill."

Duncan nodded, "Among other things. As you saw, Heaven had given His Majesty a great gift to help his people, but he was disturbed to find so many injuries attributed to them."

Henri nodded. "I was just recording the number of incidents recently." He gestured to the slightly spotted report the official was working on. The report had about eight names on it and the injury suffered. "This is for the Spring so far."

Duncan looked at Henri. "The *Spring?* But we just entered Spring less than two months ago."

Henri nodded. "That sounds about right." He gestured to the report. "These are the major injuries. Crushed limbs, removed fingers or toes, that sort of thing. Minor ones aren't even reported these days."

"What constitutes a minor injury?"

Henri removed his spectacles and rubbed the ink off the lenses. "Anything the person can walk away from."

Duncan looked at the small man, barely understanding this information. On a ship, injuries were frequent, especially amongst the men new to the profession. Once the sailing season started and folks got their feet under them, the biggest threat to a crew's health was the food and shore leave. "Why?"

Henri focused upon his glasses, like he was thinking before speaking. "Well, that's a tricky question to answer."

"Someone said it was because the miller is an evil person."

Henri kept cleaning, glancing up at Duncan. "What was their evidence?"

"She has a lovely garden."

6

Henri arched an eyebrow. "I hope that didn't convince him."

Duncan shook his head.

"Good. No, the miller isn't a bad person. She just understands what they do is a staple of the community. Although she tries to minimize what happens, and does, I think there's more to it than that."

"So, the miller is a woman?"

"Widow. Lost her husband a year ago to the mill. I swear some people forget that around here."

"And you think it isn't an evil miller?"

Henri put his glasses up to the light to check them before putting them back on. "More like an evil mill."

Henri turned back to the shelves and pulled a book about two inches thick down. "This was from last year. It's divided into quarters." He set the book on the table and slid it to Duncan.

"Are these all injuries?"

Henri nodded. "The ones that aren't deaths." He pointed. "Those are about half of the pages. Flour mills are not entirely safe places to begin with. To be honest, I had thought nothing of the situation until His Majesty asked for the injury records. I always thought it was just normal."

"No. I used to live next to a flour mill in Patras. There are more injuries here than in the capital city." Duncan opened the book. "How does she keep getting employees?"

"It's employment, steady work. In truth, the number of injuries is down quite a bit this Spring since she changed his methods. Usually by now, we'd have at least four deaths on our hands."

Duncan read some of the incidents, then closed the book after his mind starting drawing all-too-vivid pictures of them. "I think it's time I got a look at this mill."

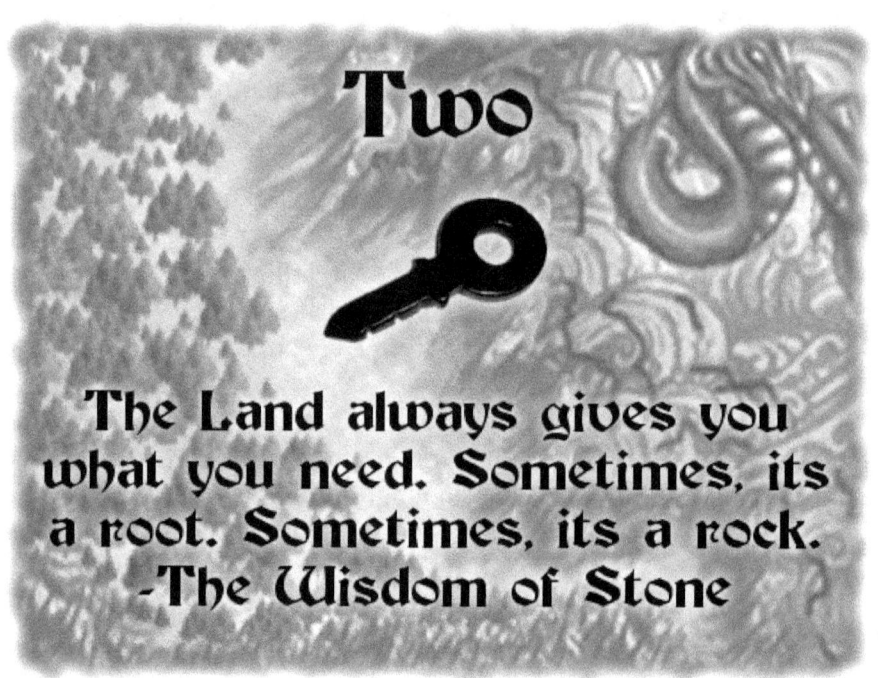

Two

The Land always gives you what you need. Sometimes, its a root. Sometimes, its a rock.
-The Wisdom of Stone

Myrgen stopped to get his bearings and sat on the stump of a tree long since cut down for wood. Given the distance from Portabella, it was possible that this tree was felled to serve them, but it seemed unlikely upon reflection. A thick, impassible forest served their needs and the hulls of the ships sunk were pretty thoroughly scavenged for wood. He had seen many planks from different vessels on the buildings in town as he passed them by. He thought nothing of it at the time, but now, the visual returned to him. Had he not been in a hurry to not be associated with the Enigma's arrival and departure, he could have stayed. It would have suited him just fine.

He could almost smell a fire somewhere in the distance, probably a woodcutter's house that took care of the nearby legitimate town. He thought the next town to the north would be St. Marguerite.

Hm. Yeah, that won't do. I guess I need to move inland.

He let the sound of the forest rustle through his soul, clearing out the dust and sea salt that had crystallized on the ship. He was more fit now than he had been in years and hoped that he would maintain it. He would certainly be able to keep his legs toned. He may end up walking all the way to the Papal City this summer. With any luck, his grandfather would be able to offer him sanctuary. It was hundreds of miles north of here, at the place where Mervolingia met Toledo... and Caratia.

He exhaled, looking down at the satchel on his hip. There would be plenty of time to think about Catriona on this trip. He'd left her side on purpose, to give her the chance to make her own decisions regarding her future without him there to make a mess of things. Alexander lied to her, brought dark forces into her world, and fired upon her ship in a jealous rage, not to mention defied her protection of Myrgen with an attempted execution. If she still felt like she needed to marry Alexander after that, she deserved what she got.

He closed his eyes against the thin line of tears that threatened him. He was hurt and lashing out at her was normal. He entertained the fantasy of her weeping uncontrollably in her chambers, or sleeping in his bed to find some comfort, but in the end, they felt like stupid, empty revenge fantasies. She would never allow herself to be seen as vulnerable to her crew. The most he could hope for is a sigh from her lips before deciding to go to sleep.

He sighed, and opened his eyes, the watery veil not really hiding the sword point the woman had leveled at his chest.

"Myrgen de Sablonierres. We meet at last."

He blinked, the tears evaporating in the presence of adrenaline. "Hello. To whom do I owe the pleasure?"

"The King of Mande, Anibal Cipriano Malatesta. He requested you personally."

Something in her voice said she was lying about that and he tilted his head slightly, narrowing his eyes to try and see why he thought that. "I wasn't aware His Majesty even knew my name."

"You have a sizable bounty on your head. He likes money. It would serve both countries for him to deliver you."

"I see." He stood, moving the sword tip with the back of his gloved hand. "Then you aren't going to kill me. I'm worth far more alive than dead."

"True." She slashed his arm, deftly tearing the last surviving shirt he owned. "But I don't have to bring you back unharmed."

He dropped to the ground and kicked her hand, sending the sword flying across the clearing. Her arrogance at getting the drop on him left her open to attack and he kicked a second time, aiming for her ribs. She dodged, throwing a kick his way before running for her sword. The foliage was thick where it landed and he knew he'd have a second or two while she searched for it. He sprinted into the trees.

Portabella was barely a half mile back. There was a steep cliff with narrow stairs. Not the best place to fight but at least there, they would be on equal footing. Her sword wouldn't help her in that place. He looked back to see her bent over a bush, grabbing her sword, then he was running out of sight. A half mile was a long ways but he could hear her following him. He jogged back and forth through the trees, hoping she didn't have a pistol. He couldn't remember seeing one.

He slowed once, listening. He could hear something, but it didn't sound like pursuit. He continued towards the pirate town, hoping to get there first. It occurred to him that she probably knew about the place but she was behind him. Her knowing about Portabella would not change anything about his plan. He saw a break in the trees and stopped, the smoke clotting his lungs as much as the air.

He stepped out and saw the black cloud just as he felt it burn his already labored chest. His coughs joined the symphony of gull cries in the air and on the edge of the cliff. As he walked to the edge, he saw the benefit and bane of the protected bay. Wind didn't really blow through there, which hid the smoke from the surrounding forest and the cliff stopped the sounds of people burning to death from ever being heard. No one could have helped them because no one could have known there was a problem.

He wondered if people had tried to flee up the cliff and went to the edge, nosing aside the vulture-like gulls waiting for the flames to cease. There were no survivors waiting there struggling to climb. He looked to see if any had fallen and saw two bodies directly below him on the ground, a green gown dumped on top of a white shirt and the red-brown of congealed blood.

Belladonna...

He fell to a knee, then sat back, the bounty hunter forgotten in the shock of the destruction. When she emerged behind him, he knew.

"You did this."

Her heard her stop and turned to face her.

"Yes." She gestured to the town with her sword. "This place has been a blight on the world for years. Pirates preying upon lost or desperate souls. Fugitives, like yourself and that man under the woman, hiding from their fates. I was ordered to destroy it." She looked at Myrgen. "This order was not an unpleasant one."

He wanted to rage against her, to scream at the injustice of it, but he stopped himself. He was too close to the edge of the cliff. He may not be wanted dead, but if he fell to it in a struggle, what happened afterwards wouldn't matter. At least not to him. He coughed, covering his mouth with the back of his hand. With the other, he leaned on the ground, balancing himself.

He felt the earth beneath his hand shift and he knew this place was once a holy sanctuary of the Land. The stairs in the cliff face, the protection of the stone, even the traps under the water were the acts of a Land Worshiper. Someone called upon their deity to protect them, and this was the result. He could feel the presence of stone beneath the grass at his fingers. Some scraps were pulled up, dragging towards the edge and he saw a piece of white stone exposed there.

He moved to stand, covering the white with his stabilizing hand, and found what he had found in the darkness tendays before; a rock. He grabbed it and pulled. The earth erupted, coughing grass and dirt at the woman with her sword drawn. She turned away, protecting her eyes as he swung the rock at her. The White Stone Sword struck her sword as she parried at the last second, the contact drawing sparks from the steel.

Her eyes went as wide as his at the sudden appearance of the weapon but she recovered first. She slashed at him, driving him back to the cliff's edge. He held the White Stone before him, countering her attacks, almost forgetting his training for the last few tendays on repelling boarders. Almost. He realized he needed to get the advantage and drew her in. Her blade slashed and he dodged, the White Stone hitting her broadside, forcing her to step to the edge. He shoved his shoulder into her pushing her over, but he lost his balance and they both were lost.

He twisted, grabbing for the edge as she fell away from him. His hand tried for anything that could save him and instinct made him stab downward with the Sword. Sparks lit the rock as it drove in, stopping him. He dangled for a moment, then felt the wall for any kind of hand hold. The top was only a dozen feet away, but it could have been a mile. A small crack rose from the Sword like smoke and he pushed a bit harder to see if that would seat it better.

The crack grew, rock falling away, creating a handhold. He used his other hand to grip in and then tried freeing the sword. It came away as if out of a sheath instead of stone, which almost caused him to lose his balance and fall to his death anyway. He stabbed the rock higher up, then used it to help him climb up the face. When he reached the top, embedding the white stone in the grass from whence it came, he pulled himself up and almost decided to let go again.

The woman was crouching there, sword sheathed. Her eyes were swirling black, like ink in water. A gold amulet hung around her neck and there was a faint scent of rotting eggs. She reached out her hand to him.

"Now, shall you come with me, or are we going to do this again?"

Myrgen exhaled and drew himself onto the grass.

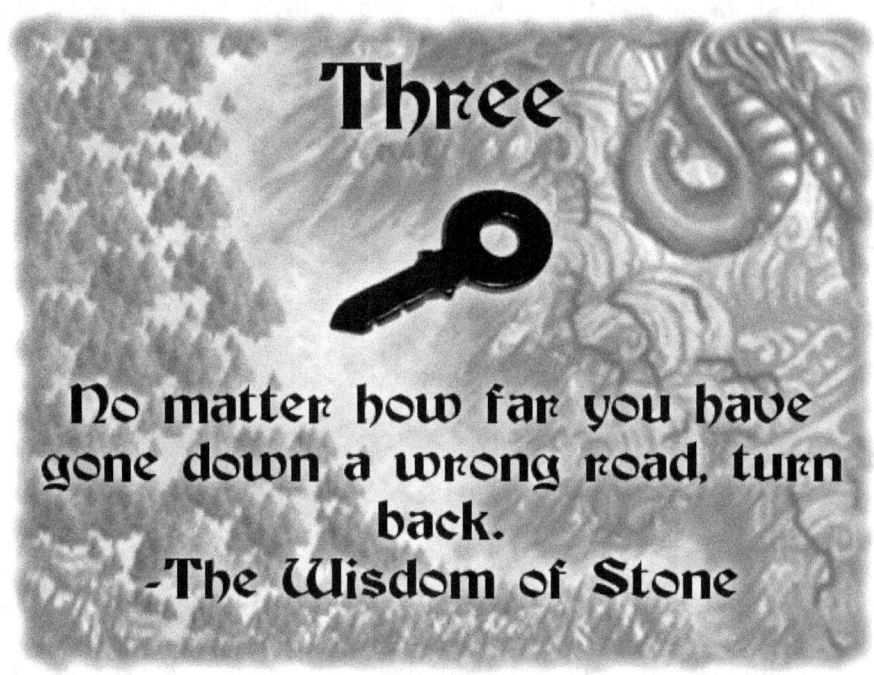

Three

No matter how far you have gone down a wrong road, turn back.
-The Wisdom of Stone

Duncan entered the St. Andrew flour mill and looked around. It was a typical mill. A water wheel took advantage of the small stream winding its way to the ocean and the millstone area was open with good ventilation. He could see that the windows had shutters for guarding against the weather on the Meal and Sack floors where the finished flour was gathered from the Stone floor and bagged or stored. He looked at Henri, who nodded to a woman motioning to a burley young man. The two walked over to her.

She was a blond woman with grey-blue eyes and an easy smile. Her clothes were rugged, canvas and buttons, leaving nothing dangling that could catch in the machinery of the mill. Her hair was fetched into a cap he had seen a lot in the working class women, designed to contain the hair while probably also stopping sweat from falling into their work. She turned to Henri as he approached and curtsied.

"Henri, what brings you by? You don't show up for flour."

Henri bowed in response and gestured to Duncan. "This is Duncan McVryce, in from Patras. Duncan, Kaelandra Durant, mill owner."

Her eyes widened. "The King's man?"

Duncan bowed. "Have we met?"

She shook her head. "No, but it's a small town. News travels." She wiped her hands upon her apron. "I wasn't able to get to see his miracles. I had things to attend to up here."

Henri folded his hands across his stomach. "That's actually why we're here, Kaelandra. His Majesty saw the injuries from the mill workers and wanted to see if he could help."

She nodded, sighing. "It's been a terrible couple years. We were just fine, minimal injuries for over a decade. Then suddenly, it was something practically every month. If we weren't so vital to the town, we'd probably have been run out."

Duncan leaned in. "What's happened?"

She gestured to the stairs taking them to the Stone Floor. "A few years back, there was an accident. We ended up having to replace the millstone. After that, I think the thing was cursed or something because we had nothing but trouble." She pointed to a large wooden drum in the center of the Stone Floor, effectively the second story. She turned to Duncan. "How much do you know about the workings of a mill, m'lord McVryce?"

"A little. I hauled flour for one back in Patras. They are usually three floors. The top floor holds the unmilled grain and the milled flour, or *meal*. The second floor is the Stone Floor where the millstone is turned by the water flow coming in from the *weir*. The buckets fill with water, which pushes them down and they empty at the bottom to be refilled and do it again.

"The bottom floor is the Meal Floor, where the wallower is set. The *wallower* and the *pit-wheel* are the gears that turn the stone above. You also set the *tentering* gear here, which determines how fine to grind the flour." He noticed how quiet the mill was on the Stone Floor, since the stone should be grinding against the lower stone. Instead, there were sounds of other stones, but the big one in the center was silent.

"Exactly. Well, a few years ago, we were sought out to make the flour for the Papal City's sacramental feast for St. Michael's Day. Princess Margaret was getting married to Henri of Navar and there was so much to do, all the mills in Patras were overwhelmed. They sent some of their work out to smaller towns nearby and we were one of those that got the overflow.

"As you can imagine, it was a great honor and we wanted to do a good job. We had so much to do that we increased the water flow from the weir. Unfortunately, the extra work caused our millstone to wear out sooner than we expected and we had some chip off. We didn't want the flour to be deemed inferior so a man overseeing things for the Church came in to help get rid of some of the debris. Unfortunately, he didn't remove the drum lid to the stone, just lifted it up. As a result, it fell and pinned him to the stone. Before we could get it off, he had been badly cut across the cheek."

Henri nodded. "I remember him. Ce'Nedra said he was very upset that his face was 'ruined'. For someone associated with the Church, it was unusual that he would be so vain. He ended up healing in town but eventually, the only women who would spend time with him were the ones paid to at the Red Sky. He became so unpleasant, people just avoided him."

Kaelandra nodded. "He was definitely someone used to getting by on his charm and good looks. He had nearly every young girl in town fawning over him, many thinking he would be a good catch to marry, being so high in the affairs of the Church. The Church means money and security. Anyway, he got hurt and we were scared to death that he would cause a lot of problems for us. We finished the milling job and then went about replacing the stone. The Church then contacted us, saying they apologized for their man's behavior and that he had been reassigned. They offered to buy a new stone for us.

"They sent the stone to us from the Papal City quarries themselves and we were so grateful. But not long after, the accidents started. The millstone drum exploded, causing a huge mess and a lot of damage. Four people were injured. That drum has housed the previous stone for over a decade. It had the mill's Fae in it…"

She stopped, her eyes taking on a slight fear. "Uh, not that anyone here trucks with Fae, of course. It's just what the locals said."

Duncan felt puzzled that she would retract her statement about Fae, but then he realized that talking like that could be seen as heresy. He smiled. "Don't worry. You might say I've had some experiences with Fae recently. I won't turn you in."

She exhaled, relaxing. "Well, it's true. His name was Woodwarbler. We could tell he was taking care of the stones because the wood would have a little tune that went with the rhythmic grinding."

Henri smiled. "A bard named Flynn came through years ago and heard it. He was so taken by it, he created a song. The young people in town even made a dance to it, the Woodwarbler's Reel."

Kaelandra laughed. "Yes! He was so pleased by that. We had the most productive and safe year when that happened." She got a bit less whimsical as she returned to the other tale. "After the drum exploded, we had to build a new one. But Woodwarbler was gone. And the mill fell silent. Then, not a few months later, the drum exploded again. This time, it was right after a harvest and several people were badly hurt. My husband was killed.

"I took over running the mill and it has been problem after problem since then. I even installed an extra shack of smaller stones we run with the water for when accidents happen, so we can continue to grind. During the year, we don't use the big stone unless we have to, during harvest. No one is allowed up here when it's going."

"Did you ever figure out what was going on with it?"

Kaelandra shook her head. "With Woodwarbler's death, we haven't had any luck at all with solving the problems."

Duncan nodded. "Have you looked at getting a new stone?"

Kaelandra shook her head. "I can't afford it. This was a gift to say thank you from the Papal City. I could never replace that. When it works it produces a very good meal but when it goes awry… well, it's like having a teen-aged daughter that can sever an arm."

Duncan smiled at her jest but it wasn't a mirthful situation. "Thank you. I'll look around and see what I can do about this."

Kaelandra curtsied. "Thank you sir. I'll get back to work."

Duncan and Henri left the mill and looked at the building behind them. Duncan cast his eyes to the second floor. There were signs of damage, even from the outside, though only cosmetic. "I wish Gwen wasn't gone. I could use her in this."

"Gwen?"

Duncan nodded. "The Glarren woman who was staying at the inn. She knows about Fae."

Henri nodded. "Well, I can ask around discreetly and get back to you. Someone might know something in town."

"That would be helpful. Judging from Kaelandra's reaction, no one's going to tell the King's Man about their dealings with the Fae."

Henri walked down to the Church and entered the chapel. The faces of numerous saints smiled from small effigies around the room with a single large statue of St. Andrew, the patron of fishermen, behind the altar. The priest came over from tending to the votive candles in a bank halfway up on the seaward wall. "Chancellor Henri, so good to see you."

"Father, I have a question you might be able to help with. Remember a few years back when the millstone broke at the Durant Mill?"

"Ah yes." The priest gestured to the nearby pew and sat down. "Such generosity from the Papal City. I suspect it had something to do with the mess in Patras."

Henri nodded. King Charles had called for the slaughter of all Emilianites in Patras and it had, in turn, spawned the murder of thousands more across Mervolingia before it was brought under control. "The incident brought in a new Pope, didn't it?"

The priest glanced around. "I was quite the conspiracy theorist back then. I believed the Papacy changed hands because the Church was so embarrassed that their Pope was deceived by a human, and a woman, no less." He scoffed.

"You don't think that now?"

The priest sighed. "I must say I was wavering in my faith before. But when the King healed all those people, all those children…" He shook his head. "It has restored my faith, I must say. Most of the town too, because the church services have been quite full."

"What was your theory about the accidents?"

The priest sat back. "What? That nonsense about that Woodwarbler creature 'protecting' the mill? Psh. Peasant tales to comfort children."

"So you don't think the mill drum was the home of a Fae?"

"Well, if it was, then the presence of a holy millstone would most definitely drive the monster away. The Church grounds have always protected the people from attacks by the Fae and other such heathen creatures."

"Heathen creatures?"

"Yes. Here, let me show you. Wait here." The priest went upstairs and came back a few minutes later with a large book. "I've been reading up on miracles lately and came across this passage."

He showed the book to Henri and pointed to a page. Henri read.

"And then the Holy Church did protect her people from the monsters outside. Those who did not come in were destroyed by the evil things the Land and Hell had produced.

But the light of Heaven pushed away all that was unholy;

The Fae monsters that tricked the people,

The Land beasts rife with claws and horns unlike any made by Heaven,

The Sea Serpents that blew vile steam and salt into the faces of the unrighteous,

Even the dragons that flew and burned the air.

None that clung to the ways of the heathens were spared."

Henri handed the book back to the priest. "Thank you so much, Father. I think that has helped quite a bit."

The priest took the book back, nodding to Henri as he left the building.

Henri met Duncan with dinner at the office with a smile. "I think I have a solution to our mill problem."

Duncan perked up at the lift in Henri's voice and the scent of Ce'Nedra's cooking. "Do tell."

"I asked around a bit. Turns out the stone being from the Papal City is the root of the problem."

"Well, that's been established. The problems didn't happen until that stone got here."

"Yes, but the thing is that the stone is from a *holy* site. That will repel anything non-Heaven oriented."

"Like the Fae inhabiting the drum."

Henri nodded.

Duncan leaned forward on the desk, making a steeple with his fingers and touching them to his lips. "Where did they get the previous stone?"

Henri shrugged, then looked at the records on the wall. He stood up, talking as if to himself. "Well, the stone before had been there for decades. There's a sign on the outside of the building that says it was built in 1543." He looked at the spines of the books. "Yes. Here. I've been going through the records and putting into these empty books the records of the town. I remembered seeing something about the arrival of a millstone. Here it is."

He set the book down on the table. "The Durant Mill was built in 1543 and the stone was cut by Szilárd Janikane and his wife Erzebet. Those are Caratian names."

"Meaning?"

"Meaning they were Land worshippers. The Land is an ally of the Fae and so when the Durants got the new stone that repelled Fae, it was conflicting with the mill's inhabitant."

"So what do we do?"

Henri shrugged. "It might be as easy as having the priest bless the wooden drum, so the two work in harmony. That would ensure that the Fae would avoid the place but it might stop the accidents too."

Duncan sat back and crossed his arms across his chest. "You honestly think that there's a miniature holy war going on in that mill?"

"Your King came through here two days ago and healed a blinded child. You going to doubt the ability of the Church to do something?"

Duncan nodded. "Alexander needed to be on holy ground to heal. It's possible what you say is true. Okay, let's talk to the priest about blessing the drum, then see about dealing with this nobleman."

Four

No road is long with good company.
-The Wisdom of Stone

Myrgen stood, trying to decide what his fate should be. He let go of the White Stone Sword and it sank into the ground like water into a well. The five hundred foot drop behind him was two steps away but he didn't believe he had left the company of the woman he loved just to cast himself from a cliff edge overlooking a burning pirate port.

"Thinking about throwing yourself off the cliff?"

Myrgen sighed. "I suspect it would not work." He nodded to her. "Your eyes are swimming black, like ink in water. You also reek of sulfur. You're a Shadowalker."

Her eyes narrowed. "That accurately describes what I've done. Sulfur, huh?" She sniffed herself. "From this side, it smells like lemons."

"That makes it seem even more like an artifact of Hell." He nodded towards Portabella. "That doesn't help."

Boots stood as well. "The King of Mande has been searching for this place a very long time. It's been well hidden. There was a traitor to the Crown there." She gestured to Myrgen. "Apparently more than one. I could probably go through each kingdom's bounty list and collect on several, had I the time to fetch their remains."

Myrgen stepped away from the cliff edge, not wanting to take a trip through the shadows. He knew from personal experience that the place was inhospitable. His last encounter with a Shadowalker had endangered the entire ship. He didn't want to risk anything Octavius or Catriona might have hidden in his bag.

Catriona…

He closed his eyes a moment.

Not now.

"So, I'm a bounty then? Are you really going to take me all the way to Mande when Patras is much closer? It would save Cipriano the trouble of housing me until the order came to execute me."

"Well, you've already escaped from Patras once. Clearly they aren't secure. Besides, I've avoided Patras. Better to take you to Vincenzia. Let the King deal with you himself."

Myrgen shook his head. "How do you know I'm not on good terms with the man? I'm a rather shrewd accountant, trained in Florentine. Someone like that might be of use to the king of a country based on greed."

"I suppose I can let His Majesty make that decision. Come on." She gestured for him to start walking east.

He went in that direction for about ten minutes with her sword point behind him. He waited for the inevitable touch of the shadows surrounding him but it didn't come and didn't come. The waiting was maddening.

"Aren't you going to tie my hands or something?"

She sheathed her sword. "Why should I?"

"So I don't escape?"

He heard the smile in her voice. "I have been in these woods a long time. I'm pretty sure I can get ahead of you no matter what. If you run or try to escape, I'll simply expedite matters and let you smell like lemons for a while. Would you prefer that?"

He felt her hand on his shoulder and almost attacked her. The thought of being invaded by the shadows again stopped him.

"No. I'm fine with walking all the way to Vincenzia."

"I got that impression." She patted his shoulder. "Now, why don't you be a good traveling companion and tell me where you were going."

Myrgen frowned. "Where I was going?"

"Yes. You left the safety of the best hidden port in the world outside of the Cyprian Isles. The only way to find Portabella is to have been there before. There is magic protecting that place from being seen from land or sea."

"Really?" *Hunh. I wonder which member of the* Enigma *has abandoned a life as a fugitive.* He snorted. *Probably Thessius. That man gets more interesting the longer I know him.*

"Indeed. You can't even accidentally stumble upon it from the cliffs. It merely routes you around it. That's how it's stayed so safe for the last three hundred years or so."

"You know a lot more about it than I do. How did you come to it?"

"That's easy. I was born there."

He stopped, turning to look at her. "You put to the torch your home town?"

She scrunched her nose. "It's not a good place to raise a family."

"Were your parents there?"

She looked directly into his eyes but didn't answer.

"By the Stones…"

She arched her eyebrow. "A Dirt Worshipper? I had you pegged for Augustinian."

"It's been a long Spring."

"Does that mean you were heading to Caratia?"

"Maybe. Hadn't truly decided yet." He started walking again, realizing for the first time that he had been swearing in his mind in the manner of a Land follower. He tried to think about when that started.

"Is that where that Sword came from?"

Myrgen looked down at his hand. He wondered if he could call it to him again. He glanced at the ground and saw it gliding along just under the surface. *If I even think it…*

He stopped himself. *If that has been entrusted to me, I can't risk it going through the Shadows. That is an artifact of the Land, sent here to protect me. If I end up corrupting it…*

"Presumably." He looked at her. "It seems pretty Landy."

"So, why did *you* leave Portabella?"

"Well, for one thing, I thought bounty hunters might try to track me down."

She smirked. "Aren't you just full of insight?"

He stopped and let her step beside him. He decided to really *look* at her. "Yes, I seem to have been given a bit of clarity of late. It comes from keeping certain company. I've learned to observe people.

"Like you. Your brown hair and eyes indicate you have Mervol blood, probably on both sides. Portabella may be hidden and safe but it's hardly made up of trustworthy folks. For all the codes of conduct pirates may have, that doesn't mean you weren't sold into slavery by your parents.

"You seem to know your way around these woods, which indicates a familiarity born of hiding and playing in them. You know the place can't be seen or found and those steps up the cliff are arduous, even for a child. That tells me that if you went up there, you stayed in the woods for a day or two at a time. You likely have a place you camped all set up from your childhood, a hiding place where you could go if you were scared or mad. I imagine we're going there first."

Boots blinked at him, her eyes clear now, but startled. "You *have* been around her."

Myrgen swallowed, knocking down the fear now rising in his throat. He started walking again. "I don't know what you're talking about."

She let him get ahead of her but didn't say anything more. The next hour passed in external silence as a war of thoughts and memories and admonishment battled inside him. *Why did I do that? Why would I allow my hubris to reveal the close connection between me and the woman holding my heart to the bounty hunter holding me hostage? Who does that? Clearly, Catriona made the right decision choosing Alexander.*

That line of thinking was replaced with scoffing and ridicule about how the stupidest thing in the world was him thinking Catriona was better off with the man who destroyed her ship and tried to secretly murder him. *Yes, she's considerably better off with that miserable pig than with me. Even I don't believe that.*

This was then flanked with equal strength forces of their near misses on the ship with kissing, and the direct hits with kissing. He was concerned he spent the latter part of the hour sighing like a bored dog awaiting the return of his master.

"So, why did you leave?"

Myrgen started, almost forgetting Boots was there. She had put away her sword at some point in the hour and he realized she had been thoughtfully quiet herself.

"I had some things to think over and I couldn't do it there."

"'There' being Patras?"

Myrgen laughed. "Well, it truly would have been much harder to think hanging from a spike on the city walls. Although I suppose I might have had days for reflection, depending upon the killing wound."

"So, you weren't in Patras right before Portabella?"

He looked around, not really wanting to inform, or confirm, where he was or what he was doing before getting into this situation. He saw a small tree house in some branches pretty high off the ground in a tree. It definitely looked like something built for and by a child a couple decades ago, and the tree had grown higher in the intervening years. He nodded to it.

"Is that yours?"

Boots stepped up beside him as he stopped to assess the structure. "Hunh. That's a bit higher than I remember. I thought things were supposed to shrink as you got older."

"Yeah, unless they are part of a living thing like a tree." He looked at her. "You're not going to make me go up there and check it out for stability, are you?"

Boots put forth a rather wicked smile, and Myrgen remembered for a second exactly how potentially scary this situation was. Then she shook her head. "No, I can check it without climbing. But I can tell from here it fell apart years ago. I guess we keep moving, huh?"

They continued towards the east and Myrgen started calculating the time it would take to get to Vincenzia on foot. She was not veering north at all so she seemed to know the route she wanted them to take, but it didn't make any sense to take it. The Cliffs of Caratia bordered Mande and there were no breaks in the terrain at all to link the two countries. Legend had it that the cliffs rose up in response to a threat from the Church hundreds of years ago and the forbidding wall repelled all access from Mande. It only allowed one path from Mervolingia on the western wall and one for York on the northern face. Even the seas destroyed ships that went to Caratia if they originated from Mande. In all her sea travels, even his sister Tanglwyst had never set foot in the mysterious country.

"I have a question. Can you travel anywhere with that amulet?"

She kept her eyes on the terrain ahead. "Anywhere I've been before."

"Have you been to Vincenzia?"

"Yes." She looked at him, her eyes dark. "You wish to expedite matters?"

He shook his head and they fell back into silence. *If she can go wherever she wants, then why take her time? She must realize the longer we take, the more likely I am to escape. If that's her intention, why capture me in the first place?*

He let that gel in his mind for a bit and during that time, he caught her looking like she was about to say something, then stop herself. He tried catching her expressions out of the corner of his eye but that didn't give him much of a clear vision of her.

What could she possibly want to ask me? She knows more about the Underground than I do, especially figuring she knew about Portabella before me. She's a bounty hunter, so she knows that arena better too. She's even been commissioned for at least two jobs by the King of Mande, so she can deal with snakes and poisoners. Why me?

Then it occurred to him.

Catriona.

"We'll stop here for the night."

Myrgen stopped and looked at the area. Defensible, water nearby, rocks for a fire pit, trees overhead for shelter. He nodded. "Good choice. Did you know this was here?"

She nodded. "Been through here before."

"So, you could have just popped here?" He flicked his gaze to the amulet.

"If I were going to 'pop' someplace for the night, I have a room with a bed and food. It would not be out in the wilderness."

Is she hoping that the longer we travel together, the more likely we are to bond? Is she hoping to gain my trust? Pretty odd behavior for a bounty hunter.

It was a good tactic though, especially given the new, less bloody path he was on. He laid out his bedroll as she tightened up the stones in the fire pit. The more he thought about it, the more he realized guessing was not the way to go. One thing he had learned from Catriona was that letting something just sit was never the right idea. When they had almost kissed on the deck of the *Enigma,* they had retreated from the situation. Most people would have just left the incident there, the end result being either angsty pining tainted with resentment, or resentment tainted with angsty pining. Instead, she came to him and asked him about it. It was the right choice then. It was the right choice now.

"What do you want from me?"

She blew on the fire she had brewing in the kindling. "Can't say. That would be cheating."

"Cheating?"

She blew. "Against the rules."

"Okay. I haven't played this game since I was a child, but I do remember the premise. Is it something you'll get from me in Mande?"

"Not if we make it all the way to the King."

"Ah." He folded his arms. "So, it isn't just yes or no answers."

She smiles. "Sorry. Try again."

"If I get to King Cipriano, will he give you what you want?"

She blew. "No."

"Are you hoping I will give it to you on the way?"

She blew. "What do I say if the answer isn't a yes or no answer?"

"You tell me to ask a different question."

"Ask a different question."

Myrgen leaned forward. "Does Cipriano know you're bringing me in?"

She started to blow on the fire, but it caught. She sat back. "No."

"If he did, would you have to bring me through the shadows to him?"

"Yes."

"Does he have something of yours?"

"Ask a different question."

"Does he have *someone* of yours?"

She looked at Myrgen, a little grateful. She swallowed. "Yes."

"A child?"

She shook her head, a little disgusted. "No."

His eyes narrowed, noting the distaste. It wasn't the distaste of not liking children. It was the distaste of not liking the person being held.

By the Stones…is it…?

"Is he holding someone who gave you Cyprian herb?"

Her eyes widened as she looked at him, almost in fear. *"Yes."*

Myrgen sat back. Now he understood. The herb was one used by unscrupulous men to force women to devote themselves to them. If they failed to, they suffered great pain. If the Patron died, the woman died within tendays. He knew of no known cure.

"Are you hoping I can help you remove the curse?"

She closed her eyes. "Ask another question."

He frowned. His eyes searched the ground and he saw the White Stone Sword just below the surface. He shook his head, dispelling the notion she was hoping for death. That didn't seem her style or she would have just accepted falling off the cliff before. He went through every associate he had that might have some clue about this and in the end, he came up with only one ally.

"Are you hoping Catriona can cure the curse?"

A small tear snuck out from under her lashes.

"Yes."

Five

One already wet does not feel the rain.
-The Wisdom of Stone

Gwen, Michael, and Tanglwyst looked at the road that went to Caratia, Toledo and the Papal City. Tanglwyst had traveled this road barely a tenday before but she had felt worse. Every step she took away from Alexander, her body seemed to rebel. She felt nauseated, and had frequent bursts of sweating or chills. Gwen had given her some willow bark to chew upon and she drank more than her share of the water. Just a day away from Patras and they were more than half empty.

Michael leaned over to Gwen as they rode, his eyes staying upon Tanglwyst. "My lady, what is the matter with her? She seems to be getting worse."

Gwen nodded, frowning. "I know. It's a spell. She is being compelled to go to someone but she can't get to him. This is the result. She's moving forward because it's the only way to reach him, and she'll continue to push on, regardless of her state."

He looked at the Glarren woman, her long, blonde hair contained well in a braid. Her pale skin and ice blue eyes were the only things that betrayed her heritage, her accent gone from her homeland and replaced with a regional Mervol one. "You know of spells?"

She looked at him, her pale features the opposite of his black ones. His dark eyes and dreadlocked hair blended well with his chocolate skin, making him stand out in the area as much as she did. "Yes. It's a family thing."

"It is one you cannot stop?"

She shook her head. "It's not a Fae spell. I don't know anything about how to break it."

Michael looked at Tanglwyst, then back at Gwen. "In this country, it's very dangerous to admit that you know of this sort of thing. The Church doesn't tolerate magic."

"You're wrong there, Michael. It's not that it doesn't tolerate magic. It simply only tolerates its own."

Michael's look flicked to Tanglwyst, barely content to let her horse trot instead of run. "I'm pretty sure that's blasphemy."

"It would be if I were Augustinian. Damn. She's doing it again." Gwen flicked the reins and caught up to Tanglwyst who was starting to run her horse again.

Michael sighed. They were done talking for now.

Tanglwyst heard Gwen riding up and braced herself for the chiding.

"Tangl, you can't push the horses like this. You'll kill them and we'll be walking."

Gwen grabbed the reins from Tanglwyst and slowed both horses. Tanglwyst let it happen, but only barely. "I know. I'm sorry. I can't help it."

Gwen looked at her friend. "I know."

Tanglwyst looked around. "Look, we're a day out. There's going to be an inn if we go closer to the road. We can stop for the night, resupply, rest the horses. Sound good?"

"Going near the road puts us all at risk. I might be able to go unnoticed but Michael stands out and you're a fugitive. If a guard patrol goes by, you're dead." Gwen glanced at the reins in her hand. "Tell you what; we'll go a *little* closer to the road and see if we can see an inn through the trees. If we do, I'll go in and get some supplies and then we'll make camp here in the woods, where we're safe. Ok?"

Tanglwyst nodded, retrieving her reins from Gwen. She knew the road near here. It was well traveled and the stables would have fresh horses. When Gwen and Michael were sleeping, Tanglwyst would slip to the inn and trade in her horse, then ride through the night. Once out of Gwen's restraints, she could get to the Caratian border in a couple of days instead of a tenday. She'd trade horses along the way until she got to the Caratian shore. As long as she didn't sleep, she could be there in a tenday. Maybe she could hire a ship once there to take her to him.

Alexander needed her. She almost regretted the time spent back in St. Andrew helping the people who came to be healed by the Miracle King. It had let him get farther away and now she was feeling the strain of his absence. He was in danger, and she was the only person who could save him.

Dominic closed the book on the desk and sat back, feeling the spikes of pain in his lower back. Suddenly, they cramped, and he cried out, springing from the chair and pressing his hands into the fatigued muscles. The charley horse refused to dissipate and he twitched and pulled at it for an eternity before it finally started relaxing. He opened the door and limped to the privy, breathing through his teeth. He was loathe to sit again, the warning of his spasms telling him to stay upright for a while, but the alternative was staring into a black, smelly pit that went down into the middens under the castle. He decided not to sit as he peed, his eyes on the artwork above the hole on the wall. He had never studied it before and now he could see it was actually very nice.

He finished and stepped back into the hall. The servants were doing their servant things, something he only cared about if it wasn't done in his room. They knew enough to stay away from anything on the desk in his chambers, a feat performed by Myrgen the Grey during his stint as Chancellor. Myrgen had a poisoned needle hidden somewhere on the desk and this had claimed the life of a servant his first tenday in office. After that, no servants went near the desk.

It was for precisely that reason Dominic had not replaced any of the furniture in the traitor's quarters. As far as Dominic could tell, there was no needle trap but it was enough to keep the servants from snooping. He knew many servants sold the nobility's secrets to the Back Streets, enabling thieves and assassins access to their lives. As a Mandian *and* a D'Medici, he knew all too well the value, and danger, of a servant with too much access.

He walked to one of them and cleared his throat to avoid touching her. "Could you please send my valet to my quarters?"

The woman nodded and dropped her scrub brush back in the wooden bucket, the sloshing water erupting suds that threatened Dominic's elegant Mandian shoes. He stepped back and the cramp in his back struck again, drawing a gasp and a scowl. It also managed to make his mood even worse. He looked at his shoes and found suds on one of them. He spit in the bucket and went to his room to clean the soap off before it discolored the red leather.

The sight of the book reminded him of his frustration. *The amulet was nowhere in that. I'm not even sure where to look next.* He pulled the amulet out of his belt pouch. The pouch carried his daily gold and he knew few Mervolingians had the ability to discern one kind of gold from another by sound. He was hesitant to wear it because he didn't want anyone to recognize it and ask where he got it. There were few people who knew their way around the catacombs and two of them were known traitors. Their assets had already been seized for the Crown. He wasn't ready to give this to the coffers.

He glanced at his shelves again, then down at the amulet. *The symbols... they look like a mistake, like the artisan accidentally struck it with a St. Giles stamp and a St. Michael stamp. Why wouldn't the gold smith simply melt this flawed piece down again? Instead, they made it into an amulet, like it was important. Sentiment?*

He snorted.

Unlikely. This amulet is worth a season's dishonest wages. No one would drop this and not come back for it unless they were being pursued. Or they didn't realize they lost it.

He looked at the catacomb door in his room.

That means they'll be back for it.

He walked over and shoved a small chap book under the edge, stopping it from moving on its hinge.

That should do it for now. But I need to get that sealed up. I don't want to lose this to its rightful owner.

He put the amulet on, tucking the gold so it lay next to his skin.

These are religious symbols. I might actually need religious texts. I need the study at Tanglwyst's house.

Dominic barely heard the knock on his door when his whole world became bright and rich with the scent of lemons.

Six

He who rides a tiger is afraid
to dismount.
-The Wisdom of Stone

Duncan looked over the Rochefort manor house. It was a nice place; three stories with exposed beams and white exterior in what some called a gingerbread style. He marveled at the appropriateness of the architecture. The monster inside may not eat children, but he certainly consumed their innocence. Duncan decided to keep to the shadows and stay out of sight. With any luck, he could get near the back kitchen door and possibly overhear the servants talking. Rich people always assumed that since servants were invisible, they were also blind, deaf, and dumb, making them the best spies in a house. You just had to know where to listen.

He slipped into the dappled shadows of the forest bordering the back of the manor and crept quietly, dodging the windows, until he got to the rear of the house. A place this small would have the kitchen as a room inside but he expected it would have a wood shed outside to shelter the fuel for the ovens. Unfortunately, the wood was just stacked against the wall instead of protected from the weather. The wood pile was not as tall as he needed and he recognized he could either listen at the back door, or hide efficiently, but he could not do both. The lack of the shadow amulet had seriously hindered his sneaking.

A small outbuilding by the kitchen caught his attention but he would be in danger of being seen because he would have to pass in front of the open door to hide there. He realized he *could* go all the way around the house to get to the other side, but worried he might miss the one piece of information he needed. Instead, he crouched as low as he could by the wood pile, tempted to adjust it to hide himself better. He heard someone come into the kitchen when there was suddenly conversation.

"Angela, how are you?" A man's voice. *The nobleman, perhaps?*

"Anthelme, I'm good! How is your voice this morning?"

Hmm. Not the nobleman. Too friendly for a servant to the lord of the house.

"A little raspy, in fact. The Lady Rochefort really put it to task last night. Why was she so insistent on me continuing to sing?"

Angela's voice grew less cheerful. "She tends to get like that when His Lordship leaves for the evening."

"He said he had some work to do. Where did he go at that time of night?"

Angela didn't answer, or if she did, she did so quietly enough Duncan couldn't hear her. Anthelme spoke again.

"I saw a messenger arrive right before noon. Any idea what he wanted?"

"He was just telling the household about the incidents with the King in town. The Lady had spoken of seeing him but the messenger told her the King had already departed by boat."

"The King? Was he the one doing all those miracles yesterday?" he paused. "Why would the Lord be so happy to hear that King had gone?"

"Because he healed all the children in town."

Anthelme's voice grew suspicious. "What did he mean when he said they were 'intact' now?"

Again, silence from Angela but Duncan understood. All Rochefort's prey were ready for him to defile again.

Angela excused herself and Duncan heard footsteps going away into the house. After a moment, he heard footsteps coming towards the back door and leaned back against the house into the shadows of the morning. Anthelme emerged and looked into the woods away from Duncan. He walked purposefully from the manor towards an outbuilding on the edge of the property. Duncan watched and when he believed he could, he slipped past the now-empty kitchen and followed the man.

Anthelme walked up to the outbuilding that looked like a small barn. Duncan couldn't smell any livestock but he did smell straw. This was probably where the family's horses were kept. He got into a good vantage behind a bunch of bushes where he could see the door to the barn and watched as Anthelme reached for the handle.

A small dark figure slapped his hand away, practically appearing out of nowhere. Anthelme stepped back, holding his hand to his chest.

"What do you want?" The creature had a sharp voice, filled with menace and snarls of disgust.

It sounds like that monster that attacked me and Gwen in the woods near here. I thought that thing was killed.

Anthelme cleared his throat. "I'm looking for Lord Rochefort."

"The Master is not in. He has gone *hunting.*"

Both Duncan and Anthelme shuddered at the term and Duncan felt sure Rochefort wasn't hunting rabbits. Anthelme looked into the woods, then back at the manor house. He stepped back again and turned away when he was about twenty feet from the building. The goblin stepped back into the shadows and disappeared.

Duncan entered Henri's office a while later. "Who's your local authority on Fae?"

Henri looked up at the tall, bald man. "The summoning and trucking with Fae is against the church, punishable by excommunication."

"Does that mean I need to talk to the Pastor again?"

Henri nodded. "They would be the only ones allowed to study them. Everyone else would just be judged."

"Thank you."

Duncan left and Henri sat back. *Fae, huh?* He got up and looked around the office. These were all town records but he had not seen anything specifically referencing straight *Fae*. There were hints about creatures like Woodwarbler, but no one had ever seen one and therefore, there were no reports of them. Henri looked out his window and saw Duncan go out of sight down the street. He stepped out of the office and made his way to the Black Cat and Anchor.

Duncan reentered the St. Andrew church and looked around for the priest. Father Allen smiled when he saw him and moved briskly to greet him. "My Lord Duncan, wasn't it? What can I help you with today?"

"Just Duncan, please."

The priest nodded, acknowledging Duncan's humility. "Of course."

"How have you been, Father? Any trouble?"

Father Allen beamed. "None at all and nearly every mass has been filled to capacity. I know it won't last forever but His Majesty has renewed the faith of those whose lives he touched."

"That's a lot of lives."

"Indeed it is! The children are happy and healthy, the mill workers are well. I am on my way to the Mill today to bless the drum. If you feel that will help the Mill have no more accidents, I'm more than happy to bring the realm of Heaven into that place."

"I think it will help. Driving these monsters from the world is a smart choice. Speaking of which, I encountered one a couple days ago. I think it either regenerated from being almost killed, or there was more than one. Either way it's behind the attacks on the children here. Do you have any way to defeat the Fae? Maybe some books on it?"

Father Allen shook his head. "I'm afraid I don't. Our scriptorium is in great need of more books. And someone to copy them."

"Oh. Damn. Do you have any books at all here?"

Father Allen looked hopeful. "I have a lot on the history of the town. That's my specialty."

"History?"

"Yes. Like, three hundred years ago, there was a terrible plague that swept through the country. Only people on holy ground did not get it and the Church took that as a sign. Most populated areas were devastated. Once it was eradicated, the population was almost one-tenth what it had been. Noble and peasant alike were affected. So, once the plague had passed, people gathered together for guidance. The Church came in and helped people sort out their inheritances, gather their appropriate tithes and then rebuild the cities. Almost every town in Mervolingia was remapped in the rebuilding."

He motioned Duncan to follow him and took him to the Scriptorium. On the walls were several versions of maps of St. Andrew and other towns he had never heard of. About a dozen cities were represented on the walls alone. Father Allen pointed to a map that was a coastal town with meandering streets, farms, and a small port.

"That's the city of Honfleur, before the plague."

He pointed to a map beside it. This one had one central building, the church, and the roads were straight, like spokes in a wheel. The Market District was well defined and the port and warehouse regions were as well. Residential areas were on the landward side of the wheel, bordering the forest. The few farms stretched north and south.

"And here it is after the rebuild, when it was renamed St. Andrew."

Duncan looked at the priest. "You mean the town was renamed after a Saint?"

"Yes. Each town was given its patron saint and it was renamed to protect the people from being attacked by monsters again. It's worked great. There hasn't been a case of a Fae or Land beast since."

"Were they common before?"

Father Allen shrugged. "We're on the edge of a forest. Those things tend to favor such natural areas. But not since we became protected by the Church."

He pointed to another pair of maps of the coast of Mervolingia. Duncan saw the before and after names of a dozen cities and villages. Patras, Rouen and Leone were the only places that were not renamed. Duncan recognized that renaming the capital, the main port and the Mervol Church seat could cause problems but all the small towns were under different names.

"Are the layouts identical in every town?"

Father Allen nodded. "Indeed. I used to be a teamster, hauling goods from St. Giles to Pardua overland. Every village is built like this. Some of the saints are in different places, but the layout is consistent."

"What do you mean, 'the saints are in different places'?"

Father Allen pointed to St. Andrew. "Oh. When the Church rebuilt, they put holy symbols of certain Saints at the ends of the roads. The roads could continue, of course. Expansion was one of the important points of the rebuild. At eight points, Saint's symbols are engraved or statues are in place." He noted each Saint at their corresponding point on the map. "Saint Michael, Raphael, Gabriel and Uriel guard the four main compass points. Brigit, Giles, George and Dismas guard the midpoints. If an area had trouble with something specific, like pirate raids or bandits, Michael and George would be put on the roads or areas with the trouble and it allegedly stopped. For us, Michael protects the harbor and George the southern road. Allegedly, there's a secret pirate port somewhere south and the harbor is pretty open to attack on the west. The northern road to Patras is pretty well patrolled this close to the capital city so those were seen as our vulnerable spots."

"And these protections keep the Fae from entering the city?" Duncan noted that the edge of the protection circle seemed to fall just inside the edge of the forest, excluding the Mill, the Rochefort outbuilding and the place where the goblin attacked both him and Gwen, and Tanglwyst.

"According to the preaching's of the Church. I can't be sure because I have no idea how much Fae activity there was before the restructuring."

"Then how would one get rid of a Fae outside the boundaries of the protection?"

Father Allen shrugged. "No idea."

"Can the boundary be expanded?"

"Not by me."

Duncan sighed. This looked like it was going to be done the hard way.

Duncan stepped out of the church and looked ahead to the Black Cat and Anchor. *Gwen had stayed there. Maybe they left something behind.* It was unlikely, but he had nowhere else to look for advice. He walked over to the inn and stepped inside. Unlike most taverns, which were gloomy, the Black Cat was very well lit. Ce'Nedra had been frightened near to death by an attack from a Shadowalker and had made sure the place had as few shadows as possible ever since. She didn't seem to recognize that the Shadowalker who attacked her was Duncan. Luckily, while in the throes of the tendrils, he had been obscured.

"Duncan, how are you?" She smiled as she greeted him.

"Good. Looking for answers though." He looked up at the second floor. "I'm hoping I can get a look at the rooms up there. Gwen may have left something behind. Are there new tenants?"

"Not right now, but several people have wanted to stay in the King's room. I may need to get a plaque. I hope it hasn't been too noisy for you."

"I have been so tired every night, I could fall asleep in the kitchen. But if anyone gets particularly rambunctious, I'll let you know."

She reached under the bar and pulled out the key to Gwen's room. She went up with him and opened the door. "I've had two tenants in here since she left and I cleaned both days. I haven't found anything of hers. What were you looking for?"

He entered the room and started looking in the nooks and crannies like the end table drawer and under the bed. "I'm not sure, really. Gwen just seemed to know about Fae…" He realized after the words were out of his mouth that this was a forbidden subject. He tried to cover it. "I think she did research or something. Probably."

Ce'Nedra smiled. "She had that sort of air about her, didn't she?" She patted his arm. "Don't worry. Her secret is safe. Why do you want to know about the Fae?"

He sighed, sitting back on his heels on the floor by the bed. "When she was here, we were attacked by one. Tanglwyst was too, but she killed hers. Gwen managed to kill the one that got us and I saw one today at the Rochefort place. There seems to be an infestation and I wanted to find out why."

"Did you check at the Church?"

"Yeah, but they have nothing there. I did find out about the history of the town and the reorganization of the city layouts by the Church but nothing about the Fae and how to fight them."

The front door to the inn opened and they heard people coming in for food. He stood, dusting off his knees unnecessarily. "Sorry to have bothered you. Thanks for your patience."

He smiled and went to Henri's office to figure out his next move.

After about two hours of looking through papers on the changes in the town since the reorganization, both Henri and Duncan were sick of reading. Duncan's back was sore and he got up and then lay down on the floor near the fireplace. Henri got up and poured himself another in an endless stream of tea.

"I've read so many accounts of incidents today, I've forgotten what I was looking for twice."

Henri laughed. "I've had that happen myself more than once. The records here can be tedious but on occasion, they turn up some fascinating things, especially if you look at the incidents as connected." He jerked his thumb in the direction of the eastern edge of the city. "The Durant Mill ended up being more than I expected."

Duncan nodded, his head bobbing on the floor as he didn't raise it up for the gesture. "I have no idea what Gwen and Tanglwyst did to kill their attackers. I hope that doesn't mean only women can kill a goblin."

"You said you and Gwen were both attacked. What happened?"

"Little monster leapt on us from out of a bush. Managed to knock me out in the struggle. When I woke up, Gwen was helping me and the fiend was dead."

"And she didn't tell you how she did it?"

Duncan shook his head, again causing a humorous sight, he imagined.

Ce'Nedra asked, "Did you see this monster with your own eyes?"

Duncan sat up. "Ce'Nedra! Sorry, I didn't see you come in."

"Well, I was doing my best to not interrupt while I eavesdropped."

Henri came over to help her unload the basket of food she was delivering and pay her. "Why does it matter?"

"Well, if he saw the one today with his own eyes, it matters. It means the beast was only half Fae. Otherwise, yes, only a woman can kill them because only a woman can see them."

Duncan sat up on his elbows, looking at her.

She shrugged. "You wanted the local expert. Here I am."

Ce'Nedra braced herself, waiting for Duncan's reaction. He had been horribly wounded, a cat's lick from death a day ago. Now, after the King got his hands on him, Duncan was up and around like he was created just yesterday. Since the king could only heal on holy ground, she was prepared for Duncan to accuse her of witchcraft. She held her thumb at the lip of the bottle she pulled from her cellar, a gift from a hearth Fae to use for protection. With a simple move, she could release the contents and stop him from being a problem.

"I must admit, I'm surprised." Duncan straightened up and nodded. "But grateful. Thank you for trusting me in this."

She relaxed, but still held the bottle in her sleeve. "What do you need to know?"

He looked at the windows and stepped over to an area out of sight of them. He lowered his voice, as if he expected someone might overhear. "There was a creature at an outbuilding of the manor house near the woods, the Rochefort estate. It was standing guard but it told a servant the lord of the house was 'out hunting'."

Ce'Nedra winched, swallowing. "I doubt he was hunting animals."

Duncan shook his head. "I agree. I don't know what parent would allow their child out unattended with a predator on the loose like this. Hopefully, he found no prey. My problem is that I know nothing of the Fae. To be honest, I never even knew they existed before a few days ago, not really. Just stories and bard song. I know nothing about how to defeat them."

She nodded, frowning. "Did you see it enough to describe it?"

He nodded. "Barely. It had dark skin and sharp teeth. It hissed when it spoke, too, like wet wood on a fire. High pitched, eerie. I definitely felt fear creep in and settle under my flesh."

Ce'Nedra stepped back. "And you said you've encountered them before?"

Duncan glanced at the window, rubbing the back of his neck.

She pointed at him. "Was that what did that damage to you?"

"Damage?"

She glanced at Henri, lowering her voice. "I was the one who found you in the alley. You had collapsed and were covered in wounds in various stages of healing. They were everywhere. I was sure you were dead. The king had Saiban take you up to his room and the next thing I heard, you were walking back in under your own power."

41

Duncan exhaled and seemed to remember something he would rather forget. Sweat popped onto his forehead and his glance back to her eyes showed fear and guilt.

She put her hand on his shoulder to reassure him, letting the bottle settle into her sleeve. "It must have been frightening. Goblins can be horrifying and it looked like you'd battled them often."

"I… used to work for the Church but I have nothing now that I can use against such things."

"Well, luckily, I do." She stepped back, releasing him. "So, when do we go?"

"We?"

Henri stood. "Yes. We." He set the pen down on the ledger. "His Majesty asked me to investigate this atrocity. I can't deny him. If you are going to do this, I fear I must accompany you."

Ce'Nedra looked at Henri. He had a quiet strength about him, and she loved his sense of humor. She was glad he was in town when the king asked for an honest official. His arrival a few years ago had been fraught with trouble, having moved to the kingdom under the lure of employment, only to find the opportunity full of thieves and liars. He brought them all to justice, but in so doing, ended any income. The Harbormaster recommended Henri for record keeper and he had worked here ever since. She suspected he fancied her, but he was rather guarded with his emotions.

"Are you sure, Henri?" Her voice was steady from years of vocal training. Otherwise, she just knew she would have squeaked with excitement.

He rapped his knuckles lightly on the ledger. "Well, it would be pretty inappropriate for me to let you go into danger alone."

"She'd hardly be…"

Ce'Nedra walked forward, being sure to step on Duncan's toes to quiet him. "I wouldn't be in danger if you were there."

Duncan had the good sense to take the hint and stay quiet though he did shift and bounce back into the wall, limping.

Henri blushed and took off his glasses and rubbed them with a cloth. Ce'Nedra looked back at Duncan, who forced a smile. "I was going to suggest only I go, but I suspect that won't be received well."

The others simultaneously expressed their displeasure at the idea and Duncan put his hands up. "Right, as I thought. So, what do we need for this?"

Seven

Sometimes, the worst battle you have to fight is between what you know and what you feel.
-The Wisdom of Stone

"Shaestael oopthey?"

Thessius' Glarren accent was usually difficult to the seasoned crewman and impossible to the uninitiated, but after sailing with the man for five years, Octavius long ago became almost bi-lingual when it came to him. Anyone who had spent enough time around him was able to interpret his speech, and he could speak clearly most of the time. The only trouble came when Thessius had contact with someone fresh out of Glarren. Then his accent returned full force. When the ship was in port in St. Marguerite a tenday ago, one of the sailors in a nearby mooring must have been from Kilmory itself. The *Enigma* would land on Caratian soil before Thessius was speaking *almost* normally.

Octavius turned to look at Thessius, then followed his gaze to the crow's nest. The ship's first mate sighed. "I've been trying to figure out a way to get her down but nothing valid is coming to mind."

"Shae's baenthey saince eelaift."

Octavius nodded. He calculated his pause to be long enough to come off as a separate thought if it was irrelevant to whatever Thessius had just said, but short enough to still apply but seem like an original thought if it actually had something to do with his comment. When it came to dealing with Thessius' accent, Octavius' conversational repertoire was made up of carefully calculated pauses.

Catriona Moriarity had been in the Crow's Nest since the ship had left Portabella. They had left Myrgen the Grey, fugitive and traitor, in that dangerous place at his own request. She had climbed there to look for him but it had been the middle of the night when they had entered the pirate port three days ago. They had run a con on the superstitious people of the place, based upon Fae magic, and needed to leave before the light of day. Even she could not have seen anything, regardless of the tool she used or her position on the ship.

"I think she doesn't want to admit how much he meant to her. And although I know she'll come out of it, I'm actually glad she's taking his absence seriously. Myrgen was a good man. He didn't deserve to be treated like that."

"Traited lake whait?"

Octavius took a risk, figuring that what was on his mind was the same as what was on everyone else's. "Like whatever made him leave."

Thessius patted Octavius on the shoulder, returning his gaze to the nest. A dark head popped over the edge and shouted down to the deck.

"Thessius! Can you find someone to relieve me?"

"Aye Cap'n!" Thessius started climbing the ropes as Catriona started climbing down. She landed on the deck by Octavius as Thessius stepped into the nest.

Her Caratian accent seemed to fit in with the multi-cultural theme of the ship. "We need to pull into the next port, Octavius."

Her first mate frowned. "Why?"

"Because I need to get off the ship."

He smiled. "What's your reason for abandoning ship, Captain?" He folded his arms, hoping she had plans to return to Portabella to hunt down Myrgen, something she could not do on the sea.

"I need to get to Caratia by the end of the month." She paused, starting to pace a bit. "It's Alan's tenth birthday. Usually we miss it and celebrate it when we get home. But I can't be late this year. It's his Naming Ceremony."

44

Octavius frowned. "Can't they hold off until you usually arrive? We rarely get there too long after."

She shook her head, wringing her hands. "The *Enigma* is damaged. Going our usual route by Yantap and Latia to avoid the Fingers of Mande will put us there two tendays after his birthday. But this time, you have to stop in Latia and take Estelle to Galadorn Forest where she can be healed. The ship needs repairs that can only happen in that place."

She walked over to the railing and leaned on it. "I need to get home fast, and the only way to do that is to go overland at this point."

Octavius stepped up beside her, his hands behind his back. "We could go through the Fingers of Mande."

She closed her eyes and shook her head. "And put the entire ship and crew in danger? Estelle is already hurt. The ruse at Portabella took a toll. I don't think you'll risk her health any more than I will."

"You think I want her *father* to see her in this condition? The last thing I need is to be turned into a salamander in a Fae forest for allowing the Midsummer King's daughter to come to harm." He shook his head as she cracked a slight smile. "No, I'll risk the entire Mandian navy before I'll let you hit landfall. Caratian wood built this ship. I want it repaired before I return her to Galadorn. Fae magic and Land magic are allies. The ship will be fine if we can get her to Zara."

She took a deep breath. "I suppose you're right there."

"We'll get you home, Catriona. Even if it means going through the Armada itself."

She smiled. "Let's hope it doesn't come to that."

Octavius looked out over the sea. "You know, we're already past the Mandian border. Landfall here wouldn't get you home any faster. Mande rejects the Land's magic."

"Yes, but I thought, I might…"

He looked at her, her eyes showing that weathered look she had managed to avoid all these years at sea. "You thought you'd go back to Portabella, didn't you?"

Her eyes shifted to the shoreline far to the east.

"Have things changed since he left? Or would you simply be dragging him back for your comfort?"

Her face solidified, her resolve returning. "You know, I hate you some times."

He nodded, leaning forward on the railing to check the wake of the ship. "I know."

"I miss him." Her voice almost wavered.

"I knew you would."

"Then why did you let him go?"

"I'm not the Captain, Catriona. You are. I didn't let him go. That's on you."

She looked at him. "Then why did you let me do that?"

"Because he needed to leave. And you needed to let him."

She looked down at her hands, then over at the hallway that led to her cabin. "I think I'm going to rest a bit. I haven't slept in a couple days now."

"I'll keep everything running."

She pushed away from the railing and went on her way.

Catriona walked over to the cabin door that was Myrgen's room and opened it. The last time she was in here, she fell asleep and dreamed of him. It had been comforting at first, but the last two nights, she dwelt on him more than she had ever thought about Alexander. She couldn't understand why she connected to Myrgen so well. He was a stranger compared to Alexander.

That's not entirely true. Myrgen let me read him. He insisted on it on more than one occasion. I've never been able to read Alexander. I may have known him longer, but with all that's happened, I don't know Alexander at all.

She wanted to lie down on his bed, but she had taken his pillow to her bed the night he left. If she was going to fall asleep, she would do so in her own bed. She closed his door and opened hers, the mid-morning light not a threat, thanks to the repairs Myrgen and Octavius had done to her chambers. The attack at St. Marguerite had destroyed the stained glass window depicting Estelle's home as well as part of the ceiling. Myrgen had stayed up for a full day to repair her, taking care to fix her cosmetically as well as cover the damage. The result was a wall with a bank of lanterns on hooks to give light when they were needed. It made it impossible to tell the time of day outside.

She walked over to the map table, the swaying lanterns rocking their light back and forth across the coastline. Going past the Fingers of Mande meant going through hostile territory. Centuries ago, the Third Dûcesa, Serene, was assassinated by Mandian spies; infiltrators into Caratia to fight the Land Worshippers on behalf of the Augustinian Church. Caratia's army found the spies and cut their throats, using their bodies in a ritual to find the others. The Land tasted Mandian blood and ran the rest of it into the sea, turning it red for over a decade. The coral and reefs that grew in the water ripped out the hulls of the Mandian ships, and formed a line of defense from both the north and the south called Callista's Teeth. Sea predators populated the area so heavily, anyone that fell overboard was lost.

Caratia was impossible to attain by land as well. Cliffs rose out of the ground, ascending five thousand feet into the air, cutting off all of Caratia from Mande, Mervolingia, Toledo and York in a matter of minutes. Only two passes crossed those mountains now; The Path to Persephone which went north into York and Slade's Watch to the west into Toledo. The resulting cliffs bore gold by the score to the surface and Mande was content to forget Caratia to pursue this gift.

Catriona found it interesting this didn't produce more Land Worshippers in Mande. Instead, the Church swept in and set up cathedrals to the Saints in every city, making the entire country the unofficial seat of power for the Augustinians. Fae were driven out, as were any other faiths. To that day, the only taverns on the continent devoid of hearth Fae were the ones in Mande.

Catriona ran her fingers along that cliff on the map. It was a mile deep except at the two passes. When she was there, she could sense every inch of the country. As the *Stapana*, the country's Champion and Protector, her duty was to keep the people safe. She could command the land anywhere a citizen of Caratia was touching, and when she was in her homeland, she knew every name, every surface, every danger. It was overwhelming. She loved being home, but she also loved being at sea where the Land could not control her.

She became a sailor to save the life of herself and her son, avoiding a man who wanted her dead for taking his eye in a fight. Eventually, he died but by then, she had gotten into alliances she couldn't easily break. She was honor bound to sail the seas with this crew, freeing those men who repaid their life debt with their own ships. If she left the *Enigma*,

Estelle, the Fae heart of the ship, would be returned to her father Corrigan, and Estelle and Octavius would be separated.

Barely a month ago, as she was about to flee Mervolingia possibly forever, the Land had told her Dûcesa, Anika, that Catriona still needed to save someone back in Patras. She had failed to do so. Though Charles' was alive in secret, Alexander had been left behind to become king. She believed she had been returned to Patras to keep this from happening, but she was too late.

Now, he wanted her for his queen. As prince, he had gone where he pleased. He had freedom to be with her. Now that he was trapped, he wanted to keep her by his side. She knew the court at Patras would be more dangerous than being at sea in a hurricane but she felt it was the Land's Will that she be at his side.

This was made harder by Myrgen's presence. Alexander had threatened Myrgen though she hardly blamed him for that. Myrgen was the reason Alexander was now bound as king, at least in part. Another party in the treachery was already dead, and the third player, Tanglwyst, was probably either on the run or under arrest. Myrgen was the only loose end. She knew that Myrgen was played by Tanglwyst, which was unsettling because they were siblings. She didn't want him to be caught again by Mervolingian forces. Alexander had already tried to behead him behind Catriona's back. With Myrgen on land, alone, she wouldn't be able to save him.

She hit the map with her fist. She hoped he was sticking to the cliffs. If so, she believed the Land would keep him safe. He was too smart to travel through Mande and he wouldn't go back into Mervolingia. She expected him to still be in Portabella if she managed to get back there. If truly was the safest place for him. Anywhere else and he'd be caught and killed. He knew that. He also knew his way around the shadier aspects of humanity. He knew how to interact with criminals. And Xeno, a traitor to Mande from at least four years ago, had remained free hiding out there. Who knew how many other political refugees Portabella housed?

She exhaled. *Yes, Portabella is truly the best place for him. As long as he's there, he's safe. As long as he's there, I know where he is. I know…*

A tear escaped its prison behind her closed eyes.

I know I can see him again.

Alexander Angloume, King of Mervolingia, opened his eyes and sat up. He blinked a moment, then threw his legs out of bed and pulled on his boots. He grabbed his doublet off the top of the footlocker nearby and tugged it on, his brownish-blond hair in a battle for conservatorship on the top of his head. He half-ran to the young blond Glarren man at the helm.

"James! We need to go through the fingers of Mande!"

Captain James Douglas looked up as the king came onto the upper deck. "Why?"

"We can get ahead of Catriona that way. Be in Caratia before she makes land. She always goes around Latia and Yndia on her way to Caratia."

James glanced at the deck, thinking. "That's right. She's an outlaw in Mande because she aided that traitor, Xeno della Lama when he left the employ of King Cipriano."

Alexander stopped. "You… you know about that?"

James turned to a man nearby, handing him a log book. "The Watch Schedule looks good." He turned back to Alexander as the Watch Commander left. James crossed his arms. "Of course I do. My uncle was the Black Sparrow. It was his duty to know ever piratical act that crossed the Sea of Erasmus. A Mandian traitor is a potential ally, especially one so high up in the king's navy. Della Lama was a practiced naval tactician. Going up against someone with that well-trained a crew would be important to track."

"What else do you know?"

"About that? Or about her?"

Alexander turned away. He really wanted to know more about how well Black Sparrow had known Catriona, but he decided he didn't need to delve right now. *Down that path lies madness.*

James stepped over to the railing scanning the shoreline. He saw smoke coming from a set of cliffs and pointed it out. "Looks like someone had a problem with a local village."

Alexander walked over to where James was standing and looked at the shoreline. "What is over there? I didn't think that area was even inhabited." He looked at James, then swallowed. "Damn it."

James looked at the king, waiting. "Am I setting a course for it?"

Alexander nodded. "Yes. That's still my territory. Those are my people. We'll make up time on the trip through the Fingers."

James gave a slight nod to his First Mate and the course was set.

Eight

Doing the right thing isn't always convenient. In fact, that's usually how you can tell it's the right thing.
-The Wisdom of Stone

It took about an hour to get to the cliffs. As they drew closer, James used a spyglass to look the area over. It looked like just cliffs until the ship got about five hundred yards from them. Then he called for the crew to drop anchor.

"We need to go in long boats from here." He pointed to the water between the cliffs and the ship. "This area is well known for ripping the bottoms out of vessels."

"I have my kit ready." Alexander picked up the Healer's Box at his feet. He had carried one like it when looking for Catriona. It had proved more than helpful in healing her various wounds through the last few years.

James ordered the long boats put into the water and authorized ten men to go with them. They loaded up, six per boat, and started rowing for the edge of the cliffs. The smoke seemed to come from behind them instead of on the top so Alexander could tell there was a hidden cove.

He had never stopped in this area when traveling by land or sea. From any distance, it looked unbroken.

As they came more into the rocky area, James put the spyglass to his eye and put up his hand. "Wait! Stop rowing."

Both long boats stopped, slowing to a halt as the oars' momentum died on the water. He focused the spyglass and took a deep breath. He handed the glass to Alexander. "There's nothing we can do here."

Alexander took the glass, skeptical eyes on James. He moved to get a better angle and put the glass up to his eye. The small amount of port he could see was a charred ruin. He knew first-hand how quickly a fire could get away from townsfolk, especially if they were focused on something else. The amount of damage he could see was total. Bodies hung over smoking stair railings visible through caved in roofs, carrion birds poking and plucking the flesh. White rafts of gulls in the bay tugged at their footing, and Alexander saw one yank off a finger from one such raft and swallow it.

He pulled away the spyglass, closing his eyes against the after-images etched on his retinas. A shudder shook him and he looked over at James. "Why did you stop? There might be survivors."

James pointed at the shore. "Did you *see* that? There's nothing left there."

"There *might be.* A child hidden in a cellar or something. If I can get to the church…"

"*There's no church there!*" He stepped over to Alexander as the crewmen steadied the craft. "Don't you know what that place is? It's Portabella. I'm sure of it. Alistair told me of it, though even he had never been there. It's protected by a veil. You're not supposed to even find it if you don't know exactly where it is. The best hideout for fugitives in the world. Dangerous. Filled with thieves and killers. They seed their bay with sunken ships, leaving just enough of the mast or bow out to guide a ship through to its destruction. They prey upon the foolish who think they can go here. The only way in is if you know the path or you row in like this." He looked at the bay. "Someone wanted this place gone."

"Who?"

James shook his head, his eyes sharp. "No idea. But they had a small army from the looks of it. Every building I saw was completely destroyed. Burnt to the point of burning itself out. Even the ships in the harbor I could see were destroyed."

Alexander put the glass back up to his eyes and scanned for any sign of life. Nothing moved but the birds. He could see one whole ship, torched and sunk, next to a husk of a dock. Part of another floated nearby, moved by the current. Two full buildings were in sight and a large ship's cannon lay point down on the street, like it fell from a roof when it collapsed. He studied it for a moment, trying to understand why it seemed out of place. Then he remembered the cannons he ordered to fire upon Catriona's ship at the last port. They rocked back, away from the edge and there was distinct scoring on the brass from the artillery. This cannon was clean.

"They didn't fire their cannons."

James had his hands on his hips. He took the glass from Alexander when he held it out.

"See for yourself."

James looked again and nodded. "You're right." He put the glass down from his eye. "This was an inside job." He looked at Alexander. "Still want to go over there?"

Alexander looked back at the ship. He wanted to get back under weigh and beat Catriona to Zara. If he was there in time before her, he could make sure he covered the expenses for the repairs to the *Enigma*. He could apologize and make amends. He breathed deep, brow furrowed. "I think it's a loss. We have to stop at the next port anyway. I'll send word back to Gomez and have him investigate. You're sure there's no church?"

"Not unless you count the prayers said at a brothel."

"Not really helpful in my case. Come on. Let's get under weigh."

Dominic opened his eyes and shivered. He felt nauseated and reached out in the cold room, feeling around for something to stabilize him. His hand met a desk and he leaned on it, catching his breath until the queasiness faded. He reached up and felt the back of his head, expecting a bump or blood but there was nothing to indicate someone had hit him. Bright light in multiple colors splayed in a familiar way across the desktop and he turned around to see the stained glass window in Tanglwyst's study. This window was made just for her and opened to overlook the alleyway where her first husband was murdered. It was the moment she was first set free and she had stepped out of the alley and bought that block. Her manor house took the entirety of the area, including a huge garden in the back and high walls to protect it from the thugs.

The fireplace was cold, proving she was nowhere to be found. Summer or winter, she almost always had a fire going. Dominic looked down at himself. He was wearing the same clothes he had been moments ago so he had not blacked out and lost a few days. Nothing hurt, so he wasn't drugged and dragged there. He had been in his quarters a few moments before, and thinking about coming here for a book. He went to the book shelf and found it, pulling it from the section on Church history. It *felt* real.

A bell sounded from the nearby church and he started, his hand going to his heart. He felt the amulet there and realized he had just put it on when he thought of going there. He closed his eyes and thought of his chambers again. The nausea returned and he felt wobbly for a moment, but when he opened his eyes, he was back in his chambers, the book from Tanglwyst's study in his hand. A servant was knocking at the door, calling out for him.

He opened the door and the servant winced, like he smelled something powerful. He looked away from Dominic. "My Lord Chancellor, you said you wanted me?"

"I did?"

"I was told thus."

"Oh." Dominic vaguely remembered asking his valet to be sent up, but so much had happened since then, he couldn't even remember why. He looked around his room for some clue and saw the chap book under the door in the prayer nave. He almost requested a mason to come and wall up the passageway, but then he looked at his hand, still holding the book from Tanglwyst's study. He smiled, and looked at his servant.

"I'm sorry. I can't remember what I wanted. Must not have been important."

He closed the door in the servant's face before he could say anything else.

Duncan stood at the back alley by the door, waiting for Ce'Nedra to return. He had started to go in, then the memory of his last conscious visit here had confronted him. He had killed Alistair there a few days before, right at the top of the stairs to the wine cellar. Before his healing at the hands of Alexander, Duncan had been falling to evil as dark as the monster he was hunting. He was ashamed now to be getting help from these people.

He wasn't sure what the mead was for, but he hoped it was a way to knock it out. When the back door opened, he pushed off from the wall where he was leaning. He took the basket from the lady and took her hand. "Good woman, I must insist that you stay behind. The king would never allow me to put you in danger."

Ce'Nedra patted his hand. "There, there. I promise not to tell him." She took her basket away and walked down the alley towards the woods.

Henri snorted a laugh. "Nice try."

Duncan leaned over to him as they followed her. "How can you let her do this?"

Henri looked at Duncan, eyes wide with shock. "Have you ever *met* a woman? They kind of do what they want, young man."

Duncan smiled. He hardly felt like a "young man" but he knew from personal experience that Henri was right. *Tanglwyst did what she wanted.*

He breathed away the thought of her and it was easier than he expected. It was better having her gone than here, in danger's reach. He knew the ease with which a life could be taken, and the speed. That used to be his forte.

He realized the irony of that belief: he *used to be* a killer, that somehow, being healed by the king had cleansed all that away. He knew he *used to* feel that compulsion to make a kill quick, if not painless. In the last month, he had killed two men, one so fast, he probably still didn't know he was dead. The other had been a special contract and the request had been for it to be ugly and painful. He hoped he would die quick, not suffering, willing to chew off a limb like an animal.

Now, here he was, hunting down a fiend in human form, one keeping company with creatures he hunted for the Church. He had every intention of killing the man when he found him, especially if he found the beast violating another person.

Ce'Nedra lead them into the woods and when they started getting near the estate, she stopped them and motioned them over. She kept her voice low. "We're almost there. Where did you see it?"

Duncan raised his head and saw it. "That one there. You can barely see it past the main house on the far side." He looked at her. "I was thinking about this. I need you two to wait here."

Ce'Nedra started to protest but Henri put his hand on her arm, eyes on Duncan. "Why?"

Duncan glanced over the estate. "Because if he's got a child in there, he's going to wait until dark to go to them. That means they are in there now, alone."

Ce'Nedra's eyes narrowed. "Or under the guard of that goblin. You said you know nothing about fighting them."

"No, I don't, but you're going to tell me."

"Duncan, it can hide from you. You're a man."

He could feel the confusion all over his face.

She shook her head. "Fae can't hide from women if they have become aware of them. I'm aware of them. I can help, but only if I'm there. You can die from fighting these things. Their bite can put you to sleep and then what would happen? You'd die and the children would continue to be prey. I won't let you do that, no matter how dramatic the story would be that was told by the bards."

Duncan smiled at the idea that bards would tell his story and he sat back on his haunches. "Ok, fine. What do we do?"

"We go with your idea, to a point. You seem a bit more comfortable with being sneaky. I haven't heard you very much when you move since we left the office. You go in and see what's there. If there's anyone being held captive, we need to free them, but only if we're sure we can escape with them. It won't do any good to go in and have no way out.

"Once you have assessed the situation, you wave me in. I'll look around and see if the goblin's in there. We'll go from there."

"What's the mead for?"

"They like sweet drinks. If it's in there and not engaged in something, you can leave the bottle as an offering. The goblin will drink it and pass out."

"Oh."

"You can also hit it over the head with the bottle."

Henri nodded. "That seems like a very reasonable plan."

She smiled. "Thank you."

They stood and Henri tugged on Duncan's sleeve, delaying him as Ce'Nedra went ahead a little. Henri leaned in. "You have something for when this very reasonable plan goes awry?"

"Nope. I think that's what will save us. Hell loves a good plan."

Nine

Fate is cruel. Sometimes, it lets you live.
-The Wisdom of Stone

Duncan put a hand on Ce'Nedra's shoulder as they got closer to the manor house. "We need to find out if he's in the outbuilding right now. Wait here. I can get in easier alone."

Ce'Nedra looked at Henri. "What are we supposed to do?"

"Wait to make sure I don't get caught."

"What do we do if you get caught?"

Duncan glanced at the couple. "Get creative."

The tall man bustled off and Ce'Nedra exhaled, frowning. "How exactly are we supposed to know if he's been caught?"

Henri smirked. "I'm quite sure it will be obvious."

Duncan crept up to the woodpile at the back of the manor. Because of the heat, they had the back door open, and the smell of roasting beef wafted unhindered from the warm interior. He ducked into a shadow and made his way downwind of the kitchen.

"…seen our lord today, milady Webb?"

"Milord Ballard. No, not today." She paused and lowered her voice, straining Duncan's attention to hear her comment. *"Not since last night."*

The young man sighed. "Did you hear anything from the Slaughter Cellar, Angela?"

"No, Anthelme. I'm sorry. Not since the King left."

Duncan heard the man leave the kitchen and walk near the wood shed. He was about to duck out of sight but he heard someone else leave the kitchen.

"Where are you going?"

Duncan saw the man for a moment. Shoulder-length brown hair was normal for this area, and it was clean and tied back but his skin had the russet color of a foreigner. He had seen a similar skin tone in the executioner of St. Marguerite a year or so ago. He was from Yndia, probably a worshipper of Karma. *Why would someone like that be here, with a child killer?*

Anthelme turned to the woman. She also stepped into view for a moment. She and Anthelme were of similar age, mid-fifties. She was definitely from Mervolingia, with curly blond-grey hair and light brown eyes. Her complexion was that medium white tone that mottled under the work of a kitchen, flushing red but fading here in the cooler air.

Anthelme glanced over her shoulder to the kitchen. "I'm heading to the Cellar."

"What if he's there?"

"Then I'll let Karma guide me. The children in town were healed from his horror, but I noticed a couple still missing. I need to look."

"What will you do?"

He started to step away but she grabbed his forearm delaying him.

"Answer me, Anthelme, *what will you do?"*

"What should have been done before now."

She frowned and stepped back, letting go of his arm. "What do you want all of us to do?"

"Just," he glanced around and Duncan feared for a moment he had been seen, "keep them out of the Cellar. If I'm not back in half an hour, go to the constable."

She nodded and went back inside.

Anthelme glanced over at the shadow where Duncan was, then went towards the outbuilding.

Duncan figured the woman would be watching the doorway, so he ducked out the opposite side, away from the kitchen door and made his way towards the outbuilding staying to the low shrubs in the woods. Once past the house, he looked around to see if he could find the man. Anthelme was crouching down by a nearby bush, looking at Duncan. Duncan decided not to pretend and checked the location of the house and his own companions.

"So, I guess I didn't hide as well as I thought."

Anthelme shrugged. "Or I could just be very observant."

Duncan's eyes searched the man. "Are you an... adept tracker?"

"No, I'm a drummer."

"Oh." Duncan sat back.

"Why would you think I was an adept tracker?"

"Well, because you're, um," he gestured to Anthelme.

"What?"

"Kinda..."

Anthelme looked expectant.

Duncan closed his eyes, sighing. "Foreign."

Anthelme frowned. "Foreign?" He tilted his head. "Are all foreigners adept trackers in this country?"

"No, I just thought..."

"And what makes you think I'm foreign?"

"You *look* foreign."

"Ah." Anthelme folded his arms across his chest.

Duncan pointed at him. "And you said you'd let Karma guide you." He pointed behind them over his shoulder. "Back there."

Anthelme narrowed his eyes.

Duncan swallowed, expecting a fight and decided to divert it. "Did you say, 'drummer'?"

"Yes. The Lord Rochefort hired me to be musical. I was flattered at first but a month ago, I was asked to do a vibrant drum and song set for dinner. I thought he wanted something lively for exercise or dancing, but he left just after I started. Everyone looked nervous when he left. I started to play and when I stopped because he left, the lady begged me to continue. When I paused to drink something, I thought I heard someone scream. I started to leave, but was stopped by Lady Rochefort. She told me the best thing I could do, for everyone, was play as loud and as hard as I could manage."

Duncan spat. "To drown out the sound, right?"

"I asked about it later, from the woman I was speaking to before. Angela said the last servant that went investigating never returned. She hoped he'd run off."

Anthelme's tone indicated Angela's suspicion that the servant never made it out of the cellar. Duncan looked towards the building they sought. "What's your plan?"

Anthelme pulled out a dagger. "I used to keep this at the ready when I was a traveling bard. I know a thing or two about using it. You?"

Duncan pulled a pair of knives from his belt.

"I suppose it's time we checked that building then. What do you know about the monster within?"

Anthelme shook his head. "Only enough to know it needs to be killed."

Duncan nodded and the two moved to the outbuilding.

Henri stretched his neck to see over the bushes. "I think he's talking to someone."

Ce'Nedra looked up from where she was crouched. "Who?"

Henri shook his head. "No idea." He looked down at her. "You want to keep following him?"

"Of course. If he needs us, we need to be nearby."

Henri ducked back down and the two continued to sneak over to the outbuilding.

The bald man slipped into the shadows of the outbuilding and looked at Anthelme. Anthelme looked back at the main house, then walked over to the door. At least he would have a reason to be in the area. The bald man seemed at home in the shadows but also acted like he expected them to hide him more than they did. He opened the door and winced at the sound of the creaking hinges. He barely got the door wide when the pain in his leg made him fall to the ground. He looked down at the shadowy monster attached to his leg, its teeth buried to the vile black gums. He slapped it and it went flying into the dark recesses of the building.

Two people ran out of the woods nearby, a woman and man from town. Anthelme was having trouble remembering their names. He thought the woman ran the inn and he might have known her from there, but his head was muddled from the pain. He looked down and couldn't feel his leg. He looked at the woman.

"I can't..."

She pulled apart the bloody tear in his pants, exposing his skin. He saw black poison running up and down his leg. The pain felt like lava in his blood and each beat of his heart caused it to scream through his veins. The scream ripped through his throat and into his tongue before he could stop it.

The woman looked at the bald man. "The poison's reached his heart. He won't last long."

The bald man looked into the darkness and growled. "Then our surprise is lost anyway." He leapt into the shadows of the outbuilding.

The other man started to follow but Anthelme grabbed him.

"The... floor... there's a ring..."

He felt the poison behind his eyes and then the world went dark.

Henri looked at the shadows where Duncan had gone. Ce'Nedra touched Anthelme's neck and then closed his now, black-veined eyes. Henri shuddered as the speed with which the goblin's bite acted. Ce'Nedra touched his hand. He squeezed hers, then left to follow Duncan.

Henri was nowhere near as stealthy as the tall man and he worried he might lose him in the darkness. He slipped in, trying to be as quiet as possible. As a result, he heard a thousand things he did wrong, as if he were walking on every piece of dried kindling in the forest. He saw a figure move in the darkness and hoped it wasn't the goblin.

Duncan motioned to him to come out of the faint light from outside. Henri obliged.

"I don't know where it went. I followed it in here but it isn't anywhere."

Henri looked around and saw straw strewn all over the floor of the building. "The fella outside said there was a ring on the floor."

They started moving straw aside with their feet and found a trap door on the far side of the barn. Henri looked around. "Did that thing go in here? There's no sign of it passing."

Duncan shrugged. "It could be they can move through an area without a trace. I've encountered one before. I think it might have even been this one."

"Where?"

"In the woods near here, about halfway to the main road out of town towards Patras."

"And you lived?"

Duncan shrugged. "It wasn't really after me. It did knock me out though."

"How did you get away then?"

"I have no idea."

Henri pulled the ring and lifted the trap door. The darkness below was disrupted by a lantern lit in the area and the smell of death, fear and urine permeated the air. There was a chink of chain against chain as they set foot into the room and Henri saw five cages on the perimeter. Three heads turned to them as they entered, two didn't move at all. Then the light above them went out as the trap door slammed shut.

The floor was strewn with foul straw here too and blood stained some of it over in the corner. From that corner, the nobleman stepped his hand gripping a butcher's cleaver. Henri backed against the steps and a stench-covered body dropped on him from above. He grabbed the leathery, bat-like skin and pulled it in front of him. His fear was confirmed as the goblin squirmed against his grip. It twisted in his hand and bit it, teeth dripping blackness into his skin.

Henri screamed and grabbed the monster's head, slamming it into the steps behind him. The stair broke into a sharp shard and Henri stabbed the goblin onto it, impaling the tiny monster. It screeched and the nobleman lurched forward at the cry. Duncan plunged his knife into the man's neck and both demons died at the same time.

Henri looked at his hand and saw the black veins starting to creep up his wrist. He dropped to his knees, squeezing the wrist in the hopes that he could stop the progress of the poison. Duncan looked around, then came back with a piece of twine. He tied it around Henri's arm, just above the elbow. The black veins were starting to slip past his grip and go up the arm to the elbow.

Duncan looked at Henri. He swallowed, then grabbed Henri's damaged hand and pulled it from Henri's grip. Before he knew what was happening, he saw the flash of the cleaver swinging through the air. The sound of the metal striking the stone floor beneath his arm hit the air right before Henri's screams of pain.

Ce'Nedra ran to the trap door and pulled on it, but it was locked from within. She heard the screams below and they frightened her. She backed away when she heard Henri. She no longer wanted that door open. She looked around and found a pitchfork, and stood by the door, waiting. After about a minute, the door rattled and lifted. She saw Duncan's head emerge, blood sprayed all over his cheek and eye.

"Help me."

She set down the pitchfork and ran to the opening. Duncan moved Henri to the opening and Ce'Nedra's heart sank as he, too was covered in blood. His skin was pale and waxy. She reached down and pulled Henri, who stumbled up the steps. He climbed out and lay down on the straw. That's when she saw the twine and the bloody stump where his right lower arm used to be.

"What happened?" Her voice went shrill with panic.

"He got bit. It was the only way I could think of to save him. I don't know if I got it all."

She looked him over but the blood was everywhere. She looked around but saw no water in sight. "I can't tell."

Duncan went back down and Ce'Nedra squeezed Henri's remaining hand. He moaned a bit, but seemed to be starting to shiver. "I'll be right back."

He nodded.

She ran to the manor house, praying to the Fae that he wouldn't die without her.

Ten

Cast about the names of Fae carefully.
-The Wisdom of Stone

Gwen pulled her horse up outside the inn and got down. Michael watched from the woods as Tanglwyst paced behind their animals. Gwen would go and negotiate feed and hopefully get something that could be reheated on the road. Tanglwyst was decidedly difficult to get to stop for any reason. Gwen had said she was tempted to hobble the horses at night, just in case. Michael had told her that unless she planned to break the horses' legs to stop the woman, it wouldn't work. Tanglwyst knew how to un-hobble a horse. The only reason they were stopping was because Gwen promised to use the speed spell to help them travel but could only do it if the horses had a solid rest in a stable.

Gwen knew Alexander was to blame for the situation but it didn't help when the person going through it was the person she had to deal with. Much more time with Tanglwyst and she was probably going to die at Gwen's hands before the spell got her. She went into the inn and let her eyes adjust. This place was just like many places along the road;

Dark despite the windows, bar, tables, rooms upstairs, cellar for roots and wine, hearth Fae to take care of the property. Gwen nodded to the Fae darting into the empty room upstairs. It gave her a nod as well before proceeding under the door to probably fluff the pillows and clean the straw in the mattresses.

She went to the bar and knocked on the top. A woman came from the back, wiping her hands on a towel. She was about to speak when the door opened and Tanglwyst walked in. The woman at the bar smiled.

"Well, hello again! I was hoping I'd see you come through here someday, just to show me you were safe."

Gwen looked at the woman. "She was here before?"

"Yes." The woman leaned in to whisper. "Left here with a scarred man of questionable intent. Gotta say, I was worried about her."

Tanglwyst came up to the pair. "I recognized the place when I went to use the privy. They don't have horses to let here." She nodded to the woman, "Unless that's changed?"

"'Fraid not. We have a small stable for the horses what visit but none to swap."

Gwen turned to Tanglwyst. "Well, stabling the horses for a night will help them. And you. Let you get some actual rest."

"Are you sure you can't cast it on them now? They can rest when we get to Caratia."

"That will kill them if they are exhausted, and the way you've been pushing them, they are almost to that brink. Look, you need the rest too. We all do."

Tanglwyst looked at the woman behind the bar. "How many rooms do you have?"

"Two right now."

Gwen nodded. "That will be perfect. I'll sleep in with you so I can help you."

"You mean keep an eye on me."

"That too." Gwen pulled Tanglwyst aside and lowered her voice. "I can put a sleep spell on you. It might be the only way to let you rest."

Tanglwyst yawned. "Will it stop me from dreaming about Alexander? Because every time I close my eyes, I see him in danger."

"I can ward against it."

Tanglwyst looked at the rooms upstairs. She shook her head, like trying to clear it. "Fine. But hurry, before I lose my resolve."

Gwen returned to the woman. "We'll take those two rooms please."

Tanglwyst looked around the room. It was a nice, small room, the kind you find comfortable enough for a single night, but not better than your own bed. She wondered if innkeepers did that on purpose. If the beds were too comfy, their guests might never leave. Her heart was still very restless and she recalled the state she was in last time she entered this place. This compulsion stopped her from entering her safe haven of the Papal City where her grandfather lived. It turned her back from assured lack of extradition to return to the place wanting her death. She knew in that minute that she loved him because the thought of the world without him was impossible to imagine. She realized the compulsion she felt right now was not as strong as it had been last time. It gave her hope that Gwen could calm the fear for a night.

Gwen came in. "Michael is prepping the horses in the stable. There's a good feeling about this place. It will help the horses to sleep in a stable, just like it will help us."

"Thank you again. I was just thinking about the last time I was here. I was so tired. I was ready to drop but I wanted to keep going. I got some bread and water and was willing to get back on the road."

"Is that why the innkeeper was worried about you? Because you were willing to travel with a stranger?"

"Well, yes, but she was right to worry." Tanglwyst looked at the bed. "Okay, you said you could put me to sleep and 'ward against' me dreaming about Alex? I don't know what that means but you made the horses go fast once. I trust you to have this under control."

"It will be done in an instant. Here, drink this. I made a little extra back in St. Andrew."

Tanglwyst took the small bottle from Gwen and sniffed it. It had a strange, familiar smell and she took a drink. She barely handed back the bottle before she felt the effects. She staggered to the bed and fell back into blackness.

Gwen pulled Tanglwyst to the side of the bed opposite the one she wanted, closer to the door, and pulled off the woman's boots and socks. Her feet smelled of travel and horse sweat. Gwen saw that her feet were calloused from the boots, like these were worn for far too long. Gwen looked inside and saw old blood stains in the base of the boots. She took a deep breath as she set aside the boots, calming her anger. This woman wasn't exactly frail, but she wasn't a farm worker or a messenger. She wasn't used to traveling like this, non-stop. At least she was already wearing the proper clothes for travel.

The part that angered Gwen was knowing that if Tanglwyst had been in her night clothes instead of on the road running for her life, she still would have walked her feet bloody to get to Alexander. Gwen looked at her friend and pulled out some stones from her pocket. She kissed them and then placed them around the room chanting in a low voice.

"Embertwist, here my plea. Take this person's dreams from me. Keep the Church's eye from her, so she might rest and become pure."

The stones shifted and glowed, setting up a perimeter around the bed. The glow was very faint but Gwen could see it. She smiled and left the room.

Embertwist watched Gwen leave and looked down upon Tanglwyst from Gwen's pillow. He felt certain the Glarren woman would have been overly excited had she known he was here so he had stayed on the pillow and not let her see him. Trickier with a Glarren woman, but he was, after all, Embertwist. Even they couldn't see or feel him if he didn't wish it.

He waved his hand and a tendril of white lights, weaving together like ivy on a wall, spun out away from her towards the south. He studied the spell, noticing how the tendrils grew thicker each second, joined by tiny, tiny veins of light from the distant source. He tilted his head.

"Church magic."

The Sinister Glove nodded from the foot of the bed.

"It has a voluntary component." He looked at his lieutenant. "She's *letting* it affect her?"

The Glove nodded.

"Why?"

"I think she's in love."

Embertwist looked down again. "Love? This isn't love." He picked up one of the strands, then dropped it like it was hot. "Is it?"

"He doesn't have to love her for it to work. She just had to have a connection to him." She pulled out a packet from her pouch and unrolled it. She pulled a lockpick from the tool kit. She inserted it in the tendrils and pulled them apart with another tool. A thin, pink one glowed at the center.

"Is that it?"

"Mhm."

"Can't you just cut it, or something?"

"Ugh. No, of course not. Look, you heard them. She's heading to Caratia. Once she passes the Cliff, she'll be in the purview of the Land. The Church has no power there. She'll be fine. The Glarren woman knows that. She's counting on it."

"Yeah, well, there's something strange about that one. I've never felt a resonance like that before."

"I know. I want to study her but I can't be around her for long. The lesser Fae don't seem to notice as much, but whatever it is, it interferes with her spells. It's a good thing you're so interested in this woman." The Glove looked at Embertwist. "So, can you do it? Can you interfere with the bond for the night?"

"Psh." Embertwist waved at the Glove. He put his hands on Tanglwyst and a thin barrier pushed the compulsion back, leaving just the thin pink tendril. He gestured to the remaining connection. "I can't do anything about that. That's Gloriana's realm. She fosters or freezes love. I take care of the more physical parts." He glanced at the Glove and winked.

She arched an eyebrow. "You offering, elf?"

"I'm starting to feel my power grow."

The Glove rolled her eyes and reached out to slip her fingers behind his head, pulling him to her for a kiss. "There's an empty bed in the next room."

"Says you. Prove it."

The room became silent as the two disappeared.

Myrgen watched Boots as she sat around the fire. She hadn't said anything for a while but she had not sat as quietly as her tongue. She was casting looks into the dark all around her. He sat up from his bedroll.

"What's wrong?"

She looked at him, as if she'd forgotten momentarily that he was there. "Nothing."

"Boots, are we being followed?"

She shook her head. "There wasn't anyone left to follow us."

Myrgen's gaze slipped to the ground. *I had almost forgotten.* He had been playing along with her, mostly out of a survival instinct. Keep the exterior calm so the captor didn't know he was plotting his escape. He did it in Patras. He'd done it in Mande. He looked at her again, making sure he retained his focus. He knew the White Sword was within his grasp if he needed it, and that had given him the strength to keep his faculties. This woman was more than just a killer. She was a mass murderer.

"Why'd you do it?" Myrgen's voice was low and didn't offer the option for more silence.

She looked at him, though her gaze wasn't as steady as his. "Portabella was a scourge on the world. It needed to be destroyed."

"Is that because of what it did to you?"

She scowled. "There were more than enough reasons to remove that place from existence. It was a haven for thieves, traitors and pirates. They preyed upon anyone who went near there."

"Except no one could find the place unless they had been there or were led by someone who was. I had heard of it but there was no record of where it was or how to get to it."

"That didn't stop them from luring the unsuspecting victims to there and then using them for profit or sport."

Myrgen caught the meaning behind the snarl. "Your mother or just repeated exposure?"

"Why does it have to be 'or'?"

"And you decided to end it, 'once and for all'?"

Her eyes narrowed and she shook her head in disgust. "What does that phrase even mean?"

"'Once and for all'? I have no idea. I personally despise the phrase. It makes no sense to me. I hate clichés. They show limited intelligence and a lack of ingenuity. There's always a better way to say something." He looked towards the former location of Portabella. "Just like there were better ways to deal with the town."

"Doesn't really matter anymore. The deed's done. The contract is fulfilled."

"Contract?" Myrgen looked over Boots, down to her shoes. Her boots were of Mandian manufacture, the leather an oxblood purple with a stacked wood heel. The strap around the base was adorned with a single shape: A horseshoe.

He looked at her eyes. "By the Stones… You're a horse."

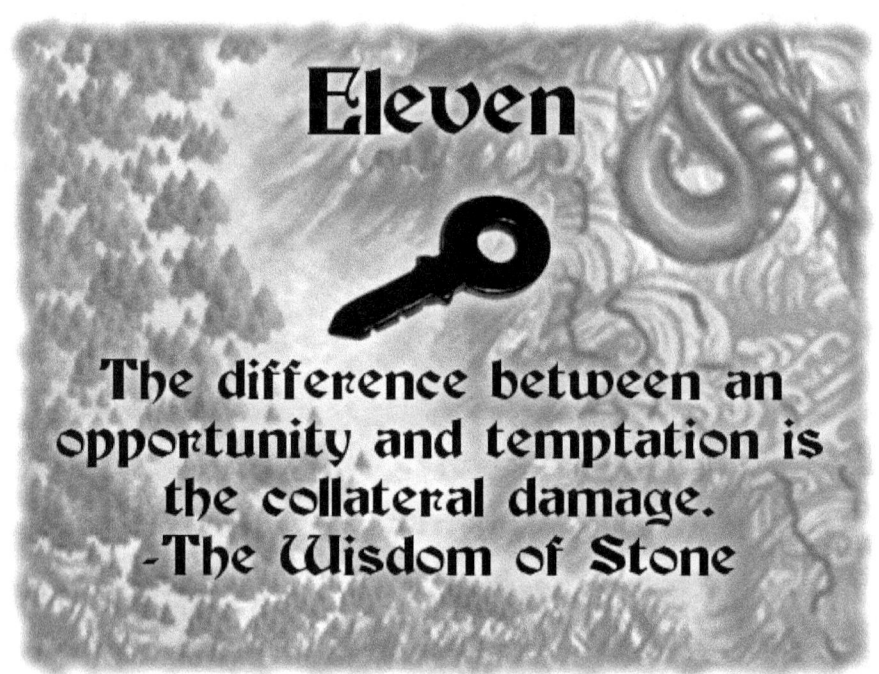

Eleven

The difference between an
opportunity and temptation is
the collateral damage.
-The Wisdom of Stone

Boots' eyes grew cold. "Whatever are you talking about, milord de Sablonierres?"

The Sangiardo Stables were a legend in the Underground. Allegedly, Giovanni Sangiardo was a priest who used to care for a special breed of horses for the Church. When he moved the operation to Mande, several deaths occurred near or with the horses. One man was run over by a wagon pulled by some of these horses, another died when knocked off of a horse riding through the local woods, a third died in a hunting accident while on a horse. Rumor started jokingly that the horses were assassins because the family members left behind inherited quite a bit of money and property.

Myrgen had it on record that he actually became an assassin broker, with the killers-for-hire being called "horses". The symbol of their connection was a horseshoe on them somewhere, like horse brass on a harness.

He'd seen them before. Professionally.

Myrgen put his hand to the ground, the White Sword touching his palm. "I should have known. Sangiardo didn't succeed last time he was contracted. It was only a matter of time before he tried again."

She arched an eyebrow and tilted her head. "Is that so? An unfulfilled contract. Those are rare."

"Rare enough to warrant killing an entire port to get me, apparently. So, I'm going to make a deal with you. I'm going to leave and you get to live."

She smirked, her movements becoming a crouch to spring. "Oh, I don't think I'm going to let you get away."

"I don't think I'm giving you a choice."

He stood and she jumped. The Stone Sword pulled easily from the fertile ground and he struck out at her. She was surprised by the appearance of the weapon and he caught her across the chin. Myrgen cut to kill but at the last moment, he struck with the flat of the sword. She was knocked aside, her chin bleeding from the stone's rough treatment of her face. He struck her again with the flat and she fell back to the ground. She started to get up again and he kicked her, this time rendering her unconscious.

He took her sword from her belt and reached for the amulet. Black tendrils lashed out and he jerked away just before they touched him. They wrapped around her and she disappeared in a puff of shadow and sulfur. Myrgen recoiled, looking around for her reappearance. She didn't, so he grabbed his things and took off into the night.

"I have a message for Grand Guard de Santander. I was told to bring it to you because he's away with the King."

Dominic looked at the messenger. His livery was of the Royal Patrol. He took the note and opened it.

"GG de Santader,

A patrol has returned from south of St. Marguerite, reporting in after investigating a large column of smoke from an unknown area. Fearing a forest fire, they prepared for the evacuation of the area.

When the column did not diminish but did not seem to get any closer, the Patrol went towards the smoke to discover the source.

They found the smoke issuing from a hidden cove the Patrol had never encountered in several years of being in the area. Consulting with local woodcutters, hunters and fishermen, it has been determined the secret village might have been the legendary Portabella.

The Patrol reported it burned utterly, no survivors.

Requesting further instructions.

-Patrol Chief Rhys Mathias"

"I'll take care of this." Dominic turned away from the messenger as he bowed before leaving. *This should be interesting. I've been everywhere with Tanglwyst. There are no ports south of St. Marguerite. But Portabella? Fascinating. Whatever magic kept it hidden must have been tied to something there, a person or building, some artifact.*

He fingered the amulet. No time like the present to test it out. Having seen the swirling eyes in his mirror and having timed it to determine how long they lasted, he decided to appear outside of town and walk the last half mile. He got his traveling supplies together and willed himself to the north of St. Marguerite.

The feeling of suddenly being out of control and out of reach was thrilling! The more he did it, popping back and forth to Tanglwyst's study, the more he loved it. It was what he imagined flying must be like. The power to go anywhere was *intoxicating.*

The landmark he chose ended up being only a quarter mile from town, so he walked slowly, despite the advancing darkness. As he got into the town, he was grateful he had waited for the swirling to stop. Otherwise anyone would have been able to see his impairment, his eyes went so wide.

Everywhere, there was fire damage. Some rebuilding was happening but there was no building in the main area that escaped the scorch marks. The smell of smoke was still in the stones and even the piers were blackened and treacherous. The people in the streets showed signs of the fire, bandages and crutches were more prominent than he remembered.

I thought the fire was south of here.

He went to the City Offices, seeing a light in the window. Morgan Wolf looked up at him as he entered.

"Dominic?"

"Morgan. What happened out there?" Dominic gestured to the tattered streets.

"We had a fire we didn't get under control in time."

"I saw the report. I thought it was somewhere south of here."

Morgan straightened up. "Different fire." His eyes narrowed. "You read the report?"

Dominic realized that, since the Patrol messenger had just arrived an hour ago, his appearance here was out of place. He decided to pull an old D'Medici trick. "I have many ways I get information. It's why I decided to leave Patras and see the damage personally."

"I see." Morgan tapped his fingers on the desk. "Well, it's out now though we kept finding little smoldering messes that have been quite persistent."

"What happened?"

Morgan blinked. "I thought you read the report."

Dominic continued the bluff. "It had some holes. That's why I came here." He decided to play a gamble, based upon the damage he just walked through. "When you request the amount of money you have, it warrants my personal investigation."

Morgan exhaled, settling back in his chair. A sturdy cane fell to the floor with a clatter and he looked at it but didn't pick it up. Dominic didn't look at the cane. "Yes. We have had several deaths from the fires and the damage to property has been overwhelming. Considering the source of the trouble, I felt it appropriate to petition the Crown for assistance."

Damn. I think he's seen through me. "Understood. Do you have a tally of expenses?"

"Right here." He pulled a thick missive out from under some other ledgers and handed it to Dominic. "That's the tally as of yesterday. Today's are being added as we speak." He gestured to the paper he was working on when Dominic came in.

"What's happened just today?"

"One of our guards was killed when a burnt support beam cracked apart. He is survived by a wife and two children. Ysabel works for me so she won't go hungry. However, the beam was part of the building Spencer was manning the night of the first fires. It housed a city cannon."

Dominic looked up from the tallies that had caught his interest. "One thousand ducats to replace destroyed lumber for homes? Are these people somehow wards of the state or something?" He shook his head, his eyes returning to the ridiculous sums requested. He saw a minimum of five thousand ducats on the first page alone. "This doesn't even include any city buildings."

"Yes, well, I wanted to take care of the citizens before I took care of the city structures."

"Pah." Dominic threw down the tallies. "Ridiculous. We're not the Church. We don't do *charity*." The disgust in his voice was a clear as his intentions of paying. "If these pathetic souls want money, they can petition the Papal City like every other poor wretch. Redo these figures and *only* factor in the cost of restoring city buildings. Everyone else will take care of their own wounds."

Morgan closed his eyes and Dominic stormed out of the building.

Gwen sat down across from Michael. "She's down."

Michael sighed. "Good. What did she ask of you earlier?"

Gwen blew out her breath, glancing around the empty hall. "You'll undoubtedly find out anyway. It's a Fae spell. It removes the ability to feel fatigue in a horse or person. It doesn't *stop* them from *getting* fatigued. They just don't realize it until the spell wears off."

"Won't that kill the horses?"

"Normally, yes, it could, if the rider pushed the horse until the spell ended on its own. The horse and rider would stop and then the horse would suddenly fall over. Luckily, I can stop the spell whenever I want so I won't ruin them. We have about a day's hard ride to the base of the Cliffs of Caratia. The way through is a climb but there's an inn at the top. We'll let the horses rest for a half day, make the climb and rest again at the top. Once she's in Caratia, the Land holds sway there. The spell will be lessened, if not stopped altogether."

Michael leaned closer, keeping his voice low so the staff wouldn't hear him. "You think the spell might be broken there?"

"It could be broken right now by her if she just chose to. Its hold is very tenuous. If she has her faith in him shaken at all, she's free of it. I think it's *very* possible for her to have her faith shaken in Caratia." She smiled, remembering the things she'd seen citizens of the Land accomplish. Stonemasons who used no mortar, fields that harvested themselves, wonder upon wonder done like it was normal. She couldn't imagine what a Caratian farmer would do in Mervolingia, or vice versa.

"So, you're a Fae worshipper."

She nodded, sitting back and turning the mug of tea on the table in a circle. She lifted it up and moved it slightly, making a new moisture ring partially on the first one. "Always have been, though making that known is dangerous in these borders. The Papal City is practically within sight of this place."

"But you seem willing to talk about it openly here. Why?"

She looked at him, her gaze relaxed, disguising the hand on her dagger. "I've never met an innkeeper who wasn't a Fae Worshipper."

Michael sat back, looking around. She saw his eyes light upon the summoning rune in the carved wooden roses along the ceiling, the Fae statue near the fireplace and the bowl of milk on the bar. He nodded and smiled.

"I find that comforting."

Gwen relaxed her grip on the knife and drank some more of her tea, setting the mug down a third time to complete the small spell-casting symbol on the table. She didn't know if she'd need it, but it was there for the night, just in case. If she put a drop of blood in the center overlapping circles, Michael's memories of her and Tanglwyst would be erased and they would escape. He'd wake up tomorrow unsure how he got there or why. A word and a gold slipped to the innkeeper and they would be gone.

"So, what is the plan then?"

Gwen finished her tea. "We need to rest up tonight. Sleep until you're no longer tired. Once we're up and ready to go, we'll ride and there will be no stopping until we get to the Cliffs."

Michael nodded, finished his ale, and bid good night to his friend.

Dominic stepped into the street and closed the office door behind him. He was sure he handled that right. It didn't matter what happened to cause this damage, he wasn't about to authorize spending that kind of money because some guards neglected a fire until it ravaged the city. He would look for the missive from Morgan when he got back to Patras and find out what the town's Vicar was talking about. Until then, he would just continue with his attitude of this not being the Crown's fault, and therefore, not going to be paid for by the Royal Treasury. Honestly, to demand payment for what was probably a lightning strike or arson? Dominic shook his head in disbelief.

He thought about why he came there in the first place but realized he had just stormed out of the only place with records and maps. He looked around and spied a guard house.

Ah! There will likely be Royal Patrolmen there. They tend to bunk down in the barracks. He strode up to the bunkhouse and opened the door like he belonged there. He looked around for a patrol tabard and found one. The partially-dressed man sitting on the bunk it was draped over had a tattoo of his division.

"Excuse me, I have a question about the burnt village that was discovered."

He looked up at Dominic. "I can probably help you. What did you need to know?"

"Where is it?"

The guard nodded to a map on the wall and they walked over to it. It pointed to a cliff coastline near the border of Mande. "It's here."

"I thought it was a bay?"

"Yes, hidden by magic."

Dominic pointed at the map. "Well, it's been discovered, right? Why didn't the map change?"

The guard folded his arms across his full, bare chest. "I don't know what kinds of maps you're used to seeing but these were drawn by a person, not magic."

He shrugged. "To tell the truth, I've never really looked at a map."

"How can you have never looked at a map?"

"Well, it's not like I've never *seen* a map, of course. I've just never had to be the person knowing where I was going."

"That explains how you got where you are now."

"It has served me quite well. One must know their place more than their location." He lifted his nose. *A particularly good snub. Well turned phrase there.*

The guard looked at him in stunned silence. After a couple moments, Dominic started to feel like he was being judged and looked back at the map. When this did not stop the judging, he cleared his throat, glancing at the guard out of the corner of his eye.

"Yes, well, c-carry on then." He waved his hand, dismissing the man but when further study of the map didn't yield any new information, he decided maybe he would try again in the morning. He returned to the offices and saw Morgan Wolf locking the door.

"Hey, take me up to that spa you run. I want to go to bed."

Morgan looked at him, his eyes dark. Suddenly, he brightened up. "Can't. Burned to the ground."

"What?" Dominic was sorely disappointed. Tanglwyst would be very sad to hear that. "That's a shame. Well, what's around here of similar quality?"

Morgan folded his arms and leaned against the door. "Well, unfortunately, with the tiny secret fires people keep discovering, it's dangerous to stay anywhere in town. You could be killed by a collapsing floor, or roof and not even know you're dead before your next of kin does." He nodded to the south. "Better to keep moving, to be honest. There's a place more your style about half a day's ride to the south. Scenic area, nestled against a cliff, right on the ocean. I understand the people there are quiet and very accommodating."

"Really?"

"Best kept secret on the coast." Morgan pushed away from the wall and started hobbling down the street towards the local tavern. It had some scarring from fire and Dominic didn't trust it.

He looked to the south. *Half a day's ride? It's already dark.* He looked around town and decided to come back in the morning. He knew of much better rooms to which he had access and it had been a long time since he'd been home. He stepped into a shadow and was gone.

Twelve

We look to the past for two reasons: to relive the best and to learn from the worst. -The Wisdom of Stone

The home of his mother, Graziana D'Medici, was nowhere near as lavish as she deserved. Her windows were plain glass, with stained glass in only the private chapel and the window above the front door. The double doors onto the veranda welcomed the scent of barely a dozen rose bushes, and only had two areas for seating. When it came to the furniture, it was handed down from royal cousins. Only a few pieces had once graced the summer palace in Veniche. Compared to the homes of the other D'Medicis, Graziana practically lived in squalor.

Part of that was the refusal to accept any part of the Giovanni fortune or estate. His father, Marco, had died years before, but the Appolodorus family held all of his lands and businesses. When he and his son passed away in a murder-suicide on Giovanni's wedding day, Dominic had figured he would inherit the whole thing. He was the only surviving son and he wasn't a bastard. Giovanni had been married to his mother originally. The fact he was marrying again when they still had a union on the books was something Giovanni had planned for the longer con. The woman he was marrying was rich. He undoubtedly planned to take all her money and probably kill her before anyone in Mande caught wind of the illegal wedding.

Or so Giovanni had thought. Dominic had no trouble keeping track of his father's activities and no interest in letting his brother benefit while he continued to be destitute, with barely ten thousand ducats to his name. Sure, an *honest* day's wages were two ducats a month, but no one truly expected a D'Medici to earn an *honest* wage. Everyone was assumed to have side wagers and unknown investments. His poor mother had no such things and yet, she tried to smile and be happy. He knew the truth though.

He stepped out of the shadows near the front gates of the city and made his way to her home, letting the inky swirls and lemons fade away in the street lanterns. He knocked on the door, half expecting her to answer it herself. She had half a dozen servants and no slaves, which was practically immoral. He would have bought her a slave when he started working for Tanglwyst but Tanglwyst Enterprises did not deal in human trafficking. Pity too. It was extremely lucrative. Dominic had resisted the urges to get into it only because he would have been fired by Tanglwyst for owning one. Now that he was Mervolingian Royal Chancellor, he would get a whole household of the things and invest in a few slaving ships as well.

The door opened and a Latian girl stood looking at him. She was about fourteen from the look of her and quite far from home. Latia was one of the islands around the Fingertips of Mande and well known for their scholars. Dominic doubted there would be any reason for a young girl like this to be here unless…

"Who are you?" His voice was crisp and dry.

"I am Fotini. Who are you?"

"I am Dominic D'Medici, Royal Chancellor of Mervolingia. This is my mother's house." He brushed past her, pushing her aside. "Where is she?"

"Fotini?" The voice came from the nearby sun room. "Who is it?"

"It's me, Mother." He pulled off his travelling gloves he had donned outside of town. He walked in to the room and saw her looking confused.

She looked past him to the young girl again. "Fotini, who is this man?"

Dominic frowned, concerned. He walked over, his tone softening. "Mother, it's me. It's Dominic." He knelt before her, her eyes searching his face. He reached out and took her hand.

"Dominic? I have a son named Dominic." She smiled, grey eyes dancing with remembered light. The wrinkles in her face expanded, deepening with her smile.

"Yes, yes you do."

"He went travelling some years back. Does pretty well, of course. I hear from him every once in a while."

For a second, Dominic thought she might be toying with him, scolding him for not writing or visiting as much as he should. Then the girl came over and touched his shoulder.

"She actually goes on about you quite a bit."

Dominic looked up at the girl.

She nodded to the stairwell. "I knew I recognized you. You're in the hallway."

Dominic stood and Graziana went back to gazing out the front window. He followed the girl to the foyer and looked at the stairwell across from the front door. On the landing was a portrait of Dominic he had made with his first month's pay after being hired by Tanglwyst. He looked back at his mother.

"What happened?"

Fotini closed her eyes. "She's gotten worse of late. When I came here a few months ago, she could remember things from a long time ago and from a few days before but she kept misplacing the names of things like her chair and her cup. My name is really Zenobia but she apparently had a cousin named Fotini that I resemble so she's called me that since she saw me. I've actually begun introducing myself as Fotini because it's easier on visitors."

"Did she suffer a blow to the head or some sort of fever?"

Zenobia shook her head. "No. I came here right before winter. My mother passed away and I was told I had a half-brother here in Florentine. That must be you."

"Half-brother?" Then it made sense. "Oh, you're a child of Giovanni's."

"From the breeding cages. I stayed in it with my mother until he died. Once we were set free, a woman visited us. She gave us money from his estate and said we could look for my brother in Florentine when we were up to it. Unfortunately, my mother never recovered.

82

Once we were out of the cellar in Cheryb, she began to cough. She lingered for a year before she finally died. I used the money to pay for everything, but it left almost nothing to live on. So I left for here."

"And my mother took you in?"

She winced. "Not entirely. I kept trying to explain who I was and who told me about you, but we never got the woman's name. At first I thought I'd be turned away, but then your mother came out of the solarium and called me Fotini. Insisted she knew me and demanded I stay. I've been helping here ever since."

Dominic was about to snarl that he would never have tolerated a vagrant off the streets to live with his mother when Graziana wandered in from the other room. She stank of feces and waddled like she was carrying something between her thighs.

"Dominic, is that you?"

"Yes Mother." He turned to her and she hugged him her voice a squeal of delight.

"Dominic, you've come home! Fotini, this is my son Dominic. You should marry him."

The stench of her fouling herself overwhelmed him and he pushed her to arms' length. "Mother, did you have an accident? Do we need to take you to the privy?"

"Oh, I should make you both dinner." Graziana started to move towards the kitchen and Dominic looked to Zenobia.

The Latian girl took Graziana by the hand and linked her arm through to guide her better. "Graziana, let's get washed up for dinner. Dominic might come by."

"Oh yes, we should. Invite your young man there to join us. My Dominic is very successful these days. He might be able to get him a job…"

Dominic watched his mother be led away to be cleaned up like an infant. He walked into the solarium to survey the damage to the chair. Someone had the forethought to cover the chair in a waterproofed canvas to preserve it, but he lifted the smelly cover and looked at the upholstery beneath. The royal crest of Mande had a yellow and brown stain covering much of the design but it looked like it had been cleaned as well as someone might. He put the cover back down in disgust.

As if his mother didn't have enough indignities.

"Your Excellency, a Don Dominic D'Medici is here to see you."

Giovanni Sangiardo looked up from his papers at the servant in the doorway. "Dominic D'Medici? Did he say what he wanted?"

"He didn't say, but he said to give you this." The servant's fashionable high heels clacked across the polished tile and he set a ring seal on the desk. Sangiardo picked it up and examined the Seal of State for Mervolingia. *Interesting.*

His eyes narrowed and he looked back at the servant. "Send him in."

The servant nodded and a few minutes later, a thin, attractive man far too young to be the holder of such an item entered. He bowed and Sangiardo stood. "I take it you've come to give me news about the owner of this ring?"

"Glad to see you know its importance."

"Of course I do. He had a contract out on him once."

Dominic tilted his head. "From who?"

"A former employer of his. It was that family's custom to kill anyone who decided to leave their services, especially under suspicious circumstances. He decided overnight to find other employment. They decided by noon to have him killed." He looked at his nails, the whites of them bright from the hand treatment he just received that day. "The family has long since died out. It's always dangerous to make enemies you can't defeat."

"So he just outlived it?"

Sangiardo just smiled. "Something like that. Let's just say they found other problems a bit more pressing." He clapped his hands together. "So, my cousin, what brings you back?"

Sangiardo gestured to the chair opposite him and sat as well. Dominic took the offer and inhaled deeply.

"I wish to change the contract I put out."

"Change it? How?"

"Well, you've never caught her and I have a more immediate target."

Sangiardo sat back, sighing. "She has proved to be difficult to defeat in a dark alley. Or a well lit one, it seems."

"Yes, well, I've had occasion to bargain with her. She owes me for looking the other way about something. I don't want her removed before she can serve that purpose."

Sangiardo nodded. "I see. Well, that will require a fee to change the records."

Dominic nodded. "Of course." He pulled out a coin purse and set it on the desk.

Sangiardo lifted it, pulled out a coin and tasted it. "Mervolingian silver. I do like the taste of foreign money." He put the coin back in the pouch and placed it in a drawer. Then he folded his hands on the desk and leaned forward. "So, who is the new target?"

"My mother."

Myrgen went through the underbrush as quiet as possible. He didn't know how long the assassin would be out but he was more worried about leaving an obvious trail than anything. If Boots had grown up in this area, she would know it. He had to avoid any landmarks or significant features like a river fork. She wouldn't be tracking him like a hound. More like a hawk.

Land, preserve me.

He stopped and crouched by a tree and listened. He put his hand to the ground, praying that it would tell him if she approached. The problem was that if she saw him, she would be on him before he knew it. He scanned the dark, hoping she was still out. He'd never been hit by a stone sword before and he knew nothing about how long she might be unconscious. He *did* know it wasn't that easy to one-punch someone. People were a lot more resilient that novels portrayed them.

He heard nothing and started heading out again. He moved a little quicker, figuring that he needed distance now instead of stealth. He was almost to a dead run when he ran into a clearing with a large boulder with a spring of water leaking from it. Some birds were resting on top of it and they took off, crying to the night. He crouched by the water and listened. Suddenly, he smelled sulfur and a hand grabbed his shoulder.

In the next second, they were gone.

Dominic closed the door to Sangiardo's home and looked down the street. He had hoped to rest in his old room, but it was such a fetid mess now, befouled by his mother's malady. The thought of going back there was horrifying. He wavered between feeling this was a betrayal and realizing it was a mercy. Regardless, he needed to be there. He had told Sangiardo to make it look like someone was trying to assassinate *him*, and his poor mother got caught in the trap.

A couple of days. That's all I have to last.

He breathed deep the scents of Florentine, the city he grew up in. So many memories beckoned him, some bad ones, but mostly good. He loved this place. Regardless of the time of year, Florentine always had flowers and spices. The hills were rife with silver, such that the mines didn't even have to dig very deep. This kept the hillsides pristine and lovely, with sanctions against the refineries being too close to the city. The more pungent area of town was to the west, away from the water and near the docks.

Florentine was one of four great cities at the Medians of the Fingers, where the land joined again. Pardua was the furthest west, closest to Mervolingia. Set in the Storm Catch, it was the first port associated with Mande. This was in the thumb area of the hand and prospered because many ships would wreck in the Storm Catch (the area between the tip of the thumb and the tip of the index finger). The Digitae Primus, or first finger of Mande guarded the Primo Mare and at the Meridian was Vincenzia. The Secundo Mare led to Florentine and the Tertia Mare held Calais.

Florentine had always been out of the way from Tanglwyst's ships so if he wanted to head home, it required taking a barge upstream or travelling overland with a caravan. With the amulet, returning home was something he had looked forward to, until he got here. He put his hand on the door to his home and listened for anyone stirring. It sounded quiet so he used his key to enter.

Graziana was asleep in her filthy chair and Zenobia was asleep in a chair nearby. They looked like imperfect bookends. Dominic went to the girl and shook her awake.

"Why isn't she in her bed?" He whispered to keep from waking his mother.

Zenobia shook her head. "She won't stay in it. She gets up in the night and comes here, looking for you."

He looked at the grand chair that had been used as a privy for so long and winced. "There must be something you can do. That chair needs to be burned."

"I can't, but you might."

He looked at her, then nodded. He walked over to his mother and knelt before her. "Mother?"

She opened her eyes as he shook her knee. "Dominic?"

"Yes, it's me, Mother. Shall we take you to your bed?" He stood and helped her to her feet.

"I waited for you, my *maritozzo*. Did you see?"

He smiled at her pet name for him, a sweet cake he practically lived on when he was young. "I did see, Mother. Thank you. I'm sorry I was so late."

She turned to Zenobia. "Fotini, did you see? Dominic is home. I used to crave *maritozzo* from the local bakery when I was pregnant with Dominic. That's why he loved it so much when he was a child." She turned back to Dominic as they started up the stairs. "Will you get some from the bakery for your grandfather? He loves them too."

He almost told her Papa had died years ago, but Zenobia shook her head. He suspected it could get her agitated to suffer the loss of a loved one when they were trying to get her to bed. "I will, Mother. I'll do that in the morning."

"Thank you dear."

They got her in her room, which was very nice still. Dominic figured she didn't spend much time in it. Zenobia brought a waxed blanket from another room and opened the bed clothes, slipping it down. She held it open for Graziana who climbed in with Dominic's help. She folded the blanket on top of his mother before putting the covers over her, protecting the bedding. Dominic felt the tears stinging his eyes as she did so, recognizing the girl's attempts to keep the house nice while still attending to his mother's needs.

He kissed Graziana's forehead and stepped out into the hallway. Zenobia followed.

"Thank you for that. The chairs in that room are far more comfortable."

"The chairs?" Dominic frowned.

"Yes. She can't be unmonitored at all. If she gets up in the night, she can fall down the stairs. I looked for a room on the bottom floor but none of the servants live here. It's all storage."

"Oh. Do you want me to sit with her instead?"

She looked at the door, then at Dominic. "No, I would just have trouble sleeping, worrying about leaving her."

"Is this all you do, all day?"

She thought a minute, then nodded. "Yes, I think so."

He looked at the door. "How do you bear it?"

"Where else can I go?" She shrugged. "Besides, it gives me something to do. I was idle for long enough. Here's someone who needs me. I need her just as much."

"You do?"

"She gives my life purpose." She smiled, which turned into a yawn. She nodded while covering her mouth and stepped back into the room.

He watched the door close.

What have I done?

Thirteen

Sacrifice has dark connotations for a reason.
-The Wisdom of Stone

"Message for Lt. Gomez de Santander."

Gomez opened the door to his room and looked at the Royal messenger standing before him. He rubbed his eyes and glanced around. The night sky was that shade of nowhere-near-dawn black outside and he was already missing his bed at home, and his wife Mauda. He was starting to regret suggesting to Alexander that he go on a Wife-Searching Tour. This was a ruse Gomez came up with to cover Alexander's absence from the palace while chasing the woman he loved. He sent out four caravans with full regalia to represent the crown, all designed to draw question as to where he would be. This kept the nobility scampering to make their daughters and dowries presentable and too busy to coup.

When Gomez discovered Alexander's illegitimate child with Catriona Moriarity, he felt in his heart it was only right to let his king pursue her. Clearly the king loved her. The way Alexander went through the abandoned house she had shared with her now-deceased husband showed Gomez a look he had only seen in the mirror. He would never deny any person a chance to have what he had with Mauda.

So they had devised a plan: Tell the world he was going to pick a woman from whatever walk of life she was in, instead of simply choosing the best foreign contract. Mervolingia supplied the bulk of the food for the entire continent and was the largest producer of medicinal herbs in the Saintlands. Anyone attacking would have to march across hundreds of miles and if they razed the fields, they would cause their own countries to starve before the next crops could be harvested for their own use. Attacking Mervolingia would cause famine and unless your country didn't need food, sane people didn't do it.

Having a Mervol king who was unmarried was a huge commodity. Thus, the fanfare caravans were put together and letters sent out two tendays ago. Gomez went with the one to the north because more people would be likely to believe Alexander himself was with the Captain of his Guard. North of the capital city of Patras, there were four counties and numerous small hamlets. Anyone Gomez found worthy was to be given a special sash and her name and visage recorded for perusal by the king. Since no one of any class was too low to be considered, families everywhere were scampering to make their children presentable.

Alexander had even given Gomez the right to have his own daughter Kayliegh chosen as a "potential bride", even though Gomez knew she wouldn't be chosen. It would open up her prospects to have that sash though. To be considered good enough for a king meant the man who *did* win her heart would be getting more than just a great wife. Their future would be set.

Gomez took the missive and closed the door. The seal was that of the Palace guard and he opened it, still too groggy to be concerned.

Sir,

A letter came to the office recently of a horrible murder in St. Giles. The information from that area is not in the recent reports but the letter received detailed a matter that deserves our personal attention. Please see the enclosed for explanation. I'll await your orders.

-Gardain Nina Richeleau, Second

He read the other letter.

"Lucia,

Forgive the brusque nature of this missive. I am distraught beyond measure and can barely bring myself to think about this, much less write it down. Putting the words on paper makes them somehow more real.

Celeste is dead. She was murdered by a..."

(Here, the handwriting changed.)

"...monster disguised as a man. A client came in to the Red Sky. He had a black scar on his face, as if a fiery stone was drug across his cheek. I thought nothing of it. Many disfigured men seek our companions, thinking wrongly no whole woman would want them. I set him up with Celeste because she never has problems with the way men look, being blind. She has a very loyal clientele because she is so enthusiastic in her work.

I heard an unusual amount of ruckus in the room and thought at first they were just being energetic. Then I heard her scream in pain and I knocked on the door. It was locked and when I pushed against it, there seemed to be something blocking it. I brought the key to open the room and two guards to break down the door. Her screams will torment me for the rest of my life, they never stopped the entire time. Eventually, we got the door open. The bed had been shoved against it with such force, it broke the frame. A rancid smell filled my nostrils, like burnt flesh.

Celeste lay on the bed under a sheet, still screaming. The man was nowhere to be seen, and the room had only the one exit. When we pulled back the covers, Celeste's body was so empty, as if her entire body had been drained of all moisture and life, her eyes were gone, black holes crying blood in their place. Her mouth was open and she was somehow still alive. Her chest had carvings through the skin and into the bones. I could see her ribs through the flesh. He had managed to take every bit of blood from her body, but kept her mind trapped there, awake throughout the ordeal.

I ran from the room and the guards managed to end the screaming. The guards said they found dark stains on her skin, like someone had spilled ink on her. They looked around for a trail of ink but no one saw any so it remains unexplained.

Lucia, don't let this man near you, or any of the girls. If he arrives, put him in a room alone and get the guards. Under no circumstances, be alone with him yourself. Take care.
    Elina"

Gomez noticed that the writer clearly went from trying to write the account herself to dictating it to someone with better control. Judging from the legibility, it was someone familiar with writing reports. That meant either the messenger service, the bookkeeper for this business or someone at the royal guard station in St. Giles. He hoped it was the latter because that would make his job easier.

He looked at the messenger. "Return to Patras and tell *Gardain* Richeleau that I will look into this personally."

The messenger nodded and Gomez closed the door to get dressed.

Myrgen fell onto the floor of the windowless room and vomited. Black shadow streamed off his skin like smoke. It took several minutes to expel all the darkness but he sat back on his heels, grateful he had avoided the extended time in the dark like he experienced in St. Andrew. He looked at Boots, who was walking around the dimly glowing room, lighting candles. The baseboards were about the luminescence of a half-moon night from symbols his vision was too blurry to discern, and the candles brightened it slowly to early morning. She walked over to a desk and took off the amulet, placing it in a drawer.

"I... thought you... couldn't remove that..." Myrgen gasped, massaging the muscles in his abdomen. Myrgen's face stayed pinched in pain as he looked around. He felt his lungs ache and the pain in his stomach wasn't subsiding. He felt like he had been in a bar fight with his intestines

"It's possible here, probably because I can't leave here without it." She sat on a chair at a table. "You might want to step back a bit."

She nodded to the pile of vomited rabbit and wild carrots they had eaten. Tendrils of the shadows he had shed slithered towards the partially digested meal. He backed away, hitting the bed with his back which didn't improve matters with his body. He climbed up and got his feet off the floor as more shadows crawled from beneath the bed. They covered the pile of still warm bile and consumed it like wolves on a deer. Within seconds, it was gone and the shadows dissipated into the air.

"Ugh... does that mean we're breathing them in now?"

Boots shook her head. "I don't think so, but then again, this place is a complete mystery. I have no idea where we are or how to get out without the amulet. No one else is ever here, so I think they're attuned to each other."

"So, you never run into Duncan McVryce here?"

"Who's that?"

He shook his head and tried stretching the stomach cramps out. "The last guy I encountered with an amulet like that. He attacked me and these shadows filled me when he stabbed me with them. I think he had one of those. I just now remembered seeing it."

She looked away, tapping her fingers on the table. "So, when you said you had encountered one of these before, you weren't talking about the amulet?"

He shook his head and the activity made his vision swim. "I... meant I had seen the shadows and the inky eyes before. I had experienced them... but without the benefits of going where...ever I wanted." He blinked. "There's no way to get outside air here?"

She looked around. "For all I know, we're under water."

He looked at the walls. They weren't made of stone, at least, not stone the Land touched. *It would explain why I can't feel the Land at all. I am completely cut off. Catriona would die in minutes here.* He had not realized how essential his connection to the Land had become but in its absence, it was apparent. He was missing a part of him right then and he hadn't even known that part existed.

"Why did you bring me here?"

"To show you what I'm capable of. I could put that amulet on right now and just leave you here. I have no idea what would happen to you. I never bring food here because I figure it would just go bad but after seeing that little display," she nodded to the damp spot on the floor where the vomit had been, "I think that wouldn't be true. To be honest, this place is a refuge, a safe haven. If I'm hurt, I heal up overnight here. If I am hungry, I no longer am here. I can't be summoned from here because the amulet is neutralized or something. At least here, I can take the *mostro dannati* off."

She knows it's a monster, and that it's damning her. Well, knowledge is half the battle. "So, you've shown me. You can put me in a room and leave me to die. I have to admit, I've been threatened with that before but right now," he nodded, looking at the sealed walls adorned with faintly glowing symbols, "yours is the most convincing. I doubt I could get out of this one without you." He looked at her again, annoyed that the pain wasn't subsiding, but at least it didn't seem to be increasing. "So, what do you want?"

"I want out of this room."

"You and me both."

She smirked. "Then you see my problem. Once outside these walls, that thing is back in control. I want it off."

He glanced at her boot, at the small horse brass on her ankle. "Did your boss give the amulet to you?"

Boots looked at the cup she had drunk from. The small leaves soaking in the drudge at the bottom looked familiar. It was barely visible through the dark liquid, but it was there, small blue-tinged leaves reconstituted in the mead.

Boots leveled her most vicious gaze at Sangiardo. "You gave me Cyprian herb?" Sangiardo merely watched her response, uneffected. "You money-grubbing, ass-licking pestilent maggot!" With every insult, she took a step towards him, but he didn't move. "I will kill you for this! I will tear the flesh from your bone in strips, fling them around your mother's crypt and stomp on them until they are little, slimy pieces of carpet!"

She put her leering face in Sangiardo's and he didn't even blink, which actually surprised and impressed her. Instead, he held her gaze.

"Try it."

Boots flexed her fingers but found she didn't possess the will to hurt this vile man.

"The fact is only one person in the world has ever managed to be released from the effects of this herb, and I'm pretty sure she won't give you the antidote." Sangiardo stood and walked away from Boots, showing his confidence in the herb's effects by turning his back on her.

"Before, you were a ruthless killer. Now you're just a love struck assassin with a shoe fetish.

"But our fates are absolutely linked. I die, you die. You are the ultimate bodyguard. I have a secret that needs protecting but someone I can trust implicitly. That's now you."

He turned back to face her, clasping his hands behind his back. "So whether you like it or not, Madame Malatesta, you will not only fail to kill me, but you will give your life for mine. And I can't thank you enough."

"Yes, but he's not the owner of the amulet. I can't say who is."

"Can't or won't?"

"Can't. I don't know. It serves someone else but I don't know who. Sangiardo was given the amulet and told to use it wisely. He put it on me. I can feel the presence, but I frankly have chosen not to investigate the owner. Unless Sangiardo tells me to, I wouldn't be able to do anything about it anyway. In my line of work, it's better to never know who ordered the contract."

"Because you might decide not to do the job if you knew who you were doing it for."

She shook her head. "No. Because I can't refuse the job no matter what. If Sangiardo tells me to do something, I have to do it."

Myrgen closed his eyes, feeling sick. "Portabella."

She nodded. "Apparently, the client said they wanted it destroyed. No survivors. You're lucky you weren't in town when I got there. And that you didn't stay."

"So, why are we going the long way around to get back to Florentine?"

"Because of what's on the other side of Florentine's coast."

He frowned, thinking. "What? The Blood Sea? Nubia?"

"Catriona Moriarity."

Myrgen's blood ran cold.

"You were with her when you left Rouen. I heard about your incident with Nicolai Moriarity and burning his body. A street person said the two of you spent the night together at the Open Lotus."

He inhaled, which hurt but less than he expected. "We stayed at the same place, not in the same bed."

"But Alexander Angloume was pretty mad that you did, and believed otherwise, apparently."

"How do you know about that?"

"The same way I know you fought Nicolai on the docks. People see things. They sell that information cheap."

"So, you know what I've been doing. Sounds like I left quite a trail." He shook his head. "I never would have been that sloppy before."

"I know. Luckily, you aren't now either."

He looked at her eyes and swallowed. "What do you mean?"

"You used to be impossible to track. You were renowned for never having anything connect back to you. Suddenly, you're attacking someone in public, burning bodies of Callista worshippers *personally*, and spending the night with known pirates. Such behavior is unbecoming a legend such as yourself." She glanced away. "But then, love does crazy things to people."

"I didn't love her then."

She looked at him again. "You sure about that?"

He sighed. "No."

She nodded. "You left her ship. Why?"

"Because I love her now."

Her eyes narrowed. "It's not supposed to work like that."

"No, it isn't. But she has this notion in her head that she's supposed to marry Alexander."

"That's why he was so mad. He loves her too."

He shrugged. "It's a regular romance novel, or common theater plot. Nothing special to see here."

"Except it's happening to you."

Myrgen said nothing and went back to rubbing his stomach. After a few minutes, he glanced at the desk. "That really is a hopeless situation, isn't it?"

She saw where he was looking and nodded. "Yeah. I mean I could just smash the thing here, but then, I'll be trapped here. Since I don't get hungry or anything, I don't have the ability to even starve to death. I would literally be trapped for all eternity."

"What if I took it now?"

She looked at him, her eyes guarded. "What do you mean?"

"Well, you tell me what to do and I take us both out of here, with you not wearing it. As soon as we're out of here, you can destroy it."

"With what?"

He reached for the Stone Sword but it wasn't there. It must have been blocked from coming here. What magic could so thoroughly stop the Land from touching it?

"I have an idea, but it clearly isn't something we can do here. The white sword that was in my hand is a gift from the Land. It might be able to destroy the thing."

She looked nervous. "It's not mine. I don't know what the person who owns it would do if it was lost."

"Boots, if the person who owns this is doing this to you, who cares? They aren't the sort of person you want having control over your life."

"What if it doesn't work? What if that sword isn't enough to break it?"

"Then we'll try again in Caratia, where the Land will hold sway."

She cocked her head. "Caratia?"

"You wanted Catriona. That's where you find her."

She looked away, fighting in her mind as her eyes darted about the room. "I… I can't go into Caratia."

"Why not?"

"You really don't know?" Her eye roll and tone indicated disbelief.

"Uh, know what?"

"I'm Mandian. We can't enter Caratia."

"Well, not to live there, I'm sure but," he gestured to the north and east, relative to where he had been before they teleported into this room, "but there's a mountain pass and the sea. It's just a political boundary."

"Spoken like someone who's never been there."

He opened his mouth but realized she was right. In all his travels, the one place he never even considered before Rouen was Caratia.

Boots used her hands like walls. "Caratia is guarded on three sides by cliffs, unbroken in every way except in two places, one north into York and one west into Toledo. The eastern side is protected by the Sea of Blood, aptly named because any Mandian vessel is destroyed on the reefs and devoured by sharks."

"You can't be serious. That has to be sailor superstition."

Her face became mocking disbelief. "Oh really? And you know this because of what?"

"Well, the... uh..." He frowned. "Come to think of it, there's nothing that Caratia really exports or imports. I never saw an order for food or textile agreements with them and they never have had a treaty brokered for anything, at least not with Mervolingia."

Boots sat back, crossing her arms. "That's why your king is so interested in snagging her in his grip. He can force a trade agreement *and* get his bloodline into the Forbidden Land."

Myrgen's stomach churned and he couldn't tell if it was because of the room or the thought of Alexander breeding with Catriona. Both had the same effect. He remembered throwing up on the ship and wondered if Catriona was feeling sick too.

"Yes, well, whatever we decide, we need to do it now. This place is... I don't know..." He tried to stand and fell to his knees. She rushed over to him, abandoning the aloof air she had managed to maintain since they met. She put a hand on his shoulder.

"Why are you doing this?"

"What? Collapsing?"

"Offering to help me?" Her eyes indicated hope, but guarded, guarded hope.

"Let's just say I'm walking a different path now. And that means giving kidnapping assassins the benefit of the doubt. But understand, you only get this one shot."

"How do I know you won't just take the amulet and strand me here?"

"Look at me." He was gasping and sweat had started to dampen his brow. "What makes you think I want *any kind* of prolonged contact with that thing?"

She closed her eyes and sighed. "Okay."

She helped him up and walked him over to the desk. He opened the drawer and the tendrils licked at the light. He almost thought he heard a hiss from it.

"You need to pick it up and then envision in your head where you want to go. It has to be somewhere you've been before though."

The first thought that entered his mind was the *Enigma*, and he rushed to repel that thought. Best case scenario, he would be shunted to the water next to the ship and would sink to the bottom of the sea without them knowing he was there. He didn't want to think about the worst case.

It has to be somewhere neutral. Something with a strong Land presence... But where?

A picture formed in his mind and he took a deep breath and grabbed the amulet. The shadows burned his flesh and he dropped it. Boots started to pick it up but he stopped her. He reached down and grabbed it again, more prepared this time. The shadows grabbed his flesh and he concentrated on the place in his mind.

A puff of sulfur consecrated his initiation into darkness, leaving the room silent except for the crackling of the candles.

Fourteen

Sometimes, the road less traveled sneaks up on you.
-The Wisdom of Stone

Tanglwyst awoke in the night. Everyone had been counting upon exhaustion keeping her down until morning, but she could hear and feel Alexander in danger with every heartbeat. Every minute she wasn't trying to get to him was a minute she would lose near the end. She fell into a slumber before she found him before. She couldn't let that happen again.

She knew she had only two tendays to get to Alexander. Gwen had told her back in St. Andrew that she was under a spell, and that the compulsion to go to Alexander was actually a lie. He wasn't in danger. He had *geased* her, forcing her to go to him despite it meaning her death. As each day passed without her being at his side, Tanglwyst would become more and more ill. Worse, the lack of sleep would make traveling dangerous because she could fall from her horse or run into predators, human or animal. She could even be caught by the patrolling guards and put in a cell, making her execution unnecessary.

Tanglwyst also knew how to break the spell: Renounce her fealty to the King and she would be free of the *geas*. Unfortunately, for that plan to work, she would have to not care for the man. The previous winter, while she was trying to heal from a broken heart, Tanglwyst had become friends with Alexander. It turned out he, too, had suffered a loss and they bonded over entertaining his niece, Marie-Elizabeth or Emmy as she was called by family. She felt herself falling for him, and he seemed to reciprocate. But then something happened and he turned inward, no longer playing with Tanglwyst and Emmy. Emmy moved on, playing with Nicolai's son Alan but Tanglwyst had no one new to play with. She told her friend Elizabeth about the way she felt about Alexander.

That was when Elizabeth gave her the wine.

Tanglwyst now understood that Elizabeth had designs on Alexander, that he was her real goal, not simply the throne of Mervolingia. Elizabeth never revealed her plan while alive but Tanglwyst had discovered the plan after finding a secret alchemy lab in the Queen's chamber. Elizabeth had obviously used some sort of Fae magic to create a place within her room for there was a secret chamber far too large to be part of the castle. She didn't even know if it was still there. She really knew nothing of Fae magic.

Gwen did though. She would ask her about it.

Right after Gwen caught up to her in Caratia.

She looked at Gwen and turned to slip out of the bed when she felt her stir. When she didn't wake, Tanglwyst got out of bed. She planned to say that she was on her way to the privy if Gwen woke up. Tanglwyst had never been happier that privies were external on inns such as these. The palace and her home in Patras had middens but that wouldn't have required more than a robe. Getting fully dressed would be appropriate for a jaunt in the night to pee.

She was careful in her silence, gathering up her things in her coat. She kept her hand on the money pouch to keep it quiet, and considered leaving half her coins for Gwen and Michael to catch up. She just wasn't sure how to do so without the metallic *ching*.

Maybe I'll leave the money with the innkeeper. She was so concerned about me, I doubt she'd steal anything.

The hinges were well oiled and made no noise, allowing her to slip away without Gwen stirring. The travel had been brutal and resting on the ground had not done the trick. The only reason Tanglwyst wasn't as unconscious as Gwen, was the *geas*. Tanglwyst left the room and sat down on one of the common room chairs near the hearth to pull on her boots. She had just gotten them on when she heard a small whine off to her left.

She looked down and looked into the big brown eyes of the cutest little dog she'd ever seen. He was sitting up, looking at her like this was his natural posture. He was black and white, with fluffy cheeks and large ears with tufts. He looked a bit like an adorable black and white fox, every part of him was happy and fluffy. The smile on her face was not even voluntary, yet she could not have stopped it from being there. She picked him up and he licked her nose.

She smiled and held him, petting him as he wagged his tail. He nuzzled into her lap and curled up on her. She scratched his ears and they both became content. After stroking his fur a few minutes, she remembered that she needed to get moving. Unfortunately, to move would mean disturbing the tiny dog, and she found that was a terrible idea. So she petted him a bit more. Soon, she realized that she actually *did* have to use the privy but the thought of disturbing the dog again stopped her.

Eventually, she realized she needed to do something. She tried to pick the dog up, but he just seemed so happy and loving there in her lap. She looked at the window and watched as the sky lightened, leaving the night and her escape behind. By the time Gwen came out, she had spent the night in the chair.

"What are you doing out here?"

"Well, I had to use the privy in the night so I sat down to put on my boots. Next thing I know," she looked fondly at the dog in her lap, petting him, "the Heaviest Dog in the World was in my lap and I cannot bring myself to disturb him."

Gwen leaned against the doorjamb and folded her arms. "You tried to leave."

Tanglwyst looked up, trying to seem shocked. Gwen shifted her eyes to the pile on the floor. "You needed your belt and money pouch to go to the privy? Your coat was also probably unnecessary, given the lack of rain or frost, at least for a 'trip to the privy' in the night."

She walked over and picked the dog up off Tanglwyst's lap. "Thank you, Sampson." She set the dog down on the floor and he trotted off to the kitchen.

"Sampson? Like the strongest dog in the world, Sampson?" Tanglwyst shook her legs to get the feeling back in them until she was sure they'd hold her, then stood and ran to the privy. She returned to the inn afterwards before she even realized she could have escaped. Gwen was likewise pulling on her boots but was somehow not impaired by having a small dog nearby.

"Okay, how did *you* escape the little dog's spell?"

"Simple. I was the one who cast it."

"You cast a spell to keep me here?"

"You're under a spell to make you leave. Seemed prudent. Besides, that way, I could actually get some rest. Being able to spread out on the bed was," she stretched, smiling, "luxurious."

"Well, hurry up then. We need to get moving."

Tanglwyst knocked on Michael's door and did the same prodding to leave on him that she did on Gwen. As Gwen gathered food for their trip from the innkeeper's daughter, she could hear Tanglwyst hurrying Michael. Her chiding caused both girls to snicker more than once and Gwen's spirits were lifted by the time they were offered breakfast.

Tanglwyst was about to say something foul about time being short when Sampson came out of the kitchen carrying a small stuffed toy. He snarled and growled at it, then dragged it to Tanglwyst, who picked it up and spent the next half hour playing with the dog while Michael and Gwen got the horses ready to travel.

"So," Michael asked once the inn's staff was out of earshot, "the innkeeper seemed worried about you. What happened when you were here last?"

"What makes you think something happened?"

"That woman remembered you despite that place being on a main road and your visit happening tendays ago. Something must have stuck in her mind about it."

"A few tendays ago, when Duncan got me out of Patras, we stopped for the night. We... got separated. I was within sight of the Papal City when I got the dreams about Alexander."

"Does that mean you didn't get *any* rest at all last night?"

"How could I possibly rest? Every time I close my eyes, I see Alexander in danger. I can't shut him out of my mind and the feeling of urgency gets worse by the hour."

Gwen shook her head. *Geases could be pretty nasty things.* "I knew I had to take steps to stop you in case you couldn't resist the call."

"I suppose I should thank you for that, though I have to say I can barely handle the time I wasted being lost." She sighed. "However, judging from what happened last time I was there, I think this *geas* thing doesn't care if the person lives or dies getting back to the King."

"What *did* happen to you?" Michael's concern showed in his voice and frankly, Gwen was curious about that too.

"I was on foot and got to the inn, exhausted, looking for a horse. They didn't have any they rented out. A man was sitting in here and he... said he had a horse."

The strange pause in her tale was confusing, like she was either changing things or leaving something out. Gwen narrowed her eyes. "A horse? Why would the innkeeper be worried about you riding with a man on his horse?"

"It turns out he didn't have a horse."

Gwen sighed. "What happened?"

Tanglwyst gathered up Gwen's satchel and handed to her. "I'll tell once we get the horses moving."

Michael was still groggy and Gwen handed him a warm wineskin of tea. They all mounted their well-fed and well-rested horses and started riding east toward the Separation Mountains.

Gwen turned to Tanglwyst. "Ok, what happened?"

Tanglwyst looked quizzical and Gwen realized the *geas* probably had her mind refocusing upon Alexander.

Gwen prompted. "With the man from the inn?"

"Oh! Yes, well, he was wearing an amulet, one I'd seen before. The man was heavily scarred and had a distinct appearance. I honestly weighed the risks against the man being very identifiable should anything happen."

"Wait, you *knew* you were putting yourself in danger? Why did you go?"

"I... I don't know... I knew it was a bad idea. I just also knew he could get me to Patras in an instant."

"An... *instant?*"

"Yes. The amulet was one I had seen Duncan use before. He used it to rescue me from Patras. He took me to a room with no doors or windows. This man took me to one like that, though I don't think it was the same one. We fought and I took the amulet off him, then used it. I imagine he's still there. There's no way out of the rooms except with the amulet."

"What did you do with the amulet?" Gwen tried but failed to keep the venom from her voice.

"I went to the palace and then to the catacombs underneath when Dominic almost found me. I dropped it. It made me horribly ill."

"And weakened you when you started walking to St. Andrew." Gwen spat.

"Sorry. I know it was an inconvenience."

Gwen shook her head. "Not for that reason. I'm just... *angry* at Alexander for this."

And at Duncan. He was the Shadowalker, and I went into the woods with him. And Alexander covered for him, knowing I would never allow him to be with us, that James would never have allowed it. Maybe that's what's happened to Alistair. He's in one of these rooms. Now I have even more reason to not want Alexander with my friend. He would kill her rather than let her be with anyone else.

"Enough of this. We need to get moving."

She drew her horse next to the others and cast the spell, petting their manes. Within seconds, keeping the horses still was impossible and they rode like a wind storm through the trees. While traveling, they couldn't communicate except through gestures and they slipped into the woods to hide their speed. As they rode, Gwen felt a presence around them.

Oh no. There are Fae in these woods. And I'm not paying proper homage to allow our passage. It was too late now. If they couldn't get out of the area in the next twenty hours, the Fae would extract payment of a nature she truly hoped they could pay.

Fifteen

What is invisible to the eyes, can be seen by the heart.
-The Wisdom of Stone

Myrgen opened his eyes at the morning sun cantering through the leaves of the trees near the rock spring where Boots had caught him. He sat up on his elbows, the sound of splashing water nearby making his bladder scream. He was better but his head hurt like he had been drinking all night, then thrown up as his morning exercise. He crawled over to the spring cascading off the rocks and drank from an area that didn't have bird droppings near it. He splashed his face as well, feeling like he must have sweated shadows all night long.

He looked around for Boots and didn't see her at first. The amulet was on the ground nearby which made him happy. He was glad she didn't try to grab it after he was unconscious. He heard a noise nearby on the far side of the spring and forced himself up to investigate. He stopped when he saw the pillar of white granite that had not been there the night before. The boulder was prominent in the daylight and had a bird just starting to build something on the top. He looked around and heard the whimper again. He moved up to the rock and then leaped back when he saw the eyes and nose in it.

Boots' eyes opened and her nostrils flared in panic. Myrgen's eyes were wide with shock and he looked around for what could have done this. He flexed his fingers, calling for the White Stone Sword and suddenly, the sword was in his hand and the boulder was gone. Boots fell to the ground on all fours, panting. Tears started rolling down her face and he knelt beside her, instinctively putting an arm around her to get her over to the water.

She drank it and then sat back on her heels, shaking her head to get rid of the experience.

"That sword thing certainly has a mind of its own."

Myrgen looked at the sword and set it down beside him. It stayed where he put it instead of soaking into the ground. "What did it do?"

"We came out of the shadows here and you collapsed. The amulet fell away from your grasp. I was worried you were dead or something so I started to reach for it. Then the stone just leapt up and covered me."

He looked at the sword and then back at her. His eyes narrowed and he stood. "That's not the truth." He nodded toward the amulet. "That thing is over there, by where I was. You were on the other side of the spring. What happened?"

She turned away, irritated. "It's pretty much the truth."

"I should have left you there." He called the sword to his hand and it leaped into his grip.

Her eyes got panicked again and she held her hands up to ward him off. "No! Please don't! I can't handle being in that pillar again."

He glared at her. "Then talk."

"You passed out. I almost pulled you over near the spring in case I needed to splash water on your face but that shadow was screaming off you like steam. I didn't want to have it grab me and...I don't know. I don't know what it would do to me. I know what it *has* done and I just didn't want to have any of that *undone*."

"What do you mean 'undone'?"

She swallowed. "Last year, I was burned in a fire I set. Some mixture I was given leaked out of the clay ball it was in and when I threw it, it ignited, following a trail of drops up to me." She moved her hair aside and he saw right cheek and neck were scarred, as if the fat underneath had boiled and broken through to escape.

"I was about to die, and the amulet brought me to the room. There, the shadows covered me and when I woke up later, the wounds were gone, like they never happened." She looked at a similar mark on her right hand and wrist.

"Last night, when you brought us back here, you went down as soon as your feet touched solid ground. The sword was at your side like it was waiting for you. The amulet fell away from you. I looked at it and pulled my own blade to run it through. I guess your sword thought I was about to attack you. It went into the ground and then, it was all over me. I couldn't move. Same white stone as your sword. It covered me, only leaving my eyes and nose. Even that, I think it did for you."

"In case I wanted to kill you myself."

She nodded. "It pushed me away from you, to the other side of the spring." She rubbed her arms and nodded. "Needless to say, that thing is," she exhaled slowly, steadying her nerves, "unsettling."

Myrgen felt the comforting presence of the sword, feeling almost like he could feel the connection to the world through it. He didn't find it unsettling at all.

"See to it you remember this then."

She nodded, recovering slowly. She nodded towards the amulet. "So, what's your plan about that?"

He looked at it. "I don't know."

"Can you encase it in rock?" She looked up at him. "It's pretty effective."

He smirked. "Maybe. I don't think that's the best idea though. That thing is poison. I don't want it leeching into the Land here."

"Well, we can't just leave it out in the open. What if a bird put it in its nest or something?"

"Or a child found it." He shook his head. "No, we can't leave it here like that." He walked over to it and stabbed it with the Granite Sword. Sparks flew off it as the sword buried the tip into the ground beneath it. The gold screamed and dissolved around it into shadow. He lifted the tip and looked at it. Black scars marked it, like it had been burned. He wiped it off on his pants but the marks didn't go away. Apparently, fighting these shadows left scars on everyone and everything.

"Where did it go?" She looked around, then touched her neck, scared. It was bare.

He stepped over to her again and knelt before her. He moved aside her hair to look at her face. The burns were still there. "Away from here. Does that hurt?"

She touched it. "No. Not anymore." She stood. "But I'll never forget what it felt like when it happened."

Myrgen found it odd she burned Portabella when she'd had such a horrible experience with fire herself but didn't feel like exploring the mind of a hired assassin at the moment. He stood as well, dusting his knees of the soft dirt.

"Well, you're free of it now. You can go on your way and stay out of trouble."

He looked around to get his bearings and she put her hand on his arm. She stepped close, her eyes seeking an answer. She leaned in to kiss him.

"What if I don't want to go away?"

Myrgen backed up, his arm getting out of her hold and pushing her back with his forearm. "Look, I'm an arrogant pig, so I'm going to assume it's simply my ego that says you were about to kiss me and let my mind assume you were distracting me so you could kill me. That makes a lot more sense than the former."

Boots stepped back. "Why would you assume I'm going to kill you? If that were the case, I'd have done it back there in the room. No mess, no anything."

"It's a lot more reasonable than thinking you wanted to kiss me. Are you going to tell me that you've watched me from afar for years, working up the courage to talk to me? Because taking a contract for my life would be a pretty interesting thing to tell the grandkids."

She blinked a moment, then started to laugh. It rang throughout the woods, startling the birds on the rock. Her laughter started him laughing and the stress of the past few days started shaking out of him. They both knew his comment, though witty, was hardly this funny, but reason required this of them at that moment, and would not be denied. It brought them both to their knees.

Eventually, she fell backwards onto the grass and caught her breath. He sat down, letting the last of the chuckles out of his lungs. His abdomen hurt from the giggling and that was on top of the heaving and unpleasantness of the previous night. His muscles cramped and that started a new round of pain-induced laughter. He leaned on his hands and tried to stretch out the offending muscles. Finally, he too ended up laying back, the last of the stretching easing the pain.

"I had forgotten how painful it is to laugh that hard."

Boots looked at him without getting up. "Yeah. That... ow..."

He looked and saw she was holding her side, like she had just run a mile from a bear. They lay there in silence as the birds sent scouts out to their rock to see if the crazy people were done yet. After a few minutes, she broke it.

"I was serious though."

He looked at her. "About what?"

"I don't want to go away."

He sat up on his elbows. "Why not?"

"Because that necklace was only part of my problem. Sangiardo can still control me."

"Control you? What do you mean?"

She took a deep breath. "Remember that question about Cyprian Herb?"

Gomez looked out over the valley before him. This path seemed designed to inspire as much awe in the traveler as possible. The low hills of grapes were being worked by numerous people preparing them for the summer. Everything was turning lush. He was still a day's ride from St. Giles but he could see it and the sea from this vantage. This area was known as Bordeaux, because it bordered the Krakten Empire. There was no earl or count here, no garrison stationed here, because the majority of the border was the Black Forest. He could even see the dark line of the forest from here, but it was more a demarcation than a feature.

He knew relatively little of Bordeaux outside of these things. From the looks of it, this area was pretty prosperous. It was governed by a talented duchess named Varia Faeleurre, one of the few women in Mervolingia to rule in her own right. Installed by Charles during his first years as king, she inherited it after using her gift of song to lull invading renegade Fae to the Black Forest, where they were trapped. Many believed she was part Fae herself until she returned from the dark woods. But all that was information available to anyone who had an interest in Mervol history. Beyond those recorded bits, Bordeaux had stayed completely off the King's desk.

Until now.

St Giles was not the capital, but it was the busiest port outside of Rouen, known for exporting the wine from the area. The soil produced a rich red grape, unduplicated anywhere else. As the only supplier of this wine, it commanded a high price among the world's nobility. The north-east corner touched the Yorkish and Krakten borders and a well-known Convent that educated girls thrived in the town practically a stone's throw from the Papal City. As such, the wine made its way into Papal services and table settings regularly, as well as supplying the northern reaches of the continent. Only via ship was the wine available to Mande and the southern isles. Wine caravans had not gone south in over a decade.

Much of that, Gomez could see, was because the southern roads were nowhere near as defensible. There were only hills as far as he could see from here, and the road was open with no hiding places like forests or even heavy low shrubs. Even from this far away, he saw heavy traffic on the road to St. Francis de Sales and the Artemisian Academy for Girls.

As he rode towards the port city, he realized he knew more about the area than he thought especially for never having seen it. His patrols began and ended with Patras. He received the reports from Sergeant Jamie South, a young South Yorker whose family came to Bordeaux shortly after he was born. They were always on time. That sort of fastidiousness indicated either a strict, military upbringing, or a mental disorder. Gomez was finally ready to find out first hand.

He got into St. Giles just as the sun was setting, extra daylight provided by the unobstructed horizon. Street lanterns were being lit and the town guards were roaming in pairs. He stopped the first set he saw.

"Excuse me. Where is the Grand Guarde's office?"

"Just at the end of the main road here, Sir. You need an escort?"

"Not if it's that easy. Thank you."

He rode down the street to the well-lit building at the end. The sign on the wall was embossed brass and looked like it was polished every day. It gleamed in the street light and proclaimed this to be the building he sought. He dismounted and opened the door. Inside, the office had three guardsmen on duty. One of them was wearing sergeant's bars on his coat. Gomez stepped up to his desk.

"Sergeant South?"

Jamie looked up and scanned Gomez' outfit. He had a trim haircut and intelligent blue eyes, like a wolf. His hair was a mix of greysm adding to the canine resemblance. He stood and put his fist to his chest in salute, adding a shallow bow. "Sir."

Gomez replied in a similar salute. "I'm Grande Guarde Gomez de Santader of His Majesty's Guarde. I got a letter about an incident involving the death of a blind woman?"

Jamie gestured to the chair across from him. "The Scarred Man Murder. How did you hear of that already? I just sent the report yesterday."

"Apparently, someone from here sent word to St. Andrew and it got forwarded to me." He pulled out Elina's letter and the missive from the St. Andrew guard's office. "I was in the area so I came to check on it myself. Beautiful countryside here."

Jamie took the letters and opened them. "Yes, we are truly blessed." He read through the letter from Elina as well as the missive from the office. He sat back afterwards. "Well, unfortunately, that about sums it up. Yes, the man went to the brothel, hired a girl that specialized in damaged clients. They went to the room together, the door was blocked closed and her screaming began. The creature I had to put down in that bed was no longer a person." He bowed his head, clearly disturbed by the memory.

"The man hasn't resurfaced yet?"

He shook his head. "No sign of him. There was a faint smell of sulfur in the room but nothing else."

"Sulfur?"

He nodded. "Elina didn't notice any strong smells on him when she gave him the room. I originally thought perhaps he had spent time at a natural hot spring or something, but there aren't any in the area within a day's ride and it wouldn't explain the lack of the stink on him beforehand."

Gomez looked at the letters on the desk and sighed. "Is there anything I can do to help?"

"At this point, the trails gone cold, not that it was ever there to begin with. He wasn't staying at any of the inns or houses in town. He showed up, went straight to the brothel, killed and disappeared in the span of an hour. Nothing left behind."

"Except the way the victim died."

"And that has left no information. I suppose the best way to help is to ask if there have been any other murders in Mervolingia like these."

"I haven't gotten a single report of anything like this." Gomez frowned. "Unless he was new to the area."

Jamie's cocked his head. "Meaning he came in on a ship?"

"It makes sense. He went straight to the brothel, which was probably something he heard about on the ship from the other sailors. Have you interviewed the sailors?"

"As many in the area as we could, but it wouldn't matter at this point. The ships that were in port then aren't now." Jamie tapped a finger on the desk, thinking. "However, the Harbormaster would have record of those ships. They tend to be regulars. This port only has a few ships that leave for the whole season. Most of the others are on return treks from Pardua and back."

"Pardua?"

"Ladyship de Holloway has a distributor for her vineyard there. Serves all of Mande. One of Lord D'Medici's family."

"Dominic D'Medici?"

"He's her chancellor."

Gomez raised his eyebrows. "Well, he's moved up in the world. He is Acting Chancellor for the Kingdom right now."

"Really?" Jamie sat back. "I wonder what the lady will do now without her best money handler."

Gomez leaned on the desk and folded his hands. "Has she been through here recently? The King was looking for her."

"Know why?"

Gomez realized he was the only person outside Alexander who knew about the Summons put on the woman. This was a town she heavily supported financially. He wanted to tread lightly here. "You may not have gotten the missive yet but the King has decided to go on a search for a wife. He has opened the options to any woman in the kingdom."

"Has he? Well, the Lady Tanglwyst is already married, I'm afraid. To Urien Atreides."

"Who is he?"

"He's another rival merchant in the area. They decided a few years ago to join forces. It's why her shipping company has been so prosperous. Almost doubling her contracts and reach. It has made them both very dominant in the shipping industry, and rather rich."

113

Gomez nodded. "Well, I think he'll be disappointed. I know they met recently."

"Well, she does have a daughter. Kyri Charissa Tanglwyst. She might be very interested in the missive for her sake."

"Maybe that's why he wanted to contact her."

Jamie smiled. "He'd be marrying into a good family."

"Well," he stood up, "I would like to see what you have on the murders, but I have been riding for a while. Is there a good inn here?"

Jamie smiled a deep, wolfish grin. "You ever hear of the Wise Wench Tavern?"

Sixteen

Many forget their duty until
horribly reminded of it.
-The Wisdom of Stone

Duncan watched the sun set on the day and his horse sighed the sigh of a travelling companion used to noisy company. Duncan was not noisy this trip. His mind was too much upon the events in St Andrew. Ce'Nedra had ran to the manor house and got help from the staff and family there for Henri. She even said his quick thinking probably saved Henri's life. Unfortunately, he was going to be recovering for quite a while. Duncan decided to leave that night to return to Patras. He wanted to get a message to Alexander.

If he could tell His Majesty about the incident, he just knew the man would return and heal Henri's severed limb. At least he would live. The lady Angela, Anthelme's friend, didn't even have her friend to bury.

Duncan shuddered, the image of the withering hand and forearm twisting in the straw like spun sugar in water, once again behind his eyes. The smell that came from it was something he had never smelled before. It was indescribable. The same thing had happened to Anthelme's body by the time the servants got to the outbuilding from the house. He became a noxious puddle in a pile of clothes that were stained beyond repair. Nothing resembling him had been left and nothing on his body was salvageable. Even the silver in his pocket was corrupted slag.

The city of St. Andrew would deal with things there now but in the meantime, Duncan had an idea. Henri was deserving of the King's healing and help and he would get Alexander back to restore him if he had to drag the king from Catriona's bed personally.

Duncan crested the ridge and looked down into the valley at the Mervol capital. Patras glimmered in the evening light. The lanterns on the streets were lit and nearly every window echoed with warmth. Duncan had not had a home in a city since he was given the amulet. The secret room was the only chambers he favored and those were destroyed with the amulet. It was possible the room itself still existed, but with no windows or doors, he had never seen outside of it. He assumed it was a vault buried somewhere but he had no idea where to even begin looking.

He heard the cathedral bell sound through the air like a bat looking for its swarm. Evening mass would be commencing soon. The Archbishop would be busy for a while. He knew they had a barracks for the cathedral guard and a rectory for the priests. The Archbishop had a room and office in the cathedral itself, an attempt from the current pope to rein in the wanton expenditures of the church officials. Gregory walked a humble road and the churches in Mervolingia followed the directive, possibly since the Papal City had a border with Mervolingia. He doubted the officials in Mande were giving up their golden fountains and silver goblets.

He spurred the horse and went forward down the road, entering through the southern gates. He thought about where he would go from there as the sounds of the city at dusk claimed him. He knew of a few inns and taverns from his days as a sailor but since Patras' only waterway was the Siene River, the dock was mostly warehouses and barges. Most of his knowledge was of Rouen, the port at the end of the Siene's journey. Tanglwyst's house was likely still under guard in case she returned so that was out. He figured the best place might be in the arms of the Church.

He rode the horse up to the buildings behind the great, glittering Cathedral to St. Michael. All the roads in the city led directly and openly to the cathedral, with the Church's holdings to the north. They were quite self-sufficient, if necessary, with stables, guards, gardens, a convent, a monastery and numerous additional resources. If the city ever fell prey to a plague again, the Church would be able to wall off their city and sustain itself until the rest of Patras died around it. He nodded to the stable hands as he rode up.

"May we assist you, sir?"

"I have a message for the Archbishop. Can you take my horse? He's had a bit of a run."

"Yes, sir."

"Thank you." He looked around and found the entrance to the offices he used to visit the Archbishop. He had never teleported into the Church's holdings, out of respect. It occurred to him now that the Church may be warded against such spontaneous visits. Having someone *poof* into existence while you were relieving yourself or taking a bath could be decidedly uncomfortable. He wondered why they didn't simply have a special room for such things, maybe with a bell to let them know someone was there. They went to all the trouble of making windowless vaults as refuges. It wouldn't take much to do the same for the Archbishop's palace.

He walked down the long hallway to the Reception Hall. Outside of the High Office was a desk that was, to Duncan's knowledge, always manned. He had been here at nearly every hour of the day or night and there was always someone at that desk. He nodded to the man sitting there.

"Father Jarius, good to see you. Can you get me on His Excellency's schedule?"

Father Jarius looked up and smiled, his face creasing in lines favored by sardonic wit. "Well, Duncan McVryce! Good to see you as well."

Jarius had a friendly voice that hid well the decades of military service. He favored veterans above most civilians though only in company, never in treatment. Duncan always believed Jarius would be a rousing drunk and an honorable barroom brawler.

Jarius looked at his ledger. "Hm. He's got several appointments this tenday. The King's Coronation is due in the fall, after he returns from his jaunt to find a wife."

Duncan paled as he remembered the last task set before him by the Archbishop: to stop Alexander from marrying the heathen Stapana of Caratia. Suddenly, he no longer felt a burning desire to see the Archbishop and report in.

"Ah yes. Any idea where he is now?"

Jarius put on the spectacles Duncan was seeing more often in the area. He had no idea if they worked but this was the fourth or fifth set he'd seen in the past few months. "The Archbishop? He's in his box at mass."

"His box?"

"Yes, he has an opera box in the cathedral. Brilliant idea if you ask me. No better place to watch the mass if you don't have to run it. Plus, if you nod off, no one will see." He smirked at Duncan.

Duncan had actually been inquiring about the king, but Jarius had no way of knowing that, so he just went along with the discussion. "Then I'll leave him a quick report. No need to interrupt his schedule."

Jarius nodded. "Written or verbal?"

Duncan thought about what would be said. If he told the Archbishop about the loss of the amulet, at least he would understand why Duncan could not be summoned. And why he was traveling overland chasing the king. He didn't want to tell him the rest.

"Written, if you don't mind. That way, it can sit for however long it needs to but not get forgotten."

Jarius nodded and passed Duncan a page and quill. He took them and the ink to a side table to write.

Your Excellency,

While in pursuit of His Majesty, the Traveling Amulet was destroyed by fire. I know where he's going and plan to head overland to intercept. Forgive me for losing such a valuable artifact. I wanted to let you know for your own safety so you would not try to summon me in an emergency. Thank you for your trust.

Duncan McVryce

He read it over and nodded. It was good enough. He blew on the ink to dry it, then folded it so the paper wouldn't smudge it. He handed it to Jarius. Jarius nodded and put the paper in a pile of other documents.

"Anything else?"

Duncan thought. He wanted originally to ask about where to stay in Patras, but upon being reminded of his previous task, he no longer wanted to be somewhere the Archbishop might walk in and start asking questions.

"No, I'm just reporting on my way to finish my last task. Thank you, Jarius."

The priest smiled and nodded. "You be careful out there, Duncan. I wouldn't ride during the night, but I'm not a young fightin' man anymore like yourself."

"Not sure I'm a young fightin' man these days either. I'll see you next time." Duncan waved goodbye and headed out into the streets.

As the sun set behind them, Gwen started looking around for a place to stop for the night. Inns on the road were spaced half a day's ride apart on the busy roads, catering to wagons and carriages while still being spaced well for messengers who were riding harder. Unfortunately, the "main road" and the group parted ways miles ago. This road went to Caratia, a closed country with no external trade agreements through this route. The main road turned towards the Papal City, a much more lucrative path.

As a result, there were no lights at all on the road. They hadn't passed an inn since the crossroads. Gwen looked at the cliffs before them and a tiny light glowed at the summit. That was a hard ride uphill in the dark. At this speed, it would be death to them and the horses. Gwen touched her horse's mane and all the steeds started slowing down.

Tanglwyst started to panic and looked at Gwen. As the horses slowed to a trot, she spoke up. "Why are we slowing down?"

"We have to stop." Gwen pointed to the cliffs. "We can't climb that, not in the dark. We need to let them rest."

Tanglwyst looked at the summit, then back at the road. "Where are we?"

"No idea. We left the main road shortly after morning when it moved towards the north. No one comes this way. There's no reason to."

Tanglwyst sighed. "He's that way. I can feel it. Not directly." She pointed southeast. "There. But moving our way."

Michael nodded. "Good. How wide is Caratia, Gwen? Will we get there in time?"

"It's a few days across."

"Will we be there in time?"

Gwen didn't respond.

Tanglwyst pulled the horse to a stop. "Wait... I know where we are." She looked deeper. "I know where we are!" She turned the horse towards the woods and spurred him on.

Gwen tried to call out but she was away before it would have mattered. She looked at Michael and the two of them followed her. Before long, they saw a flicker in the woods, a fire beating back the darkness. Tanglwyst pulled up her horse at the edge of a clearing with several tents and armed men sitting around. She got off her horse and one of the men stood up.

"Lady Tanglwyst?"

"Marcello!" She hugged one of the men, a tall, portly blond man with a curled moustache and beard. He hugged her back and then pushed her aside as Gwen and Michael got off their horses. "Friends of yours?"

"Yes. This is Gwen Douglas and Michael deNoir. They're family."

"A Glarren woman and a Nubian? You have an odd family lineage, young lady."

She smiled. "We are on our way to Caratia. Can we stay here with you? Safety in numbers and all."

Marcello bowed. "We are at your service," he straightened again, "provided, of course, that it's acceptable to our captain."

She put her hand on his arm. "Of course. Thank you. Where is Tulio?"

A tent flap moved aside and a short, dark haired man stepped out. His brown skin was robust, as was his stature, and his eyes and face broke into a comfortable smile at the sight of the visitors.

"Ah! We have company!" He walked over to Tanglwyst and took both her hands in his. "So good to see you again."

"Once I realized where I was, I knew at the very least it would be safe to camp here."

Michael waked over. "Where are we, exactly?"

"The Disputed Forest." Tulio gestured to their surroundings. "It is my domain. And you are all welcome. Please, come and sit."

Gwen looked around. The sense that there was a moderately powerful Fae in the area had faded but had not left completely. She left the horses reluctantly to stand by the fire.

The men passed stew around and bottles of mead. Michael listened more than spoke but answered questions about how he came to be in Tanglwyst's company. Tanglwyst did not hold any information back when it came to her escape and their previous dealings, something that seemed to catch Michael off guard. More than once, at the revealing of a secret, he looked at Gwen and she shared his apparent concern. Tanglwyst was giving up too much too easily. There was a Fae spell involved here.

She slipped over to Michael and crouched down beside him, taking a bowl of the stew to cover her conversation with him.

"Michael, I think there's another spell going on. Tangl is…"

"Talking too much. I know. What kind of spell does that?"

"I have *heard* of something but it's only a rumor. Something old. Mages used to get people to speak the truth but those people were destroyed in the Church's Cleansing, according to my research. I don't think there are any alive now."

"So, this isn't a Fae spell?"

Gwen marveled at how easily her companions had fallen to accepting the existence of Fae magic. "I suppose it could be, but I don't see the purpose in it. Why would these people care about what's happening with us?"

Michael shrugged. "Maybe she's just very comfortable here. She trusts these people. She knows they are also fleeing from the road patrols. That man speaks with a Toledan accent. They called this the Disputed Forest. I suspect they are all thieves, hiding from the law. She was doing likewise. And she has a way of connecting with people."

Tanglwyst began the tale of her encounter with the Scarred Man and Gwen stood up. "Excuse me. I'm sorry to interrupt but we need to feed and water the horses and set up our bedrolls. Is there a place we can do that?"

Tulio nodded and motioned towards a large ten foot tent. "That is our 'guest room'. You are welcome to use it. We have no other guests tonight."

"Guest room?" Gwen frowned. "What kinds of guests to you usually get?"

"The kind people pay to get back. Wouldn't do for them to be harmed in the process."

Michael stood as well and went with Gwen over to the horses. Tulio took Tanglwyst's hand and gestured towards the tent he came out of. "Come, my friend, I'll show you," he said in response to something they apparently were discussing.

Gwen and Michael started to move towards her but two of the larger men stepped up to stand on either side of the door. They stopped, concerned. Gwen didn't like that there was a spell involved here. Unfortunately, she wasn't sure how to handle this now. She stepped up to the guards.

"We can't let our friend out of our sight. She has a spell on her."

The guards looked at her but did not move.

"Tangl!"

Tanglwyst's voice came from inside. "Gwen, I'm fine." The flap moved and Tanglwyst looked out, holding a map. "What is it?"

"What are you doing?"

She held up the map. "Looking at our route tomorrow. Why?"

Gwen folded her arms. "Don't you think it's something *we* might like to look at as well?"

"That's why I was bringing it out." She stepped out with a large map of the area. "Here. Come look."

Gwen and Michael came over and looked at the map. Tanglwyst pointed to a spot on it.

"This is where we are right now. This is the way to the pass into Caratia. Tulio says we can take this if it will help. They already know the area."

"I see." Gwen turned to Tulio who stood in the doorway. The interior of the tent was lavish. Shelves holding books, rolls of paper, clothes and bottles lined one wall. She saw a bar attached to two of the wall poles that had clothes hanging on them. She also saw the end of an actual rope bed on a frame, complete with a mattress.

"Thank you, Sir." Michael's tone was diplomatic, something Gwen wasn't quite feeling at that moment.

"You are my friend's family. That makes us family too. Come, sit and drink." He gestured back to the fire and put a bottle of mead in each of their possession. He raised his in salute. "To reconnecting with family."

The men in the circle raised their bottles and shouted their agreement. Tanglwyst raised her bottle and Gwen and Michael reluctantly did as well. Gwen took a mouthful of mead but did not swallow it, planning instead to discreetly put it back in the bottle and then later accidentally spilling it. Michael drank, probably counting upon his size to delay any alcoholic effects.

Gwen was more interested in Tanglwyst's actions though. Gone was the nervousness she displayed on the road when Gwen ended the spell on the horses. She was relaxed, chatting, laughing. Gwen had worried that the Fae spell of the little dog wouldn't have counteracted the *geas* but it had. It seemed the *geas* might have a weakness against Fae magic. Perhaps, for the night, Tanglwyst might finally get some rest.

Boots and Myrgen walked until dusk, the last hour or so picking up dead wood for a fire when they stopped. Myrgen spent the time thinking about what a turn of events this had been and that when he decided to leave Catriona's side, he had never expected the next few tendays to be spent traveling with a paid assassin. He honestly had expected perhaps a few assassins in Portabella, but nothing on the road. He definitely hadn't thought he would be moving towards Caratia in the hopes of delivering said assassin to her.

He wondered how the reunion would go and couldn't find a balance between a gushing romp across fields of flowers into each other's arms, falling together in a desperate kiss, and having her dismiss him as she showed off her new wedding ring. In the end, he felt he would have to just let things happen as they would. Trying to guess the future was merely revealing his own lack of faith in himself and her.

Boots had been equally silent throughout the day, occasionally touching her neck with varying degrees of concern and relief. He didn't see fear in her, but her being who she was, he didn't expect to. Something a bounty hunter would have to master is the ability to disguise fear from a mark.

They came upon an area sheltered by a canopy of trees. These were pine trees, indicating they were moving out of the lowlands and into higher altitudes. The ground was covered in brown needles and it looked like a good place to camp for the night. He looked at her and nodded to it.

She nodded back and dropped her firewood, shaking out her arms. He piled his as well and they gathered handfuls of needles to act as kindling. The ground was also littered with pine cones and those proved to be better fire starters than they had found before. He packed a few away in his satchel for later, in case he parted company with Boots before entering Caratia. He paused for a moment, staring at the burgeoning fire.

Is that really what I'm going to do? Is that what I'm supposed to do now? Just let this person wander around Caratia, trying to find Catriona simply because I'm not ready to see her yet? What's it going to take to be ready?

He didn't know, and in the end, he needed to let things unfold at their own pace and hope the Land would give him guidance with each challenge.

Neither she nor Myrgen had wanted to fuss with tracking down game so Boots pulled out some roots they had come across on the trip that day, along with some mushrooms she knew were safe. The terrain was getting out of her realm of familiarity and soon, they would have to reply upon fresh meat every night for their meal. That meant stopping earlier or planning to hunt during the day. She decided to set a trap for the night while he built the fire, to see if they could have something for the morning. With any luck, they would have fresh meat for breakfast. Otherwise, the area still had birds.

She had yet to really cope with the discomfort of sleeping on the ground. She was acting tough while she was traveling with Myrgen, but she had sneaked out in the middle of the night every night to rest in the bed. She had a thread on him so it always let her know when he was about to stir simply because she had told it to. Now she felt that absence, that loss of connection to him and it unsettled her. She felt utterly alone for the first time in months.

"Where do you want to bed down?"

Boots was startled out of her thoughts and looked at Myrgen. She cast her gaze around and sighed. "One spot is pretty much as good as the next, isn't it?"

He laughed. "Well, yes, that's true. Do you want the slightly flattish area near the edge of the canopy, the slightly *less* sloped area near the trunk or do you just want to reject the whole idea and sleep sitting up against the trunk?"

She smiled but didn't really feel it. She nodded towards the trunk and he acknowledged it by taking the spot on the other side of the fire. She felt the weariness of the day's travel set in as she sat down. Her eyes closed before she could stop them.

She heard a sound and blinked, looking around. Myrgen was asleep on the other side of the fire and the trap had gone off, waking her. She put her hand down to stand and felt something beneath it. She lifted her hand and the amulet was there, unscathed. She jerked her hand away and it did not respond, didn't attack her like a wolf, didn't seep into her like a fetid disease. Instead, it just lay there, available and quiet, like it was waiting.

She reached out and envisioned the room with the nice, soft bed. Suddenly, it was around her and she was in the same position on the floor as she had been in the woods. The amulet was in the same place, not magically in her hand or on her neck. The place was pleasantly lit, and there was warm, fresh roasted pheasant and a meat pie on the table. A bottle of Bordeaux was open next to them.

She looked at the bed and Myrgen was there, resting. She stood and walked over to him. She wanted him to be okay with this, to be safe here too. She touched his shoulder and tugged on him. He rolled onto his back, his face and chest eaten away by shadows.

Boots started awake, clutching her chest. The amulet was not nearby or on her neck. It had been just a dream.

Probably brought on by this being the first night without it.

She shook herself, trying to knock away the visions the dream had called up. The image of Myrgen, dissolved by the darkness, lingered in her mind and was etched into the backs of her eyelids if she closed them. She moved closer to the fire to try and get warm.

She was pretty much done sleeping for the night.

Seventeen

Blood and bone are fragile, but the mind is strong.
-The Wisdom of Stone

"*Blood of the Father!* Michael, she's gone."

Michael turned over on the bedroll at the strange method of swearing, and looked around him. The encampment of bandits was gone and he sat up, scanning the area for proof they were anything other than a dream. He found none. Gwen was up and kicking over stones and deadfall that would have been stacked up into a firewood area had there been a large group camping there. Even the grass was not trampled.

"Wha… How? There was…"

"I know." Gwen frowned. "Remember I told you there was a Fae around? It was them, or at least one of them."

"Who?"

She looked at the trees. Two horses were tethered to a couple branches. They had eaten down the grass within reach. "That's the trouble. It could have been any of them. Or *all* of them. They were really making sure I couldn't tell which one too." She picked up a stick and threw it.

Michael got up and dusted off his breeches. "What do we do?"

"Well, the horses look refreshed so there's that. My use of the Fae magic must have drawn them to us. I'm still unfamiliar with the way Fae look in this area." She glared around, raising her voice. *"They couldn't have done this to me had I been in Glarren."*

The trees offered no answer or secrets. Michael stepped to her, putting a huge black hand on her shoulder. "Gwen, what do we do?"

She looked into his dark eyes, still scowling. "Well, we know where she's going. She has no choice. It just angers me that these Fae would feed Tanglwyst's obsession." Her eyes shifted to the surrounding forest.

Michael patted her shoulder and walked over to the horses. Gwen let out a loud sigh of resignation and joined him. They got on the horses and started riding east.

The Sinister Glove watched as Gwen and Michael mounted up. She looked around. The sun was high in the sky. The Glarren woman would be hours behind Tanglwyst, just enough behind that she would get the message, but not far enough behind to put Embertwist's prize in danger. The Glove's master had already used the woman to dispose of one of darkness's agents. She had proven useful. The Glove now saw why Tanglwyst caught her lord's attention. Her lineage was connected to something that resisted the shadows call. Alexander had touched the shadows. Having the leader of the largest kingdom in the world fall to the shadows would only end in a war that couldn't be won.

Tanglwyst needed to get into Alexander's life and stay there.

The Glarren woman was a challenge though. There was something about her. She was definitely Glarren but there was something *else*, something *more*. She wasn't immune to the touch of the shadows. In fact, she might be even more susceptible than most people but the Glove didn't know why. For her not to know why was baffling. Knowing secrets was her stock and trade.

The illusion of the band of forest thieves was an easy one for someone like the Glove. Of course, there were only three others in the world "like" her. The other Fae Lords also had their lieutenants, but their purviews were not secrets, at least not other people's secrets. Sure, Corrigan's Voice of Command knew every military strategy, Gloriana's Glacial Breath knew every way to preserve and heal, and Calpurnia's Elegant Solution would have known every secret of magic but only the Glove could know the secrets in the world that people tried to hide.

At the moment, she lacked only a few secrets when she sought them. One of those secrets was exactly *what* was different about this Gwen. She had potential within her but the Glove had no idea what that was. The only way to get that information was to put her in positions that would get that enigma to reveal itself. This situation with Alexander's *geas* might be what it took. Nothing else had worked yet.

Getting them into Caratia was the first step. The Land was an ally of the Fae and like all other forces, they fought against Heaven's control of the world. The end of the Soulless War marked the last time the energies of the world had worked together. After it was over, the Church had decided all the others needed to be destroyed. Their purge, called the Cleansing by some, had caused the world to be reshaped. Places where Fae had walked freely were warded structurally to allow only the Divine. Fields and waterways were blessed, driving away the Land and the Sea's influences.

The only thing that stood against Heaven at this point was Hell and the Glove believed that was only because Hell served Heaven's purposes. It was a monster the Church controlled, one made up by them to frighten humans to do what they were told. Hell wasn't real. It was just a construct of Heaven, imbued with power by the Divine. Yes, it had its own feel, its own flavor, but it was still part of Heaven. It certainly wasn't part of the Land.

Because Heaven had wiped away all other influences, it made Hell a very efficient tool, but in the end, it was only doctrine and painted images, given a realm of influence by its counterpart. Without Heaven, there would be no Hell. It was amazing what a rendering of blood and fire could do to the human mind, branding it with a stench of seared flesh and pain into the imagination.

That was the true power of Heaven. If you had humanity's thoughts, you had their creativity, and with it, you ruled the world. The only way to get it back was to capture their attention and turn it away from what they were trained to trust. And the only way to do that was to *show* them what could be. But Heaven wasn't going to just let that happen. It was going to fight it.

There was a war coming. It was time to get armed.

Tanglwyst rode hard until she saw the Separation Pass road looming up ahead. The road had been much easier to ride alone. One rider could be passed off as a messenger and she had not feared the few patrols she had seen. Somehow, she knew she would be safe. Her horse had a new piece of horse brass on the harness, no doubt put there by Tulio. The disc of "horse jewelry" was cast brass with an image of a ship in full sail, unimpeded by terrain. The horse rode like it was young and fresh, itching to a hundred miles behind it. When she would slow down to get her bearings, his would sneak up to a run pretty quick. It was like he shared her desire to get to Alexander.

She pulled him to a stop and looked at the signs before her. To the left were the roads to Toledo and pointing back the way she had come was a marker for the Papal City. She was farther down this road than she had been three tendays before. Back then, she had turned away when she could see the spires of her grandfather's home. Now they were more than a day's ride away. She wondered if Alexander's *geas* would have worked if she had been inside the holy walls before he called.

She thought briefly about the amulet that allowed her to return to Patras so quickly, but as she looked at the huge cliffs of foreboding stone before her, she remembered it would not have helped her here.

In all her years of traveling, she had never been to Caratia.

Every year she tried, the weather was horrid, threatening to capsize the ship after leaving the Fingers of Mande. Even coming from the north was no better. She could put into port at the edge of Cantiville, the very last port in York before Caratia but had never gotten past the Great Cliffs. Yorkish crafts were able to penetrate the waters, so she and Dominic had decided to let them handle the trade and left that country alone. It wasn't like they didn't have enough to do.

It crossed her mind to turn back, to go to her grandfather in the Papal City. She knew she would be safe there. Then she looked ahead at the very daunting road up the face of the cliffs. The small village of

Cliffbase was waking up and she didn't want to risk getting caught behind a slow moving cart going up the face of the mountain. She nudged her horse in the direction of the pass and gave him his head.

"I think I see her." Michael pointed up the cliff. They were still an hour's ride from Cliffside by the signposts they had passed but he could see a lone figure going up the mountainside. The face had a few switchbacks but this road was not meant for carts or carriages. It was meant for defense. There was little more than a faint line indicating a path at all and no steps.

"Yes, but she's moving quickly. She has a charm. I can't believe the Fae did this."

Michael sighed. Gwen had been in bitter silence the entire morning. It was very unlike what he had seen before this day. As they had gotten closer to Caratia, Gwen seemed to switch between being excited to be there and being irritated as having to go. He figured the two emotions weren't mutually exclusive. Hopefully, getting Tanglwyst to Alexander was going to work out like they hoped.

"So, what's the trouble if she gets there before us? You want her to be in contact with Alexander, right?"

"I suppose. But not before I talk to Catriona. I need to make sure Tanglwyst isn't used as leverage."

"What do you mean? Catriona couldn't care less about that woman."

Gwen snorted. "Alexander revealed his intentions. He plans to use Tanglwyst against Myrgen to get him to leave Catriona. With Myrgen out of the way, he'll have easy access to my friend and, well, I know from personal experience that he can talk her into anything. Even marriage."

Michael shook his head. "We never expected this much trouble when we started all this."

Gwen gave a genuine smile. "Well, that's the problem with adventures. They're never fun while you're having them and you don't always know what's going to bring one on." She nodded to the mountain. "That, however, is an adventure, to be sure. And I think it kind of follows her."

"So she's cursed, then?"

Gwen laughed. "That's one way to look at it. Either that or she's drawn the eye of..."

Michael looked as she suddenly went silent.

"Oh for 'Lumen's sake... How could I have not seen it before?"

"Seen what?"

"Tanglwyst. She's caught the attention of a Fae Lord. That's how she escaped." She looked around. "From the looks of it and given the time of year, and what has been done to us, it's Embertwist."

"Who's Embertwist?"

"The Fae Lord of Spring. He's the ultimate trickster. According to my uncle's writings, he was the reason the Soulless plague didn't spread and conquer the world."

"The Soulless plague?"

She nudged the horses forward again. "I'll tell the tale tonight. Right now, we need to catch up."

Tanglwyst pushed forward, grateful at every step that she was not the one doing the running up this cliff face. She was reaching the halfway point when she looked down and saw Gwen and Michael entering Cliffside. Her horse didn't seem to mind the climb outside of being impaired by the road. If it were possible to leap from rock to rock like a goat, he would have ascended the mountain within a few hours. As it stood, she would be at the top by late afternoon. The other side would be all downhill and she would progress much faster.

When she finally got to the top, she was surprised to see an inn, sitting there as if expecting her. Its windows were open and the smell of fresh bread flowed out of them. She could see pies cooling on a counter inside. The horse got onto level ground and galloped past the place, causing her a moment of regret. As she started down the other side, suddenly, the harness fell off the horse and he fell forward. She went over the top of him and hit the rocks, tumbling down the road. He slid and hit the rocks beside her but his larger mass propelled him over the rocks and he fell beyond. She heard his screaming end by a meaty slap and the crunch of bones.

She dared a look over the edge and confirmed the worst. Her steed was dead, dashed upon the horrid teeth of the entry into Caratia. Her tears begun and she turned away, giving them up to the stones that had stolen her friend. If this was what this place was like, she regretted ever coming here.

For the first time since beginning this journey, she saw Gwen's point. This was a horse Gwen had given her and she had ridden it to its death to get to Alexander. She had pushed it past its lifespan like it was merely a tool and not a living creature. What kind of monster had he driven her to become?

Her arm hurt and when she decided to move, she screamed out in pain. A sharp jab in her side worried her and her lower leg was bleeding. She felt blood trickling down her cheek and she called out, hoping she wasn't too far away from the inn to be heard. After a few minutes, a tall, thin man with black curly hair and a sharp nose looked on the road.

"By the Stones! Symonne! Get some bandages!"

Eighteen

Knowing the truth doesn't always grant you the wisdom to understand it.
-The Wisdom of Stone

Giovanni Sangiardo closed his eyes and thought of Boots, summoning her. He waited for the puff of sulfur that never came and opened his eyes.

Apparently, she was dead too.

That was all four lost. If he couldn't use anyone else to fulfill the contract, he would have to do it himself. This was not a task the horses would do. As far as he could tell, Graziana D'Medici had never been evil to anybody. The horses were holy animals. They would not harm a decent human being.

He had learned that the hard way. When he first saw the magnificent beasts, he was a monk in the Papal City. The Pope's Steeds were in the charge of this monastery, St. Anne's Stables. They were pure white chargers, four stallions and four mares. He cared for them for six years, cleaning the stalls, making the feed cakes, grooming them, and feeding them. In all that time, he never saw anyone ride them, not even to exercise them. They ran around the pastures just fine, were able to be saddled and bridled, even were led easily to the blacksmith at the monastery for shodding, but no one ever got on them. Even the Pope never rode them, and Sangiardo had been through two reigns.

More confusing than even this was the harnesses. Each horse had a harness with a piece of horse brass on the chest. The horse brass was a strange series of lines and marks but he couldn't figure out what they were. The harnesses were never allowed to be taken off either, no matter what. The horses never chafed or had any problems with the leather rubbing away their hair and never seemed to mind them either, so he was never worried.

When he wasn't tending to the horses, he studied glyphs and symbols in the library of the monastery. One day, he decided to look up the symbol on the harnesses. He spent a tenday on the task before giving up. It was just not something recorded. Then, one night about a tenday later, he woke up in the night. He realized the symbol might be *multiple* symbols superimposed. He got up and snuck out to the stable. He needed to examine the brass where he could compare it to the different Saints.

He went up to one of the horses and unbuckled the horse brass from it. No sooner had it left the flesh of the animal but a strange light gathered around it and then it just dissolved into thin air. He looked around, afraid someone would have seen it, but no one did. He couldn't explain it, so he went to another horse and did the same thing. Again, it dissolved into light and then there were only six.

About that moment, it occurred to him that this was actually a problem: two horses missing and him standing there with the brass from both. He panicked and tried to figure out what to do. Since he was the only one in general who ever cared for the horses, he figured he had about half a day before this was discovered. He could be halfway through Toledo before he was discovered missing.

Eventually, he realized that running would just make him a target and the Church had a long reach and many weapons. Instead, he realized there was more than one stable in the city. If he grabbed two horses from elsewhere, he would be able to hide his mistake, especially if he put the blankets on them they sometimes wore. If he could find two horses with white legs, he could hide the truth.

He went to the closest inn with stables and as luck would have it, there was a brown and white one whose lower half was white. The stablehand was asleep, it being after midnight, and he slipped in and out with it quickly. He put the harness on it, just in case anyone saw him. No one ever rode or even saw these horses. This symbol would be enough to get the town guards to look the other way.

As soon as the harness was secured, the light from before returned and the horse transformed before his eyes into one of the white horses he had been tending. He even thought it recognized him. It tossed its head at him and whinnied, waking the stablehand asleep in the straw nearby. The young man wiped his eyes and stood.

"Can I help you, sir?"

Sangiardo had his wits about him by then. "No, I've got this now. Apparently, this one decided it wanted to see the city and got out of the St. Anne Stable. Came here to visit. Unfortunately," he glanced at the horse's tummy, "she released one of your animals when she pushed her way in."

"What?" The lad looked frantically at the stalls and then ran out the stable. "Did you see where she went?"

Sangiardo pointed in a direction and the stablehand ran off. Sangiardo waited until he was out of sight, then he put the other harness on another horse. He led the two Papal Steeds into the alleyway, then went back in and set the other horses free. As the poured out of the stable, he walked quietly back to the St. Anne's Stable.

He had put the horses back in their stalls at the monastery and not mentioned the incident. Then he got a letter from a relative in Florentine telling him his parents had died and that he needed to come home to settle their accounts. As he looked at the sizable debt his parents had left, he had a thought grow in his mind. He showed the letter to the Abbot, who released him temporarily from his duties to attend to the family's matters. He packed his things and left town.

He waited two days at the Crossroads Inn, then slipped back into the city in the middle of the night. He collected the harnesses off of every Steed and put a piece of common horse brass in each stall. He then set fire to every patch of straw right around the brass, making sure it turned to slag or was at least unrecognizable as common. He crept away and let the stable burn as he left town again. Not wanting to tip off his host by smelling like smoke, he kept travelling south towards Mande. After a day, he got a room at another inn and asked about bathing. "I'm so sick of smelling like a campfire," he said and the innkeeper believed him.

When he finally got to Florentine, he looked over the nags his parents had at their stables. All were sway-backed and old, definitely not the sort of animal a noble would want to be seen upon. He put the harnesses on the four they had and watched them transform into beautiful beasts that would demand respect. It didn't take long for people to notice the new rentals and within two tendays, the horses were making enough money to pay on the debts owed. After two months, he was able to buy another horse.

By the time the new year came, he had all eight horses stalled and being rented out to nobility. Even King Cipriano himself rode one, even tried to buy it, but he said the horses were his only income and he needed to pay his debts first.

Then the deaths started.

A few people who rented on of the horses suffered fatal accidents while riding. The horse ended up running one into a tree branch, while another fell and was kicked. When Sangiardo heard this, he was horrified, and not a little frightened that the authorities would demand the horse be put down. However, the first family was not broken up about it. In fact, they slipped Sangiardo a tip that paid off one of his creditors altogether.

After that, people with relatives they wanted killed showed up in hopes that the stable was actually an assassin service. This was good money until the day he took a contract for a city official who was refusing bribes. When the horse got under that man, he actually ran amok and stomped to death the person who put out the contract.

Shortly after that, he started looking around for a *real* assassin, not willing to give up the money the service brought in. That's where he found Boots.

And that's why he wanted to get her back now.

Nineteen

Enemies and allies hide equally
well in crowds as shadows.
-The Wisdom of Stone

"Come in."

James poked his head into Alexander's room. "We're pulling into port now."

"Thanks."

Alexander gathered his things into his satchel as the ship bumped and groaned into place. He heard the anchor drop and put on a long coat, preparing for the weather. He needn't have bothered. The sun warmed the decks and the men as they lowered long boats into the water. They were anchored in the harbor about half a mile from the piers. Alexander almost asked why they were so far out, but a single glance answered that question.

The port of Calais was packed. Every merchant ship in Mande seemed to be there, prepping for travel. He forgot that Catriona often left early in the season, when merchant ships wouldn't dare risk their cargo. That was three tendays ago and now, the season was launching.

A small beach had four other long boats on it, being watched by two guards and a young man behind a desk under a small but impressive shelter.

They got to shore and Alexander went with James as the crewmen beached the two boats. James nodded to the young man behind the desk.

"Good afternoon."

The assistant harbormaster smiled, well-manicured teeth showing off for the newcomers. "Welcome to Calais. Is this your first visit to our fair city?"

Alexander realized too late that the man was speaking Mandian and not Mervol. Catherine had of course taught all her children the D'Medici native tongue, but Alexander had always struggled with anything except Mervol. It had blocked his ability to search for Catriona, drawing it out for years. Had he been able to adequately convey his ideas, it should have taken no more than a single summer to reunite them.

Alexander also noted that James' Mervol was so excellent, Alexander had not even realized the man's Glarren roots. The coaching and practice that must have been necessary to take a young man from talking like Thessius, to talking like a Prince, was beyond impressive.

James returned the smile. "Resupplying. Looks like we got here just in time."

"This is our busiest month. Just tell me how much of what you need and we can arrange for it to be taken out to your ship."

Alexander was impressed. "You deliver the goods?"

The assistant nodded. "It's part of the docking fee, in fact, to encourage ships to use the port regardless of the fullness of the dock. It is much quicker than filing everyone through the actual docks and more efficient." He pointed to the bay. "See that barge? It has the standard supplies most ships need."

James and Alexander looked where he was pointing. The barge to which he referred was larger and better stocked than James' entire ship. Alexander leaned over to his captain. "Did you see that when we pulled in?"

"I thought it was another ship."

"I can see why."

James looked around. "I've been here before for the season launch but it wasn't this bad."

138

The assistant folded his hands, smiling. "It's been getting bigger every year. With His Majesty Cipriano in town, all the nobles have turned out."

"Shouldn't they give you a proper roof over your head then?"

Alexander shook his head. "I doubt they'd spend the money for it. Why pay upkeep on a structure all year for something a tent could do for one month?" He turned to the assistant. "Excuse me, where would I find a messenger service?"

The assistant pointed down the docks. "Head up the main street going north there. You'll find several services."

"Thank you." He nodded to James who started listing the needs of the ship.

The street indicated was as busy as the docks and when the assistant said several, he was not kidding. The first eight storefronts on the street were messenger services. He saw one that catered to Mervol businesses and went in. There were four other people in line ahead of him and the man at the window was telling the messenger in the uniform his missive as the messenger wrote it down. A woman came out of the back and sat down at a second window.

"Next."

Alexander gathered his thoughts, not wanting to listen in on the private matters of strangers. The man at the counter paid his coin and the man in front of Alexander stepped in when he was called.

"I'd like to send a message to Patras. To Gabriella Minozzi, the Danse Academy. 'I received word of the destruction of Portabella. Now that area should be safe to travel in again. I will await your return schedule. I look forward to seeing my family again."

"From?"

"Marcurio."

"Six ducats."

Marcurio paid him and the man took the note into the back. Alexander was a little surprised to find out this information had gotten all the way to this port when they had only seen the still burning ruins a few days before. He stopped Marcurio on the way by. "Excuse me, did you say *Portabella* was destroyed?"

"Indeed. King Cipriano announced it yesterday in the Afternoon Missives himself. Usually, the daily missives are announced by his Steward."

"And they've confirmed this?"

"I assume so." Marcurio shrugged. "I am not the person who knows such things."

"But you're sure enough to ask your family to come here based off it."

The man shrugged again and Alexander got the impression that was what he did best. "I miss my family. I moved here from Patras after my company expanded. My wife got a job at the Danse Academy teaching nobles. I am embarrassed that she must work at all. So, it is time for her to come home."

"Will she have a job here?"

"Not if I can help it."

"Next."

Alexander looked at the messenger, then nodded goodbye to Marcurio who went on his way. He stepped up to the window.

"So, Portabella is gone?"

The messenger nodded. "According to the missives coming in and out of St. Marguerite. Of course, the devastation spread to that small town too, judging from the requests for food and supplies."

Alexander sighed. "Oh, I heard they had a dock fire or something. Nothing too bad."

"Well, far more widespread than a little dock fire. According to the reports coming and going, most of the village is gone."

Alexander's eyes reflected his horror. "Wait, what? I thought they put it out."

"No. Been burning for days. Several dead from the fire getting into walls and roofs. Apparently, they put one out and another springs up. They suspect alchemist fire. That stuff burns where it touches. It's a problem if they don't extinguish it immediately."

Alexander felt his color drain away. *What have I done?*

"Sir, did you want to send a message?"

Alexander blinked, coming back to his task. He had originally meant to send word to Gomez about where he was on his quest, but now this had his full attention. "Yes. Yes, I do."

The man wrote down the address. "First recipient?"

"Dominic de Medici, the Royal Palace in Patras."

"Message?"

"Send assistance immediately to St. Marguerite. Whatever they need, be it men, money, food or supplies. Spare no expense."

"From?"

140

"Alexander."

He finished writing the message and set it aside. "Next recipient?"

"Catherine D'Medici. Same message. That will confirm it if he tries to 'chancellor' his way out of it. I also need one sent to Gomez de Santander, same address. That one needs to also say I'm in Calais, and will contact him when I reach my destination." He folded his arms, arching an eyebrow. "That should ensure the job gets done."

The man started writing the information and slowly stopped. The woman at the other window also stopped. They both turned to look at Alexander and about that moment he realized he had just revealed who he was in a public place. Not just any public place, but in a country where he had not announced he would be arriving. This could be seen as spying by the king.

"From?"

"Uh, also, Alexander."

"Eighteen ducats."

"Eighteen? They're all going to the same place?"

The man behind the counter leaned on it. "Yes, but I imagine you want to make sure these letters get into the hands of their intended. That means getting an audience with the Queen of Mervolingia. Since you didn't choose to use a royal messenger, I assume you are traveling incognito. To preserve that, it will be full price."

He thought for a moment about correcting the man as to Catherine's actual title of Queen *Mother* but he was in Mande. They probably saw her as Queen even now. Alexander pulled out the coin and put it on the counter. "Well put."

"I could have charged fifty."

"That you could have. But I would have never used your services again."

The woman leaned over. "And that would indeed be a tragedy. Thank you for your business, Your Highness."

Alexander left the building, putting his hand on his coin purse to keep track of it. As he made his way to the dock area again, he passed a jewelry shop. In the window was a beautiful ring of silver with an amethyst in it. It caught his eye immediately. He looked and saw James still talking with the assistant harbormaster, looking a lot like he was haggling over prices. Alexander entered the shop.

"Good afternoon! May I help you?"

"The silver ring in the window, how much?"

"Ah sir, good eye for beauty but not necessarily for substance. That is white gold."

"White gold?"

"Indeed. The gold veins in the Digitae Primus run almost white. It is the only place in the world where one can get this."

"That looks like an engagement or wedding ring to me. You're right on the docks. Does that get you much business?"

"Indeed it does. Most sailors have been on ship for days or tendays. When they step off, they are often thinking of someone special to spend the time with. Plus, this way, the gold shipments don't have to go all the way through town and a band of pickpockets. The docks are very well patrolled at all hours and I pay for extra protection. Even after all that, I still come out ahead being here instead of further in town." He smiled. "So, would you like that little beauty in the window?"

Alexander smiled. "I believe I would. I'm looking for a wife. Might not be a bad idea to have something on hand should I find one. How much?"

"Three hundred ducats."

"Ah. Well, I still need to fund this expedition I'm on."

"I do have a reliable messenger I can send it through. I can have it waiting at home for you."

He looked at the window and saw James walk past, looking for him.

"Excuse me." Alexander stepped back out into the street and tapped James on the shoulder.

"Ah, I thought I saw you around here. The supplies are being delivered. We have time for a meal if you like but I didn't pay the full docking fee so we can't stay the night."

"The crew will be less than pleased about that."

"Well, that's why the landing party was so small. I didn't release them for shore leave. You see, Your Majesty, you happen to be in a bit of a hurry." James looked at the window. "What were you looking at in here?"

"A few pieces. Just in case."

He looked at the amethyst ring, hands on his thighs as he leaned in. "Well, that's pretty. Not Catriona's thing, but just about any other woman would love it." He stood and looked down the dock shops for a place to eat and pointed. "That looks good. Come on."

142

James took off and Alexander looked once again at the ring. James was right. *Mandian gold, and a purple stone? Who was I buying that for?*

It was made all the more disturbing that Catriona had not crossed his mind the entire time. He dragged his eyes from the display and followed his captain.

Catriona eased by the island of Latia, going around it instead of between it and the Digitae Secundus. She knew the way was impassable. The sea was thick with kelp forests that ensnared larger ships' rudders. Only flat boats with a shallow draw could fish there safely. The kelp forest spread for miles east and west, almost to the other *Digitae*, leaving the *Secundus* the only Mandian fingertip without a trade port. Then, years ago, an undersea quake has caused a jut of land to rise, almost connecting the peninsula's city, Aquila, with the island of Latia. A bridge was built to promote trade and give Aquila access to a port within half a day's ride. The populace believed the earthquake was a gift from Heaven.

After construction, Aquila permeated the village of Brine Harbor, changing the people with an influx of money. Simple fishermen and gardeners became dependent upon buying everything instead of growing or catching it and folks forgot how to survive on their own. More than one family fell prey to seeking greed, to the destruction of all they loved.

As the ship went past the small island, she realized it was even bigger than before. Gone was the forest where she first met her late husband, replaced by tall houses and elaborate manors. She had fought against that, suggesting the bridge to prevent destruction of the forest. Apparently, it was all for naught.

Octavius came up to her. "First time I've seen that place since we started sailing."

"And the last. These waters are too dangerous for us. A Caratian ship in this area is suspicious. The patrols will shoot us into splinters. Can Estelle help?"

Octavius shook his head. "I don't know what's going on but she's sleeping more. I thought she was getting better but I'm not sure now. Of course, she won't let me see any damage. I really wish…"

Catriona didn't need to look at him to tell he was wishing Myrgen was here to look at her. He was the only person to ever see her true self. The discussion had already come up to take her to Galadorn but she had refused. She was still too afraid of what her father would do if he saw her injured like this. Catriona, knowing Corrigan like she did, had to concur. They would return in the fall, and possibly stay in Galadorn over the winter to restore or replace the stained glass window.

Octavius looked at his captain. "Well, we aren't drawing much. We could probably outrun anyone who caught us. It's really the only option since we can't use a disguise. She did offer to disguise us if a ship saw us."

Catriona smiled. "I have a way to get us through without expending Estelle's energies."

She went to her chambers, her eyes falling only briefly on Myrgen's door like they usually did, and looked around. She snapped her fingers, remembering, and went to the seat by the back of the ship. The bench seat of the chart table was covered in a custom woven tapestry and it likewise would need repairs once they stopped for the season. Still sporting tears from the devastating attack in St. Marguerite, she had stitched them closed as best she could. But she was no seamstress and she worried about making the repairs too permanent and ruining the material.

She lifted the seat and pulled out a box. She set the box on the table and unlocked it. A purple and silver flag was neatly folded within. She grabbed it and ran back outside. She handed it to Octavius.

"I never thought I'd use this again."

"Wow. I didn't even know you still had this. I figured you got rid of it in Rouen." He handed it to Thessius who took it to be raised.

As it reached the top of the mast, the brilliant colors of House Holloway and the Tanglwyst Trading Company announced their allegiance.

Twenty

Tragedy will either bind us or break us, but no one is unmarked.
-The Wisdom of Stone

Gwen and Michael pulled up to the Drum and Nightingale Inn as the sun left the sky for the night. It was a new moon and there was no chance Gwen would risk the horses on an unfamiliar road in the pitch dark. Tanglwyst wouldn't get far if she didn't stop for the night.

Besides, it's not like I don't know where she's going.

They got down and tied the reins to the post outside. The hearth was warm and the food smelled good. She opened the door and was greeted by the pleasant sight of Tanglwyst sitting in an upholstered chair. The pleasant feeling drained away when she saw the number of bandages on her. The plump, red-haired woman beside her came over to them.

"You must be Gwen and Michael."

Michael nodded and Gwen looked at Tanglwyst. "What happened to her?"

"She went riding by at a full gallop. You just don't do that on this mountain. The road on the other side, well, it just isn't a fast road unless your life is expendable. There's only one fast way to Caratia from here."

"Oh no."

"She went over and did some damage to herself. The horse didn't survive."

Gwen grew quiet and Michael spoke up.

"Is anything broken?"

The woman looked over at her charge. "She has bruised her ribs and has a nasty sprain in her ankle and wrist. She's got a few bruises that will take a while to heal and we're watching her to make sure the bump on her head doesn't put her into a death-sleep. I've got an herb tea in her right now to help her heal."

Michael walked over to Tanglwyst but Gwen stayed back. Tanglwyst turned to him as he came over.

"Michael. Gwen. I'm so sorry I left."

"What happened?"

"I couldn't sleep so I got up. Everyone was gone. The horses were nearby and mine was wearing a new harness. I took advantage of the situation and got on the horse. He wanted to run, so we did. When we got to the top of the mountain, he was still running. We went right past here and he…"

She turned to Gwen. "I'm sorry Gwen. I truly am."

"Shut up."

Michael looked at Gwen and she knew he was surprised. But at that moment, Gwen didn't care. She was *done* caring.

Michael took a few steps towards Gwen. "Gwen?"

"I don't *care* if you're sorry. I don't *care* if you're *hurt*. You *murdered my horse*." Tears started filling her eyes but she bit past them. "You just couldn't do it, could you? You used *my* friend to *death*, serving your own purposes, regardless of the cost. You used us just like you use everyone, just like you always have.

"You could have still sought Alexander *without* the compulsion. You *chose* not to. I'm done with you. I'm done with all of this. Alexander is a monster and the fact that you *know* this and refuse to let go of your…" Gwen looked away.

Michael put a hand on Gwen's shoulder. She felt cold anger throughout her heart and soul and she didn't like it at all. She felt betrayed and hurt and such loss for her horse at such a *senseless* death. It wasn't even a noble one. Worse, she felt betrayed by her faith. A *Fae* did this. A *Fae* put a spell on her horse to aid the obsession of a tyrant. Words could not fill the burnt hollow of her heart right then.

The red-haired woman sighed and a tall, thin man with black hair and brown skin of Toledan birth came out of the kitchen, wiping his hands. He looked at the situation and put the cloth on the bar.

"This looks like a weary crowd. What do you say everyone just back away and take a room. We have enough for each of you. Get some rest and sleep it off. No one should make any decisions under these circumstances."

Michael nodded. "That's a good idea. Gwen, go to bed. I'll get the horses stabled."

Gwen felt numb but recognized the wisdom in the man's request. She followed him to one of the rooms and took the key without comment. Once she was alone, she sat on the bed and cried.

Duncan pulled in to the Crossroads Inn and dismounted. A young man outside, maybe mid-teens, took his horse. "Staying the night, sir?"

"Yes, if there's room. I don't want to head to Caratia in the dark."

"Caratia too? Is there a festival or something?"

Duncan took off his gloves. "What do you mean?"

"Well, we never get folks heading to Caratia. Everyone always heads off to the Papal City from here. But you're the second, well, actually the fourth person in two days that has been heading that way."

"Fourth? Were two of the others a blond woman and a redhead?"

"Yeah, with a black fella."

"Black?" Duncan was confused. "Like black skinned?"

"Yes."

"Odd. They must have picked up a companion on the trip." Duncan shrugged. "Well, that will help them stay safe. How far away is Caratia from here?"

"Well, technically three days. I know a shortcut through the woods though. Knock off half a day to the Separation Pass. You ever been there before?"

Duncan patted the horse. "Nope. Never even been near the place. I tend to keep to the Sea of Erasmus."

"You ain't Mandian, are ya? Een a little bit?"

Duncan shook his head. "No. Why?"

"They can't go in. My pa was half-Mandian and I can't get past the inn at the top."

Duncan raised his eyebrows. That was going to be a problem Alexander never expected. His mother was pure Mandian, straight from the source. If this boy couldn't go there, the King would die on the rocks of the Blood Sea.

"On second thought, son, I think I won't be staying after all. Where's that shortcut?"

"Do you know how far away we are from Caratia?"

Boots looked at Myrgen, then nodded to the mountains nearby. "Technically, it's right there. Just on the other side of those cliffs. We've got about a two tenday trek north from here, or a one tenday trek east, then the Sea of Blood is our only obstacle."

"My sister never went to Caratia the couple times I sailed with her. We always stopped at Mande or Krakte." He looked at the foreboding cliffs. "So, if we just climbed straight up, it would be a day to the top?"

"Uh," she looked at him like he had suddenly sprung a leak and was streaming milk from his ear, "yeah, I suppose."

He sighed.

"No."

He looked at Boots. "What?"

"No. We aren't going to climb a sheer cliff face."

He opened his mouth but really couldn't come up with a good counter-argument, so he closed it again. "Meanie."

"Yes, I'm such a torturous villain, I'm not going to allow you to try to climb a sheet of glass a mile high so you can fall to your death."

Myrgen folded his arms across his chest and pouted visibly. Boots smirked and went back to roasting the rabbits they had caught that day. She stretched her back and felt the light bruises on her spine from sleeping on the ground. Once again, her mind went briefly to missing the amulet and the room. She sighed, remembering the dream but pushing it aside.

"Missing your room of luxury?"

She nodded, not looking at him. *No point in lying about it.*

He nodded too, then went back to looking at the mountains. Her eyes cast across him and she regretted not truly having an experience like his to relate with. Her closest emotion to love was the imposed loyalty to Sangiardo. It interfered with any other emotional connections she might make. She had a brief dalliance with the idea of her and Myrgen, but when she gave it more than an instant's meditation, all she felt was ice in her chest. Her mind might romanticize the idea of someone else, but in the end, it dissipated like a fart in a breeze.

"What's he like?"

She looked at him. "Who?"

"Sangiardo. I've never met him. I never even heard of him until I had a Horse try to kill me."

"What happened to him?"

"Who? The Horse? My friend Michael got his hands on him and ended the contract."

"Ah. That was you." She poked the meat of the rabbits' thighs. "I had heard we lost one. There's only me left, to be honest. Your lover took out the other two in his stable."

He looked down between his knees at the ground, like he didn't like being reminded of the woman he loved.

"What's *she* like?"

He shrugged. "Tough to nail down. She lives by her own code of conduct and I don't really understand it. She's smart and loyal to her people, whether they're her crew, her friends, her family, or her countrymen. And she's stubborn and arrogant and aggravating in her certainty that she's right. And the worst part is when she *is* right, because then she becomes *insufferable.*"

Boots smiled. "Most people do. Sangiardo made a decision that he's regretted, but you can't get him to go back on it. He'll burn as a witch or be buried in a pauper's grave before he'll admit he made a bad call on something. Though he never *says* it, the only Cardinal Sin in the Gospel according to Giovanni Sangiardo is Admitting He's Wrong."

They laughed a moment, then Myrgen tilted his head, looking at her boot. "You're the only Horse left?"

She sighed and nodded.

"I thought there were, well, more than four."

"He has more than four *actual* horses. In fact, there are eight of those. But the assassins were only four."

"And he hires out the real horses for actual riding?"

"Yes. But they are part of the team too. In fact, they're all he has left now, except for me."

"Can you tell me what happened?"

She took a deep breath, trying to figure out how much to say, then shook her head. "There's not much to tell, really. He tricked me into drinking Cyprian Herb, then made me kill for him. I had been handy enough with a blade to stay alive in the Bloody Alley. He recruited me in a way I couldn't refuse. Since then, I've been doing his dirty work."

"Did he drug the others too?"

She nodded. "None of us could leave and we couldn't kill him. We talked about it a couple times amongst ourselves but we knew it would never happen. Besides, it was a death sentence to us if anyone actually *had* killed him. Now, of course, it's just me. I think he had aspirations to have as many killers as he had actual horses but he never got that far."

"When did you get the amulet?"

"Oh, I think about three months ago. He got it from someone who paid him a retainer fee. It enabled me to travel all over the world, if need be. Sangiardo sent me to places for contracts which I fulfilled, then returned instantly to Florentine where I was seen publicly. There was no way to connect him to these distant murders."

Myrgen frowned. "Who would have enemies that far away?"

She shrugged and yawned. "I don't know, but I'm going to eat and sleep. That sounds like something for *you* to puzzle out."

Twenty-One

**Never let someone you care
about leave your company
without knowing that fact.
-The Wisdom of Stone**

Gwen awoke in the soft bed and stretched. She felt her eyes still puffy from crying the night before, and they were probably red too, but at least she had spent her time mourning her furred friend. The innkeeper had been right: she felt better. She got out of bed and got dressed. She wasn't quite sure yet how she was going to handle things with Tanglwyst, but she did feel like she might have a clearer head for the task. She used the chamber pot in the corner, then went out to the main area.

Fresh bread and sweet jam sat on the table and Michael was eating it like he'd not seen food in months. Tanglwyst was sitting with him and when she saw Gwen, she stood. Gwen came over and sat down, not yet sure whether she was still mad or if she was over that. Tanglwyst seemed to understand that. She gestured to a mug in front of her that had tea in it, and Gwen nodded. Tanglwyst hobbled over to the bar and spoke to the man from last night, calling him Tomas.

Gwen turned to Michael. "How's she doing?"

"Broken, but sane at least. She plans to stay here for a few days, then head on down the mountain to the Papal City."

Gwen blinked, taken by surprise. "She's... she's not going to Caratia?"

He shook his head.

Tanglwyst set the steaming mug down by Gwen. "No. I'm not. You were right. The person I thought I knew, the person I met this winter, could not have done this. This is someone new, and I want nothing to do with him."

Gwen was at a loss. "But, all this...?"

Tanglwyst nodded. "I know. I'll pay you for your time and losses. It's the least I can do."

"That's not necessary."

Tanglwyst shook her head. "No, it is. Alexander has become a tyrant, and frankly, my loyalty has always been to Mervolingia, not some random person sitting on a throne. Alexander is obsessed with Catriona and he's capable of using one of his own people like a tool." She looked at her hands, wrapped around the mug. "When you said that last night, you really hit the mark. I realized I have been the worst version of myself for too long now. When I started thinking about what Alexander had done to me, how he was going to use me to hurt my own kin," she shook her head, "I just couldn't do it."

Michael drank his morning mead quietly while Gwen and Tanglwyst sipped their tea. After a moment, he decided to ask what was on his mind.

"So, do you think Catriona will be a tyrant too, or will she balance Alexander out?" He looked at his two friends. "I don't really know her but you two do."

Tanglwyst and Gwen scoffed in unison. Tanglwyst spoke first, at Gwen gestured giving of the floor. "Catriona will never bend her knee to Alexander, no matter what. She has too much integrity for that." She pointed her index fingers around her mug. "When she worked for me, I put her in charge of my Black Fleet. It was my 'preemptive salvage' fleet. I intended it to be how I got things that people didn't exactly want to part with on their own.

"But Catriona wouldn't take certain runs, no matter what the reward. She only went places that had a purpose, too. She would refuse a larceny job in Calais but would take an identical job in St. Marguerite."

Gwen pointed to Tanglwyst. "I know which ones you mean. There was a friend of hers in St. Marguerite that she needed to check on. She helped his crew recover from a captain that went mad. They ended up rescuing Ambrois' brother from a life of crime in Portabella. Instead, she gave him a job on one of your Black Fleet ships. After sailing a season, he decided a land-based life was best for him and settled in Rouen. Ended up at the orphanage there. Turned out, once he had people relying upon him, he became very responsible."

Michael sat back. "Impressive."

"That's why she's going to be fine against Alexander's machinations. She won't compromise."

Gwen sipped her tea. "So, what are you going to do instead?"

"I'm going to see my grandfather at the Papal City, like I originally intended back when this all started happening. I'm going to ask him about this."

"What are you going to tell him?"

Tanglwyst sighed. "Everything. The Church won't endorse a king if they believe he's unworthy and I need advice on how to handle the resulting civil war once the king's claim is rejected. Plus there's Catherine to deal with, though she may be the solution. She ruled Mervolingia for decades keeping the peace."

"So, you're not going to Zara?"

"No. I have no reason to anymore."

Gwen reached out her hand and held Tanglwyst's. "I'm glad you finally saw through Alexander's lies."

Tanglwyst squeezed Gwen's hand. "I'm sorry it took all this for me to let go of the man I fell for."

Gwen sat back. "You... loved him?"

Tanglwyst sighed, casting her gaze at the ceiling. "I was starting to. He was kind and sweet and generous. He played with me and Emmy every day. I would have followed *that* man into Hell itself." She shrugged. "But apparently, that was just an act. This is what he's really like."

Michael shook his head. "No. He isn't. Something's wrong with him. A spell might be on him too. I've known Alexander for a couple of years now. He's a kind, compassionate man. I don't know what's going on, but I'm hoping we can break that. You might be able to help with that, my lady. Remind him of who he used to be."

Tanglwyst shook her head. "I'm not the person who can do that, Michael. I met him this winter for really the first time. I don't have years of experience with him like the two of you. I don't know what will trigger that change. At this point, I'd be dead weight. Besides, I need to heal up and you guys need to get to your friends. You need to protect them from what he's become."

Gwen nodded and Michael acquiesced. They stood and got everything ready to go, leaving Tanglwyst to finish her tea. When they were ready, they came over to say goodbye.

Gwen hugged Tanglwyst. "I know the Alexander we all know is still in there. I saw some of it in St. Andrew when he healed all those people. If we can get that man back, it will be better for everyone. But you need to know something: Alexander has a gift, outside of the healing one. He can talk people into anything. Catriona is not immune to that. That's why I'm leaving for Zara right now and not taking you to the Papal City. I need to show her the truth about him."

"If you can do that, it might end his obsession. If he lets go of her, then he might be the king he should be. It would stop the slaughter of thousands in a senseless war.

"Now, off with you. I need to rest."

Gwen and Michael smiled and left the Inn.

Myrgen looked through the trees and stopped. He hit Boots' shoulder with the back of his hand and pointed. She nodded, smiling. They ran up to the small cottage in the woods along the edge of the forest. The lights inside were cheerful and someone was making stew. They knocked on the door.

A man about his mid-forties opened the door and Myrgen immediately felt a kinship with him. His hair was brown, as were his eyes and he smiled when he saw them.

"Visitors?"

Myrgen nodded. "Please sir, we've been traveling for days. Do you have a pile of hay where we can bed down out of the weather for the night?"

"I have better than that, young man. Come, come inside." The man gestured to a pair of rooms off the main one, each with a bed in it. "Please, go ahead. Since my children are all grown, the house just feels so empty."

Myrgen turned to his host. "What about your wife?"

The man turned wistful. "Wilgefortis? She passed away several summers ago. I loved her very much."

"I'm sorry."

The man returned from his memory and waved his hand. "That was several lifetimes ago, son. Several lifetimes. Now, please, are you hungry?"

Myrgen and Boots both said "*Yes!*"

The man chuckled and gestured to a table. "You get yourself settled in the rooms, then join me. I'll get more bowls."

Myrgen walked over to the spare rooms, making sure they were extra and that the man wasn't giving up his own bed. He saw another bedroom down the hall and relaxed. "Which one do you want?"

"The one with you."

Myrgen did a double take. "What?"

She leaned in to keep their conversation private. "I'm not trying anything."

"Then what is it?"

She glanced at her hands. "I've had the same nightmare ever since the night at the room. I keep seeing the amulet, right next to me. It flickers in firelight and the shadows keep whispering that it's there for me, should I ever need it." She held out her hand, as if to catch something. "All I have to do is call it."

Myrgen grasped her hand, roughly calling her away from that line of thought. "That will just damn you again. Why would you do that?"

"I wouldn't, at least not knowingly. But if I did it in my dream…"

"Boots, this is a fight you're going to have to fight every day of your life. Period. I know. I fight a similar one myself. I can't be there for you every night. And frankly, if you're inches away from bringing that thing back into your life, I don't want to be anywhere near you. Those shadows would have me in my sleep and I've been under their influence before when I couldn't wake up. I won't go through that again."

She nodded and grasped his hand. "You're right, of course. Yes." She looked at the two rooms. "Well, I'll take this one, then."

Myrgen nodded. "Good." He put his satchel and coat on the pegs by the bedroom door and went out to the main room. The man was petting a sizable dog of mixed origin.

"I'm Myrgen, and this is my friend Boots."

"Welcome my friends. My name is Raven. And this is my friend Lauriel."

Boots walked through the woods to the house conveniently placed there. She knew her salvation was inside but she also knew she dragged the shadows behind her. If they got in there, everyone would die. She felt the amulet around her neck but it weighed on her like she was carrying a full grown person. It was hard for her to breathe.

She looked down and saw she was indeed carrying a whole person: a full grown man with light brown, thinning hair and a bulbous nose with a wart on one side. He was tall and had his legs wrapped around her waist and his arms draped around her neck. He looked familiar and in that instant, she knew who owned the amulet.

She woke up, the dream still lingering in stark detail. She looked around for a piece of paper and found one in the end table nearby. A graphite was next to it and she grabbed both and started scrawling. The man in her dream was someone she knew but had never met, because his visage was stamped on every coin in Mande. The man around her neck was King Cipriano.

She thought about waking Myrgen but then it occurred to her that if the shadows were still watching, they might use this opportunity to spring. Regardless, the dream had awakened a memory that was buried.

She had gone with Sangiardo to Vincenzia for a meeting with a high ranking official at the palace. They were escorted to a large study and two guards inspected the room, then stood just inside the closed door. After a few moments, a side door opened and the man in her dream walked out trailing a gold robe embroidered with the seal of Mande. He wore expensive silk from head to toe and the gold leather shoes adorning his feet cost more than her entire arsenal.

King Cipriano looked at them and Sangiardo took a knee, pulling Boots with him. Cipriano looked down on them, then with a gesture, dismissed her. The guards took her out and stood outside with her while the king and Sangiardo spoke. When he came back out, the king wasn't in the room anymore and Sangiardo was putting something in his coat. Shortly after they returned to Florentine, he gave her the amulet.

That must be who it belongs to. That's who's behind this. But why?

She thought about the jobs she'd been given since receiving the amulet and being told what it could do. Yes, she had said to Myrgen that King Cipriano would be happy to see him caught, but she had been trying to puff herself up to be a threat. Only now did she realize she had been closer to the truth.

But he doesn't know about Myrgen. No one does.

Unless the amulet told him before it died. Still, she had never received orders through the amulet, nor had she communicated with anyone through it. She was the only one with access to the windowless room so she couldn't even have gotten messages through there. All communication had been through Sangiardo himself when she would return.

Even if Sangiardo wanted her back right now, which he might, she couldn't return. More importantly, she couldn't even tell him where she was without that amulet. She couldn't explain anything. She knew she'd die if he did but other than that, she had no way of even knowing if he was healthy. He had sent her on long trips away from him before. She could be away from him so the herb didn't stop that. She always suspected that if he ever consummated their relationship sexually, she would not be able to leave his side. Luckily, he had always kept her at arm's length, probably for that reason.

Boots lay back on her bed. For the first time in days, she didn't dread going back to sleep.

Twenty-Two

Fine silks and spices can dress up even the lowest quality of meat.
-The Wisdom of Stone

James and Alexander sat down in the restaurant and a woman came over to them. She smiled. "Welcome to my home. We have many different wines to go with your meal. Would you like a wine list?"

Alexander looked at James. "Are you sure we can afford this place? They have more than one wine."

"My uncle told me there was a place like this here. I wasn't sure it was real."

The girl chuckled and handed them a piece of hand printed paper that had been waxed to seal it. It had several wines listed and James pointed to one. "Is that a true Bordeaux?"

"Yes it is. We have a supplier."

Alexander looked at the price. "Sounds good. I haven't had a Bordeaux since Patras."

She nodded and left. The establishment was busy and the conversations loud. Mandians that were working people tended to be boisterous, family people. They loved life and it was out in force that day. There were so many people, Alexander listened instead of trying to talk. They would be back on the ship soon enough. It would be quieter there.

Several people had dressed in their finest and everyone was in a festive mood. When the girl returned with their bottle of Bordeaux, Alexander motioned her closer. "Is it always this busy?"

She looked around. "This is mostly for the festival. King Cipriano loves to celebrate the opening of the sailing season."

"Wait, Cipriano is *here*?"

"Indeed! He comes here every year at this time to watch the merchant fleets launch. There's a lot of partying and he even lights fireworks after dark. You have never been here for it?"

"No, and I'm afraid I probably will miss the up close of it tonight too."

"That is too bad. It is a wonderful show. I will bring your food now."

James smiled. "I wonder what we're getting."

"Probably something that compliments the Bordeaux."

"I'm not sure I know what that would be."

Alexander laughed and picked up the bottle to read the label. "Lions in Saltire. Interesting."

James took the bottle and poured it.

Alexander tasted the wine and looked at the glass, surprised. "I know this."

"Mhm." James sipped his. "Wanna know why?"

Alexander nodded and took another drink.

"It's Tanglwyst's label."

Alexander set the glass down. "By the Saints, she's just everywhere, huh?"

"She merchants this area pretty heavily, yes. Her reach goes away the farther east you go. At least by sea. Her overland caravans go to York."

Slow roasted beef on a bed of rice arrived and Alexander had not realized just how long he'd been living on hard tack until that moment. The food was delicious and would probably never taste as good under any other circumstances. The girl was attentive and James and Alexander joked throughout over who she was interested in. Each man pointed little clues in the other's favor. By the time they saw their crewman looking for them, they were almost willing to stay the night.

Alexander paid while James spoke to the crewman in the street. When he stepped out, the man from the messenger service pointed Alexander out to some city guards. They walked towards the group. Alexander tapped James on the shoulder and nodded to the guards.

"I have the feeling we'll be here for the festivities after all."

Alexander walked into the summer palace in Calais. It was covered in gold and beautiful, detailed paintings. One thing about the Mandians: they could afford the very best artists. Where the walls and ceilings were not illustrated, there was white-gold leaf. Apparently that was the biggest source of wealth in this area for it to be used to this lavish extent. He wondered what the palace in Vincenzia looked like.

He was led to an office not unlike the one he now had in Patras. Two guards stepped in with him and stayed in the room. A man in a long green robe and tall matching hat was holding a folio with papers in it. He knocked on a door on one side of the room and it opened. He whispered loud enough that Alexander could hear it, "He's here, Your Majesty."

The man stepped back and King Annibal Cipriano Malatesta stepped out of the room. He wore a sweeping robe of gold and green with the Mandian arms on it: Three ships above a lush meadow surrounded by mountains of gold. Upon his head was a circlet of white gold and emeralds. Cipriano bowed to his equal.

"Your Majesty of Mervolingia. Welcome to my country."

"I thank you for your welcome, Your Grace."

"It would be far more fitting had I but known you were coming."

Alexander nodded. "My apologies, Your Grace. I did not know we would be visiting or I would have sent word personally."

Cipriano waved his hand. "It matters not any longer, cousin. We have met up now, and in time for you to see our festival."

"I would be honored, Your Grace. However, the ship I'm on had a deadline for its cargo. We were only going to be here a few hours to resupply."

"I'm sure they will understand. If it spoils, I will reimburse them. They must have known there could be complications when they took on your passage." Cipriano poured some wine into a green glass goblet and motioned for Alexander to sit in a chair at an engraved table. "If the worst happens, there are many, many ships in my port. We can take you wherever you need to go."

Alexander didn't want to reveal that he was traveling to Caratia just yet so he nodded as he sat. "That is most kind of you. Thank you."

"So, tell me, what brings you so far from home before the pleasure sailing season actually kicks off?" Cipriano poured some wine into a second goblet and the steward brought them both to Alexander. It was tradition for a host to pour for all, then offer the guests their choice. It was a tactic used to prove the guests weren't being poisoned, a practice born of necessity in this country. "I understand you are off looking for a wife?"

Alexander picked the second cup poured and sniffed it. "Wonderful bouquet."

"It's from a vineyard by the border. The area is perfect for grapes."

He tasted it and found it to be everything he expected from a Mandian wine, rich, red and bloody. He leaned forward, setting the goblet down. "Yes, you heard right. I have decided to marry whomever I choose. I'm too old to have my mother arrange something."

"Yes, and her choice for your brother turned out not to be a good fit. You are smart to insist on choosing your own mate."

Alexander inhaled, making sure he didn't take the bait, if that was what the king just offered. He didn't need to become angry in his first diplomatic situation. Instead, he nodded and smiled. "Exactly the point I made to my mother."

"Well, it turns out I might have an offer that will suit both your desires." He motioned to the door he just came out of and a young girl of about ten years old joined them. She was wearing an expensive green velvet gown with a metal plaque belt of white gold set with emeralds. On her head was a circlet like her father's.

"This is my daughter, Gillian."

Gillian curtsied, her dark curls gently bounced, mirroring her dancing hazel eyes.

Cipriano leaned on the table. "She's not *quite* of marrying age just yet, but that doesn't mean she's too young to be engaged."

Alexander's eyes darted back to Cipriano. "Your Grace, your daughter is lovely as the sky, of course. However, I have another prospect in mind at present." He turned back to the princess. "After I investigate that one, my lady, I may ask to call upon you. Would you like that?"

"I would be honored, Your Majesty." Her voice was cherubic and very young.

Cipriano smiled. "With those charms, I doubt the Stapana will be able to resist your proposal."

Alexander tried not to react to this secret being known. He blinked slowly to buy time on how to react.

Cipriano didn't wait. "Yes, Alexander. I know of your romantic quest. I know quite a few things, in fact. Such as the name of your heir, Alan Moriarity." He inspected his manicure as he continued. "There are those who believe you have plans to legitimize this young man as your son."

"You have an awful lot of interesting notions."

Cipriano scoffed. "Oh please. This is all the same sort of information you could get on me and mine with any steward's help. So here is what I propose: My daughter is far too young for you. Her mother, rest her soul, would never tolerate her being given in marriage to a man three times her age. The woman you are interested in is definitely a much better fit.

"However," his blue grey eyes narrowing, "I also know that the Church will not endorse this marriage to a heathen without her conversion. That's always such a tricky business. Converts are notorious back alley practitioners of their previous faith. The Stapana would not tolerate being denied her Land Worship."

"You are astonishingly well informed, sir."

"I pay a lot of money to be so. I have connections keeping me informed as to the inner workings of the world. Those connections can be turned to *your* advantage as well, cousin."

"And what would I have to do for such a boon, *cousin?*"

He nodded to Gillian and she left the room, closing the door to the chamber she came from. "I will assist in the acceptance of your marriage if *you* will assist in betrothing Catriona's son to my daughter."

Alexander frowned. "You want Alan and Gillian to marry? I thought you were against arranged marriages."

162

Cipriano shrugged. "Mine was arranged and I loved that woman immensely. I shall until the day I join her, and beyond. But I also understand that a young girl's fancy can be swayed by the wrong boy. Alan has your bloodline, and his mother's. He was raised by someone you treasure above all others. I believe that has created a person worthy of my little girl."

Alexander nodded. *He's just looking out for his daughter. I can't say I blame him. Alan could hardly marry Emmy, after all.* "I'll tell you what I'll do: I won't say I'll arrange a betrothal, but I *will* invite Gillian to spend time with us over the summer after Catriona and I are coronated. We'll come here for this festival, and take Gillian back with us. She can stay for a few months, getting to know the family. If she and Alan enjoy one another's company, I'll see if Catriona can be swayed."

"That is all I ask."

Alexander finished his wine and stood. "Well then, Your Majesty, I should get to my ship and get under weigh. The longer I'm away from Caratia, the less likely I am to bring both our hopes to fruition."

Cipriano smiled and stood as well, offering a bow of respect. Alexander was escorted from the room and the palace by the guards.

Cipriano opened the door to his bedroom and called his daughter out.

"Did you get what you wanted, Daddy?"

"I hope so, my dear. You'll have to meet the young man and decide for yourself."

"But if I marry him, Mandians will again rule Caratia, right?"

Cipriano smiled and nodded. Gillian bounced out of the room and Cipriano stood. The girl understood what was at stake here.

For centuries, my people have been denied passage into Caratia. I will be the king that sets foot on her soil again.

Twenty-Three

Anyone who believes the only real danger is in your mind had never met a Fae Cat.
-The Wisdom of Stone

Gwen and Michael headed down the mountain into Caratia. As they passed the body of her horse, she said a blessing over him, asking the Fae to carry him to their home. Michael waited patiently, understanding the importance of committing a fallen animal back to the earth. In his faith, something he had not practiced since being captured and taken from Nubia, humans and animals ran together across the plains. They bonded as family. You treated your companion animals the same way you treated your children.

When she finished, they heard a sound from the forest below. It carried across the air like it was projected at them, coming at once from everywhere and nowhere. It sounded like a cross between a roar from a lion, a jaguar's scream, and a wolf's howl. He had never heard anything like it. Gwen smiled.

"Looks like my prayer will be answered."

"What *was* that?"

"One of the natives of this forest, the Fae Cat. They are large predators that roam in packs in this forest. Lethal killers with poisonous claws."

Michael looked around, wary. "Why does anyone live here?"

Gwen laughed. "Because these creatures are the servants of the Land. They are Caratia's forest guardians, protecting this part of the country from anyone who gets in that doesn't belong here."

"How do they know?"

"Well, some of it is instinct. They know when people are here with evil intent. The Dûce and Dûcesa can also declare someone an Enemy of the State. If that enemy tries to leave through the forest, they are hunted down relentlessly."

"That..." He shook his head. "So, the Crown of this place can execute someone by using the creatures that live here?" He looked at the trees and rocks. "Do they control the plants too?"

Gwen got on her horse and started down the mountain as another roar-howl echoed a little closer.

Duncan got to the base of the Pass as dawn hit the roof of the Cliffbase Inn. Riding all night had left him exhausted and he felt better stopping here than back at the last place. Every once in a great while, he would think about the amulet and the ease with which he used to travel the continent, but it was always fleeting. He had been addicted to a drug that was destroying him and now that it was out of his life, he felt alive.

He helped those people back in St. Andrew. He helped a town get rid of a serial killer and rapist of children. He helped get his king on his way to find the woman he loved. Now, he hoped to help Tanglwyst get back home, or at least to safety. Alexander would still be sailing to Caratia. Duncan figured he might be able to catch up to Tanglwyst, take her to the Papal City like she originally wanted to, then head over to reconnect with Alexander.

In truth, if he found Tanglwyst before he met up with the king, he might be willing to just leave Alexander to woo his lady on his own. After all, James was with him. He was probably pretty safe. Gwen was heading to Caratia to meet up with James and then the siblings could go about their business. All would be well.

His eyes closed and he saw Alexander dashed upon the rocks to the Blood Sea, James' ship in pieces as the sharks turned the water red.

He started awake. That's right. He can't enter Caratia. How the hell am I supposed to save him if I can't get to him?

He looked at the inn and smelled bacon, and the down-to-earth scent cleared his head. The idea of Alexander not being able to enter a country was ridiculous. He couldn't believe he had put credence in that boy's tale. Caratia was a country rife with legend because it was secluded. Superstition required mystery. He doubted the boy's duties would have allowed him to leave his mother's business long enough to ride this far and another day farther up the mountain. He dismounted and went inside.

Myrgen got out of bed, feeling refreshed for the first time on land. As usual, his first thoughts were of Catriona and the crew of the *Enigma*, but after that, his next thoughts were of breakfast. He went out to the main room where Raven and Lauriel were in the kitchen. Raven smiled at the newcomer. Lauriel didn't notice, his attention fixated on the bacon in the pan.

"Sleep well?"

"Like I was in my own bed. Thank you for opening your home to us."

Raven nodded to the other bedroom. "Your companion didn't seem to have as easy a night. I heard her up about halfway to dawn."

Halfway to dawn? Odd expression. "She has a lot of things she's thinking through. Tends to interfere with things like sleep."

"Ah. I hope they are things she will be able to get through."

Myrgen nodded, looking at her room. "Me too."

Boots opened her door, pulling on her coat. "That smells amazing."

Raven nodded to her. "It should be ready by the time you get a plate and sit down."

Myrgen and Boots did as instructed, doing their best not to attack the eggs and bacon like savages when it was served. Raven and Lauriel shared their food and when the initial wolfing down was done, he collected the plates and put them on the floor for Lauriel.

"So, where are you two headed?"

Myrgen wiped his mouth. "Haven't made that decision just yet. Right now, we're just trying to sort out our options."

"Well, if you end up in this area again on your travels, please stop by and visit longer."

Myrgen nodded. "I will indeed."

Boots looked behind her at the cottage. She had felt such a gentle safety within its walls unlike anything before, including the windowless room. She had been able to look at things with clarity. In thinking about the amulet, she had realized the owner. She was now trying to sort out if she should tell Myrgen.

"You okay?"

She nodded. "Yes. Just…"

"Did you have another dream last night?"

"More like a memory." She looked at him. "I think I know who owns it."

"Who?"

"Cipriano."

Myrgen's face betrayed his shock. "The King of Mande?" He focused again upon their road.

"It was a way to get assassinations done in distant places and leave no trace. If I had a way to disappear back to Florentine in an instant, no target was beyond his reach."

"Even royal ones. All you would need in your hand is a missive and a Royal Messenger tabard to gain access to anyone."

Boots nodded.

"If I may ask, where did he send you?"

"I went a few places in the last few months. Portabella was a test, to see if I could get into secret places. He didn't know I grew up there and had an in. By now, he would know of the destruction of the place."

"You didn't report it to Sangiardo?"

"I had other things to do."

Myrgen nodded. "Ah. Right. Me."

"It's turned out profitable so far. Besides, the information would have reached everywhere by now. The smoke from the fires would have been seen on the ocean."

Myrgen closed his eyes a moment, and Boots let him. She had killed people he knew. Myrgen was the kind of person that mourned a friend's passing, even if that person was someone he only knew for a day. His profession before revolved around making connections fast.

"Do you know what else he had planned for you?"

Boots shook her head. "No, but I have been traveling all year. Anywhere I hadn't been yet. I was to get there by whatever means I needed to, then return. I had been to Patras, Vincenzia, every major city in Mande, in fact. Cheryb. Sangiardo was talking about sending me even farther once the sailing season started. Kilmory, Yantap. Even to York and Krakte. Get there, come back. Now I know he was establishing return spots for the amulet when I finally got it. I couldn't go where I'd never been."

"Can someone else use those spots?"

She shrugged. "I don't know. I only know of the one amulet."

"But if you knew it, and you took someone…"

She nodded. "That stands to reason."

"By the stones." Myrgen stopped, exhaling.

She put a hand on his shoulder. "It's gone now. You destroyed it. He can't attack anyone through me anymore."

"Who's to say he doesn't have more?"

She frowned. She couldn't really answer that. They started walking again and saw a couple spires of smoke in the distance, several miles away. It looked like a village near the cliffs. She nodded towards it.

"Looks like we might get a bed tonight too."

Myrgen squinted at the horizon. "Maybe. I wonder how close we are to the Pass."

"Still a tenday away."

"Yeah, well, maybe Raven's cottage grew legs and walked in the night while we slept."

Boots laughed and they pressed on.

Duncan felt refreshed after breakfast and looked out the window at the Pass. He stopped the young woman serving drinks as she walked past. "Excuse me, how long does it take to get up that?"

She looked out the window. "I understand it takes a day."

"You understand?"

"I've never felt the need to go up there. It is a steep climb and there's just an Inn at the top. Once a year or so, the people who run it come down here for supplies. They stay the night and head up the next day. Sometimes people make trips up there, stay the night and return, but I have no idea why."

"They only need supplies up there once a year? How much do they buy?"

"Not as much as you think. I believe they come down for human contact. They can't get much up there."

"Does anyone ever come down from Caratia outside of those people?"

"No, no one from that place ever comes here." Another patron called her name and she acknowledged them. "Excuse me."

Duncan let her go, drained his ale, and left for the Pass.

Michael looked over the world he was walking through. It was untamed and rich in color. The sounds were powerful and terrifying, and he felt strangely at home. He had not been back to Nubia since he was taken even though Myrgen had offered a few times. Michael knew the challenges of entering into Nubia. Many tribes had already moved higher onto the continent, but the protections only worked from the sea. Overland, slaves were taken all the time.

When he was taken, he had feared the unknown, but had always felt his spirit would never be claimed. He had never expected the kindness Myrgen showed him, the trust. He had expected pain, torture, even scarring. He told himself that he could weather anything his captors did to him.

That why he was so unprepared when Dominic…

Gwen looked at him. "Whatcha thinkin'?"

He shuddered. "About home."

"Patras?"

He shook his head, moving a branch aside. "The other one."

"Oh. How long ago were you there?"

"It's been a while. I usually don't think about it but here, in this place... It reminded me."

She nodded. "It's nothing like Glarren, not in appearance. These trees are different, the soil, the animals. The only thing the same is the connection to the Fae." She smiled, looking at the sky and her surroundings. "I had forgotten how cut off from it Mervolingia was."

The sun shone on her hair and he noticed the glint in the pale, spun gold. Her eyes were ice blue, a color he had never encountered before. Oh, some women in Mervolingia and Yndia had blue eyes, but these were glacial. He thought of children with her eyes and his skin and tripped.

"Michael? Are you alright?"

He stood, brushing himself off. "I just was too busy looking around. I wasn't paying attention to the dangers of... roots."

She took his hands and looked at them. "That's a *Cimbrus* tree. It has poisonous sap."

He looked with concern at his hands and body. "Is there some reason why this place is so deadly?"

She dusted off his legs. "I don't see any cuts." She looked at him. "You're lucky. We need to keep an eye on things here."

He nodded. She was right. This place was too inhospitable to be distracted.

Twenty-Four

We don't always know how we get somewhere.
-The Wisdom of Stone

"We've got company."

Catriona looked up from her notes at Octavius. "What is it?"

"Mandian patrol. Eastern horizon."

"Have they seen us?"

"They turned our way, so, yeah. They're on an intercept course."

"*Szar!*"

Octavius blinked but she didn't apologize for swearing. She went up on deck and took the spyglass from Thessius. She swore again.

"How far are we from the Blood Sea Shoals?"

"Still a day, Captain."

"Can they catch us?"

"Board us? No. But they'll be in range to fire upon us."

"Why did they change course to intercept? We were flying the flag."

"That might be the problem, Captain. I'm sure word of Tanglwyst's treason has reached her Mandian allies by now."

Catriona put the spyglass down. "I need them closer to find out, but having them closer puts us all in danger. We're still in Mandian waters so I have no power here at all."

They watched the ship for the rest of the morning and by lunch, the patrol ship was a lot closer than a regular patrol would be. Thessius swung down from the crow's nest.

"Captain, it's a race-built."

Catriona's swearing became a stream of Caratian. Race-built galleons were a new style created in Mande's shipyards. Sleeker and smoother on the sea, they weren't good against storms, but the damned things could outrun one.

At this rate, they would be fired upon by sunset.

Thank the Saints for Cipriano.

Alexander got out of bed and went out onto the deck of the *Raven's Watch*. The delay at the palace had worried James because he had only paid for four hours of docking and the cost for overnight was prohibitive in many ways. Cipriano's signature, refunding all docking fees for the ship, coupled with the fireworks show had enabled them to get back out to sea despite it being after sunset when they left. Once out to the unobstructed ocean, they could sail all night.

"How goes it, James?"

James looked up as Alexander came up to him. "Well. We made good progress last night." He pointed to the north. "That's the Second Finger and the small isle of Latia we're passing now. We'll be to the Third by sunset."

Alexander had a pang of guilt for a moment at the name of the island and he shook it off. *Nicolai is dead and he deserved his fate.* "Excellent. We should be there either before her or within a day of her arrival."

James folded his arms. "Have you considered what you'll do if she rejects you?"

Alexander leaned on the railing facing land. "I've never let my mind linger on that."

"I doubt that. You've had a pensive look on your face every time there's a delay. You are clearly thinking she might tell you no."

"I'm hoping she will see how important she is to me after chasing her halfway around the world."

"And if she doesn't? I mean, you did fire on her ship. If you did that to me, it would end our friendship."

Alexander started, slightly amused. "We're friends?"

James smiled, then grew serious. "I mean it, Alexander. What if someone was killed?"

Alexander shook his head, despair clouding his eyes. "I don't even want to picture that. If someone was killed or hurt... Let's just say she wouldn't be the only one never forgiving me."

"Captain, do you have a minute?"

Both men turned to the First Mate. James nodded and left Alexander to his thoughts.

"Sir, there have been concerns about our heading."

James folded his arms across his chest. "Why?"

"Because some of our crewmen have asked to be let off in Naplles if our destination is Caratia."

"Why?"

"You don't know?" The First Mate looked around. "They can't set oar in Caratian waters. They'll be killed by the sea itself. They're Mandian."

"What does that have to do with anything?"

"Have you ever been to the Blood Sea before, sir?"

"Well, I sailed with my Uncle for a couple years..." He blinked. In fact, he never *had* been to Caratia, or to the Blood Sea. They had always gone to Glarren and back to Yndia via the Sea of Erasmus. "Hunh. So, tell me what it means to be Mandian going to Caratia?"

"Centuries ago, when the Great Plague swept through, King Alphonse Pulcini I ascended the throne after the sickness claimed his father and brothers. He claimed the plague came from Caratia, across the plains that were once there. They marched towards Zara, setting fire to all the crops before them to destroy the plague. He claimed Heaven was angry because Caratia was populated by heathens.

"It is said the First Dûcesa waved her hands and the Separation Cliffs sprang from the ground, cutting the entire country off. Alfonse's forces would not be stopped. They went via sea and started destroying every ship they encountered, bent on cleansing the heathens and claiming that area for Heaven. But the Dûcesa had made a pact with Callista and the first Caratian ship they encountered repelled even canon fire. Mandian blood hit the water and every ship with Mandians on it was ripped apart on the rocks that sprung from the deep. Sharks claimed them all but never laid tooth on any Caratian, even if they were bloody from fighting.

"Ever since, the Sea has run red the second a Mandian goes anywhere near it."

"That sounds like a remarkable story. And Mandians have stayed away ever since?"

"Well, of course. It turned out what Alphonse really wanted was the gold and silver that ran in large veins throughout Caratia. When the Cliffs rose, they brought that ore to Mande. They couldn't get to the country anyway so they instead took it as a sign that Heaven rewarded them with the spoils they sought."

James' eyes narrowed. "So no one from Mande can enter the area?"

"No sir, not even if you were born elsewhere. If you have a parent or grandparent of Mandian descent, you cannot cross."

James looked at Alexander, still over by the railing. "That just might be a problem."

He walked back over to the king.

"So, Alexander, you ever *been* to Caratia?"

Alexander jumped. "Sorry. I was caught up in my thoughts. Um, no, not really. I've met Drake and Anika once, but that was in Patras when they were bringing Alan to Patras last year. It was right before I found out Nicolai was alive. I thought she was bringing him to live in Patras because she was planning on being with me."

"But you've never been to *Caratia* before. How about the Blood Sea?"

He shook his head. "Honestly, I never tried. It wasn't until after I sailed with her a few times that I realized that was where she spent her winters. She had never told me. I spent years in seedy ports on the Fingers looking for her. I finally found her in Cheryb. She told me not to look for her again because it was dangerous out there and she didn't want me hurt or captured."

"I have the feeling that didn't stop you."

"No. I kept at it, heading north along the coasts. Ran into her at St. Marguerite, then again in Rouen. The last time she let me sail with her for the rest of the season, to Glarren and northern York. We never went south of there because there's a land bridge that is risky to cross along the straight between York and Glarren. There's a big port city that spans the bridge on land but it's an actual road between the two countries in the summer. The only time you can sail across it is in the spring."

"I see. Well, I know you're not going to be okay with this, but we need to stop in Naplles before we head there."

"Why?"

James thought about whether to convey the tale or not and in the end, if he was going to be responsible for Alexander, he needed to tell him. He explained the story he had just heard.

Alexander leaned back against the railing. "Is that true?"

"I have no idea. I've honestly never been there. Alistair never went. There were always enough other places to explore."

"Yes, no ship ever went north from Mande. They went east to Nubia so I always assumed they just plundered the entire continent. I've received silks from Yokotama at the palace from mother's family so I guess it always seemed they had access."

"Alistair always said you could trade for anything in Mande. They must have a supplier." James leaned his forearms on the railing. "So, how do we handle this?"

"Do we have any proof that this seafarer's superstition is even true?"

"As much as any other one."

Alexander folded his arms. "Then I imagine that's the first step."

Duncan saw a messenger service spot and thought about Alexander. He stopped outside the door. *Couldn't hurt to ask.*

He stepped inside and looked around. There were places to sit and write, with quills and inkwells and paper. The walls were decorated with nine maps, ranging from a detailed map of Patras to a map of the Known World, all done by the same artist, someone named *Magdalena.*

He stepped up to the desk. "Hey, can you get a message to a ship at sea?"

The messenger was a simple-looking fellow, with neat clothes and a tightly cropped light brown haircut. His eyes indicated an innocence born of people who didn't need much to be happy. He raised an eyebrow.

"Uh, no. I don't know of anyone who could do that."

A voice came from behind the messenger. "There is one way."

The messenger turned around and a dark-haired young woman with similar facial traits leaned against the desk.

The young man frowned. "You mean the folks at the summit, Mag?"

She nodded. "Folks who need to reach someone in a bad place can send a message through the service at the inn up there." She looked at the Pass.

"How do they do it?"

The messenger shrugged. "I don't know. I just know that sometimes, people come through here with messages, trade out horses, and head up the mountain. They come back down a day later. They don't even stay overnight. They swap out horses again and leave."

Duncan looked over his shoulder and then back at the siblings. "One other thing: Is it true that no Mandian can enter Caratia?"

The messengers shrugged. The man said, "I've never seen one that I know of. Why would someone from Mande be clear over here?"

Duncan nodded goodbye and left.

Why indeed.

As sunset neared, the patrol galleon drew to within gun range. Catriona had the cannons primed and ready in case they were hostile, but she wasn't willing to fire on them unless they needed to. She wanted to get them close enough to read their captain but that range was getting shorter and shorter as the sky started to darken.

She had held the spyglass to her eye for almost the entire last hour but she kept seeing only sailors doing their jobs. No officers, which probably meant they were either eating dinner or a missive had come in. The ranking officer on deck had been given orders to pursue this ship but that was all she could tell in the last hour. Wherever they were, they had to change shift in the next half hour. Unfortunately, by then, it would be too dark to read them.

Suddenly, the ranking officer called a sailor over and pointed to the *Enigma*. He had a spyglass as well and she could see he had registered something of alarm about her ship. He became agitated and the other sailor looked at her ship, then ran off. Barely a minute later, several officers ran on deck and the Captain took the spyglass as the others squinted into the rising shadows. Octavius raised his hand to start the crew preparing to fire.

Then the captain shouted something and the other ship dropped anchor. Catriona put her hand on Octavius' shoulder, staying his hand. The officers were milling about, very worried but the light was at that shades-of-grey level where details were fuzzy, and the setting sun behind them ended her chances of getting anything else. She put the spyglass down.

Why did they drop anchor?

The odd behavior continued as more time passed. They were still within gun range on both ships and would be for a while but they were letting her sail away. They had the same technology for looking at her ship as she had for looking at theirs. This close, they could have identified her, but they didn't respond like they recognized her. They responded like…

"Thessius, Go out to yard arm on the east side of the ship, jump off and swing out as far as you can. Tell me what you see."

Thessius scaled the main mast and crawled out to the end of the yard arm, grabbing a rope and tying a bowline knot on the way. He tied a second one up the line a bit, then grabbed that and backed up a few feet. He ran to the end and jumped off. As he got to the end of the rope, he put his foot in the lower loop and used his momentum to twist his body and look at the ship.

He swung back onto the ship and landed on the deck. "Caipen, weer ay playg shaip."

Boots and Myrgen looked at the sparkling lights of the village, earthbound stars mirroring the night sky. Myrgen smiled.

"Looks like we might make it in time for dinner."

"That's both a blessing and a curse. I'm running low on money." She shrugged as he looked at her. "I never expected to be away this long. At least not without access to money."

Myrgen frowned. "Yeah, I never thought of that. What do you want to do?"

She reached down and touched her rapier. "How much could we get for this?"

"Your sword?"

"We need to eat, and after last night, I am *certain* I need a bed as often as I can get one. If we can sell this, we have traveling money for the trip."

"It will leave you unarmed."

"You'll have a sword if we need it."

Myrgen paused, thinking about what this meant. They were no longer prisoner and captor. They were companions, allies. The plot he suspected Boots of concocting, of convincing him to befriend her and then being willing to go with her had worked. He worried that he didn't feel trapped.

They got into town and heard the tink-tink of a blacksmith working. They sorted out the direction of the sound and walked that way. The forge was glowing orange and the large man behind the sound was outlined in the fire. He stopped striking as they walked up.

"Can I help you folks?" His hair was cropped short to keep it from the fires and out of his eyes and he wore a sweat and soot stained shirt with tiny holes in the sleeves from the sparks. A heavy leather apron covered most of the rest of him.

Boots had unslung her rapier to prepare it for trade. "We're travelling and got lost. We've lost our money and need to make some. Can you pay me for this?"

He took the weapon and looked at it. "Lost your money?"

Myrgen looked guilty. "I... fell in a river. She managed to get me out but I dropped our other satchel."

The blacksmith looked at him.

"And my weapon..."

The blacksmith took a deep breath. "You sure you can afford to part with this? It's your only remaining protection."

"We figure once we get into Caratia, we should be fine."

"You headed up the mountain?"

Boots nodded. "Any idea how far we are from the Pass?"

"Well," he nodded to the mountain behind them, "it takes a full day to get up there. That's a nasty road too. I wouldn't try it at night."

Myrgen stepped more into the light, his hand up. "Wait, where are we?"

"Cliffbase." He pointed to the mountains. "That's Separation Pass."

Myrgen stepped back out into the street while Boots negotiated the sale of her sword. There was a distant flicker at the top of the mountain, like a single lantern in a window.

It's right there. I don't know how we got here or what I'm going to do now, but the time has come to get my head right. Tomorrow, we'll be in Caratia.

Duncan got up to the Drum and Nightingale and turned to look at the world behind him. This was the highest in the world he had ever been and the view was beyond astonishing. All of Mervolingia was laid out before him. He could see all the way to the Erasmus. He could see the steeples of the Papal City and the glittering lights of Toledo. He could see Bordeaux and he imagined he could see St. Giles. All he knew and loved was beneath him, save one thing.

He walked the horse to the other side of the cliffs to look down into Caratia. It was like looking into a pit of writhing monsters. The sun did not shine upon this place, and all was in shadow. Far away, what seemed like the same distance as the lights of St. Giles, similar lights danced alone in the night. He saw nothing to indicate any other civilization outside of what were probably a few campfires through the unending black where the moon had not yet shined.

He saw a flicker in the forest floor about a day away into Caratia. That's probably them. They must not have made as good time while trying to struggle through the woods. The roads of Patras are considerably better maintained. I can't even see a way through that pit of darkness.

He looked back at the small inn. He dismounted and went inside.

Symonne looked at Tanglwyst's wounds. "These look good."

"Good enough to travel tomorrow?"

Symonne looked less than pleased. "I would prefer you stay put for a while longer, but you should be alright," she pointed at her charge, "*if* you travel slowly. There's an inn at Cliffbase. Rest there tomorrow night. From there, you should be able to find regular resting places all the way to the Papal City."

The door opened to the inn and a dark figure stepped in. He looked at the women and the largest smile erupted on his face. "Tanglwyst!"

"Duncan?"

He came over to her and hugged her. She flinched and took in a sharp breath as he pressed upon a bruised area. Symonne pulled him away and he looked at her bandages like he had neglected to see them before. He stumbled back.

"I…'m sorry. What happened? Where is Gwen?"

Tanglwyst waved Symonne off. "I'm fine, Symonne. It was just one of the bruised spots. Gwen and Michael went on to Zara."

"Without you?"

Tanglwyst took a deep breath and nodded. "It was time."

"Are you going to join them?"

She pursed her lips and shook her head.

Symonne looked at Duncan. "You look hungry and tired. Let me get you some stew."

Tanglwyst brightened. "I have been dying for some more of that honey bread since last night."

"I'll make sure we have some. You two chat." She went back into the kitchen.

"So, what's going on?"

"I just finally let go of Alexander."

"Let… go?"

"Yes, so he couldn't control me anymore."

Duncan pulled a chair over to her. "What are you talking about? Control you how?"

"You don't know?"

"Know what?"

Oh no. This is going to be a long conversation.

Once the patrol ship went on its way without so much as a shout out to the ship, Catriona and Octavius ran into his quarters. Estelle was there, almost transparent, her eyes closed in intense concentration. The illusions in their cabin were gone, revealing bare walls and sparse furniture and a lone, bunched up sock in a corner. Catriona and Octavius both started towards her but she held up her hand. It shook from the effort.

Both heard in their heads, *Don't disturb me.*

Octavius' face was a canvas painted with pain and worry and fear. *What are you doing?*

Protecting us all. Do you think I'd be in better condition if we were boarded or pock-marked with cannon fire?

Catriona put her hand on Octavius' shoulder. *How long have you been doing it?*

Long enough. Now, please go. I need my strength.

Octavius looked at Catriona and nodded. "I'll stay with her."

She squeezed his shoulder. "I'm so sorry."

"Just… let us know when they're out of sight."

She nodded and left.

She went to her cabin and looked around. The sense of loss hit her like chain shot, and she felt herself ripped apart. If anything happened to Estelle…

She closed her eyes and fell to her knees. They were bruised from this posture, she'd done this so often since they had left Portabella. The feeling of despair was overwhelming. First she lost Myrgen, now Estelle was fading. Turning back towards Galadorn would put them back in the path of that patrol ship and that would drain her even more. Estelle didn't look like they had that much time. She was giving her life to save the crew.

There was a splash on her hand and she realized she was crying again.

Just when I thought I was all cried out.

She let them fall for a few minutes, then shook it off. She had work to do. Caratia was a place where Fae were not attacked. They could revitalize there. Estelle didn't control the wind in the sails or their tack into the currents.

But her crew for damn sure could.

Gwen and Michael sat back against the trees and listened to the night. Periodically, they would hear the Fae cat howls but Gwen had been amazingly undisturbed. He decided to ask about it.

"So, you don't seem worried at all about those things."

Gwen looked at him. "No, not really. They know me here."

"The Fae cats know you?"

"Sort of. I'm not an enemy of the Land and I have Fae connections. They know I'm allowed to be here."

"What about me?"

"You're with me."

"And if I wasn't?"

She lay back against the tree again. "That's not a position I'd want to be in."

Michael sipped the soup he had been handed, looking over the fire at Gwen. "Thank you. For everything."

She looked at him. "You deserve it. You've been very helpful to me." She looked away into the fire. "I'm sorry about what has happened to you."

He tilted his head. "What has happened to me?"

"I was thinking about it today, how you were taken from your home. Mandians?"

He looked at the soup and nodded.

"I figured. No one else really does slaves."

"My people used to. Our culture was very advanced. When tribes would go to war, slaves would be taken from the prisoners. It was common to have them ransomed back, but sometimes, they stayed. They became part of the tribe and their children were full citizens. It made the tribes closer, in the end. Then the Mandians came and they negotiated the same way we did. But then they didn't follow through. It ended up being lies. They were only in it for the money and they didn't care about the people. We were cattle."

"I'm sorry." She glanced down at the water in her cup. "I mean, I know it wasn't anything having to do with me, but I'm still sorry you lost your family."

He nodded. "Thank you. Your family is very important to you."

"Well, yes. Are there people who *don't* feel that way?"

He pursed his lips. "I'm afraid so."

She squinted her eyes, thinking. "Yeah, I think we *both* know someone like that. Dominic doesn't much care for his family."

Michael swallowed, shifting. The memory of Dominic's visits still churned his stomach. He had set Michael up in Gwen's house while she was helping Alexander, but the man's motives had been more into abuse. He made sure Michael knew that the slightest idea of revealing the atrocities Dominic was perpetrating would result in Michael's death. Worse, Dominic had also threatened Myrgen.

Gwen dipped her head, looking in Michael's eyes. She patted his leg. "What did he do?"

He shook his head. "Nothing I didn't let him do."

"Why did you let him do anything?"

"Because I could take it."

She leaned back. "You don't really strike me as the kind of person who just takes abuse."

He smiled, though he felt it not reach his eyes and he averted them. "You never worked for Myrgen."

He yawned to make sure she didn't think the subject was one that he wanted to continue to discuss. She yawned in response.

"How do we want to do watches?" He nodded to the fire. "I figure we need to keep that going to ward off the predators."

"Well, this close to the mountain, we should be safe. They have better things to eat tonight than us."

Michael almost asked what, then he remembered the horse. That had set her off enough to walk away from Tanglwyst, even in her weakened condition. Gwen was a kindred spirit to Michael. She wouldn't have walked away from a friend in a challenging situation.

"Why did you walk away from Lady Tanglwyst back there?"

"She decided she wasn't going to Caratia."

"Before that."

Gwen rolled her eyes. "I used to think Alexander was the sun and the moon. He was kind, sweet, generous, helpful. He was amazing. He searched for Catriona for years before she ran into him in a port in

Cheryb. He arranged for a back room meeting with her. I was there when it happened. She was so shocked, and excited when she saw him, but when he asked to go with her, she refused."

"Why?"

Gwen shrugged. "It's not her style. She doesn't keep people around her that don't owe her something."

He frowned. "Is that why she is helping Myrgen?"

"Probably." She leaned on her knees. "Dammit. I really wanted her to be happy."

"What makes you think she won't be happy with Myrgen?"

"Well, he's a ruthless monster, the likes of which Dominic admires. No one decent would like a person like that."

Michael snorted. *Had she really just said that?* She looked at her things as she was packing them down, completely oblivious to the fact she just insulted him.

He shook his head and set out his bedroll. He was done talking for the night.

Twenty-Five

Give me your blood, that I may
know you are my kin.
-The Wisdom of Stone

Duncan awoke, but did not get out of bed. The things Tanglwyst had told him about Alexander still sat heavy in his mind. He had wanted to protest, to tell her he had seen the good man, that Alexander had healed Duncan from a horrible addiction and destroyed the monster within him. He wanted to tell her she was wrong about him.

Unfortunately, she was also right about some of the things. He had cast a spell upon her that she could only break if she gave up her fealty. That would be difficult because a traitor with no fealty was exactly what the judiciary courts needed in the incident with Charles' murder. If she let her fealty go, she would be held responsible for every crime Elizabeth failed to go to trial for. Even though she never uttered this line of thought, he could not believe she had missed it. She knew what the consequences would be.

He was more concerned that she had held onto it this long and had only now let it go. That meant something life changing happened. She was severely wounded, beaten pretty badly. It must have something to do with that.

But she was attacked by a goblin in the woods. Was Alexander really the cause of that?

That made him even more confused. How could this man, who healed all those people, be the same man willing to *geas* this woman into getting so injured, more than once, that she could have been killed? Risking her life with another shadow traveler, walking through the forest where a goblin attacked her, forcing her to turn around and chase him to the other side of the continent while she grew less and less likely to be able to reach him. Alexander had sentenced Tanglwyst to death and was going to make her work hard for her own execution.

I want to talk to him, get his side of the story. He knew telling that to Tanglwyst was probably his *own* death wish, but the good man was worth the fight.

"No, Duncan. I'm going to the Papal City where I'll be safe. If you want to talk to Alexander, go ahead. He'll have a reasonable explanation for it and you'll be drawn in. I just don't want to be there to get drawn in too."

"You can't travel alone to the Papal City."

"The hell I can't." She pointed to Caratia. "Have you seen that place? That is a nightmare, waiting to claim me and you and everyone who *isn't* a part of that world. I want nothing to do with it."

He took both her hands. "You're injured. You'll be vulnerable, bait for the thieves on the road. You won't make it that far."

"Then come *with* me. Leave Alexander to his fate. He doesn't need you." Her eyes pleaded and he hung his head.

"Symonne, how long before she can safely travel?"

"At most a tenday, maybe earlier if she isn't too active."

"Here." He pulled out a pouch of coins and handed it to the innkeeper. "Keep her here and safe, would you?"

"Duncan, you can't." Tanglwyst tried to reach for the pouch. "Symonne, I can pay for myself."

Symonne nodded. "And you need that coin for your trip to the Papal City. I'll make sure he has provisions and will tell the Land he's there for a reason."

"I'll be camping. Did you see that place? There isn't another village until the sea. I can't pay a rabbit to be my dinner. This money will be better used here."

Tanglwyst shook her head. "At least take a few coins for when you get into town."

"No, because by then, Alexander will be there and he owes me back pay. I'd rather have nothing on me to give to a robber."

Tomas smirked. "Well, there won't be bandits but hiding from a Fae cat will be easier if you don't jingle."

Tanglwyst's face went determined. "Never mind, I'm going with you."

Tomas, Symonne, and Duncan all barked, "*No,*" and Tanglwyst's face returned to normal.

"Look, what could you possibly do out there to make it easier on me? Be bait for the monsters?"

She frowned. "Fine."

He looked at Tomas. "There's rumor that you have a messenger service up here that can get a missive to someone on a ship."

Tomas folded his arms. "Yeah, I got one of those."

"You're writing Alexander? What are you going to tell him?"

"From what I understand, no one of Mandian blood can get into Caratia."

Tomas nodded.

"Well, that's a problem because Alexander is half-Mandian. I need to warn him away from this course."

Tomas nodded and went in back.

Tanglwyst leaned over to Duncan. "You think you might dissuade him from pursuing her this way?"

"If it gets to him in time, maybe. I don't even know if it's true but so far, everyone I've spoken to has reinforced it."

Tomas came back in the room with parchment and an elaborately colored quill of blues and greens with a pink and a gold stripe across the upper third. "Do you know the name of your recipient?"

"Of course."

"Their *real* name, their *unique* name?"

Duncan blinked, not understanding the question. "Uh, King Alexander of Mervolingia. I'm pretty sure there's only one of those."

Tomas nodded. "That does sound quite unique. Now, the only other thing to discuss is payment. To do this is expensive because the messengers must fly through dangerous air."

"You deliver this by bird?"

"We have a very reliable network. It can take a bit of time though."

Duncan sighed. He wasn't going to be able to get a message to him after all.

Myrgen and Boots woke up in the common room at the inn when the bustle of the breakfast crew drew them from sleep. Although they got a good sum from the blacksmith for the rapier, prudence dictated they conserve it because there would be no other things of value to sell. So it was a silver each to roll out their bedrolls on the hearth and eat breakfast the next day. At that rate, they could last a month.

Boots had tossed and turned a little in the night, and Myrgen woke up every time she twitched. He was apprehensive for some reason, which, over breakfast, he decided was due to the idea of venturing into Caratia. He had left Catriona to find himself and he had not yet done so. He was not ready to see her, to speak with her. Moreover, he highly doubted she was ready to speak with him.

They left the inn with two loaves of bread and some cheese for the road and headed up the mountain.

Tanglwyst hugged Duncan and he waved goodbye to her caretakers. His horse was fed and rested, which was necessary after that ascent the day before. Tomas came out and gave him a wreath of ivy woven with red and blue flowers. He put it over the reins of the horse.

"Don't lose these. They'll mask your presence in the woods."

Duncan got astride the horse and took the reins, keeping the wreath between him and the horse's neck. "Thank you for taking care of her."

"She'll be right here when you come back."

Duncan nodded. "I'll hold you to that." He looked down the descending road. "Anything to watch for there?"

"You know that trip you took to get up here?"

"Yeah."

"That way is worse."

"Got it." Take it slow.

He nudged the horse and started down the mountain.

"What are you thinking?"

Boots looked at Myrgen. "What makes you think I'm thinking at all?"

He stopped, catching his breath and realizing maybe silence was the smartest course. "Because you're being quiet, though," he gasped," now that I'm talking, I see your way is much better."

She smiled and leaned against a rock announcing the one-quarter mark up the mountain. There was a bench of stone here and she nodded to it and crawled over to sit.

"I was thinking of," she swallowed, "home." Her voice indicated that the effort and thinner air was starting to make its mark. She too was breathing hard. She squinted up the mountain. "Do you think they have these turn outs every quarter of the way up?"

"Maybe even more frequently."

He was wrong.

By the time they got halfway up, the road narrowed to almost single file. He could see horse tracks up here that seemed pretty recent but didn't have the spare breath to bring it up to Boots. *Riding a horse up this would be a nightmare.*

They stopped for lunch at what was probably a little more than halfway and they could see no one following and no one descending. Myrgen was grateful because there was no way to pass them either way without someone getting killed. As they cleared their way into the last quarter, he had his second or fourth wind and his heart started pounding as he let his mind wander to tomorrow. They would stop at the inn on the top and then start their descent into a forbidden land he was quite certain he wasn't ready for.

He looked at Boots and she seemed to be having similar thoughts with similar distress. When they were about one switchback from the top, she stopped and Myrgen saw she was shaking.

"I can't do it."

Myrgen came back down to her. "What do you mean you can't do it?" He pointed to the top. "It's right there. Just a few more feet. Then we'll stop for the night."

"It's not that. I can't move."

She looked down at her feet. Every part of her was shaking. Myrgen put his hand on her shoulder.

"Do you need to sit down? Rest a minute?"

"You don't understand. If I take *one more step* up this mountain, I will be ejected from it." Her face started to tear up.

"Ejected?" He realized the Land was arguing with her. He knelt down and called the White Granite Sword into his hands. He handed it to her. "Here. Lean on this. It's from the Land. It will protect you."

She put her hand on it and steadied herself on his shoulder. It seemed to do the trick. She stopped shaking as much and looked up to the summit. "It really is right there, isn't it?"

He smiled. "Yes. We're almost there, Boots."

She smiled, a thin, exhausted smile. "Call me Entivia."

"Entivia." He pulled her satchel from her shoulder. "I'll carry this the last bit here." His exhaustion showed its power and he dropped it. He leaned down to pick it up, letting go of her for just a second.

She launched into the air like she had been kicked by a giant. He grabbed for her but caught the blade of the Granite Sword. It sliced through his palm and didn't even slow down.

"Entivia!"

"Myrgen!"

Her scream carried up and then it stopped. Myrgen ran down the road, taking the faster way of sliding past the switchbacks. He called her name over and over, hoping to hear her reply. By the time he got to the bottom, he had not found her. He climbed back up the lower switchbacks well into the night, calling her name but he never heard her voice.

Boots hit the tile floor hard, knocking the wind out of her. She opened her hand and the amulet tumbled out onto the floor. She rolled over onto her stomach and tried to get to her knees at least but couldn't manage.

Myrgen...

The Granite Sword lay on the floor next to her, his blood coating the blade, bright red against stark white. A very expensive gold leather shoe stepped over to it and an elegant hand with white gold rings on two fingers picked it up. Boots followed the hand up to Cipriano's face, eyes sparkling like the jewels he wore.

"Well, I remember you, young lady. You're that horse of Sangiardo's."

She tried to speak but her breath had not yet rejoined her body.

"I understand he sent you on a journey to enter Caratia. Not that he told you that directly, of course. His spies saw Myrgen the Grey enter and leave that pirate port of yours. We both knew you would try to escape his yoke.

"That's the trouble with Cyprian herb. If you don't actually consummate it, the pesky little recipients might try to exercise their 'free will'. Not that you could ever truly escape it, of course. Except for one way, really."

He looked down at her and stabbed her through the heart with the sword. Her body fell prone again, her cheek splatting on the tile. A tooth hit the tile and chipped off, skittering away a few feet. A blood pool started marring the floor beneath her.

Cipriano went over to the book shelf and pulled a well-thumbed book off of it. He set the book on his desk and opened it, the other hand still holding the sword. Boots' blood mingled with Myrgen's and dripped onto the floor next to him. He leaned it against the desk where the remaining drips managed to touch his shoes and hem. He didn't care. He flipped through the pages until he found what he sought.

On the page was a drawing of the White Granite Sword in the hands of a large, barrel-chested man with thick eyebrows and mustache. He was being pulled into a black space behind him and he was tossing the sword to a woman of similar heritage. The caption underneath read:

The Stepan Slade Stormchest throws his badge of office, the White Granite Sword to the First Dûcesa at the final moments of the Battle of Persephone. She died soon after, leaving Caratia without a leader.

He smiled at his new acquisition. If he walked into Caratia bearing this sword, the Land would not know he was Mandian. Then he would run it though the heart of every royal there and claim the heathen lands in the name of himself and his family.

Long live the king.

Twenty-Six

Let nothing impure touch your soul. The great stone will cast you out of my arms.
-The Wisdom of Stone

Octavius stepped out onto the deck of the *Enigma* and walked over to Catriona's cabin. He checked Myrgen's old room first on his way by. He had found her there more than once since the man had left their company but since the situation with the Patrol, she had been unable to sleep. He hoped she was there because it was keeping her connected to the world. When he didn't see her, he sighed and went down the hall to knock on her door.

"Captain?" He looked around her dark cabin, then stepped back out to light the lantern hung on a peg by her door to help navigate the room. The loss of the stained glass window was overwhelming now that Myrgen was gone. Octavius felt Catriona would have a better go of it if she had that window to cast beauty and light into her life. The lantern flared and he stepped into the room again. The scent of old wine, dirty clothes, and an unemptied chamber pot overwhelmed him and he left the door open to help air out the place.

He had not been in here since Myrgen left and the toll of his loss was evident to him for the first time. Her cabin was a disaster. Her clothes were dropped on the floor, scattered wine bottles rolled against the corners of the room. The chart table was covered with papers, scribblings of Myrgen's from his time here. There was also the small printed book she gave him to catalogue the supplies so he could report what the attack had cost the ship besides structural integrity. He picked up a couple other pages and he saw the graphite was smudged, like it had been rubbed or touched. He shook his head.

Captain, you should never have let him go.

He looked over at her bed and was shocked to see she was not in it. He looked around the room, making sure she had not passed out anywhere, then left the room. He blew out the lantern and returned it to the peg. He walked back to the deck and looked around. From above him, he heard her voice.

"Octavius! We're there!"

He looked up and saw she was sitting in the Crow's Nest. She had driven the crew harder than he'd ever seen her since the patrol ship, not stopping to sleep unless she fell over. Her voice had gone hoarse and only Ambrois' insistence of hot water and honey had saved them. For over a day, she had whispered her orders to Octavius who conveyed them. He had only recently gone in to check on his wife now that her voice had returned.

They had gotten through the Blood Sea Shoals easily, the teeth that took out any Mandian rigs retracted for the *Enigma*. She had done her due diligence and paid the blood toll to pass the teeth, proving her blood was not forbidden. When the blood touched the sea, sharks came up and swam through it, dispersing it. The way to Zara was cleared immediately, leaving a smooth path into Caratia. This was the practice every time they returned to her homeland, regardless of the direction they came from.

Thessius walked over to him, stretching out his back. "Thaink 'e Goddess' Fins wayr elmos' thayr. Shay's bayn crayken hayr whaips sense thet petrol shaip."

"She's concerned about the ship."

Thessius looked like he was about to reply but Octavius stepped towards the main mast and Thessius slinked away, knowing an unwinnable battle when he met one. She dropped onto the deck.

Octavius frowned. "I just got the tally from Ambrois. We're almost out of food and water."

"How many days?"

"One."

She closed her eyes. "What do you want to do? Myria is nearby. We could stop."

"Relaunching might be the problem. She's pretty weak. And dropping anchor could rip her apart right now."

She nodded. "Ration the water. We can't afford to stop."

Myrgen sat on the ground in the morning light, having spent the night scrambling in search of Boots. After the moon left the sky in darkness, he stopped looking. She was gone. No body, nothing. He thought of her dream and had a spark of hope that she survived, but then the cold of reality hit him. They had barely escaped the monster before. It would never let her go a second time. If she returned to find him here, she would likely as not be the murderess he first met. Probably worse. He looked back up the mountain and stood, shouldering the satchel. He turned south and walked away from Cliffbase.

Alexander was talking with James when he heard a splash over the side of the ship, followed by a few more. He frowned, looking towards the edge when the man in the Crow's Nest shouted, "Man overboard!"

James and Alexander ran to the railing but all three men were swimming hard towards shore. They were rounding the tip of the Fourth Finger and were about as close to land as they were going to get before they put into port in Zara.

"*Damn.* They really did it."

James and Alexander turned to the sailor who made the comment, a ginger lad of about seventeen.

"You knew they were going to jump?" James looked to be controlling his emotions like a master.

"They said so last night. 'If that captain doesn't pull into port when we pass Trieste, I'm over the side.'" The young man turned to laugh with his shipmates. The color dropped from his entire body when he saw his audience was his captain and the king.

"Why?" Alexander was having a little less success with controlling these emotions. *If this causes another delay…*

The boy swallowed. "They're Mandian. Lots of them are. Full blood or part, they know they can't pass into the Blood Sea. They'd rather risk the sea here than die for sure there."

James squinted after the deserters. "How many?"

"All told, sir?"

"Yes."

"About twenty."

Alexander growled. "Twenty? That's one third of the crew."

"Do you think they'll all jump, boy?"

He didn't speak and just nodded.

"You gonna be one of 'em?"

He swallowed again. "My grandmother is Mandian, sir."

James didn't nod or look at the boy. "Dismissed."

The boy ran off and Alexander stepped up next to James. "Odd coincidence. My grandmother is also Mandian."

"You going to jump over the side too?"

He looked into the water. "Probably not." Alexander breathed through his anger. When he was calm, he looked at James. "So, this thing is just a superstition, right?"

"Probably."

"But is believed enough to propel healthy men over the side of a perfectly sound sailing vessel."

"Mhm. Appears to be."

"So," Alexander leaned on the railing, "what do we do?"

"Have you ever even been close to this Blood Sea?"

"Not before today."

"So you have no idea what this entryway is like?"

Alexander shook his head.

James sighed. "Then I guess we need to find someone who does before they are all off the ship."

Duncan guided his horse back onto level ground and they both sighed in relief. The way down was steep and littered with the bones of a large animal. It wasn't until they came across the head that he realized it was Tanglwyst's horse. His animal had been skittish ever since the first blood smear and when he saw the way the head was mauled and dragged around, he felt pretty skittish too. It got dark faster this close to the cliff wall and the forest seethed with hissing, growling life. They were going to need a fire.

He found a spot that looked promising and began figuring out the perimeter. He put together a few small piles of kindling around him and set up four small fires to protect him and the horse. He was hoping the wreath of flowers Tomas had given them was indeed capable of keeping the monsters at bay. He wasn't sure he could tend these fires all night alone.

The hardest part was going to be in keeping the horse calm in the event of an attack. This animal had been great for the entire trip here, but this was hostile territory and this horse had been pampered with a stable and hay every night on the road. Duncan gave him a horse travel cake to eat and settled in to tend the fires. He hadn't heard any howl-cries all night and hoped that meant the Fae cats were full up on horse. This might be the only night before he arrived in Zara where he could sleep.

"You asked for me, Captain?"

"Yes, Cheston. I want to know what you can tell me about the Blood Sea."

"Not much I'm afraid."

"You mean you haven't been there before?"

"I have, but never beyond it."

"What happened?"

The sailor scratched his jaw. "I came there with a couple other ships, heading to Nubia. They were slave ships, though I was just interested in getting work. I couldn't afford to be picky. So the head of the expedition says they are going to a different part of Nubia, one where no one has 'harvested' before. Like they were *crops*. So he points to the spot on the map and the captain of my ship says that's the Blood Sea. Sez none of that crew were gonna make it, least of all the expedition leader.

"But they don't listen. So when they get to the edge of the sea, there are tall thin rocks that look like teeth kinda *guarding* the way. The line goes all the way out of sight. It looks like you might could maneuver a ship between them, provided you were narrow. But these weren't narrow ships. They were slavers. So the captain sends out the guns. He figures the teeth aren't real big or thick. They can be shot out at close range.

"He pulls up alongside them and fires the guns. Water and rock goes sailing all over the place but it seems to work. He sends out a longboat to check the depth of the teeth now. One of the sailors jumps overboard and swims down to get an idea. He sez the tooth is down about the depth of a man but that the anchor might be able to smash it the rest of the way. Everyone pitches in and we get the anchor over the spire and around it. The wind starts pulling the ship away from the spire and after about half a day, they get it to break off far down enough to pass the ships through.

They start sailing and one of the crew notices he's bleedin'. Then a few others noticed they were bleedin' and it fell into the sea. Everyone on the ship that shot the tooth starts bleedin' into the water. Then a tooth from out of nowhere shoots up through the slavers and everyone's falling overboard. It tears apart the *Destiny's Barter* and the *Sychophant,* leaving just our ship, the *Respectful Knave.* I suspect it was because we hadn't raised anchor and gone near the reef.

"Then the sharks came in. Big as the slavers. Ate every one of the expedition people and a few others. Lots got onto our ship but I can tell you now that no Mandian that went in the water came out of it."

"What happened when you got back to port?" James leaned forward on his chair.

"One of the sailors in port at Naplles said that the Teeth require you to give it a blood sacrifice. If ya don't, it will take it."

Alexander stood up, outraged. "Like kill a person?"

Cheston shrugged.

"Thank you, Cheston. You may go." He looked at Alexander once the sailor had left. "I take it you're against cutting a sailor's throat and dumping them into the sea?"

"It's ridiculous. There's no reason for it. Stones don't just emerge to rip apart a ship."

"You are sitting here, right now, telling me that something like stone teeth protecting a bay is impossible when you healed a city full of people of destroyed eyes and severed limbs by laying hands upon them. I take it only *your* religion has any truth?"

Alexander shook his head. "Maybe that's the key. If we don't believe it, it can't hurt us."

"Yeah, because if we don't believe in something, it can't be healed before our very eyes or put someone to sleep so you can escape."

"Fine. So what do we do?"

"Pull into port and send a message maybe?"

"In seven years of trying, I was never able to send Catriona a message she received."

James scrunched up his nose. "That sounds like an awful lot of attempts." He rubbed his palm with his thumb. "Well, I'm not worried about the deserters. Frankly, we're under weigh. You and I alone can practically sail this ship into harbor. It's getting it started that is the problem."

"Let's hope it doesn't come to that." Alexander folded his arms, thinking. "The young man on deck said about twenty men were going to desert. That leaves what? Twenty or so who won't?"

James nodded. "I think I see where you're going with this. We need to talk to someone who's been here before."

The two men left the room and started questioning the crew. Eventually, they found one man who had been on a ship that turned back after chasing a ship that made it through. The man told them he heard the captain of the other vessel cut her hand and cast the blood on the water and the teeth sank into the sea.

"Sank?" James shook his head.

"*Her* hand?" Alexander perked up.

"Yes sire. We were chasing the *Enigma*. It's a Caratian vessel. Aided a Mandian traitor so we chased her down. She got away."

James pointed to Alexander. "You said she avoids Mandian waters because of aiding a traitor."

"Yes. Xeno della Lama. No one knows where he is now but it was suspected he might…" He paused, realizing something. "James, he was suspected of being in Portabella."

"So Cipriano finally found someone willing to betray the man." James saw Alexander's puzzled look. "Can't find it if you've never been there. Trust me, many authorities have tried."

Alexander shook his head. It seemed like a decade since they had passed the burning village. They turned back to the sailor. "Did you see what she did?"

"No sire, I was just a sailor. I wasn't in the Nest nor did I get to look through the glass. But I heard the officers talking about it. Ships are hard places to keep secrets."

Alexander noted this and resolved to minimize the information he let slip. The last thing he needed was an international incident because of something he said on this trip. "Thank you. Captain, do you need anything else from this man?"

"No. You're dismissed." James walked over to the chart table and looked at a few different maps. Once the sailor was gone, he motioned Alexander to join him. He pointed to a drawing of the area they wanted to enter. The map had all sorts of monsters and indistinct coastlines associated with it. None of his charts had anything consistent except the row of stone teeth blocking it regardless of the direction you came from. One map explained that fog stopped the coastline and interior of the area from being mapped from a distance.

"Now I see why Alistair never came this way. He was protecting her."

"Protecting her?"

"Alistair and Catriona were a couple, before she returned to Latia. I found reference to it in a journal. It was after she had left her son with the Caratian couple but before she found out her husband was dead. He probably sailed her to see the boy. But he never would have taken a group of sailors across the teeth." He took a deep breath and looked at Alexander. "They took a small ship. Probably just a two person."

"Like a row boat?"

"Doubtful. That's still a long ways to row. No, it was rigged like a ship, I'm sure. Sails, oars, a small anchor. I know the kind."

"Do you have one?"

James smiled. "Not yet."

"There's a port nearby. We can buy one in Trieste or Naplles."

"And risk a single seed from a Mandian tree or plant getting into the soil there? I think that place is too protected even to risk that. But I think we can do this." He walked over to the desk and pulled some papers from a drawer. He brought them over to the table. He scanned them and pointed to an entry. "These."

Alexander looked. "You're kidding."

James shook his head.

Alexander looked again and nodded. It would be the only way. "How long?"

"At least a day."

Alexander groaned. *Another day...* "Can't we just risk it?"

"You're asking me to choose to endanger everyone on this ship for your obsession?"

"Well it wouldn't be a very good obsession if I wasn't willing to risk other people, right?" He sighed. "But no, of course not."

"That's good. That was growth." James smiled. "However, I'll tell you what I *will* do. We're going to build this ship *at* the teeth. We'll test it before we launch, meaning we'll row you out and see if the teeth will let you pass at all. If it looks like they won't, we won't bother. You'll simply have to wait for her to leave.

"However, if you *do* pass, we'll make this ship and set sail."

"Do we really have everything we need here?"

James nodded.

"Okay then, let's get to the teeth."

Book Two

I will give you a heart of stone, so
that you will better know my voice.
-The Wisdom of Stone

Twenty-Seven

Know your allies.
-The Wisdom of Stone

Myrgen saw the flickering lights through the trees before him and his stomach growled loud enough to spook a bird out of a nearby shrub. He stepped through the low branches and saw Raven's cottage. He could smell some meat roasting on a spit and let it compel him to knock on the door. The gentleman opened it and smiled.

"Myrgen! So good to see you again." He glanced around outside. "Where's your friend?"

Myrgen swallowed. "She went home. The traveling was too much for her."

"Ah. Well, not everyone is willing to look into their own soul too deeply and traveling does inspire that. Come! You're just in time for dinner."

He entered and collapsed into a chair at the small, two-person table. Raven made up a plate for him and Myrgen didn't eat it all in one gulp like he thought he would. Raven didn't insist on much conversation which was helpful because Myrgen didn't feel capable of actual speech. He was in mourning and the loss of Entivia after losing Catriona just felt overwhelming when he let his mind wander near it. At the end of the meal, Raven gestured to a room he used before and Myrgen just fell into it.

He awoke the next day feeling better, once again the smell of bacon and eggs filling his nostrils. He went out and greeted his host.

"How did you sleep, my honored guest?"

"Quite well, my honored host."

"Good."

Raven slid two eggs onto a plate next to a stack of bacon clearly designed to feed a small army of teenaged boys. He presented the plate to Myrgen and poured a goblet of milk for him. Hot water bubbled in a hearth kettle and Raven gestured to tea, to which Myrgen nodded. That was likewise brought over and set before the man. Raven sat across from him with a similar set up and smiled.

"So, what would you like to talk about this morning?"

Myrgen blinked slowly. "What kind of Fae you are."

Raven paused cutting into his eggs. "What makes you think I'm Fae?"

"This house has reconfigured itself to fit the fact it's just the two of us. The table is smaller and there's only one other bedroom now. You have served fresh eggs and milk for breakfast but you don't have any chickens or a cow. And your hair is green."

Raven pulled a strand down in front of his eyes, then smoothed it back into place with a sheepish grin. "Oops."

"Is this even food we're eating? Or is it a delicious illusion and I'll find I'm starving later?"

Raven shook his head. "No, this spell provides for the body's needs. The food is real, just like the beds."

"And you just live out here, helping travelers?"

"Not really. We just happened to cross paths."

"Twice?"

Raven frowned. "Eat your swine."

Myrgen laughed and took a bite of breakfast. He figured he had already eaten here a couple times. Any spell this man had meant to trick him with had run its course.

Raven joined in and took a swig of tea. He frowned at it and touched it with his finger. He scalded himself on the hot water but when he tasted the brew again, he smiled. "I definitely prefer cider."

"Spoken like a man who doesn't need the recharge to get moving in the morning."

"Well, drink up then because you have to get moving this morning. I need to show you something."

Myrgen arched an eyebrow but continued to eat. *What could the Fae Realm possibly need to show me?*

Lauriel came in from outside and Myrgen saw this pretense was also gone. This animal was hardly a large dog, not this particular shade of green and brown with a back that looked like it was made of sharp grass. His feet were the color of very rich soil, almost black, with white flecks. His teeth and claws were impressive, like they could burrow through stone and bite through steel. His eyes were as sharp as his weapons, that scary intelligence that one never wants to see in a predator before them.

Lauriel nodded to Myrgen and lay down by the fire. Myrgen nodded to him.

"The illusion was a smart idea on that one."

Raven looked at Myrgen, at Lauriel, then back at Myrgen. "Why?"

Myrgen let the oddness of that question wash over him. Clearly, exposure to Lauriel had brought on the picturesque ignorance of familiarity. Myrgen shook his head and continued to eat. When he was done, he picked up the mug of tea. It was still quite hot so he poured some milk in it to cool it down. He sat back.

"So, why are you here, Raven? Did Catriona send you?"

Raven picked up his cider and sipped it, glancing away. "Who's that?"

"Estelle then?"

Raven's eyes snapped to Myrgen. "How do you know my sister?"

Lauriel looked at Raven, then Myrgen.

"We met at sea. She was attacked and she showed me her damage so I could fix her."

Raven set his mug down. "Attacked? Is she okay?"

"She was torn up pretty bad. We repaired her but I don't know how she is right now. Catriona was heading back to Zara. I know the plan was to do repairs there. She refused to return to Galadorn for them, even though that was the only place to replace the window."

"The stained glass window the ship was fitted with?"

"Yes."

"Replace? So it was destroyed? Did they save the pieces?"

Myrgen shook his head. "The thing was blown apart by a cannonball. There were only shards left, barely enough to identify it was ever glass. We threw them over the side."

"Oh no. We need to go."

Raven got up and started frenetically grabbing items and shoving them into a leather satchel. He went into the back bedroom for a few minutes, then came back out. He put a hat on his head and took a large stick out of the closet near the door. Myrgen stood and shouldered his own satchel, then followed Raven outside while Lauriel brought up the rear.

They walked over to the cliff wall behind the hut and Raven put his hand on the stone. A doorway opened into it, revealing a cave. He stepped in and looked behind him. Myrgen glanced back and the hut was gone.

"Where are we going?"

Raven stopped a moment to cast a small light spell. "We need to head to Zara. I need to get to my sister. And I need to explain a few things to you on the way. I know who you are, Myrgen. And I need to teach you how to deal with it."

Lauriel rolled his eyes and Myrgen caught the expression out of the corner of his eyes. Raven looked at Lauriel and frowned.

"He says I'm not a very good teacher."

"How bad is 'not very good'?"

"I'm… *confusing.*"

Myrgen nodded to the dog. "Can he explain it then?"

"No, he can't. So I won't tell you anything. I'll just show you."

They walked through the cave, turning to what Myrgen figured was north. They were going up a bit as well for about ten minutes, then down for another twenty. Soon, the passage opened into a cavern with an opening to the outside. Myrgen glanced out and found the position of the sun to show they were on a north-facing wall of a mountain, looking out over rolling hills of green. The cave they entered had been facing west. Separation Pass was a day away and before that, the southern wall was a tenday, supposedly. Myrgen figured this was just another illusion. Traveling with Fae was very disorienting.

"Where are we?"

Raven looked at him. "About three thousand years ago. I think. Or York."

Myrgen blinked, confused. He tried again. "Which…? What is this place?"

"The past, in memory form. But physical. I don't know how old this is. All I know is that it made an impression on the Land and when it showed this place to me, I saw fire. A lot of it. And I knew I needed to show the next one this place. That's you, I think. I mean, you're not dead being here so it must be you." Raven cocked his head. "That made sense, right?"

"Uh, no."

Raven frowned. "It has something to do with the bringing up the giving or giving up the bringing. That was it! Giving up the Bringing."

Raven smiled, satisfied with that correction.

Myrgen looked at Lauriel. Lauriel rolled his eyes and sat down. He nodded towards an area behind Myrgen.

In the center of the cavern was a strange sarcophagus-like structure with a lid. The walls were painted in ancient runes and pictures depicting a sacrifice that was placed in the sarcophagus. The place smelled very strange and sharp, and Myrgen felt overwhelmed with a sense of fear, anger, and sadness. He started to lean on the lid to catch his breath, but felt fear and hatred associated with it and shied away. Instead, he stumbled to the entrance to get some air.

It was afternoon now, and he was on a southern wall, facing south. Below him was a huge country with forests and trees. Water sparkled to his left a few miles away and he could see a city off to the left as well, settled on the shore. Fields stretched out to the south around the city which seemed to consume the entire coast. They were about halfway up the cliff wall and there was no road to help them wind their way down.

Raven came up to him and put a hand on his shoulder. "You need to remember this place. It will be important later."

Myrgen nodded, unwilling to risk opening his mouth and chance vomiting. He felt a bit like he did when Boots took him to the secret room and back. At present, he wasn't sure if it was the intensity of the emotional scars left there or the Fae presence, but he was not willing to ever go back there. Even as he thought that, he realized that he most assuredly would return. He looked back at the cavern, sitting there looking onto some other country like it was a scant forty feet away. As he watched, it faded and turned into just a natural cavern, shallow and dark.

Raven started moving the down the mountain and once he felt stable enough on his feet, Myrgen joined him.

By the time the *Raven's Watch* got to the Teeth, James had lost over half his crew. A few chose to use the longboats leaving only one behind, which James had guarded personally. This ship and its provisions were made entirely in Yantap, so he knew nothing here was Mandian. He also had enough supplies to remove some of the wood on the ship from areas which were replaceable with other timber so that the small-masted craft could be made, provided it was possible to pass the Teeth. James gave instructions to his First Mate to take the *Watch* to Naplles and he would meet them there, should the small craft be taken to Zara.

They lowered the longboat into the water and James and Alexander got in. They rowed over to the spires of rock that were frightening sentinels to the Blood Sea. As they approached, they saw movement on the other side, like whales just below the surface. Fins broke through and he realized those were sharks, almost the size of his vessel with his crew on it. They could capsize a boat like this one by swimming too close. Alexander saw them as well and shifted, his movements and light sweat betraying his fear.

"Having second thoughts?"

"Oh, very much, yes. Those things are on the other side of those teeth. They can't get to us, right?"

"If my ship can't get through those teeth, those sharks can't get to us. Thank your Saints Calista doesn't have giant eels serving her or we'd be dead already."

Alexander straightened, looking at the monsters. "Those are Calista's servants?"

"According to legend. When a sailor dies, he is buried at sea. If he was a good servant of the sea goddess, mermaids come for him and make him a merfolk. If they were a horrible person, they become sharks and must serve her through terror until they counter their wrongs. Some choose to never atone, and they become these massive beasts of destruction that you see here."

"What if a woman is a servant of Calista?"

"Same standards apply. Calista doesn't change her results based upon gender. However, it is said that if a woman is raped and then killed by a sailor, Calista will bring her fresh water. When the water touches the woman, she is transformed into a nyad, to frolic and play in the rivers and streams away from sailors who would hurt her. If any man goes to a nyad with ill intent, they have the power to call forth the storms of the sea to destroy the threat."

"Calista seems like a rather vindictive person."

"Well, since you are about to enter her maw, you might want to watch your tongue."

When they got to the spires themselves and started rowing between two of the teeth, the activity of the sharks grew. They sliced through the water before the boat and one came up to the craft and pushed it against the spikes. James reached out instinctively, his hand touching the spire. It cut into his hand and blood was left behind on the pillar. He watched it absorb into the surface, some of it running to the sea. He waited to see what the sharks were going to do, well aware that they needed to abandon ship to the Mandian side if they hoped to survive.

The shark swam up to the pillar with the blood and swam away, circling nearby. James shifted in the boat so Alexander could get near the pillar and be to the *Veil's* side to protect him. Alexander swallowed and touched the pillar.

The Power of Sovereignty covered him and he felt its presence. He felt his blood purified of his mother's taint, because he could see the difference. His father's blood was Mervol blood, as if it were poured directly into his veins from the soil and sun themselves. His mother's blood had not been purged of all other bloodlines when she became Queen and he now saw that was her personal choice. He realized in that moment that when he married Catriona, she could purge her blood of the Caratian taint and become fully Mervolingian. With that knowledge, she would be accepted by the people and Church as not a heathen.

She could be his.

He touched the pillar and pulled his palm across it, giving it a taste of the pure royal blood he owned. The pillar read it, and saw it was not Mandian. The pillar gave the blood to the sharks and they also acknowledged it, and swam away. He exhaled, relieved, and the glow receded, leaving him as he was before.

He sat down, facing James.

"We can go now."

James nodded. "Yeah, I got that. What happened? What was that glow?"

"It's the Power of Sovereignty, that my brother passed to me when he… died. It protects me from threats." Alexander nodded to the bloody pillar. "Just now, it purged me of all non-Mervol blood. Apparently, it's a process that the king and queen undergo at their coronation. I just needed it sooner."

"But if that happens at their Coronation, why did you have any non-Mervol blood in you at all. Your mother was coronated."

"She chose to keep her Mandian blood. I don't have her ties anymore. Of course, no one knows that but us. Her family will still treat me like a cousin." He looked at the oars then at the shoreline, the fog nearby lifting in a path towards the continent. He pointed to it. "It looks like the way is opening. What do you say we get moving?"

James looked back. "Don't you want to turn this into a ship?"

Alexander looked back. "Not really. We've passed the test. Let's just go. If we both row, we'll get there faster."

James shrugged and shouted his orders to the ship. The First Mate waved and they started getting under weigh. James pulled the oars into place and moved so Alexander could take the left one. With a nod, they moved the boat into the water and onto the path the sharks had given them.

Raven stopped their descent long enough to point to a fire near the base within the woods. Myrgen nodded and they finished their controlled avalanche through the underbrush and stones. Raven had a gift of finding the most direct route through things and the terrain didn't slow him down. Myrgen did not possess this gift and felt more than once that the next bump would end in a broken limb. Raven noticed his apprehension partway down and had Lauriel walk next to Myrgen to stabilize him. After that, the only thing slowing Myrgen down was his own awareness of his mortality.

Raven leapt onto the ground at the end of the slide like a performer coming on stage. Myrgen let go of Lauriel just before the end and caught a root with his foot, sending him sprawling. He slid up to the edge of the fire where a sturdily built man with lush hair and an impressive mustache sat, roasting a rabbit. Raven walked right by Myrgen like his posture was not unusual and greeted the man. Myrgen didn't hear what they said at first, his ears still ringing from his fall. He stood up, shaking off the new collection of dirt on his clothing.

Raven gestured to him. "And this is Myrgen. He was coming here. He forgot."

Myrgen frowned. "I didn't forget I was coming here."

"Then why did you turn back?"

The man nodded to Myrgen. "You are welcome here. Please sit and relax."

Myrgen bowed his thank you and came around to the other side to get a better look at his host. He was surprised to see a second rabbit on a stick a little lower, also roasting. "I'm sorry, you look like you already have a companion with you."

The man poked at the rabbits. "No. The Land told me you would be here."

Myrgen turned to ask something of Raven but the strange man and his dog were already moving very fast into the forest. "Did the Land also tell you Raven would not be staying?"

"It said you would be hungry."

Myrgen smiled. "Well, it definitely seems to be looking out for me."

"Perhaps it has plans for you then." He pulled the lower rabbit away from the fire and handed it to Myrgen. "So, tell me, what brings you to Caratia?"

"A strange man with green hair and a scary dog."

The man looked at him a moment, the broke out with a huge inspirational laugh, the kind that drives darkness from the corners of a man's heart. Myrgen laughed along with him, unable to control himself. He had so much to be sad about, yet this was the moment where all that was washed away.

"Yes, that animal has the air of a predator indeed. And they are companions, not master and pet. I believe the dog has as much say in the directions they go as the man does. Possibly more so."

"Well, he seems to understand better the situations of people around him." Myrgen carefully pulled the meat from the rabbit, careful not to burn his fingers.

"He took off so quickly. Barely a hello."

"I believe he had a family matter to look into."

"Ah. Well, his family is very challenging. He adopted Caratia a few hundred years ago and has frequently stayed when we were undergoing difficulties."

Myrgen swallowed the piece in his mouth so he didn't choke on it. "A few hundred years ago?"

"Yes. He was the Stapan of the second and Third Dûcesas."

"How any Dûcesas have there been?"

"Well, many. I believe the current one is possibly the sixtieth. It has been a long time since we started this process."

"Is the regime matriarchal?"

"Do you mean is it always ruled by women? No. It is governed by whomever the Land chooses. The Dûcesa usually has a Duce, like now. If the Land chooses a Duce, he will often find a Dûcesa within his lifetime. The current Dûcesa was chosen first, but was waiting for the Duce to arrive through the Trials."

"The Trials?" Myrgen shook his head. "Forgive me, I know nothing of your country. I want to learn though."

"Ah. Well, you would not be here if the Land did not want you here. So, I will tell you all you ask, if I can.

"The Trials are the way the Land chooses its representative here. Several people are called from all walks of life. They have challenges put before them and the Land watches how they overcome them. At some point, the Impending, as they are called, learn that they are on the Path of *Választás*, the Proving Trials, or Trials of Succession. That is the third step in their Trials. At that point, they can choose to leave the *Választás* and go about their lives."

"Why would someone choose to leave the Trials?"

"Oh, they can leave for any reason they see fit. They are already married, or they have a business they cannot leave. Perhaps they simply have no interest in being the Voice of Caratia. It could be that they do not think they are worthy and do not wish to die."

"Die?"

"Yes. The Trials can be deadly. It can end in the person's death. In fact, in every *Választás* held, someone dies."

"Are the challenges that deadly?"

"They can be. The current Duce had to capture a criminal, then defeat a terrifying beast. Then he found out he was in the *Választás*. He thought about declining the honor, but then he met the Dûcesa and he decided she was worth the risk."

Myrgen smiled. "A woman worth dying for. Those aren't that common. I've met a few that almost killed me, but that's not the same."

The man laughed again. "So, you seem to almost have the weight of the known world on your shoulders. Why are you so burdened?"

"I recently lost two people who were dear to me. One I left, the other left me."

"Companions, or lovers?"

"One of each, though neither was really consummated. I had a woman I loved who had a challenge of her own to deal with. I decided I would not be an excuse for her not to address the situation. I also didn't believe I could handle it if she chose the other man."

The man sighed. "Unrequited love."

"That was the trouble. It *wasn't* unrequited. She was just trying to interpret what the Land was telling her to do. I was in the way. So I removed myself so she would be better able to hear the will of the Land."

"And, with you gone, she might realize what she lost."

Myrgen wobbled his head. "I wish I could be so noble as to say that never crossed my mind. But in truth, I have thought over that decision every day and had to talk myself into it again as a morning ritual. I almost feel that, should I truly see her again and she has not made up her mind, I will make it a *Választás* worthy of bard song."

The man slapped his thigh. "That is a good attitude to have. If she is a woman of the Land, she will not bend if she does not choose to. If you are mistaken about her feelings for you, the Land will help her make it known. The Land gives its people hearts of stone, to better hear its Will."

Myrgen smiled at that. "In other cultures, having a heart of stone means you are unfeeling and uncaring."

"That is because the other cultures do not want their people to know the voice of the Land. If they listen to the Land, they will not hear the demands of Heaven."

Myrgen nodded. He had not heard the demands of Heaven for well over a month. He didn't care if Heaven ever tried to communicate with him again. The Church was false. His sister would poison him into unconsciousness and take him to the Papal City to be exorcized if she heard him say that aloud, but it was how he felt. He had never really put it into words in his mind before, but there it was.

"What are the Trials? Do they have a set pattern?"

The man stretched, muscles threatening the sleeves of his shirt. "Oh, let's see... No there is no set pattern to them, no order. There is the Trial of Love, the Trial of Duty, the Trial of Loss, the Trial of Fear, and the Trial of the Choosing, the *Kiszemel*. The *Kiszemel* is the final stage, where the candidates gather in the town square at Zara. There, the Land will place a square stone for every candidate that has passed the *Választás*. Until the moment they step onto the stone, they can still choose not to accept the burden. If they step onto the stone, they have said they accept the will of the Land. Then the Land chooses, and consumes the ones it did not choose."

"Consumes? You mean they die?"

"The earth falls away from them and they enter *Nyáriföld*, or Summerland. They are returned to the Land from whence they came and are used to nourish and strengthen our people." He gestured to Myrgen. "So, yes, they die. It is why they must face the other Trials before then, to be prepared when faced with their death."

The Trial of Love... Of Loss... Duty...

"Hunh. I think I might know someone going through the Trials."

The man looked at him. "What makes you think so?"

"Well," Myrgen leaned forward, setting the mostly eaten carcass beside him, "She has suffered loss recently. Her husband was killed right in front of her, but he had already left her for another woman. She had just about accepted it when he was murdered in the street. Then she was faced with a horrible situation where she needed to choose between her heart and doing what she believed was her duty to the Land.

"Then she suddenly disappeared from a ship at sea and had some sort of encounter with her deity. We were all worried because she was simply *gone*. She acted a little different after that, which makes me think she might have learned that she was in the *Választás*. Thinking about it, it makes sense."

The man leaned forward. "You think these are signs that a new *Kiszemel* is coming?"

Myrgen looked at his companion and thought about what he was saying. *If he thinks there is a regime change coming, the current Duce and Dûcesa will try to kill anyone standing the Trials. I need to handle this very carefully, especially if anyone not chosen dies.*

"Well, how long do the Trials usually take? Are they quick?"

The man leaned back. "No, not necessarily. The current Duce's Trials took several years."

"Years?" Myrgen sat back as well. "Maybe this is just something the Land does to its people then. Gives them things to help them grow and be stronger."

The man nodded. "Yes, that is possible."

"How often do the Trials happen?"

"When the current Duce or Dûcesa dies."

"And they are both healthy?"

The man nodded. "As far as I know."

"Then no. This person is just receiving guidance from her deity. I hope she hears the right message."

"I hope you are as well."

Myrgen smiled. "Me?"

"It seems you are being tested too."

"Psh. I'm a foreigner here. I wouldn't be tested by the Land. It has better things to do than to bother with me."

"The Land knows all upon its surface, just as you know if an insect is crawling upon your skin."

"That is an unsettling image."

The man grinned. "Then visualize this: If it chooses, the Land can focus all its attention upon a single hair on its arm. What if that hair was *you*."

"Okay, you win. That's a worse image."

The man laughed again and Myrgen joined him.

"Come. It grows late. We still have time to get to a warm bed."

Alexander and James landed the boat on the shore and pulled it up onto the beach. Neither of them had planned to travel out this day so they were decidedly low on provisions. They had seen lights on the shore to the west shortly after clearing the Calista's Maw, as they dubbed it, and it had taken the rest of the day to get them to the town. The idea of how they would pay for things came up about an hour before shore and the idea that the longboat might be traded for a few provisions was the plan settled upon.

The village was of the fishing variety, from the looks of it, and they found an inn simply based upon the noise. A single tavern and inn served the docks and town alike. Everyone looked like they knew each other, especially based upon how they scanned James and Alexander when they entered. A woman at one of the tables stood when they came in.

She spoke a language they didn't understand and they were faced with their first real challenge of going to an isolated foreign country with no love for outsiders. James looked at Alexander.

"What did she say?"

Alexander shrugged. "No idea."

"You don't speak Caratian?"

"No. Why would I?"

James blinked, a stunned look consuming his face. He frowned and cleared his throat. He said something that Alexander didn't catch, similar in sound to what the woman spoke but not quite right. She looked confused and he looked around. He held up a finger and went to the bar. The woman looked at Alexander, who shrugged.

James crouched behind the bar for a moment, then came back with a small sprig of what looked to Alexander to be parsley. James looked at him. "This is glibweed. It will allow one of us to speak this language."

"Only one?"

"It was all the Brownie had today. He said he could gather more tomorrow but right now, we only have the one."

The woman was looking at the glibweed and at James and Alexander. She seemed to know what it was and was patiently waiting to see who would be her contact.

"I don't know enough about the boat or the price it will fetch to negotiate. You should use it."

James nodded and ate the weed. He turned to the woman and spoke, gesturing to Alexander, outdoors and a few other things that he couldn't make out. The woman nodded as did the eight other people nearby who were listening. One of the men, a tall, slender man with very few teeth, looked at Alexander and shook his head. Alexander gave a chastised grin which seemed to be the right answer. The woman patted James on the shoulder and gestured to the man behind the bar to go outside to the shore.

The man came back in a few minutes later and nodded, replying to her question. James gestured to him and Alexander and pointed to a room. She nodded and they got a key. James took them to the room.

"Well, we have room and board for tonight and a few foodstuffs to get us to Zara. It will take a couple days on foot."

Alexander sighed. "Would it be quicker to use the boat?"

"Without food or water? No."

Alexander looked worried and James patted him on the shoulder. "Look, if she hasn't gotten into bed with him by now, it isn't going to happen with the hustle and bustle of docking and getting the ship repaired. Being in dock doesn't free up your time. It fills it."

"Maybe. I just…"

"One day isn't going to make the difference."

"Fine. You have glibweed in your teeth."

James bared his teeth, showing off the bit of green. "Does that bug ya?"

They opened the door to the room and discovered two one-person beds. They both were happy they wouldn't have to share and settled in for the night.

Twenty-Eight

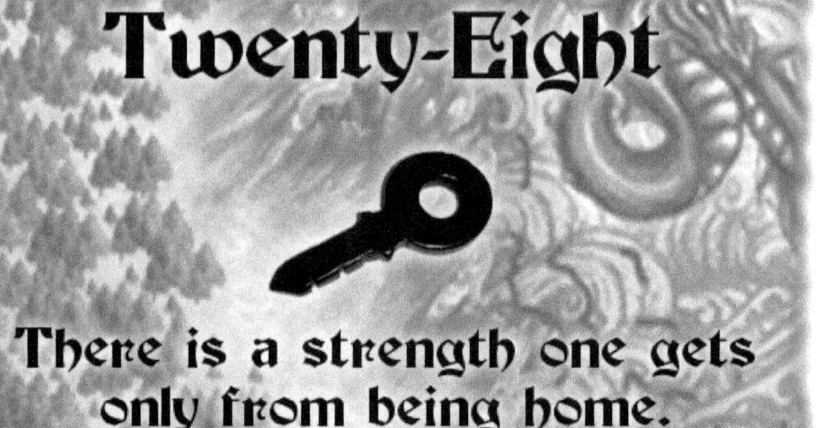

There is a strength one gets only from being home.
-The Wisdom of Stone

Gwen awoke as the sun was starting to light the sky. Michael was climbing down from a nearby tree. He was packed up and ready to leave.

"What are you doing?" She rubbed the sleep from her eyes.

"Looking." He picked up his pack and shouldered it. His hands were gloved this time, something she was glad he had. The close call with the *Cimbus* tree had worried her. He nodded, then started walking.

She sat up. "Hey, what are you doing? You can't just go off into this wilderness. You'll get killed."

He pointed east. "The city is there, about half a day away. The trees between here and there are ones I am familiar with. There have been no tracks of the Fae cats and there are human footprints. There's a hunting lodge about a mile in that direction. I'll be fine."

His voice was strained and he seemed angry. "Is something wrong? I can get up and be ready to go."

He turned back to her. "I would prefer we parted company. I wouldn't want you around the friend of a 'ruthless monster'."

She was so stunned, she couldn't think of anything to say before he disappeared into the woods.

Myrgen and the man walked towards the lights of the coast, and Myrgen became aware of the fact that the sun was rising. He hadn't realized they were far enough away to walk all night. He had spent the time detailing the loss of Boots and the way things went there. The man nodded at all the appropriate parts, interjected questions about the shadows, and successfully refrained from advice unless Myrgen specifically asked, which he did not. Myrgen realized he simply needed to vent, to talk through the lesson of Entivia Malatesta to learn from it.

The man did confirm that she would not have been able to enter Caratia, being Mandian. Myrgen felt a sense of relief at that information because it meant that Alexander would never set foot on Caratian soil. It also meant that if Catriona did marry him and had a child with him, that child could never enter Caratia either. He figured that would be a factor that would matter to her.

As they approached the now fading lights of the town, Myrgen yawned. "I didn't realize we were so far away. It looked closer."

The man smiled. "The Land wanted you to speak, so it made the road exactly as long as it needed to be."

Myrgen stopped. "What do you mean?"

The man turned to him. "Where did you start this journey before you met me?"

He thought. "Well, a day's walk south of Cliffbase, at the bottom of the pass."

The man knelt on the ground and drew a rectangle. About two-thirds of the way along the west side of the rectangle, on a long edge, he put an X. "So, this is Caratia. You were here. You walked a day to get to Raven's. How many days walk is this edge to Raven's?"

Myrgen crouched beside the drawing. "Well, Entivia and I walked for a tenday, I believe to get to Cliffbase."

"And Raven took you through the mountain to where?"

Myrgen thought about it. He pointed to a spot on the other side of Raven's hut. "We came out here, I think."

"Why do you think that?"

"Because we only walked for half a day, with a little stop off at a cave burial site on the way. It was just about mid-afternoon when we emerged from the mountain side. I remember thinking at the time that the sun was in a weird place for my direction sense."

The man pointed to the dimming lights. "And where is that?"

Myrgen shrugged. "A village on a lake. I fear I have never seen a map of Caratia so I don't know."

The man smiled and pointed to a spot directly across from the town of Cliffbase. "You are here." He pointed to a spot about two-thirds of the way along the shorter top edge. "This is where you came out of the mountain. The burial site is near the Persephone Pass at York." He pointed again to the waking village. "That is Zara."

He stood and dropped the stick he used to draw the map. Myrgen looked at the map, then at the lights. He shook his head.

"Wait, *Zara?!* How did we get to *Zara?*"

"The Land wanted you here. Come, I will introduce you to my family. My wife should be up by now."

"Wait, how far away is that?" He pointed to the Separation Pass on the map.

"To an outsider? A few days, if they survive. Caratia is not known for its hospitality."

"And here?" He pointed to Raven's cottage.

"Again, to an outsider, two tendays."

Myrgen pointed to the bottom edge of the map. "Here?"

The man smiled. "An outsider would never get that far."

The path they were on gave way to a well-traveled road coming from the south through a forest. The water he had seen was not a lake at all, but the sea. He could smell the brine as they got closer. The road turned to cobblestones of a goldish-brown color and the buildings went from farmland to storefronts after a mile. He passed a tavern called the Land's End, an inn called the Fae Lock, and a blacksmith called Anvil Dragon. The city was waking up and smell of food and bread and iron filled the air. The roofs were a red stone and the buildings were a myriad of colors from malachite to hematite to quartz. He imagined the jewelers pulled perfect stones from the ground.

Ahead on a rise was a huge castle built into the side of the mountain, overlooking the city. The stones were grey, with red veins like lava running through them. In the shadows, they glowed faintly. Large gates were wide open leading into the courtyard and as they walked up, several other townsfolk walked up as well. The man greeted them with a smile and a nod and Myrgen figured they all worked together at the castle. He took an older lady's basket as they entered.

"Here, Gerta, let me take this to my wife for you."

"Thank you, my boy."

Myrgen smiled at the comment. Older people always felt anyone younger than them was a child. His companion was probably in his fifties, but this woman was likely in her eighties, so to her, he was but a lad. Myrgen was probably in swaddling clothes. The man stepped inside and it was about this moment that Myrgen realized he had been calling him "the man" in his brain for the entire night. He never caught his name and after a while, it seemed rude to actually ask. He started listening for someone to say it, but of course, now that he needed them to, no one was.

The man waved down a passerby. "Where's my wife, David?"

"In the kitchen, my Lord. It *is* morning."

"That it is. What was I thinking? Come on Myrgen. I want you to meet her."

Myrgen followed him as he strode through a door at the back and through another to the kitchens. They were alive with activity, smells and steam dominating the atmosphere. A short, lovely woman came from behind a flour covered table, wiping her hands upon her apron. "There you are! I was wondering how long you planned to be gone."

"You know I had a deadline, my Love. The Naming Ceremony comes this tenday." He kissed her lips. He turned to Myrgen. "Myrgen, this is my wife, Anika."

Myrgen bowed, bringing her hand to his lips. Then he paused, a little shocked. "Excuse me, but what are the chances your name is very common here?"

Anika smiled. "I'm afraid I am the only one I know. How about you, Drake? Are there others like me?"

"There is no one like you, my dear."

Myrgen blinked and his mouth hung a bit. He had just spent the last twelve hours boring the hell out of the Dûce of Caratia. No wonder the man had such insight into the Trials. He was the one who lived through them.

And that meant…

"Excuse me, but I was wondering, has the Stâpâna come here yet?"

Anika glanced at her hands and shook her head. "No. We expect her in time for the Naming Ceremony but we have not heard from her in a month. Not since I sent her back into that palace in Patras."

"By the Stones, that was you? You sent her back?"

"She was not done there. There was still someone she had yet to save."

"Oh no." He closed his eyes. "I'm sorry, but she failed to do so. Alexander ended up becoming King of Mervolingia."

Anika put her hands to her face. "Oh no. I'm so sorry."

"It's worse. Nicolai attacked her and she fought him. She won, but in the end, he was killed by an assassin in the street. Catriona thinks the assassin was trying for Alexander but missed and took Nicolai's life instead."

Drake and Anika looked at each other. "Then that means she is no longer married."

Myrgen thought he caught a hint of joy in their voices and faces. "Worse. It means that Alan has no father again."

"That is true." Anika looked quite saddened by that. "He is a strong boy and his father was not a good man to him anyway. I do not think he will be too broken up about it. The problem is how Catriona has taken the loss. Do you know?"

Myrgen looked away, embarrassed. "I'm not sure I am the right person to answer that question. I think she needs to be the one to discuss that."

Anika arched an eyebrow. "I see. Well, Drake, I'm in the middle of getting breakfast ready so why don't you take, Myrgen was it? Take him up and find him a room?"

"Of course, my dear. I can hardly wait to have some of your fine cooking." He swatted her rear as she turned back to her tasks and Drake led Myrgen from the kitchen. "Now, let's get you set up."

"Sir, you don't have to do that."

"Of course I have to do this. It would be inhospitable not to."

Myrgen stopped them in the hallway. "You said something in the forest, about you thinking I might be being tested too. I doubt that personally, but if it were true, wouldn't that mean… Doesn't that mean

224

I am, or rather could be, the one who might," Myrgen ran his fingers through his hair, which actually caught due to being dirty and a bit snarled. "I'm sorry. I'm usually a much better speaker than this."

"You are worried about the Trials and that it probably means my death. I understand. But the Land is testing *all* of us, my friend, and I do not fear its judgment. I owe my life to the Land and it has taken care of me and mine for twenty years in this wonderful home. If you are to live in Ashstone Keep, you should at least know your way around the rooms." Drake gestured for them to walk again. "So, do you have any hobbies, Myrgen, anything you like to do?"

"I'm a bit rusty at present, but archery and riding are two sports I enjoy. And I like to paint."

Drake arched his eyebrows as he turned another corner in this place and opened a door. "Paint, eh? Are you any good?"

"Yup."

Drake smiled and turned to the servant who passed by them. "Rose, could you tell the staff that this gentleman, Myrgen, is going to be staying with us and needs clothes, accoutrements and bedding set up in the Iron Archway, if you please." He turned back to Myrgen as the girl cast an appraising eye across his disheveled form. Drake gestured for Myrgen to enter and he was pleased to discover a bathing chamber with steaming tubs of tile and showers cascading into the tubs. The place was warm and stacks of towels were scattered around the room. The water smelled fresh and clean, with just a hint of mineral.

Drake got undressed and Myrgen followed his lead. The tubs were near each other but not too near and Myrgen gave the man his privacy as he chose a different tub and got undressed. The waterfalls coming off one side looked inviting and he stepped into one to rinse off. The scream Myrgen gave at the freezing cold water caused Drake to laugh until he cried, able only to gesture to the tubs so Myrgen could get warm again. Rose, the young red-haired woman who was cleaning his room, ran in at the sound, his dirty travelling clothes in her arms. Apparently, she had snagged them from the floor when he was not looking. She was blushed as she saw Myrgen rushing into the bath.

Myrgen submerged entirely after the dousing by the glacial water and came up when he had stopped hearing Drake's booming guffaws. He poked his head up as Rose turned away and left again.

"The water comes from the mountain," Drake said when he was finally able to speak coherently again. He wiped the tears from his eyes as he fought the last throes of laughter. "There are heating tubes in the floor and under the tubs. We usually step into the cold water when we are overheated here."

Myrgen finger-combed is hair in vain. "I was in an incense house in Rouen recently. They had showers in the rooms before you got in the baths, to 'get the large chunks off', as someone put it." He blinked, remembering the last conversation he and Catriona had. "Since I have apparently been traveling blind for a tenday, I didn't want to be soaking in filth. I've had enough of that in Mervolingia."

Drake looked at Myrgen as he ducked under the water to rinse his hair again and when he emerged again, it looked like the Dûce had taken the hint and decided not to pursue the subject. Myrgen was grateful. He was tired of the tale of his foolish attraction for the Queen of Mervolingia and how that ended in his exile for treason. He was also uncertain what to say to Catriona when he saw her. She was on her way and he surmised she should have been here by now. They must have run into trouble or something. Either that or they actually stopped to buy supplies. The stores from the ruse in Portabella probably got them only so far and the next place to stop would have been Pardua or Veniche if they needed to repair after a storm. He tried not to worry, but he felt his stomach rumbling just the same.

Either that or he was extremely hungry. Probably the latter. He saw a basket of fruit and grabbed a soft fruit that looked like a fig or peach, or both. He devoured it and it took the rumblings away. His body reacted to the food like it was on the verge of too much and he splashed water on his face to rinse away the stray juices. By the time he had done so, he noticed the water had refreshed in his bath. He looked around and saw one hole cycling water into the bath, and another draining it away. *Brilliant.*

He looked around for soaps and got scrubbed, paying attention to the important, stench-collecting parts. His hair was finally clean after several washings and he felt refreshed and alive again. He had not realized how numb he had become. He finished and stepped out of the bath, fetching a towel to dry off. Drake had done likewise, his activities hidden by the steam and silence. The waterfall worked as a sound blocker in case people wanted to be contemplative and he had not heard anything from Drake since the laughter had ceased. He couldn't help feeling this place was brilliantly laid out.

Drake met him by the door. "Feel human again?"

Myrgen nodded. "Quite." He looked around for his clothes. "My things? I can't find them in the steam."

Drake put a hand on Myrgen's shoulder. "Don't worry. Those things needed washing anyway. I'll have Rose come by and get them on her rounds. The towel will be good enough for now. I'll show you to your room."

Myrgen glanced back and then followed his host out into the hallway. They walked along the lower floor and Myrgen saw several people coming in and out of the great gate and into the courtyard. Young couples and old promenaded through the flowers or sat on benches and occasionally, children ran into the garden, chased each other around, then fled back through the doors. Myrgen looked up at the turrets that rose into the sky, self-consciously insuring the wrap of the towel was secure. The eastern one seemed to gaze at the sea itself and he wondered how far he could see from up there.

Drake stopped before an open door where a couple servant girls were scurrying about. Surrounding the door was an iron archway built into the stone and the brick next to the door cited this feature. "Rose, how much longer do you think?"

"After breakfast, Noble Father. Go eat."

"Will do." He gestured down the hall to another, more ornate door.

"Rose is your daughter?"

"Not by blood. 'Noble Father' is one of the terms for my position, as father to all the Land's children. We have never had children of our own." He opened the door on a beautiful bedroom of carved wood and wrought iron. It smelled like gardenias, cast from the amount of the bouquets of them around the room. The window ledge held several potted ones and all around were vases filled with the things. "What about you? You have any children?"

"Not anymore. My son and his mother were killed two years ago in the St. Michael's Day Massacre in Patras. He had become an Emilianite and they killed him for it. His mother took her own life after he was buried."

"His mother. So you never married?" Drake went over to his closet and pulled out a large robe which he handed to Myrgen.

"No. I was holding out for someone better, someone of higher station."

"Did you find her?"

Myrgen shrugged, putting on the robe and removing the towel. "Does it really matter? I failed them, not being there to protect my son when he needed me. By the time I got to the house, the attackers were already there. I took one of them, but they slew my son before my eyes before I could take the rest. Those men did not survive the encounter." He folded the towel and held it a moment. "Drake, if you don't mind, I feel the need to rest a bit."

"What about breakfast?"

"I'm afraid I don't have much of an appetite. Will you give my apology to your good wife?"

Drake nodded. "I'm sure she'll understand. We'll get some clothes together for you by this evening."

Myrgen bowed. "Thank you, Noble Father." Myrgen was struck by how easily he was falling in with this man. He had barely met him not half a day ago, yet he trusted him like he had known him all his life, like he was indeed his Noble Father.

He turned and left the room, a little lost in his thoughts. He had left Catriona's side to seek the path upon which he should walk, but then he had lost that precious time for insight because he got kidnapped by Entivia. Then to lose her like that after all they had been through. He shook his head and sighed.

At least I don't have to worry about that taint showing up here.

Still, it saddened him. He felt like she was a soldier under his care and she died on his watch. First Catriona, then Entivia. He dared not make another friend while his luck was so bad.

He stepped into the room as Rose and another girl were finishing the making of the bed. "Sir, the room is not quite ready yet. You should go have some breakfast."

"If you don't mind, could I trouble you to come back later? I'm a bit tired."

She looked about to protest but her companion interrupted. "Of course we can, Sir. The bed is made and we need some time to gather clothes your size anyway. Get some rest. Come along, Rose."

Rose gave the other girl an angry look but grabbed her basket of cleaning cloths and left, closing the door behind them. Myrgen smiled, then sat down on the bed, falling backwards into it. It was soft, softer than anything he'd laid upon in a month and it smelled a bit like home to him. He sat up and took off the robe, then slid under the covers and into sleep.

Drake pulled on the white shirt embroidered with winged lions and tucked it into his clean breeches. He looked up as a servant opened the door for Anika, who was carrying a tray of food, enough for at least three people.

"Where's Myrgen, Drake?"

He looked down at his breeches and fastened the waist. "He went to his room. He has been through quite a lot so let's make sure he gets to sleep as long as he needs."

"How far did you have to go?" She put the tray on a table between two ornate wooden chairs.

"To the Sepulcher."

The Sepulcher? What was he doing there? How did he even *get* there?"

"Raven took him through the mountain."

Anika sank onto the chair. "Raven Grasshair? Why was he with Myrgen?"

"Because he needed to show it to him."

She looked at the pot on the tray and poured a dark liquid into one of the cups. "Coffee?"

"Yes, please."

She poured some into a second cup. "So, Raven Grasshair shows someone the Sepulcher, you get a vision that the Választás are beginning, I get a dream of the same. What do you think?" She tried to keep the worry out of her voice but failed.

He came over to her, taking the ceramic pot from her hands and turning her to face him, taking a knee before her. "Yes, I'm afraid they are."

Her lips got tight and her eyes fell. "How long?"

"I don't know. It depends upon how quickly the Trials pass for all involved."

She put her arms around him and hugged him. "Are you going to stand with the others?"

"I'm not sure yet. I can opt not to stand, even at the very end, but either way, I will not be Dûce any longer."

"I don't care about that. I just don't want to lose you."

He kissed her hair, breathing in her scent. She smelled of cooking spices and apples. "I don't want to leave you, but we will do as the Land requires. Just as we always have."

Anika gave him a squeeze. "Perhaps I shall stand with you if you enter the square that day. That way, if we die, we'll at least be together."

He turned her face to look in her eyes. "That is a lovely thought, but this is part of my Trial as well. How I handle this challenge is as important as every step I took to be by your side in the first place. For some reason, the Land has chosen Myrgen to be here. There is something about him that I need to know, something that is very important. Eventually, I'll know what that is, but right now, I just know it is vital that I keep him here, at Ashstone." He stroked her hair and kissed her lips.

"And understand, Anika, if the Land takes us both, I look forward to standing by your side, watching over our people from the spirit world as much as I have cherished standing by your side watching over them here. I never want to be away from you."

She smiled and kissed him again, then squeezed his hands. She picked up the pot and started pouring the coffee again.

Drake sat down and picked up a biscuit, putting her favorite jam on it. "Myrgen mentioned someone else being tested. I believe it is Catriona of whom he speaks. If so, I think I might not stand in the square and see if I could serve as Stâpân instead."

Anika sat, her hope glaring on her face. "Could that really be what is happening? I would prefer that to the other option."

"I don't know. What is going on now is unprecedented. Even the First Dûcesa died before her successor was chosen. Perhaps I will too." He handed her the biscuit and got one for himself as she fixed his coffee like he liked it.

"Well, if I decide not to join you, I'll be certain to make sure you have a beautiful plaque in the study before I run off to Toledo with some young stallion."

"Will you? That would be most gracious of you. Make sure you put it next to that sculpture of the Third Dûcesa. I would *love* to be next to that for all eternity."

She handed him the coffee and smiled lovingly and he died again in her eyes, just as he did every day he saw them. He knew they could not live apart. He had gone into the woods to begin preparing her for life without him, but he knew better, especially now. She said she would stand beside him if he entered the town square. He knew if he commanded the guards to hold her while he stood, she would use the power granted her by the Land to open a pit beneath her to be with him. He knew this because he would do no less to be with her if she were called. They had been blessed with true love, and no matter what happened they would always have that.

Tomorrow was the Festival of the Planting. With any luck, they would be able to talk to Catriona directly.

The following dawn drew shouts of celebration from every man on board. Catriona nodded to Octavius as they pulled into the port at Zara. The dockhands swarmed the *Enigma*, recognizing the ship of the Stâpâna. The ship creaked dangerously as she was pulled into the area where she could be dry-docked. Octavius observed every bump and groan like it was going to be the death of her. Catriona concurred, feeling less and less the connection to the ship as they got to shore. The last mile seemed almost to be coasting on dreams of ether.

She swung down onto the docks, not waiting to get into position for the gangplank. She shouted to the dockhands to stop.

"My ship has undergone a battle and has been damaged. Is there a spot for her in dry dock?"

The Harbormaster came over to her and they hugged briefly. "A battle, Stâpâna?"

"Yes. She has gotten weaker and weaker every day. We must get her repaired."

He looked at a ledger then pointed. "This way, my Lady."

They walked to the end of the harbor to the dry dock area. There were only two slips and both were occupied. The harbormaster pointed to the bay two ship lengths away. "We can put her there until we are finished with these. It should only be a month."

Catriona shook her head. "She can't last a month."

She looked out at the area, then at the beach around the dry-dock. She took a deep breath. "We will see to her needs then."

The Harbormaster nodded and backed up.

Catriona went to the ship and shouted to the crew to disembark. She wanted as little extra weight as she could get for this. The crew took only ten minutes to clear the ship and they stood on the docks, waiting for further instructions. Catriona went to the ship and touched it. The only person still on board was Octavius and he was in his cabin with Estelle. She told them to hold on.

The ground under her feet shifted, the sand pouring from the landscape around her to fill the area under the ship. Then stone pillars rose from the sea floor, lifting the ship from the water while supporting the cradle she had made with the sand. A large basin surrounded the ship, filled with sand to keep the ship upright and she moved the entire structure through the streets to the area on the other side of the dry dock. Once there, she commanded a stone wall to protect her on all sides and a roof to shield her from further sun damage. Only the end facing the town street was left open and that was for extracting the supplies.

She exhaled, feeling better. Octavius came out to the deck railing and smiled.

"Is she alright? Did I hurt her?"

"She wasn't hurt, but she didn't wake up either. I'm taking that as a good sign."

"What do you need from me?"

Octavius leaned on the railing with his forearms. "I need you to go see your son. We're here. We're safe. I'll take over now. Go."

The music flowed like wine from the fountain in the middle of the room, the ball guests dancing, glittering gold for the men and sapphire blue on the women. Catriona sat beside Alexander in her throne, uneasy about the multitude of people in the huge ballroom. It wasn't that there were so many people, or that she didn't know them all, but that she had to be polite and gracious to them, even her enemies.

It was that she couldn't read their faces.

A thousand people were attending the ball, masked in all manner of creature depictions. It was almost pagan. A man dressed as a crow asked the King's permission to dance with his Queen, and Alexander deferred the request to Catriona. She accepted, the glittering gems which were the eyes mirroring her disguised unease.

The Crow danced her around the room, looking at her but not really talking to her. He just watched her, his unyielding gaze penetrating her own soul in his intensity. She looked away from him, her eye caught on an overlay of lace on a nearby gown. The overlay was sheer, but was flocked in a spider web pattern.

She looked to the other side of her and saw a ruff bug, a small pin worn on the large Yorkish ruffs in defiance of the rules of fashion which dictated the wardrobes of the world. The ruff bug was a spider, and Catriona wondered if the two people actually came together to the ball.

Then, she was traded in the dance to a man with heavily embroidered silk sleeves. The sleeves were white, but the embroidery was a corruptive black, again depicting an arachnid, and Catriona felt unease at this unpleasant shade of her own color of choice. Never in all the years had she worn it had she ever felt such a desire to be away from it. The Crow recaptured her and now she saw the tiniest of webs across the eyes of the mask.

There was an underskirt encrusted in jeweled spiders, and a subtle web design in a veil on another woman. Suddenly, the theme was everywhere, and Catriona needed to get out of the room.

The dance ended, and Catriona graciously thanked the Crow with the glittering eyes. He still did not speak, maintaining his silence until he had escorted her to her throne. A final bow and he looked up at her, and then opened his mouth to say thanks. A worm, bitten in half, lay upon his tongue, and she started at the unexpected sight. The Crow smiled, and blended back into the crowd.

Catriona leaned over to Alexander. "I'm going to check on Alan."

Alexander turned to her and touched her hand. "I'm certain he's fine. He's probably in bed already. You'll wake him."

"I know, but I just want to check on him."

Alexander kissed her hand and replied, "As you wish, my Love. Shall I go with you?"

Catriona shook her head. "No, that's not necessary. It will call attention to us if you do. I'll be right back." She left via the staging area behind the thrones, but her egress caught nearly every eye in the room. Alexander asked a lady to dance and the party progressed without her.

Catriona walked to a study near the throne room and closed the door behind her. Inside, she moved aside a tapestry and pressed on a brick, opening a secret door into the catacombs under the palace. She lit a candle in the room and took it into the passageway.

Her blue velvet dress brushed the sides of the passage as she walked through familiar pathways and she heard the skittering of vermin as the fled the light. She came to a crossroads and looked around. The passage to her left led to the palace holding cells, where she had rescued Myrgen. Before her lay the passage where the burnt out church was and she could see a warm glow misting the filthy air in a beckoning quest.

She turned to her right though, towards the sleeping chambers. Catriona opened the secret door to reveal an area with several shelves around the edge, shelves that once held twenty-three candles to illuminate a portrait. She closed the door behind her before opening the other one, the one which went into her son's room.

Alan lay sleeping on the large bed, his playthings and studying scrolls put neatly away by his servants. She slipped over to his side and sat on the bed, setting the candle on the bedside table. She noticed a shadow skittering away from the light up the wall, and she followed it to see where it went.

The wall seemed coated in some kind of black, shimmering paint, iridescent in the subtle light and she lit the candle next to hers to increase the light. To her horror, the light revealed thousands of spiders crawling over themselves to animate the wall. The living rock went all the way up to the ceiling and threatened to rain down upon them in a storm of poison.

Catriona carefully picked up Alan, who awoke with a start and the young boy looked around the room, suddenly on the verge of a scream. Catriona felt him clench and she shushed him, motioning him not to make a sound lest the noise cause the monstrous sight to become worse. She stepped onto the floor, staying in the pool of light for the creatures seemed to avoid it. She started to set Alan down, but the movement on the wall started to swarm towards that area. Her ball gown occupied the entire circle the light cleared, leaving no room for her son. She clung to him, terribly aware of the fact her skirt was an open area beneath that fabric scaffold, leaving her vulnerable. She needed to remove her skirt on order to save her son.

She started to set him down on the bed, but then saw the spiders had descended onto the sheets and blankets, trapping them both. The candles started to flicker, and Catriona saw silk from the webs coming down upon the flame in an attempt to snuff the candles. The tactic wasn't working and Catriona watched as a larger spider lowered down into the glow of the candles. She shifted Alan in her arms and smacked the spider across the room, hearing it hit the far wall, dislodging several comrades upon impact.

The movement from her hand hitting the spider caused one of the candles to blow out, and Catriona's eyes grew wide as the horde of insects sacrificed some of its own to snuff the other candle...

Alan screamed as the dream ended.

Drake's head snapped up, startled from sleep by Alan's scream. Alan petted the wolfhound's enormous head and the dog shuffled up closer to the boy's pillow. At first, Alan was worried Anika or the Real Drake would rush in to see what was wrong but a few minutes passed and there was no intrusion from concerned parents, foster or otherwise. Alan was disappointed and he got up to use the chamber pot. The hound watched him as he attended to his needs, then jumped down from the bed. He went over and sniffed the chamber pot and Alan pulled on his dog's collar in disgust. He put on house shoes and a robe and went to the window.

His room was on the third floor, with his mother's room on one side and Drake and Anika's on the other. The sky was lightening and pink at the edges on the left. It looked out over the harbor, like most of the rooms the family stayed in, so he could watch for his mother's ship. The *Enigma* was always the most beautiful ship in the harbor when she was here, and Alan was looking forward to heading into town today to shop for something for his mother's return. Drake had said she was due in any day but they weren't certain she would be home in time for his naming ceremony.

He felt something on his face, like a small hair or string, and grabbed at it, jerking away in residual fear. There was no source for the stray strand of web, but it brought back the visceral reaction to the dream. He liked Prince Alexander. His father had taken him to the palace a few times and Lady Tanglwyst had introduced him to Marie Elizabeth, the King's daughter. They had spent several days playing, although Alan thought it strange that his mother would be in the dream with the Prince. He didn't think they knew each other.

Alan thought about the differences between the two castles and decided he liked Caratia's castle better. It was still really big, but here, Drake and Anika played with him. Alan had never seen the King or Queen play with Marie Elizabeth, although Prince Alexander had come in and played with them often. He had been really nice to Alan, although sometimes, he was sad when Alan was around. Alan had asked him why once and Alexander said Alan reminded him of someone he loved.

After that, Alan's father had brought him to the palace often. His mother never went with them though, which made the dream that much weirder. His mother was a brave ship captain, fighting evil and swinging from ropes, looking into people's souls and learning their bad secrets. Drake had acted out the letters she had sent every time they came. His favorite was the one about the lady with the little skulls on her garters.

He knew his mother was powerful and strong. He also knew, from personal experience, that she could indeed see people's secrets. Once, Alan had hidden some food from dinner in his pocket because he didn't want to eat it and she'd found it. He had told Alexander about it the next day at the palace but Alexander had said all mothers could do that.

There was a glint on the harbor and Alan looked closer. Sometimes ships would come in during the night and moor at the docks and he would discover them in the morning. He couldn't wait to go on his mother's ship when he was older. She had told him he needed to learn to ride and fight and read first, that those were important things for a sailor to know. He knew Octavius was smart and he had said he would teach Alan math when he got to be on the *Enigma* with the rest of the crew. Alan liked math. He knew charts and stars needed math to know what they were telling you. It was like another language.

Learning languages was something else Alan did a lot. He already knew the tongue of the Yndians, the Mervol, Caratia of course, and even some Mandian because his mother said you needed to know Mandian to be a sailor. Something about it being a trade language. Alan had studied the map of the world a lot. He had little flags on pins of where he had been and different ones for where he wanted to go. He glanced at the wall the map was on and saw all the flags move a little as the sky got a bit brighter. Most of the flags were in the seas, because he wanted to go on a ship. He didn't even get that sick when he was on the water because his mother had shown him how to stop that by looking at the horizon.

Alan scratched his leg and yawned. The Festival of Palántázás, the Planting, began today and all the farmers and gardeners would be in town buying and trading seeds and seedlings. Because it was also a celebration of the Fae Lord of Spring, there were magicians and acrobats and tricksters planned for the day. This was a good time for a Naming Ceremony.

It was too early for the merchants to be setting up their booths yet, but Alan decided to get dressed anyway. He wanted to be ready, just in case she came home today. He pulled on the hose that went with his festival clothes, black and gold, like the flag of Caratia. Drake had said he might get to open the festival today himself! He liked to use the spyglass he had by the bed to look at the flags of ships that came in to harbor and draw the flags he saw. Then, he would ask Drake who they were. Drake knew everything.

He leaned against the table that had his book of ship flags, getting his balance as he pulled on his hose. Alan pulled on the gold shirt and the black doublet, then pulled on the breeches of black with gold fabric showing through the slashes. The gold shirt and the gold under the slashes were stamped with the winged lions of Caratia, ready to pounce on one another. He combed his hair and heard sounds of merchants beginning to open their booths. Since several of the merchants for this festival were farmers, they were used to getting up really early, but the sailors were more fun listen to. They had stories, where farmers just talked about the weather.

Alan's face puckered up like he had tasted a lemon. The bottom button on his doublet wasn't in the bottom hole, and he had to undo them all. He started at the bottom this time and got halfway up his chest before he looked out the window. His face erupted in a cheer and Drake barked at the sudden glee as he saw Johannes and Ambrois come in through the gate to the courtyard. He ran to the door and up the hall to the next door, throwing it open. "Drake! Anika! She's here! The *Enigma* is here!"

He ran back to his room and pulled on his boots, bouncing with the effort. Drake bounded around him, excited because Alan was excited, which was enough for the dog. His one boot wouldn't go on and he stomped his foot down to force it in place. The boot relented to Alan's superior might and he threw open the door to hurry Anika and Drake up.

"Hello, Alan," a smooth voice said and Alan looked up into the face of his mother. She took a knee before him and he threw himself into her, his excitement unfettered. The two hugged and hugged, Alan not wanting to let his mother go. Eventually she extracted herself. "What are you doing up so early? It's barely dawn and you're already dressed."

"Drake said you might be here today. He said I get to open the festival too!"

"You certainly look lordly! What a beautiful outfit. It looks very much like what Drake would wear."

"Really? Do I look like a Dûce?" He looked his own clothes over, and then looked at hers. "You are coming with us, aren't you? Today, to the festival?"

"Of course."

"What are you going to wear? Anika made you an outfit. It's made of this gold stuff, like my shirt."

Catriona smiled. "I don't know. I'll have to look at it."

A feminine voice ventured into the conversation. "As long as you're willing to try it on." Anika and Drake came out their room and smiled at Catriona. She went over to her Dûce and Dûcesa, exchanging hugs with them. "We were afraid you would miss it."

"No, Noble Mother, I would not have missed this for the world." Catriona stroked her son's hair. "So, let's go ahead and have a look at this gown, shall we?"

Twenty-Nine

Beware couples with a long
history.
-The Wisdom of Stone

Drake nodded to the women and smiled. "I'll leave you two ladies to get ready. Catriona looks like she may need to get cleaned up and I have to do likewise." He kissed Catriona's cheek. "Welcome home, dear."

He waited until the door closed and then turned to Alan. "Why don't you go get some breakfast? We don't want you having a growling stomach during your naming ceremony."

"Okay." He scampered off without the slightest provocation beyond that.

Drake went to Myrgen's room and knocked on the door. He heard a call out and entered.

Myrgen was rubbing his eyes, looking around in the barely dawn light. He sat up and waved at Drake. "Time to get up?"

"Yes, you've been asleep for two days."

Myrgen stopped rubbing his eyes and dropped his hands. "Two days? By the Stones, does everything in this country defy the laws of time?"

"Yes, well, when the Land uses its magic on a human, they frequently have to recover. It's overwhelming for someone who has lived here all their life. I can't imagine what it would be like for someone uninitiated. You clearly needed the rest.

Now you need to get up. Alan's Naming Ceremony is today and I need you to escort a lady into it."

"Are you sure he's going to want me there?"

Drake looked through his now well-stocked wardrobe. "Of course he will. Why wouldn't he?"

Myrgen hesitated. "I guess it's just that… He doesn't know me."

Drake looked over his shoulder at Myrgen. "Trust me, that doesn't matter to the boy, or to us. Now hurry. We don't have a lot of time if we plan to get things done in time. Now, wash up."

"Anika, I can't wear that, any more than I can wear the green one you sent me." Catriona dried her hair as she looked the gown up and down, judgment showing in her face. The red overdress was splashed heavily over a golden underdress on the dress form Anika used to make clothes for her adopted daughter. The form was resized every time Catriona returned home but most of the styles could be taken in or let out a bit as it was put on. Anika had planned this outfit very carefully for maximum impact on the visual senses. Her plan was to get Catriona overwhelmed by gaudy color so she would see the real gown Anika wanted her to wear as a good compromise.

Both dresses on the dress form were over large hoops, which was good because the sheer weight of the fabric would have nearly crippled anyone actually trying to wear the things. The shape of the bodice was far too straight to be a normal woman's curves, hinting at the corsetry involved. Caratia's usual fashion consisted of long, beautiful gowns that hugged the curves, showing them off. The headdresses were simple and elegant, unlike other countries where the haberdashers had apparently discovered a strong vein of whatever haberdashers used to make hats stiff. In northern Mervolingia, the style involved tall cones or elaborate wire support frames which looked like butterflies or horns. Anika's own garb this morning was far more reasonable while still being elegant.

"But you always wear black, my dear. I thought this occasion of all of them might be a good time to debut a new look, like me." Anika unbraided her long auburn hair in preparation for being bound into a black silk and filigreed gold ceremonial headdress which allowed the Dûcesa's hair to flow down her back in waves. She had already donned the golden kirtle made of stamped silk and was undecided about whether to wear the black velvet coatdress now, or wait until the ball and feast for that level of finery.

She had a drape that would probably be the best choice for the day. The drape, a new design she was unveiling today, was rather like a scarf in that it was absurdly long and somewhat rectangular, made of lightweight material, in this case, silk. It was thinnest at the center for about two feet, and then it was gathered in a pin at each of the shoulders and allowed to cascade off down the back. The pins allowed it to drape across the cleavage of the breasts and soften the look, and the excess fabric off the back flowed out like a cape when she walked.

"It isn't a question of color, Anika," Catriona said, rolling her eyes. "How can I possibly protect the family if I'm weighed down with a ton of skirts and hoops? Where are the pants I usually wear? The shirt I usually wear? Those can be made of color, if its color you must have, so long as it allows me movement." She glared in disgust at the dress form. "I'm not even certain I can carry a sword in this. It's impractical for the Stâpanâ to be wearing something so... so..." Catriona gestured at the dress form's attire with both hands, her face displaying her distaste.

Anika smiled, having heard this argument before, continued to ignore her ranting. *This time, you will not win, my Dear.*

"Besides, Anika, the man actually died, at my feet, a month ago."

Catriona's demeanor altered and Anika saw a difference, something she had never seen before in her daughter. "Catriona? What's wrong?"

Her daughter looked up, her eyes damp. "I have to tell Alan his father is actually dead, killed in the street by an assassin. I don't yet know how to do so."

Anika held her daughter's hand. "He will take it well. The man was a drunkard and you were leaving him anyway so he could be with his mistress. It's not like Alan doesn't know that. We told him on the trip here. For Nicolai to be dead merely makes the gesture more final. At least we won't have to worry that you're unhealthy conscience will decide it is best to return to his side."

"No, my unhealthy conscience is telling me to do something else entirely. Which brings me to a very important question. Anika, when you sent me back into the palace in Patras, do you know who you sent me to help?"

"Excuse me?"

"Well, I thought you sent me back to save Charles's life so Alexander would not have to become trapped as King of Mervolingia. If I had been able to stop Alexander from accepting the Power of Sovereignty, he could have come with me and we could be together. But that didn't happen." She turned and walked over to the gowns on the form, taking the arms and holding them to the sides as if she were actually inspecting the things.

"What *did* happen was I found another man there. He was being held in the dungeons and he is noble and just, a strong person. I helped him escape and he started to come with me here, to Zara." She turned from the dress and Anika saw her eyes were damp with emotion. "He was even so bold as to challenge me, to tell me the choices I planned to make were wrong and that I was being an idiot. As a result of this, he left the ship a tenday ago, but I still think about him every day. I wish I knew if he was all right."

"And who is this man whom you have rescued?"

"His name is Myrgen the Grey."

Anika blinked, her sharp green eyes hardly believing what she was seeing. *Catriona is normally so in control if her emotions, her body, her responses. Could this be why Myrgen is here, now, why the Land told my husband to keep him here? Drake needs to know this.*

Anika picked up a jeweled necklace and donned it as Catriona pulled the gore-colored gown off the perfectly good golden kirtle beneath it. The necklace was in Anika's keeping because of its significance to the Land of Caratia. The stone at its center, a deep onyx flecked throughout with pure gold, had risen out of the ground when she was a young woman tilling the fields of her father's farm. It was the Heart of Caratia, and had been undiscovered for a decade when she came across it. In addition to marking her as the Dûce's intended, it also connected her to all in Caratia who held love in their hearts, and made her the Matchmaker for all who needed help with such things. Right now, Catriona needed help. Catriona had never touched the stone, even accidentally, citing she did not need matchmaking because she was already married.

Perhaps Drake can get more information from the stranger. They were currently in another room, choosing clothing for the festival to replace his traveling clothes.

"I see. That is very interesting. Two men whom the stone could have meant. I, of course, would have to have either one or the other around to see which one the stone intended. Where is he now?"

"I left him in Portabella."

"Our captains always avoid that place. Why would you leave him there?"

"Because it was the safest place for him. A port where the authorities could not reach him? It seemed ideal. He said he needed to understand the path being laid before him and he could not do that on board," she lowered her eyes, almost closing them, "with me."

"Why would he say that? What was happening with you?"

Catriona fluttered, composing herself and regaining control. Anika took a deep breath, not certain yet if she should be excited or horrified. Land's Will or not, if that man had hurt Catriona, he was *not* going to be staying in Ashstone. "Honey, why don't you start at the beginning? How did you meet him?"

"So, you mentioned Catriona, our Stâpâna, the other night in the woods. How did you meet her?"

Myrgen looked at his questioner, unsure how to answer. The man pondering clothes for Myrgen was the ruler of this country and General of the most frightening army in the Saintlands. He was an imposing man without the title, and having him broach this subject at this time seemed almost out of place.

Myrgen had stripped down and was scrubbing up using special soaps Drake had brought with him. The cleansing was designed to infuse the Protectors of the Land with the ability to survive scrutiny, long courts and physical attacks, and Myrgen was assured everyone standing court was going through a similar bathing process at the same time. Special oils had been added to the water that scented him with spice and sexuality. He felt refreshed and extremely able to focus. Apparently, the bath a couple days ago had involved ritual cleansers which were designed to destroy vermin and he was most grateful.

Myrgen wasn't exactly certain what had happened to his clothing, but at this point he hardly cared. This man seemed to know every need, every thought Myrgen had for this festival day, and Drake was focused upon getting him presentable.

Now this impressive, incredibly insightful and helpful man had asked him a question, almost out of hand, that Myrgen had dreaded being asked. He had instinctively known what Myrgen needed in every turn and, although this was the sort of information Myrgen would have killed to keep unknown before, he also knew he was no longer that man. Myrgen also suspected trying to lie to this man was about as possible as lying to Catriona. The way the Land was reaching out in his life, Drake probably already knew the answer. This was a test.

He took a deep breath, ready to face an enraged noble with probably the most frightening set of dungeons known to man. "I kidnapped her. We met for the first time when she awoke in the holding cell I put her in."

Drake turned and looked at Myrgen. He stroked his moustache and nodded. "Good choice. Conventional means would not work on this one."

"Excuse me?" Myrgen's confusion as blatant as his confession.

Anika said, "Yes. You would not go with a man that did not impress you. Anyone who could kidnap you, then live to tell the tale, is obviously worth your time. You brought him on your ship?"

Catriona nodded, perplexed.

"And you were going to keep him, yes?"

"Well, I hadn't planned on it. I mean, not on the ship, not at first."

"Why not?"

"According to her and Octavius, she hasn't saved my life. As you know, she has saved the lives of everyone on her crew and I don't hold that distinction."

"She told you this?" Drake held up two long coats and looked at Myrgen. The grey one was very utilitarian but not appropriate for court. The blue one was almost black and would be identifiable as not black when next to the royal family. It would be a subtle distinction, not to bring exclusion, but rather *inclusion* in the family line up. Not quite family, but close. "I think I like this one for you. Can you wear the gold shirt and pants?"

Myrgen tightened the long foreign breeches around his waist with the ties and wrapped them back and forth around his waist to take up the extreme length. The legs were wide enough to almost look like a skirt and the shirt went inside the pants which had open sides that showed off the shirt well beyond the hips. The robe Drake was holding up would conceal those openings nicely. The pants and shirt were of stamped gold silk, embossed with miniature discs that reminded Myrgen of the wind, and the robe was of similar material but not stamped. The boots he wore almost seemed out of place but he didn't think anything Drake had would fit him. The man had enormous shoes.

"I'm not certain what to do with these ties. Are they supposed to be this long?"

"Here, allow me. These were a gift from a lord of Yokotama who opened trade with us last year. I do not wear it because it is supposed to be pleated in the front and back, and I remove those." Drake patted his tummy. "He educated me on the way to wear the ties though." He stepped over to Myrgen, tossing the robe over a nearby chair. The ties were intricate and the knot was a work of art by the time Drake finished. The pants were indeed pleated and gorgeous in their flow. They were comfortable and Myrgen decided to look into more of these style clothes at some point. The movement they allowed was amazing. Myrgen felt regal in them while still feeling he could draw a bow or a sword with ease.

He lunged as if holding a sword and was quite pleased. Drake noticed and smiled. "I like that the first thing you tested was your ability to fight in these unfamiliar clothes." He clapped Myrgen on the shoulder. "It's good for a Dûce to think of such things."

Myrgen squirmed at that comment and grabbed the robe.

Drake helped him into it. "So, was it Catriona that told you this, about the ship?"

"Huh?" Myrgen looked at Drake a moment, and then shook his head as he found the original conversation. "Oh. No, it was Octavius. I figured if anyone would know how things operated on the ship, it would be her First Mate."

Drake smoothed the robe's shoulders. "What does the crew think of you?"

"They teamed up and assaulted him, Anika. Apparently, he let it be known to Octavius what our relationship was, our history, and the crew took him below decks and had a brawl."

"They ganged up on him?" Anika frowned, not liking the sound of this.

"Well, no. They fought him one at a time."

Drake said, "So they let you have a chance then? To prove yourself?"

"Well, I suppose so. Yes. Things were much better after that, too. They treated me as an equal."

"And Catriona allowed this?" Drake's eyebrow arched but his lips smiled at Myrgen's back as he checked the look of the robe.

"Of course I did," Catriona replied. "If I hadn't, they would never have respected him. They needed to initiate him into their ranks and they didn't have that bond of rescue to fall back upon. Had I tried to stop it, I would have impeded that."

"So, in effect," Anika said, lacing up Catriona's gold gown, "you *did* save his life there. Had you not done what you did, the crew would have probably killed him when you were asleep, to protect you."

Myrgen said, "Probably. They are *very* protective of her. Every one, to the man." Myrgen turned to face Drake, looking him in the eye. "Seems to be a common trait in people she meets."

Drake recognized what Myrgen was saying and acknowledged it with a nod and a blink. "Yes, she does. To the man." Drake clasped Myrgen on the shoulders. "Now I need to tell you about the duties I expect of you today. I must escort a dignitary who arrived this morning and so I need you to escort Anika to the Great Balcony. I'll take her arm then and you will escort the other lady. Understood?"

"Sure. Sounds easy."

"Okay. You wait here and I'll go get Anika. Finish getting your hair ready and things. Don't forget to clean your teeth and tongue. And be sure to wear your sword. You just put it in the belt there at your waist."

Sword. He thought of the Granite Sword and contemplated calling it to him. In the end, he chose to use the one Drake had brought him. If Entivia *was* still alive, it was her only protection.

Hunh. Toledan steel. I wonder why it wasn't made in Caratia?

Anika put the long Caratian coat of stamped gold on her daughter, completing the monochromatic look while still looking regal. It had a higher hemline in front that draped to a long one in back, allowing the underdress to be shown off. "So, they fought him and he survived. Then what?"

"I took him back to his cabin to heal his injuries. Well, it turned out he could heal himself. Something he learned in Yantap, of all places. So I asked him to teach it to me and we sort of, well, *kissed.*"

"You what?" Anika blinked, then sat back, waving her hands. "Wait, wait, wait. Let me try that again. *You* what?"

"It was an accident, I swear."

"Excuse me?" Anika put her hands on her hips. "How do you *accidentally* kiss someone?"

"Well, the first time, he…"

"*The first time?* How many times has this man done this?"

"Twice. We don't dare kiss a third time. We were told, well, *he* was told the third kiss would seal our destiny together."

Anika took her daughter's hands. "Let me ask you something, dear. Did you tell him you loved him?"

Catriona looked about to protest the idea a moment, then closed her eyes. "No."

"Why not?"

"Because I can't be sure the Heartstone didn't tell you the person I'm supposed to be with is Alexander. If it is, it would do no good to tell Myrgen I love him. I would still have to leave him behind to serve the Land."

Anika looked worried. "Oh no. It might be true then."

"What?"

A knock came at the door and Drake called out. "Anika, are you ready?"

Anika opened the door. "Yes." She stepped out into the hall as Catriona put on her Stâpâna sword belt.

"It's all set. You go with him. I'll go with her. We'll get them together at the balcony."

"Good. You need to distract her from the subject. Tell her what you learned about her possibly being tested. She just told me she sacrificed love for duty."

"Will do." He kissed her. "Does she know he's here?"

"No, I want that to be a surprise."

"As you wish, my dove. Alan's probably still in the kitchen so can you get him? We'll be starting here soon."

Michael came into town as folks were gathering in the streets. The flow of foot traffic seemed to be towards the large grey keep on the hill. A portly man with long, straight black hair and no chance of a beard stood in the doorway of a tavern, his thumbs hooked in the belt. He wore a pleated skirt Michael had seen in one of Myrgen's books. Michael nodded to him.

"G'deh. Ye saim te be frem Nubia, sair, but ye comin' fren th' wrong direcshen."

Michael nodded, recognizing the Glarren accent. "I got lost. What's going on?"

"Brekfest. Ye hoongry?"

"I'm afraid so. I didn't get a chance before I left this morning."

"Well, c'mon then. Ye shoul' get eh belly full a'fore the dey gets goin'." He held out his hand to Michael. "Brian Barnum, et yer servis."

Michael shook his hand. "Michael deNoir. You're from Glarren?"

"An' ye seem ta be frem Mervolingia, though I ain't never herd o' one as derk as you being from ther." Brian gestured to the crowds and the two men started joining the throng.

"I'm an import. What's happening at the castle there? Seems like an awful lot of people heading that way."

"Aye. T'is indeed eh speshel ehccashun. T'is the Naiming Ceremehny."

"Naming ceremony?"

"Aye. Ev'ry month, th' keds tainrin' ten yairs eld go thru a ceremehny wher' they' lairn their true naimes." Brian nodded, his eyes earnest. "T'is a laife-changin' ehvent."

"And everyone gathers for this ceremony?"

Brian nodded.

Michael looked at the castle as they filed in through the gates. He didn't see Myrgen anywhere, but many folks were going into and out of what looked to be the grand hall. His stomach growled.

"I have a few friends here."

"Thail probehbly be et th' taibles. This wey."

He took Michael into the hall and he saw what had to be half the town eating and talking. Brian took him over to the tables of food and handed him a plate. Michael looked around for Myrgen or Catriona but saw neither in the crowd. He could no longer concentrate when the bacon got put on his plate. He took a bite to tide him over until they sat down.

Well, it's not like I won't stand out here. I shouldn't be hard to find.

Thirty

Obligation and loss darken the eyes.
-The Wisdom of Stone

Drake entered the room as Catriona finished buckling her sword in place. She looked up at her Dûce and smiled. "Noble Father."

"My Stâpâna." He beamed at her. "You look stunning. It is nice to see you in a dress for this occasion."

"I was going to protest but I thought it would be appropriate for Alan's Naming Ceremony. Don't blame me if there's an attack and it gets ripped."

"Would you prefer your conventional uniform, Stâpâna, and save this gown for tonight's Ball?"

She looked at him, stunned. "You mean I can?"

"Well, you'd have to hurry, but I'll let you. You are the Stâpâna. If you prefer to wear clothes you can work in, then wear them. You will most definitely be on duty, despite your connection to the Named."

She turned her back to him and started fiddling with the sword belt. "Here, get me out of this thing."

She dropped the sword onto the bed and Drake loosened the ties. She rushed to her wardrobe and pulled out her *hakama* of black silk.

"There's a gold set in there as well, if you would like to wear that."

She looked inside and saw the gold shirt and gold *hakama* next to it. They would be very appropriate for this with her black coat. She smiled and looked over her shoulder. "Thank you, Noble Father."

"It is the least I could do for someone facing the *Választás*." He turned his back so she could get dressed and she was out of the gown before she realized what he had said.

She blinked at him, the concept overwhelming her. *The Trials? For Succession?* She looked down at the garb in her hands, the trappings of womanhood dropped to the floor while the uniform of her station was being chosen in its stead.

Now everything she had been put through of late made sense. Alexander, returning to rescue Myrgen right as he became a citizen of the Land, the point of doubt in the catacombs where the Land led her when there was no light. She had put her heart's choice on the ground so he could leave her, sacrificing love for duty. Even the incident with Alexander in St. Marguerite now fit. He had been unable to bed her and she had felt he was not the right one for her at the time. Had they actually completed the act, he might have gotten her pregnant, sealing a connection to her for life and taking her from the Land's service.

She wasn't being asked to *leave* Caratia. She was being asked to *stay* and in the biggest way possible.

She looked at Drake and her heart broke. *If the Land is calling those to the square, then Drake... And here I was carrying on like a child in love. How did Anika not slap me for my joy when Drake is most likely very ill?* She couldn't think about that. Not right then. She had things to do and this was supposed to be a happy time. She looked down and put on the shirt. "How long have you known?"

"That the Trials were happening? A little while now. I got a vision from the Land as soon as our horses touched the mountains after fetching Alan in Patras. Anika had the same as a dream. We don't know yet what it means, but the theory has been posited that, if you are being called, then perhaps I am supposed to take your place. There must be something you bring that is necessary, something I cannot."

She pulled on the *hakama* and tied the ornate knot that designated her as the Land's Protector. She straightened the shirt and pulled on the long black coat. The shirt was low cut enough to remind people she was a woman but loose enough to not hinder her movements. She pulled her sword and scabbard from the conventional belt and Drake turned at the sound. She put the sword in her belt tie and went over to her mirror to make sure her hair was pulled into a utilitarian style. It was not and she pulled the pins holding it in the fancy style Anika had done, brushing it into a braid with practiced speed. She stood back and inspected her outfit.

Very dutiful. At least now I know the point behind all this pain. Her conversation with Anika had made her feel her love for Myrgen again, but this revelation with Drake had broken her out of her whimsy. She had a place in this world, and it had changed from what it was when she was Named Stâpâna. She turned her hardened eyes upon her Dûce. "If the Land does choose me and you are available for that position, that will be fortunate. I don't want to lose you, Noble Father, but we both know the Land's Will is law."

"And if it does not choose you?"

She smiled, but the smile did not reach her eyes. "Then it won't matter. I'll be taken into the earth and used to fuel its endeavors. At that point, my blood within it will be more important to its plans than my blood within me."

He stepped forward and put a warrior's hand upon her warrior shoulder. "That is part of the Trial as well. Come, we must not be late."

He opened the door and the throngs of people in the courtyard filled the air with their voices, bouncing down the stone corridors of Ashstone to greet them. Catriona looked around as a servant saw them and signaled to someone in the garden. "Where's Anika?"

"She'll be escorted in from the other side. We decided it would be nice if Alan came in with her."

She nodded. "I like that." She envisioned Alan escorting the Dûcesa on the day of his Naming and how that would be very special for him. She stood beside her Dûce and saw figures in the dark assembling on the other side of the castle. There were no windows on that side, like here, so the corridor was dark. It occurred to her to change that. It was inappropriate for such a security risk to be tolerated. The music came up, introducing the Royal Family and Drake and Catriona waited for the servants to give their mutual nods, cuing the processional to enter at the same moment.

They stepped forward and Catriona felt at once great sadness and great joy. Her son was becoming a man today, joining the ranks of those who knew their place in the world. She remembered her own Naming Ceremony when she was declared Stâpâna, where her last name, Morganosa, was revealed. She still did not know the origin of the name and had looked forward to asking about it someday but never did get around to doing it. It changed everything when you knew your place and the trivial things no longer mattered.

But this new knowledge frightened her. If the Trials were taking place, it meant Drake and Anika's rule was coming to a close. They had always been there for her. She wanted to be there for them as well. The worst thing that could happen would be for Drake to have to stand on the sigil and be taken. It meant that Drake had become ill with something that would weaken and kill him. It was the only explanation for the Trials happening while he was still alive. He looked fine now, but the Land would surely call for the new servant before he was too sick to stand. It would let him die with dignity.

She stepped into the light with Drake as Alan stepped out of the other corridor alone. She leaned over to Drake. "Wait, who's escorting…"

Then Myrgen stepped out with Anika on his arm.

And the world stopped.

Octavius watched his wife sleeping, so thin and frail she was transparent. He was beyond knowing what was wrong. When Catriona dry docked them, he had gone through the entire structure trying to find what was still burning or broken. A small, persistent fire had lasted for days before, never growing but never quite going out. He worried there was something like that he simply had not found.

But now it looked like she was going to pass from this world, and he would likely join her. The idea of living without her, of never hearing her voice in his head and heart again made him not willing to draw breath another day. He would stay with her until she was gone, then leave.

A sound behind him called his attention and he turned, expecting to chide Catriona for not being at her son's ceremony. The person before him came as quite a shock.

"Raven?"

The green-haired man knelt beside Estelle and reached out for her. His hand passed nearly through her. "I was told recently that she had been injured and that the window was destroyed."

"By whom?"

Raven's expression was grave. "Myrgen. Myrgen de Sablonierres. Rather critical player in the upcoming scuffle."

"Scuffle?"

"Myrgen said you kept none of the shards. Is there *any* chance one survived *anywhere?* Embedded in the floor, caught under a table. Anything?"

"Uh," Octavius blinked, thinking. "Possibly. The cannon ball went through Catriona's quarters and landed in Myrgen's right next to it. There could be…"

Raven stood and ran off. Octavius looked at Estelle, unaware he was even there, then did likewise. He found Raven in Catriona's quarters, pulling at the boards covering the back. Octavius stood stunned as he yanked on them. "I need these off. Help me."

Octavius pulled on the boards as well. "Why?"

"I need light." The board came off in his hands but they were encased in a stone shelter, away from the light and sea spray. He looked out. "Oh."

"There's a lantern right here."

"Yes, a lantern!"

Raven waved his hand and an almost summer day glow blazed through the room. Raven cowered from the brilliant light, shielding his eyes, as did Octavius. His eyes had just grown accustomed to the gloom. After a minute, they resumed the search. Raven checked the cushions, the table, the floor but was disappointed. He looked at the covered hole in the wall to Myrgen's quarters.

"What's through there?"

Octavius looked. "Those are Myrgen's quarters."

"Myrgen was important."

Octavius blinked. "Yes."

"Very important."

Octavius frowned.

"Very important." Raven ran into the other room and looked around, drawing the micro-sun with them. He smiled and ran to a corner. He leaned over the cannon ball, still in place in the corner where it was in a small hollow dented into the wood. He rolled it aside.

There, embedded in the wall, was a small green piece of stained glass that looked like a leaf. Octavius gasped. "It's one of the leaves from her tree."

Raven held it up in the artificial light. "Yes. I crafted this one myself."

"I could have sworn we moved that thing."

Raven shook his head. "She didn't want it found. She held it there, the object of her destruction, and hid it from view whenever someone looked for it." He took out a small leather pouch and put the leaf inside, tightening the leather around it and tying it in place. He handed it to Octavius.

"We need to take this with us now." Raven stood, brushing off his pants.

"With… us?"

"You want to save her, don't you?"

Octavius's eyes sobered. "Yes."

"Then we must hurry. We need to get to Galadorn."

Thirty-One

And all will know their place in the world.
-The Wisdom of Stone

Myrgen stopped when he saw Catriona emerge from the dark next to Drake. She was wearing an outfit very similar to the one he sported, only hers was black and gold, denoting the Royal Family connection. The dark blue on him still complemented the grouping, and he looked at Anika to see if she knew this was coming.

Her eyes met his and she looked pleased at his reaction.

Yeah. She knew.

He looked across at Catriona and opened his soul to her. *It looks like they both knew. Look at Drake.*

Catriona blinked at him, appearing a bit dazed, then dragged her gaze to Drake. A blink later, she exhaled and returned her gaze to Myrgen, adding a nod. Their respective nobles tugged the couple in the direction of the stairs that would lead up to the third floor balcony and the ambushed couple acquiesced. As the heralds saw the royal couple emerge from the hallways on the second floor, one of them climbed the stairs to speak to the Dûce and Ducesâ. Myrgen knew the herald would be discussing court business with Their Graces and Catriona slowed, respectfully out of earshot. They met at the foot of the stairs where Alan waited, bouncing back and forth on the balls of his feet. Drake left Catriona's side to take Anika's arm and Myrgen stepped back to stand a few steps away.

He hesitated to look at her, but found he could not keep his eyes from her. He distracted himself by going over to the railing and looking down upon the assembled people in the courtyard.

The sun was fully up and folks had been milling about, chatting with distant cousins and local nobles. Royal servants traveled around in Kingdom livery, offering food and drink of various flavors and temperatures, for many folks probably their morning repast. He recognized a few faces here and there, Thessius, Sebastian, Ambrose. In fact, Catriona's entire crew was in attendance at the castle, save Octavius. That didn't surprise him. Octavius was undoubtedly by Estelle's side. This set Myrgen's mind at ease because it meant he would actually know someone here besides Catriona and Drake, just in case his emotions started running high again.

He felt as well as heard her come up next to him. "Captain."

She seemed to be having the same trouble he was. "Chancellor."

She glanced at him, then back to watching the people, trying to look as though there was nothing unusual about the situation. A humming of discussion dominated the castle, bouncing off the walls and trotting down the corridors, diffusing the conversations enough to keep them semi-private. Myrgen saw a sea of colors and textures, standing on stairways talking to suitors, or describing fencing maneuvers to young students. It was similar in appearance to Mervolingia's courts except it *felt* different.

The faces and hands of those below were tanned from working in the sun or calloused from chopping wood, or threading a loom. These people worked for a living, and their presence here seemed strange to Myrgen who was accustomed to delicate waifs, male and female, flitting about court like useless thoughts. Music played from several groups below, all in synch with one another, despite the distance between the groups. The gardens were in bloom as well, and the visitors were incredibly respectful to the flora adding a heady aroma to the entire piazza. It made for an impressive scene, far outshining the

Mervolingian courts which, by comparison, now seemed artificial and contrived.

Myrgen glanced at the royals to see how their business was progressing. The senior herald speaking to Drake and Anika noticed him and Catriona standing at the railing. He motioned over another, more junior, herald standing nearby taking notes. The senior spoke quietly to the junior who then went down to the courtyard to another robed man sitting at a table. The junior herald gestured up to Myrgen and Catriona. The scribe looked up and nodded. He picked up his quill, a brilliant blue item made from some sort of native bird, and wrote on a card. When finished, he read the card and his eyes grew quite wide. The junior herald got the freshly penned card from the scribe and likewise read it, then quickly moved up to the senior herald and handed him the card. The senior herald whispered the information to the royal couple. The Dûce glanced over at Catriona and Myrgen, then back to Anika, whose eyes were also wide. Drake nodded.

I wonder what that was all about. "Are all these people here for the Naming Ceremony?"

Catriona nodded, smiling. "Yes. There are several children being Named today."

"Oh, this isn't just for him?"

She shook her head. "Of course not. The children who were born earlier this month than him will be named, then those born the same day. Those born after this day can choose to be named after him, or be named first next month."

"This happens every month?"

"Of course. You ever have a month go by in Mervolingia where a child was not born?" She turned to look at Alan and the others gathering on the stairs, dressed in their finest. Many had wreaths on their wrists of flowers or colorful cords. "See the bracelets? Anika and Alan made them for the other children. She makes them every month."

Myrgen felt his eyes sting a bit, realizing this monarchy was so foreign from what he knew. Anika knew the names of the children, knew who they were and what they loved. He thought for a moment about the Trials and shook off the meaning. He sighed, knowing soon he would have a conversation about it with Catriona but he did not want her to read him now. Not now.

Myrgen noted the hugs from the other children. "The Prince is quite well liked."

"I am glad for that."

Alan and the others turned as Drake and the senior herald came to the stairs to speak to the children. He recognized instructions when he saw them, what to say, where to stand. Alan gave his spot to a shorter girl so she could see and hear better. She was wearing pink, purple, red, and gold and her bracelet matched. Myrgen thought he detected a slight sigh when she stepped in front of him.

"He's a good, strong young man." He looked at his own crush. "You should be proud."

Catriona returned his gaze. "I am."

He wanted so much to touch her face and she seemed, for a second, to move in a similar way. Then they both remembered their place and broke the contact. "So," she nodded towards Alan, "have you talked to him yet?"

"No. I really haven't had time. I honestly just got here myself, effectively."

"It's a bit of a trip overland from Portabella."

Myrgen's gaze dropped, the weight of the word too heavy to keep his head up. "Yeah, you could say that."

Catriona was about to ask something but the herald motioned them over.

"It's time. Take your places, please." The herald gestured to Myrgen. "Sir, could you stand on this side of the Presentation dais, and Stâpanâ, would take the other side? Your Graces, will you stand in front?" He nodded to his junior herald and the junior nodded to someone else. The music came up from the multiple groups in the courtyard and the people grew quiet.

They escorted the children to the top of the stairs by the Great Balcony. Drake and Anika moved to the right side of the first child, a young girl with extremely curly red hair. Myrgen looked to Catriona for what to do, two warriors by attire, yet a man and a woman by all other accounts. Did he offer his arm, or gesture for her to precede him?

She saw his dilemma and bowed in respect, then preceded him to the left side, gesturing him to the right. There was a small dais directly behind the railing overlooking the crowd, and Myrgen flanked it with her, a half step behind and to her right. She stood with her hand resting on her sword, looking towards the children, and he took up the same stance. Drake seemed pleased, Anika less so. She reached up to finger her amulet but Drake took her hand and looked over at the herald.

The senior herald took a step forward to the large balcony used for public speaking at the castle and cleared his throat. The music in the courtyard below faded into silence and the herald's voice resonated, "My Lords and Ladies, the Dûce of Caratia, Drake Zápolya, and Ducesâ Anika Borbála Zápolya, Keeper of the Heart of the Land."

All eyes turned to see the ruling couple and applauded their arrival as they stepped to the edge of the balcony to be received. Drake waited a moment for the applause to die down.

"Family, we come here today to honor those being named. We have long watched you all grow into great people, and today you become one with the Land. Today you learn you are part of something vast, something ancient. Today, you learn the opportunities you have and you can choose where you wish to go. Today, you learn your name."

He nodded to the herald as the crowd cheered. The herald, not moving from the Dûce's side, held the card the scribe had made. "My Lords and Ladies, the Stâpanâ Catriona Angelique Morganosa, High Protector of Caratia, and the Former Lord Chancellor of Mervolingia, the Honorable Myrgen de Sablonierres."

Myrgen's head snapped up at the sound of his old title and full name, something even the heralds in Mervolingia rarely used. *How did they know?*

Catriona leaned in as they stepped forward to greet the crowd, her voice low. "The Blue Quill the scribe is using comes from a bird we use here for delivering messages. They have an innate ability to take a message to whomever you tell them to. They can find anybody, no matter where they are. As such, their feathers can be made into quills and used to determine who someone is, so long as they are alive. Neither the bird nor the quill will work on the dead. Hence, the Ritual of Guilt."

Myrgen waved and bowed, then stepped back. "You'll have to tell me more about this magnificent land of yours later."

"I will." She looked into his eyes. "I promise."

The crowd continued to applaud as she stepped back into her place by Myrgen's side. She rested her hand on her sword again and he did likewise. Catriona noticed the new blade.

"The Duce's blade? You will be explaining that later."

"I will." He looked in her eyes. "I promise."

The herald nodded to someone in the courtyard. The musicians counted a beat of four and then began playing drums in a slow, light beat, like a heart. Flutes joined in joyfully telling of youth and play and then harps added to the cheerfulness of childhood. Drake nodded and the first girl was escorted by Anika to the dais. The herald took a card from the pile in his hand, one with a very slight glow to the writing.

"Martuska Gizi Agotsz."

She closed her eyes as her name was spoken and when she opened them again, she looked different. The color in them was a little darker, a little less naïve than when she stepped up.

Applause rose from the crowd, strongest from the immediate family. The girl took her name card from the herald and smiled at Myrgen and Catriona. He congratulated her as she walked by to stand at the bottom of the stairs on the other side.

Drake escorted the next child, another girl, as adorable as a five year old and only slightly taller. Her blond curls reminded him of Emmy at the palace.

"Graezte Mészáros."

Again, the same change in her eyes as the last girl, and Myrgen wondered what they were seeing that he had not. Could it be that the Quill did not write his name as it should be, but as it currently was?

As each child came forward and was named, he saw that transformation. When they stood beside the others on the right hand set of stairs, they did not fidget or whisper to each other, but stood, contemplating. He felt envious of their sudden comfort with their world and their maturity. It almost made him want to stand at the bottom of the stairs on the left to find out what they were seeing.

Three more children were named and he remembered every syllable. Eufrozina Gabrielle Varga. *Adorján Vörös. Mihály Czinege.* Misha *Virág Zsoldos.* Each child changed as they walked past him and each one graciously accepted his congratulations. After Misha, Alan's crush, he realized there was only one child left to name. Alan had let the other children be named before him, setting them as his elders. Myrgen smiled at the gesture.

Alan swallowed and Drake nodded. Alan stepped forward slowly, shaky at first, then moving stronger as he approached the railing before him. With each step, the music grew louder, stronger, as if growing up. The notes on the music grew deeper, longer, and the drum beats became heavier, more mature.

The Herald said, "My Lords and Ladies, Principe Victor Tiberius Morganosa."

Then the singers drifted in, low humming in time with the music so they were, at first, indistinguishable. The voices seemed to frolic, chaotic and disassociated, but then, one by one, they joined together in a harmony that caused Myrgen to want to take a knee. Rather than fight the urge, he did just that. Alan saw him do this and stepped onto the dais as those below them took a cue from Myrgen. The singers hit their crescendo in furious passion and at that moment, a breeze ruffled the leaves of the fruit trees around the courtyard, sending a spray of blossoms up to the balcony to descend upon the young people on the balcony stairs. The audience gasped and smiled at the Land's acknowledgement of the Named. When the music stopped, there was a beat of silence before all within earshot applauded. Victor Tiberius smiled at the musicians and gestured to them, applauding as well.

He turned to Drake who nodded and Victor Tiberius stepped down and preceded them down the stairs to stand with the others. As Myrgen stood again, the herald bowed in admiration of the man's timely gesture. Catriona gripped Myrgen's shoulder as the herald followed the royal couple and the Principe down the hall.

"Remind me later to thank you for that."

She looked into his eyes and he saw more than just affection dancing in those gold flecks. He saw unconcealed yearning, like he had felt between them in St. Andrew. He found his mind going places he dared not explore at this moment and he nodded.

"Count on it."

The couple followed Drake and Anika down to the courtyard and Drake raised his hands for silence. "My good friends and cousins, I welcome you to our home for this very important occasion. Our Principe has acquired his True Name, and in so doing, has become a man. We celebrate this along with the families of our other children. Welcome to the world."

Joyous noise filled the courtyard and well wishes were flung like confetti over the young people as they dispersed back to the crowd. Eventually, the sound drained away and Drake gestured to Catriona. "This day does Caratia welcome home another of her children. As you have noticed, our Stâpanâ has returned from overseas. Welcome her home today when you get the chance during the festival."

A smattering of applause and discussion rippled through the courtyard until Drake again held up his hands. "And as many of you young ladies have noticed, the Land has brought a distinguished *unmarried* visitor to our shores." He winked at a couple young women who had gathered near the stairs, their eyes fixed on Myrgen. The ladies tittered, blushing. "Please show him the best our country has to offer, and we just may be able to steal him away from Patras!" The crowd applauded and Drake spoke to the herald to start assembling the royalty for procession into town.

As Catriona and Myrgen arrived next to her, Anika said, "We had to find out from the *herald* you were the Chancellor of Mervolingia?"

Myrgen smiled and leaned in to take Anika into his confidence. "My apologies, Your Grace. I have been scrubbing decks and holds for so long, I forgot I was important."

"Really? I thought you came overland to us." She looked at Catriona, then at Myrgen, a little fire in her eyes. She toyed with her necklace again and Catriona's eyes grew wide and scared. She put her hand on the Ducesâ's arm.

"Let's not be too intrusive right now. I'm sure His Honor has lots of tales to regale us during the feast." She let go of Anika and took Myrgen's arm. "Actually, I have something of greater importance for you to do right now, if you don't mind, Chancellor?"

He nodded, recognizing a rescue when he saw one. "I am ever at your service, My Lady."

Catriona walked with him to the stairs and took him to the third story, to one of the rooms. She knocked on a door and it was opened by the Principe.

Myrgen swallowed. *Time to face the music.*

Thirty-Two

I have heard the Voice of the Land. It knows my name.
-The Wisdom of Stone

"Sorry. I had to use the pot."

"That's fine. Dear, I brought someone with me, someone you haven't met before but you kind of know him. He wants to know if it's all right for him to be here." She looked down the hall and motioned to someone, and Victor Tiberius Morganosa noticed the man standing, head bowed, a little way down. He was the foreigner Drake had brought with him from the woods.

"Hello Your Highness." He knelt next to the boy, looking nervous.

"Hello." He wondered why the man was so nervous and he narrowed his eyes at the man. "I know you. You're from Mervolingia. Your name is…" Victor Tiberius thought for a moment and Myrgen let him. "Morgan?"

"Myrgen. I've heard a lot about you, from your mother." Drake and Anika came up from the courtyard, looking for the group. Catriona glanced up at them and then back at her son.

"You lived at the palace, in Patras. I remember seeing you in the halls there when Nicolai brought me to play with the Princess."

Myrgen nodded.

"Why would you want to know if it was okay for you to be here?" The wolfhound came up to Myrgen and sniffed him.

Myrgen looked at the dog and gave him the back of his hand to sniff. The dog's tail wagged as it did so. Myrgen looked back at the boy and Catriona put a hand on his shoulder. Her touch was reassuring from the way the man relaxed. "Well, I need to tell you something. Last time you were in Patras, something bad happened to you. Do you remember?"

Victor Tiberius looked at him and nodded. Drake and Anika watched carefully to see what was going on. Catriona looked up at them and then back down at the exchange. Myrgen swallowed and continued. "Well, I'm afraid that was my fault."

"Yours?"

"Yes. I was asked to do something bad, and I didn't say no. That makes it my fault."

"What were you asked to do?"

"I was asked to pretend to take someone away from their home, to scare someone into doing something they probably wouldn't do. Once I found out you were caught up at the same time, I couldn't let you go, even though I wanted to."

"Do you mean Lady Tanglwyst?"

Myrgen nodded.

"She didn't get hurt, did she?"

Myrgen shook his head. "No, she didn't get hurt. She's home now, safe and sound. I think she's sorry too that you got caught up in her game."

"I don't remember seeing you. Did you come to see me?"

Myrgen shook his head. "But I asked my friend Michael to keep an eye on you and make sure you stayed safe. I also gave him this dog to keep you company." Myrgen rubbed the dog's right ear. "You've done a good job raising him. I can see he's healthy and happy with you." Myrgen returned his eyes to the boy. "I'm sorry. I hope you'll forgive me, but I can understand if you hold a grudge."

"Sure." Victor Tiberius shrugged. He wasn't actually trained to know what a grudge looked like, nor how to hold one. "So, you're the one who gave me my dog?"

Myrgen nodded.

"Thank you." Victor Tiberius hugged him, which seemed to shock the man, and it took a moment for Myrgen to recover. The wolfhound nosed between the two of them and started licking Myrgen's face and Catriona stood, satisfied.

"And you were worried." She crossed her arms, smiling and arching her eyebrow.

Myrgen just smiled back over his shoulder at her and hugged the little boy while the dog made a mess of his hair.

Catriona stroked her son's hair, trying to undo the damage from the licking. "Come on, we need to comb your hair now."

He looked back at Myrgen. "This is my mother's room. It's right next to mine." Victor Tiberius opened the door and let Myrgen into his mother's room.

The stained glass in the window depicted a scene of the sea and a black ship cresting the waves. It was, appropriately, the first thing one saw upon entering. A large fireplace dominated the wall to the left and a wardrobe commanded the right wall. There was a portrait of Drake and Anika and another of Victor Tiberius about five years old flanking the wardrobe. Chests of drawers and tapestries flitted about the room almost carefree in their placement. There was a large map of the world over the fireplace, impressively familiar to Myrgen. He saw Yndia and walked over to it to look for Yantap. He pointed at it and said to the boy, "Hey, I've been there."

"Are you a ship captain like my mother?"

Myrgen rubbed the back of his neck, smiling. "Not exactly. Your mother picked me up in Mervolingia and gave me a ride to another port. But I've been on ships before."

"When are you going back?"

Myrgen frowned. "Actually, I'm not."

"Where will you go then?"

Myrgen bit his upper lip, looking at Catriona. "I'm not sure yet."

Catriona looked at Myrgen, her eyes fighting something out in her mind. Victor Tiberius looked at Myrgen. "Well, you should stay here then. There are fifty rooms and you can watch the ships come in every day. And there's woods and hunting too. There's a festival today, to honor the farmers and gardeners."

Victor Tiberius yawned and the pause in streaming information gave Catriona a chance to interject. "It seems you have been invited to stay." Her eyes glittered with a bare hint of smile tracing itself upon her features, tinting her voice.

"It seems I have." He took Catriona's hand and kissed it. "Thank you."

Drake and Anika came in from the hallway and hugged Myrgen, causing the dog to jump up and down. Drake patted Myrgen and pushed away. "And I thought it would take a beautiful woman to convince you to stay."

He looked at Catriona who was being hugged by Anika at the moment. "It did."

Victor Tibérius watched Myrgen look at his mother, and realized he had seen that look somewhere else: Between Drake and Anika.

He heard the herald call out for the Royal Family and Drake stepped to the doorway, motioning to the man. He appeared in the doorway.

"Noble Family, the Processional is forming."

"Thank you, Teklar." Drake turned to Victor Tiberius. "It is time for us to walk. Come, take your place."

They started to walk out and Victor Tiberius took his mother's hand, tugging on it for a moment. She turned to face him, then dropped to a knee to be closer.

"What is it, my *gránit szív?*"

"I really don't want to go back to Patras. Please don't make me."

"Why would I make you?"

"Because Alexander might make us have to. So, please, don't make us have to go there."

Her eyes got wet and she closed them. "Alright. I won't."

"Good."

He exhaled as she stood, grateful that he would not have to become king of Mervolingia after all. The Principe smiled and stood beside his Dûce as the others took their places and walked with head held high towards the courtyard.

The procession into town consisted of people who had served Caratia as former Stapans, Stapanas, or Champions. There were no living Duces or Dûcesas save Drake and Anika. Myrgen got introduced to the nobles who would be right before the Stâpanâ and the Crown. The people closest to the Royal Family were a former Stâpan named Thomas and his wife Adria. He was a furry blond man, about five foot five, and very sturdily built. He had the appearance of a man who, once he started moving in a direction, would not be stopped by anything less than the sudden appearance of a mountain in his path. His wife reminded Myrgen of that mountain, her dark hair framing strong features that were probably the only things that could take on Thomas. He bowed to them as Catriona introduced them, and Adria asked in Mervolingian, "Is this your first time to our fair country, Your Honor?"

Myrgen nodded, replying in Caratian. "Yes. I am most impressed with her."

Thomas nodded, approving the praise of his country. Adria grinned. "Ah! You have mastered our tongue despite this. I, too, am most impressed. I'm certain our customs must seem rather peculiar to a foreign visitor."

"Perhaps," said Myrgen with a wink, "but the feeling of this place encourages understanding, even from a foreigner." It occurred to him that the language of Caratia, though not something he had used often, had always struck him as a strong language, indicative of its armies. He wasn't even sure he had ever been taught it, seeing as no one he knew outside of Catriona had ever been here. It had not come to mind that he had been speaking it all along, since coming out of the woods. He realized Catriona's crew had spoken every language he knew, and, in the case of Thessius, one or two he wasn't sure he had heard before.

"I doubt you'll be considered a foreigner for long," said a young voice from behind them.

Myrgen and Catriona parted to allow Victor Tiberius into the conversation. "Your Highness," said Myrgen with a bow. "How do you like your new Name?"

"It's great! Thank you Mother." She smiled and he turned to Myrgen. "When the herald said my name, I thought it was very powerful sounding and that was amazing. Then Caratia told me the story behind it."

Myrgen cocked his head. "*Caratia* told you?" He looked to Catriona and the other couple for an explanation. Catriona directed him back to Victor Tiberius.

"Yes! I felt a breeze on my face and I heard the whisper of the wind. It told me that, when I was born, there was a bad man who tried to kill us. Mother was badly hurt, but she took the man's right eye, making him have to run away. Because she was unconscious, the midwife who helped her needed a name for me. She said it was to call me by some name because she didn't know how long before my mother woke up. Except that they needed a name for my baptism. Prince Alexander was there, and he suggested the name Alan."

Catriona blinked, amazed at this revelation. "*Alexander* suggested the name?"

Victor Tiberius nodded. "Yes. His favorite grandfather was named Alan Youngforest."

"Amazing," said Myrgen. He looked at Catriona. "I take it you did not know this?"

She shook her head. "No."

Victor Tiberius continued. "Caratia told me you had been in a church with Father Benjamin while healing and that you chose the name Victor Tiberius there, but that you knew, with this bad person chasing you, that knowing my True Name would be dangerous, so you kept that hidden, and let me go by Alan instead."

Myrgen frowned. "So you were baptized as an infant?"

"As Alan, yes. I think it's why Alexander chose me."

Myrgen glanced away at that, not sure it was a good thing. "Will it be hard to go by this new name?"

"No. But I think I'll go by Tib, for short. Victor Tiberius is too much for everyone to say."

"Tib. I like that. But please forgive me if I accidentally call you by your old name every once in a while." Myrgen felt a twitch in the back of his mind every time the name Alan was used, like he was forgetting the old name for some reason.

Tib smiled and glanced at his mother and the other couple. Adria shook her head.

"It is clear you are a foreigner, and because your ties to your country are strong, you may indeed be able to call him by that name, but he has told Caratia what he wishes to be known as, and as citizens of the Land, we will not make that mistake."

Movement ahead of the former Stâpan and his wife cued them to move as well, and Catriona looked at Tib. "Do you wish to go in front or behind me, My Prince?"

"In front, if you please. That will allow you to better protect the Dûce and Ducesâ, as well as myself." Catriona bowed and Tib moved forward as the queue progressed.

Myrgen frowned slightly. He leaned over to Catriona and whispered, "He's different somehow, isn't he? He spoke so properly there, and with command. Isn't he only ten years old?"

Catriona looked at Myrgen. "That is part of the magic of the Naming Ritual. He is now connected to the Land, and therefore knows his place in the world. It is a comforting thing."

Remind me to sign up for the process, then. Catriona and Myrgen took a step forward. "So, what is this festival like?"

Catriona smiled. "It is to celebrate market-gardeners and farmers, and the arrival of the Fae Lord Embertwist. As each season has its own patron, those who are sponsored by this festival are honored by the Land. They receive invitations to the castle to progress into town with the Dûce and Ducesâ, and are expected to dine with them all day, beginning with the morning repast, as we witnessed just now. They are not required to come but they are all invited."

"Wait. *Every* farmer and market-gardener in the kingdom received an invitation?"

Catriona laughed as Myrgen's face contorted under the image of writing out so many invitations. "Well, not exactly hand-written. There are signs the Land gives them."

"Signs the Land gives them?"

Anika spoke up behind them. "Yes, Myrgen. The Land chooses Caratia's Caretakers, and their place in the world. All the servants are chosen by the Land."

"I apologize for not understanding, Your Grace. We do not do this the same way in Mervolingia. Our royalty are born to the right lineage. The Crown is passed on from father to son."

Tib asked, "But if it is passed on through the hands of Men, how do they know the man who wears the Crown will do what's best for the kingdom?"

Myrgen blinked, again astonished by the boy's sudden maturity. "They don't."

Tib frowned. "I like our way better."

Myrgen nodded. "So do I."

Adria smiled. "You are from so far away, how did you come to Caratia?"

270

"A," Myrgen glanced at Catriona, "dear friend offered me a job working here after my old job went away. I took some time to think about it and I plan to ask them if the offer still stands."

"Oh? Doing what?"

"Running the accounts for her business."

Adria and Thomas looked at him, then at Catriona, then nodded. "Oh," they replied in unison and then suddenly got interested in something the people in front of them were saying.

He touched the sword the Duce had given him and glanced at Catriona.

She looked down at the sword. "You promised."

"What? Now?"

"We have a long walk to the tournament area. It seems as good a time as any."

"Well, it's not that long a story. The Duce gave it to me to wear for the ceremony. I had no idea it was his personal sword."

"Yes. That is from his days as a general in the Caratian army. It is the sword he used for his Trial of Loss."

Myrgen frowned, looking at the sword. He felt his own sense of loss regarding his sword. He thought about calling it to his hand, knowing it would come. But he didn't, just in case Entivia was still in there somewhere and needed it to protect herself. "I noticed it was Toledan steel. I was surprised to find it was not of Caratia."

"All of our steel is Toledan, just as all of their armor is Caratian. It is our alliance with our Land-brethren."

"Toledo sits on the edge of the Papal City. I have always assumed they were Heaven worshippers."

Catriona nodded. "That's exactly what you're supposed to think."

Myrgen nodded. "Keep your friends close and your enemies closer." *Makes me wonder which I am.* "So, that puts this into perspective." He raised his voice a little. "Your Highness, it seems you are a man now. I believe it would be more appropriate for you to carry this sword in my stead."

He lifted the baldric sword belt off his shoulder and handed Drake's sword to the boy.

"Why?" Tib looked at it, a little in awe, a little confused.

"Because, young sir, I am a foreigner here and I do not yet know my place. I don't know what the Land has in store for me, if anything." He held it out to Tib. "But you do. You possess an insight I have not

271

yet received. I was given a sword and I used it to protect someone. It is with them now and until it is returned to me by the Land, I think I should not carry any other."

Tib took the sword and hefted it. It moved easily in his hands, garnering appreciative remarks from the fighters around him.

Myrgen saw he was struggling a little with the weight of the blade and took his hand. "Here, hold it like this. It's designed to be used from the wrist."

"Like this?" Tib moved it easier and smiled.

"Yes, exactly like that." He felt good, teaching this boy how to defend himself, like something Myrgen had to say was once again valuable. He stepped aside and let him practice a few swings and jabs, then looked up as the line began moving again. "Looks like we're on deck, Tib. Time to put it away."

The line moved forward and Myrgen and Catriona held back a bit. Catriona looked around her, taking in the crowd lining the streets. "That was very fatherly of you, Myrgen." Her voice was low, but conversational, in case anyone was listening.

A cold chill ran down his back from her voice. His guts leapt into knots. "Excuse me?"

"The way you interacted with him. It was very father-like."

He scanned the crowd as well, suddenly aware of this being a very vulnerable opportunity for someone to take revenge upon the boy. "It seemed to be the right way to interact with him. He is a boy, after all."

"Yes, he is." They walked a bit further. "You chose not to tell how you got to the ship in the first place."

"It wasn't appropriate. I also didn't tell them why I left." He looked at her. "That hasn't changed, has it?"

She met his gaze. "Not yet. Anika needed one of you here to use the Heartstone."

"Is that the pendant on her neck?"

"Yes."

"So she could use it right now?"

"Yes."

Myrgen felt his eyes drawn from hers, his attention pulled towards the crowd. "Is it loud? Messy? Painful?"

"I don't know. I've never had it done."

"Have you *seen* it done?"

Catriona shook her head. "No. She usually does it in private, I think. I don't know."

He lowered his voice to keep from alarming the people around them. "Are you feeling like this is a very vulnerable place right now?"

"Yes." She kept her voice low, making sure only Myrgen heard her. "It's like there's something there, or something coming, but I don't know what."

Myrgen looked at Drake and Anika, at Tib. "Why don't the others sense it?"

She looked at them, then at him. "It's not their job to know."

Myrgen was about to question, when she flicked her eyes at the sword he had just given to Tib. Drake had given Myrgen the Sword from his own Trials.

By the Stones, he made me his Champion.

Thirty-Three

The Land does not know the future. It only knows the past, and the present.
-The Wisdom of Stone

Gwen came into Zara on the Woodland Road just in time to hear the cheers from the castle. Gwen smiled. *The Naming Ceremony is today! I hope Catriona made it.*

She ran up the hill to the castle and managed to get to the gates of the courtyard just as Tib was being named. Gwen applauded along with the rest of the town as the ceremony concluded. She saw Myrgen and Catriona next to each other and this made her smile. Maybe Myrgen wasn't so bad after all. She looked around for Michael but didn't see him.

The family went into their chambers and the courtyard was very full. Gwen heard her stomach growl from the lack of fresh food, even over the din of the chatting populace. The smells of fresh baked bread, cooked meats, and the colors of multiple fruits and vegetables assailed her senses. She went into the hall and saw Michael sitting at one of the tables. She grabbed a plate and got some fruit and meat, nibbling on some grapes to quiet her stomach. She walked over to him and sat down across from him.

"I see you got here okay."

He looked up, surprised. He set down his fork. "Yes. Surprisingly, I didn't die on my own. Imagine that."

"That's not what…" She sighed. "Look, I'm sorry. I didn't mean to offend you."

He looked down at his plate. "I'm sure you didn't even know you had." He looked over at the people outside. "Did you get the chance to watch the ceremony?"

"I saw Alan's." She glanced at her food. "Catriona and Myrgen looked good."

He nodded.

Gwen glanced out the doors. "They're lining up for the processional. They'll be practically stationary for an hour. Everyone in town picks up a ribbon flower and unfurls it as they walk to the town square. The merchants with booths go first so they can be there when everyone arrives. Then, the families and friends of the Named, finishing up with the Servants of Caratia. Once they are there, the games and tournaments begin."

"It sounds very festive." He looked at his empty plate and picked it up, standing.

"Are you going to see them?"

"I was going to offer to help in the kitchen actually. It can't be easy to clean up after all this."

"Perhaps I'll see you at the town square then."

He nodded and left.

"Your Excellency, there's a message from the Palace for you."

Archbishop Alfonse looked up at Father Jarius and waved him over. The courier followed him in and handed the official letter to him. Alfonse nodded to both men and Jarius saw the messenger out, already pulling a coin from a pouch to tip him. Alfonse found the gesture slightly offensive. It wasn't like the royal messengers were destitute. He looked at the seal and saw the Royal Chancellor's stamp upon the wax.

Ah. The Will of the King. About time.

When the Power of Sovereignty transferred, the new king had to effectively name an heir should anything happen to him. Usually the Will would be delivered a month before the King's Coronation, but Alexander had slipped away to search for his bride. It could be months before he handled the Affairs of State. The Archbishop had taken matters into his own hands and commanded a transcription of the Will be sent to him by the Palace.

He frowned at the thickness of the missive. It wasn't large enough to be the full Will. This was probably a single piece of paper. He opened it and read it.

Your Excellency,

I regret to inform you that the King has filed no such Will with the Office of the Chancellor to date. I expect him to handle that matter when he returns.

Thank you for your time,

The Honorable Lord Dominic D'Medici

Acting Chancellor for Mervolingia

"Pah." Alfonse threw the missive aside in disgust. "Acting" Chancellor. Fool clearly knows nothing of the office he's pretending to hold. I will have to remedy that by assigning the King someone competent.

He stood and went to the mirror over the water basin in his office. He poured the water in the vessel and chanted the proper incantation to cause a different face to appear in the mirror. An old man in Cardinal's robes appeared before the Archbishop. Arturo Constantine was the Keeper of the Relics at the Papal City. He would be able to help Alfonse.

"Your Excellency." Alfonse bowed to the man in the glass.

Arturo was a sharp-looking man in every way. His eyes were intelligent and he had a disapproving gaze that could carve diamonds. His voice was able to carry anywhere in the Papal library, regardless of the shelves of wood holding stacks of sound-absorbing paper. His hands and face were spindly things with skin stretched over lethal bones. He looked like an arsenal.

"Your Excellency Alfonse. What do you want?"

"The King of Mervolingia has accepted the Power of Sovereignty but has not yet sent his Will over to me to be approved. Do you have the file there?"

"Of course I do. What a foolish question." Arturo walked off, muttering to himself about how the Power of Sovereignty was the purview of the Church, Mervolingia was the only one who got it, etc, etc. He said all this loud enough for Alfonse to hear it while pretending to say it to himself. He toddled back with a piece of vellum, marked in blue ink. Alfonse knew the ink would change to gold once he approved of the Will.

"Here, here. What do you want to know?"

"Just the pertinent information. He's off gallivanting around the countryside, looking for a bride. I need to know whom to contact if he gets himself killed."

"Ah, I see. Foolish royals. No sense in any of them." He scanned the page. "Ah yes, here it is. Alan Moriarity."

Alfonse blinked. "Moriarity?"

"Yes. Must be some cousin or something. His mother is Mandian."

"Yes, but the second he accepted the Power, his blood was purified. He's strictly Mervolingian now."

Arturo looked at Alfonse, then back again at the document. "Well, still. There you are. Now, go away."

The mirror went dark, then returned to show Alfonse' face.

Moriarity. This is unacceptable. No wonder he hid it. He was planning on having the marriage be done before he ever returned. He doesn't understand the risks to the country he's presenting.

Alfonse shook his head. He went to the window of his office and put the flag of his office out onto the sill to air out. Then he went to the front desk.

"Father Jarius, I'll be heading to hear confessions now."

Jarius nodded and Alfonse went to the cathedral to wait for a response. He didn't have to wait long. Within minutes of sitting at the pews before the confessionals, he saw his Back Streets contact enter the church. He stepped into the proper booth on the very end and Alfonse entered the side for the priest.

"Bless me, Your Excellency. What do you need from us today?"

"I need an intermediary sent to my chamber within the hour, ready to travel. Non-Mandian."

"Of course, sire. I have just the individual."

"Good. I don't have time to wait."

The confessor left and Alfonse exited the booth. Duncan was given his orders to break up Alexander's little romance tendays ago. If Alexander has gone off and defied the Church with this woman...

He seethed, very angry that the King would put him in this position. He couldn't possibly expect to get away with this. Putting that woman on the throne would destroy the kingdom, opening it to Emilianite rule, like had already happened in York. The Arrogant Queen had killed the Church representative on the Night of Long Knives, when she had every enemy against her killed inside ten hours of darkness. Of course, there was no proof of this, but she stood unopposed the following dawn. The Church had not had a foothold in that country ever since.

Mande was dedicated to the Church, but its motivation was always money. Mande was a mercenary, willing to stay loyal to the Papal City only because it paid well. With the hordes of gold lining the walls of Mande thanks to the Cliff Rise, the worship of the Saints seemed almost a courtesy and not out of reverence for the teachings of the Church. It was unstable and therefore, not trusted.

The only thing keeping Mande in check was the presence of the Church in Mervolingia. The Bread Basket of the continent, Mervol crops fed the known world, so even York and Mande dealt fairly with them. Should Mervolingia ever turn on her allies, the world could starve before it crossed enough land to claim the fields. A civil war would be devastating. Men leaving the growing fields to fight for one side or the other. Saints forbid they learned of the growth properties of the farmers of Land Worshippers.

It had taken a century of training and changing the cities to get the influence of the Augustinian Church to be absolute in this country. Fae worshippers were burned as witches, Land Worshippers were thrown from cliffs into the sea, Calista's followers were turned to ash and scattered to the wind, ensuring they would never achieve their afterlife. Not that any of them had an afterlife that was not the Church's teachings. Anyone who was not a Saint Worshipper simply went to Hell.

He returned to his office and Jarius looked surprised that he was back so quickly.

"I'm expecting someone for a more in depth counselling session. When they arrive, please send them in. They should be here shortly."

He walked to the back of the office and opened a locked cabinet with a key at his neck. He pulled out an envelope marked with a number two. There were four others in the safe and Alfonse did a double take when he saw the number.

There should be six.

He looked and one of the envelopes, number three, had been turned to ash.

That was Duncan's.

He shook his head, fully expecting the news to come any day now that Duncan had perished in a fire. It was the only way to destroy these things. The others were assigned to specific people as well, and he was not yet ready to recall them, although one of the envelopes had the thickness of being filled. Apparently, the Will was not the only thing the King had been lax about.

He closed and locked the safe, then held out the envelope. He summoned the amulet to him and the container filled. He pulled out the Scarred Man's amulet. It had a small thread of gold silk on it, like someone rich had been wearing it. *Well, whoever it was, it wasn't to whom I gave it.*

A knock on the door preceded Jarius's face and Alfonse waved in his visitor. The door was closed behind him as Alfonse recognized the man. It was a monk from the Order of St. Giles in town. This pleased Alfonse because those men had one purpose: to do Heaven's Will. He stepped over to the Archbishop and kissed the offered ring of Office.

"What do you need of me, Your Excellency?"

"I need you to use this amulet to find the previous owner. Once you do, you then need to proceed to this symbol." He pulled out a book with the symbols of specific churches and pointed to one.

"After that, you are to leave that place and find the child named Alan Moriarity, and kill him."

He turned away from the monk and retrieved the flag from the window sill, folding it and putting it in a chest nearby. "The King is trying to start a war that will consume this country by defying the Will of the Church. He is on the edge of becoming a heathen. This will send the message that his *only* loyalty is to the Church. Do you understand?"

The monk nodded.

Alfonse explained how the amulet worked and turned it over to its new owner. "The previous owner may object to you having it now.

However, he clearly lost it, so he is no longer worthy of it. Kill him if he tries to stop you."

"It shall be done."

"Thank you."

He dismissed the person and the monk put the amulet on and disappeared in a puff of sulfur. The Archbishop stood by the window until the stench dissipated and returned to his work.

The monk entered the room and the soft lights came up, showing the sparse furnishings and small provisions. A man looked at him from the bed, scarred simultaneously into being obscured and unforgettable. He sat up and lunged at the monk. The monk tripped him, then hit him in the back of the neck, dropping him to the floor permanently. As he gasped, the monk knelt beside his now paralyzed attacker.

"The Archbishop has a job for us. Unfortunately, you decided to behave as if driven insane by your imprisonment. Now I must do it alone. I cannot use you if you are a monster."

The Scarred Man looked up into almost yellow eyes, trying to move unresponsive limbs. The monk stood and then brought his foot down with a cry of deep, penetrating rage. The heel shattered the bones in the Scarred Man's neck and he stopped breathing.

Shadows crept from every corner towards the body, avoiding the monk completely. He spat at the tendrils.

"Filthy vermin."

He touched the amulet and disappeared.

Michael dried his hands, the dirty water from the most recent set of dishes draining from the sink. The folks in the kitchen for clean up were from all walks of life. He had heard several people talking over their jobs and duties of daily life and been asked several things himself about his journey through the *Verfoltus,* or Bloody Forest, as he learned it was called. He felt it aptly named and said so.

"Will you be heading down to the festivities, Michael?" The willow-thin woman named Amanda smiled as she inquired, belying her lovely singing voice which he had already heard today.

"I was going to head down as soon as I was no longer needed here."

"Then please, I have a friend who could use the company." Amanda took him by the arm and walked him over to Gwen who was just depositing her own dishes in the bins outside the kitchen. "Gwen, do you know Michael? He's a friend from Mervolingia."

She turned to look at him and raised her eyebrows. He looked at Amanda, then smiled. Gwen looked a little nervous at the confrontation.

Amanda nodded. "I saw you two talking at the table. Margaret saw you come from the west, Gwen and I know you went through there. You two obviously traveled together, and had a tussle. It does no good to hold a grudge. So, Michael, you need to go to the Town Square and Gwen, you need an escort so you don't get into trouble. You two can play nice for a few blocks, I'm sure."

Michael nodded to Gwen. "I'm sure we can." He looked at Gwen's pack. "May I carry that for you, my lady?"

"You have your own burdens to carry. I can handle mine." She looked at Amanda. "Thank you for thinking of me."

Michael walked with her to the doors and exhaled deeply. "I feel like a goat."

She looked at him, confused, then glanced at the tables behind them, laughing. "Yes, the Land does not let her people go hungry."

"I kept taking things I had never seen before. Some of their breads are... I don't know how to describe them."

"Robust?"

He pointed at her. *"Robust.* Yes. Perfect."

She smiled and he relaxed. Things looked like they would be okay between them.

"You got here well before me. I was surprised to see you not up there with Myrgen."

Michael went quiet, his gaze scanning the crowd. "I thought about it but I... didn't want to interrupt him. He's not generally without something to do."

"I guess today was no different then. He was up there on the balcony with Catriona, dressed like a high ranking guardian. Apparently, he's been trusted by the Duce and Dûcesa."

"He's good at making friends."

She looked at him, drawing his eye. "Aren't you excited to see him?"

He sighed. "Yes. I just…"

Gwen patted his arm. "You will fit right into his plans, I'm sure of it. It will be like you never were apart."

They made their way to the square and when they saw the Royal family, Gwen motioned they sneak up. Michael shook his head and gestured for her to go ahead. He didn't want to surprise someone whose duty it was to protect the local duke and duchess.

Gwen managed to get almost on top of Catriona before she saw her, then the glee they held for each other was evident back in Patras. Michael wiggled his finger in his ear to knock away the ringing from the high pitched squeal. Myrgen was smiling nearby, almost doting, and Michael stepped up next to him like he had never left his side. It took almost twenty seconds for him to notice.

Myrgen's eyes went wide with joy at the sight of his friend and Michael beamed, despite his plan to stay stoic and reserved.

"Michael!" Myrgen hugged him like they were brothers and Michael returned the gesture in kind. "I cannot tell you how much I have missed you."

They separated and the four came together. Catriona nodded greeting to Michael. "Good to see you again, Michael."

"It is my pleasure, my lady. Gwen has been very excited to see you."

Myrgen slapped Michael on the shoulder. "Come, let me introduce you to some friends." They walked over to the sun shade near the edge of the tournament field and Michael saw Alan sitting with an older man and woman in modest finery. Alan jumped up when he saw Michael.

"Michael!" He ran to the large Nubian, who knelt down in time to catch the boy. They hugged at least as long as he and Myrgen had and the dog he had given him looked like it had grown three feet since he saw it last.

"Drake, Anika, this is Michael! He gave me the dog!"

The man stood and bowed. "So it is you we have to thank for increasing our food bill by an extra cow per tenday?"

282

Michael smiled, not entirely sure that wasn't true. "He was a gift from Myrgen. I was merely the conveyance."

"I am Drake and this is my wife, Anika."

"I am honored to meet you both."

"You are welcome to join us. Please."

"I would enjoy that, my lord, but first, if I may," he turned to Myrgen, "I would speak with you in private."

Myrgen nodded. "Of course."

He gestured to an open area nearby, just out of earshot of the rest of the world donning armor and hawking wares. Michael checked to make sure they were not being overheard.

"It is about your sister, sir."

The priest in the Augustinian chapel heard the sound of someone in the graveyard and stepped out, curious. The only way in, officially, to this area was through the chapel itself, though it wasn't like the low fence kept out anything but chickens and rabbits. Still, with the Naming and the Farmer's Festival today, he wasn't expecting mournful visitors. He saw a man outside in the graveyard dressed in monk's robes. He was touching the symbol on the base of the statue of St. Michael.

"May I help you, Brother?"

He stood and turned to the priest. "Where am I?"

The priest blinked, even more confused. "You… are in Zara, in the country of Caratia."

"There is an Augustinian church in a country of heathens?"

The priest sighed, a little put off by the term. He had come here a decade ago after traveling with the Dûce from Toledo. He was on his pilgrimage from the Papal City, having been released from his duties after the stable he cared for burnt down. He felt the need to try something new, and had been given leave to build a small church in the area for those sailors who worshiped the Saints. He had kept the peace the entire time, knowing what a blessing this truly was and had shown the utmost respect for the dominant faith of the country.

"I have a dispensation from the Dûce. How did you get here if you did not come via ship?"

"I have been sent by the Archbishop of Patras. You are local to this place?"

The priest frowned. "Yes. Been here for ten years now. *Peacefully.* I intend to keep it that way." He folded his arms across his chest. "Now what are you doing here?"

"I have a message for King Alexander of Mervolingia."

The priest blinked. "The king? Here?"

"I understand he has an appointment with someone named Alan Moriarity."

"Alan?" The priest thought for a minute. "The Prince is named Alan. Or at least he was until today. He was one of the people being Named."

"That would be the one. Thank you for your help." The monk stepped over the fence and walked into the street.

"Hey, wait! You didn't tell me how you got here."

But by the time the priest got to the street, the monk was gone.

Gwen had taken Catriona aside as well when she saw Michael talking to Myrgen and when she had finished, Catriona looked at Myrgen. They exchanged a look and she saw he knew as well. Tanglwyst had been under a life-threatening spell and was recovering from injuries at the Drum and Farthingale. She sighed.

Gwen touched her shoulder. "I'm sorry. I know he used to be a good person, but, now," Gwen shook her head.

"I know. Come, let's take a walk."

They stood and went down to the docks. Catriona pointed to the giant stone building housing the ship. There was a ladder to access it now and they climbed up it to go inside. On the deck, Thessius met them.

"Gwain! Good ta see ya, lass."

She hugged him. "Good to see you, Thessius." She leaned over to Catriona. "He's been near someone from Glarren recently?"

Catriona nodded.

"Caiptin, 'ave ye seen Octavius?"

Catriona shook her head. "No, not since we put the ship here. He's gone?"

"We haiven't sain haim ell dey."

Gwen knelt down and touched the ship, then got a horrified look on her face. Catriona knelt as well and felt for him. The ship was empty. But not just empty of the crew. It was a corpse, cold and soulless.

"…no…" She stood and ran to Octavius and Estelle's quarters, throwing open the door. They were just as bare. There were signs he had been here, but there were no signs he stayed. There were no things taken from the drawers and only a journal on the bedside table. She picked it up and read the last entry.

Estelle grows weaker by the hour, and so do I. I won't be able to live without her. She has been my sustenance for too long. She no longer wakes, no longer responds. I can barely see her. She gave everything to get us here, but she is dying. I can't save her. I can't stop it.

"No…" Tears ran down Catriona's face in droves. *"No!"*

Gwen hugged her and they sat alone for a while.

Myrgen felt the hairs on the back of his neck rise and he looked around, alert. Michael noticed the change.

"What is it?"

"Something's wrong. Where's Catriona?"

They looked around and didn't see her. Myrgen went over to the sunshade and bowed. "Drake, Anika, where's Catriona?"

The couple looked around. "I saw her and Gwen walking towards the docks a few minutes ago."

"She just left you here?" He looked around. "Where's Tib?"

The slight panic in his voice brought them all to their feet. He had been encouraged to enter the archery contest when they got to the square and a bow and arrow had been kindly loaned to him by Thomas. He picked it up and nocked an arrow.

Michael pointed to a crowd at a nearby jewelry stall where Tib was standing, looking at something the proprietor was holding. Next to him was the girl he had taken an interest in at the ceremony. *Misha.*

He looked around for the threat, not understanding why he knew something was wrong. Then he saw it. A man dressed in Augustinian monk's robes was standing talking to a woman at a vegetable stand. She was pointing to Tib. The man nodded and walked directly over to him. He had the gait of a predator and his hands were flexing like he was preparing a fast, deadly strike.

"Tib!"

Tib and Misha turned to look at Myrgen, as did everyone else between them, grinning faces not knowing death was approaching. The only one still moving in that moment was the monk. Myrgen drew on him and let the arrow fly in the split second that there was no movement. As the monk raised his fist to strike Tib down, the arrow embedded in his left temple, dropping the man before the world knew there was a threat. Never had Myrgen had such clarity of mind and vision but the instant it was done, the world restarted. There was a flash of light around the man's neck, but when they got over through the screaming crowd, the monk was there, quite clearly dead.

Drake and Anika ran over to the scene and Tib took Misha's hand. Myrgen looked around for Catriona and Gwen but didn't see them.

"What happened?" Anika's question showed her concern but her actions showed she realized the situation was handled.

"I felt like something was wrong. After Catriona left, I just felt... alert. Then I saw a man dressed in Augustinian robes. That's unheard of in Caratia."

Drake nodded behind him. "There's an Augustinian church here. I met the priest years ago and let him build it here for the trade."

The priest ran out up to the group and saw the monk on the ground. "What happened? Is the Prince hurt?"

Everyone looked at him. Drake recovered first. "How did you know he was going to attack the Prince?"

"He said he had a message for the King of Mervolingia from the church and that the Prince was going to deliver it for him."

Michael looked at Myrgen. "That's an ugly message."

Myrgen nodded. "Why send it? What was the Church trying to say?"

Michael shook his head. "That information died with him."

Everyone from Caratia stopped and Myrgen and Michael noticed the silence. They looked around and Drake nodded to two guards that arrived. "Bring him." He looked at Myrgen. "I need you to go find Catriona. She'll want to be here for this."

Thirty-Four

You're much easier to question when you're dead.
-The Wisdom of Stone

As the guards took the body to the square, Myrgen looked around for where Catriona might have gone. He figured she was probably taking Gwen to see Octavius and looked in the docks for the *Enigma*. It wasn't until he had checked every slip that he saw the giant stone building on the other side of dry dock. He walked up to the structure and climbed the ladder, Michael on his tail.

They entered the ship, both in awe. The stone edifice was encompassing the ship, completely stabilizing it. It didn't creak or shift or do anything normal but there was something about it that felt... mundane. He shouted out and moved towards Catriona's quarters. He saw the mess of the destroyed shutter over where the window used to be, and his chamber door standing open, but no sign of the captain. He went down to Octavius' chambers, expecting to ask him if he had seen her, and found Catriona and Gwen in tears.

Gwen hugged Michael and Myrgen went to Catriona. He looked around but nothing of Estelle remained and he realized why they were crying. He closed his eyes, his own heart breaking. Michael unfortunately knew nothing of the situation, and Myrgen assured him with a nod that he would explain later.

"Catriona, there's been an incident. You need to come with me."

"What kind of incident?"

Myrgen took a breath, trying to prepare her. "Tib… Someone tried to hurt him."

Both women stopped breathing for a second as they got to their feet. "Hurt him?"

"Maybe worse. He was stopped, but we don't know who sent him."

Catriona looked at Myrgen, red and puffy, but her emerald eyes darkened to a jade. "Not yet." She started for the door and he grabbed her arm.

"You can't interrogate him. He's dead."

"Good. That means he can't lie."

The others followed her to the square, her stride determined. Gwen looked nervous, Michael confused, and Myrgen concerned. He felt like she did, and wanted to question the priest in the Church. He was surprised for a moment when she walked right by it. Then he figured she needed to check on Tib first. He felt better when Tib ran to her and she knelt before him to hug him. She looked at him.

"I assume the Ritual will be done?"

"Yes, momma."

"Where do you want to be for it?"

"I think I'll stand with Misha. She'll have to go through it too."

"Ok, go." She shooed him away and stood, proceeding over to the Royal family.

Drake stood over the body. An arrow protruded into the man's temple but he had no other wounds. She looked at her Duce. "Who shot him?"

Drake nodded to Myrgen. "Do you want to question him, or should I?"

She looked around the square. Several people were talking quietly amongst themselves but most of the people were lingering nearby, wanting answers. She looked to Anika. "What do they want? A report, or to witness?"

Anika looked over the faces of her people, her hand on her stone. She returned her gaze to her Stapana. "It's mixed, as I would expect."

Drake shifted his feet. "It's not like the witnesses aren't going to relive it anyway, Stapana."

"So be it." She looked at the body. "I'll question him. He attacked my kin."

Drake motioned to a couple men, who brought over a couple of empty crates from the dock area. They set the boxes down and lifted the body onto them. Catriona drew her sword and walked to the other side of the boxes, so the body was visible to the populace. She raised her blade.

"Let the guilty speak. *Beszél.*"

She dropped her blade across the neck, severing the monk's head. Gwen glanced away and Michael scanned the crowd. Myrgen figured they would erupt in cheers at the beheading, but everyone stayed quiet, even attentive, like they were listening, waiting for something. She picked the head up and turned it to face the crowd.

"Who are you?"

The eyes opened. Myrgen almost screamed, and Michael stepped back. Gwen sighed, as if she had been through this before. The mouth on the head moved.

"I am Caster Delacroix, of the Order of St. Giles."

"Why did you come here?"

"I was sent here to deliver a message to King Alexander of Mervolingia."

"By whom?"

Myrgen closed his eyes, but he could still see the entire scene like he was staring the monk in the face. He turned away and saw the priest on his knees, his eyes covered. He was shaking and whimpering.

"Archbishop Alfonse, of Patras."

"Why?"

"Because he had ignored the instructions of the Church regarding Catriona Moriarity, and has continued to pursue her."

Myrgen looked at Catriona at that statement. Her gaze grew even more cold. It was a look on her that he didn't like. He nodded to Michael and they walked over to the priest.

"Come on, Father. Let's get you in the Church."

The priest looked up at them. "I didn't know."

Myrgen glanced at Catriona as he helped the man to his feet. "Yeah, I don't think that's really going to matter."

Michael looked at Catriona as well and escorted the priest inside. Myrgen put a hand on his friend's shoulder. "Stay with him. I want to talk to her before she talks to him."

"The way she looks?" Michael nodded. "You're a braver man than I. I only fought a lion."

Myrgen snorted a laugh and left the men.

Gwen looked at Tib, standing by a girl. The two were frowning at the spectacle near the square. She still remembered his name used to be Alan, but she didn't feel inclined to call him that. She walked over to him and he hugged her.

"It's good to see you, Gwen."

"Hi. You guys okay?"

The girl nodded. Tib held her hand. "I know why he tried to hurt me."

Gwen glanced at the Ritual of Guilt. "Why?"

He looked at the girl. "Misha, this is my friend Gwen. Do you want to walk over to your parents?"

She nodded and went over to a couple, who hugged her. He turned and walked towards the docks, which were largely deserted while the Ritual was going on. Gwen walked with him.

Once they were out of earshot of others, he stopped. "Alexander named me his heir to the Mervol throne."

"He what?" Gwen sighed and rolled her eyes, putting her fists on her hips. "What am I saying? Of course he did." She shook her head, even more disgusted at the levels to which Alexander was willing to go. He was effectively holding Catriona's son hostage. All he had to do was let her know that he'd kill himself without her, and she would go with him to stop Tib from being King of a land ripped apart by civil war.

"It's only until he has a child of his own. Then I'm not the heir. We need to get him to fall in love with someone and marry them."

"Yes, well, that's not a fast solution. That could take a while." Of course, that's provided he doesn't convince Catriona to be the one to make the next heir.

"Well, we need to do something. Right now, if anything happens to him…"

Gwen looked at Catriona as she dropped the monk's head into a basket and took it over to a fire that was part of the Ritual. The head and basket were burned while it was still connected to this plane. This burned the accomplices of the Guilty, branding them so they could be easily found. The populace listened but there were no screams.

Looks like he was acting alone.

Gwen took a deep breath, wondering if Myrgen was going to be there for Catriona after the Ritual was done. That seemed to be the position he favored at the moment, like Michael was favoring Myrgen's side. At least the Ritual of Guilt didn't damage her, not like her forcing the truth from someone did. When she needed to take something from an unwilling mind, it took something from Catriona as well. It forced her to be cruel, to use her power to cause pain. Worse, that lingered for a while after she had to do it. Her eyes went from clear emerald to a more opaque jade. Her heart went cold, her judgment merciless. When she had to rip the sins from another's soul, Gwen worried Catriona would not return.

That was why Gwen had been so grateful that Alexander had come back into her life. Catriona had read a man against his will and even after the situation had been handled, her eyes had stayed dark. After the meeting with Alexander, her eyes had cleared. Yes, she had returned to a state of wallowing in her guilt over Nicolai, but every time Catriona saw Alexander, her eyes had regained their sparkle. It saddened Gwen that he was no longer worthy of that role.

Tib was right though. If anything happened to Alexander while he was on this "quest", the consequences would be terrifying. Looking at this young man, he knew the ramifications.

"Does your mother know?"

"You mean, have I told her? No. I just found out at the Naming. I haven't had the chance."

Gwen sighed. "Let me know if you want me there when you do."

Tib smiled. "Thank you."

Jarius ran into the Archbishop's office when he heard the screaming. Alfonse was on the floor, writhing and clutching his face. The stench of burning flesh contaminated the air, though Jarius saw no smoke. He knelt beside Alfonse, then pulled his hand back.

His face…

Myrgen walked over to Catriona, bowing to Drake and Anika on his way. "Well, that was extremely unsettling."

"Think of how it affected him and his allies."

"His allies?"

"Yes. The Archbishop Alfonse of Patras."

Myrgen blinked several times, processing. "He experienced that too?"

"More." She nudged her chin a little higher, a look of arrogance that, again, didn't look good on her. "He felt it too."

Myrgen looked at the fire spitting from the flesh cooking in it. "How long?"

"Just the first burns. It identifies their accomplices so we can track them."

"Thank the Stones I never had anyone do anything in Caratia."

He looked around the tourney field. Folks were already returning to their business and the tournament was getting set. Combatants were talking to field heralds, merchants were starting to call out to customers. Normality was resuming. By tonight, this would be part of the gossip, tales told by those who were there to those who missed it.

He looked at her again, saw the red rimming her eyes. They were fading back to that glittering emerald with the gold flecks. He touched her shoulder.

"Are *you* okay?"

She took a deep breath, and the strength just drained out of her. Her eyes started to dampen and she shook it off. "Not entirely."

He glanced at Drake and Anika who were settling into their chairs at the sunshade. Gwen was with Tib and Michael was coming out of the chapel. "Hang on a moment."

He walked over to Michael and drew him to Drake and Anika. "Your Graces, this is my best friend, Michael. He has stood by me for several years now. I'd like to take the Stapana and talk with her. Will you mind having Michael stand in our stead for a few minutes?"

"No, of course not. See to our daughter. Please."

"Thank you."

"Oh and Myrgen?"

Myrgen stopped.

"I think you won the archery contest."

"Where would you like to talk?"

Catriona looked at the tournament field and down to the docks. She simply wasn't certain she could go back in the ship again. It had been her home, and now it just a dead, empty shell. But he deserved to know. "I need to show you something."

She walked with him to the dry dock area and he looked up at the structure. "I saw this for a moment before. What is this?"

"I made it when we got here. She needed to be out of the weather and water. It was going to be a month before they could get to her."

Myrgen stopped. "You...made what?" He pointed to the stone building. *"That?* You made *that?"*

"I have a connection to the Land here that I didn't have in Patras."

"I'll say."

He walked over to the ladder and she gestured for him to climb. He did and turned around partway up when she didn't follow. "You aren't coming?"

"I can't go in there again."

"What am I looking for then?"

"It's in their room."

His eyes got very apprehensive and he went up without her. He was up there for about ten minutes when she got worried and climbed up. She found him sitting on his bed, holding the cannonball. The journal was next to him on the bed. His eyes too were red.

"This was it. This was the thing that killed her."

She nodded.

"Why was it still here?"

She shrugged. "I remember almost removing it several times after you left, and I kept remembering it being removed. But there it is."

"They really are gone, aren't they?"

"I haven't seen him since I left for the castle. Neither has anyone else."

He frowned. "Did a man with green hair come by?"

Thirty-Five

Anyone who angers a Fae has chosen a strange path. Avoid them.
-The Wisdom of Stone

Alexander took a deep breath. He could smell something different than the sea for a change: Roasted meat. He hadn't cared enough to know the name of the village they docked in before. All he really cared about was Zara. He had a strong feeling he was close to her. If he could get to Catriona today, he knew he could convince her to marry him and return to Patras. There was nothing for her here of value, not like he could offer. This single thought played out in his mind over and over since getting through the Maw. He *would* make it happen, by sheer will alone.

"You've been quiet."

Alexander looked at James and smiled, relaxing. "I have been somewhat preoccupied."

"Thinking about what you're going to say?"

He frowned. He had simply been telling himself she would go with him. He had not yet once thought of how he would phrase that. "I probably should go over that, huh?"

James laughed. "You might want to play out a few scenarios in your head, just to be sure."

"Right. Well, after I kill Myrgen, it should be easy to tell her to come back with me. She's always listened to me before."

James snickered. "That sounds great. Do you have a back-up plan, just in case that brilliant one doesn't quite take?"

"You think I should have brought flowers?" The both laughed and after a moment, Alexander nodded. "To be honest, I'm not sure. All I've thought for the past day was that I was almost there and that I could do this. The concept of *how* has been dodging me."

"So talk it through. Tell me what you've got."

"Well, I'm thinking I should lead with an apology. I haven't had the chance to say that yet."

"Good start. Then what?"

"Well, if I get that far, I've got her, I think. I need to pay for the damages, of course."

"Of course."

"Then, offer a bride price to Drake for her."

James' eyes narrowed. "Are you purchasing her? I wasn't aware she was simple chattel."

Alexander sighed. "I am at a loss without her in front of me. I always know what to say in a given situation. I can't plan it out."

"That seems unwise but frankly, you know her better than I."

"I hope so. My biggest fear is that I have so ruptured our relationship that I cannot heal it."

"I might recommend *not* leading with murdering the person she rescued from you."

Alexander laughed but his heart went cold.

Why not? It worked with Nicolai.

Octavius walked with a purpose, lightly rubbing the shard in his pocket through the leather. He wanted to pull it out and touch it, let her know he was there, but he was worried the glass might be too fragile.

She had protected it with her last breath. He didn't want to risk it. It was all he had left.

All this time, we thought her essence was in the sap. I'll bet that was on purpose. She was a tree in Galadorn. Why wouldn't we think sap was the connection, especially magical sap that never ran out?

Lauriel growled next to them and Raven stopped. Octavius heard someone coming through the woods. For a moment, it sounded like Alexander. He had a spike of fear stab his spine and he grabbed Raven, pulling him down behind a bunch of scrub. Sure enough, he saw two men walking and chatting. One he didn't know, though he looked like a relative of someone. The other was his wife's murderer.

"It's him."

Raven looked at him. "Who?"

"That's Alexander. That's the one who shot your sister."

Raven's eyes turned cold and he put his hand on Octavius' shoulder. "Wait here. I'll be back."

He slipped out of view and disappeared.

Alexander took a step and his foot sank in the ground, like he had stepped in a mud bog. Plants started growing around the edge of the area, the grass becoming greener and the trees becoming more lush. He stumbled and fell to a knee which also sank into the ground quickly. He tried to struggle but every movement drove him further down. He looked up to James just as he realized Alexander wasn't with him.

"James, *help.*"

James took a step towards his companion but his foot started to sink into the ground. He managed to grab a flowering branch and pulled himself free. He looked down and his foot only showed dry dirt, as if he had accidentally kicked a pile of newly churned earth. He looked around for something to extend to Alexander. Within seconds, Alexander was up to his shoulders, his arms above his head to keep his hands free for James.

The young man found a large branch nearby and grabbed it, extending it towards Alexander. It hit the ground before the king as if it were simply solid ground, the dead branch coming back to life before their eyes. Both men started at that discovery and Alexander put his hand on it. The branch sank into the ground before him as if on water but when James tried to pull it back, it was buried. Alexander couldn't keep himself up any longer and sank into the ground up to his neck.

That was when they saw the cat.

A small, black cat walked over to Alexander and jumped onto the branch sticking out of the ground. It sat down looking at him. Both James and Alexander stopped what they were doing, not sure what they were seeing.

"I don't have time to deal with you right now. I have to save my sister, whom you shot."

The cat's gaze did not waver but Alexander looked to James, who moved to a different position to look at the animal speaking to them. He took a step closer and the cat held up a paw to James. "Don't make me summon your mother, boy. She won't like it."

James stood straight and backed away to a nearby tree.

"My companion Lauriel is going to stay here and watch you until I come back. Let's hope I return before you starve to death. On the other hand, that might be the kinder fate for you. I wouldn't be surprised if my father came back with me for our little chat."

Lauriel came over to him and stood, growling at Alexander. The cat jumped down from the branch and walked over to the shrubs where Octavius was crouching. After he was out of sight of Alexander but before he was in sight of Octavius, Raven returned to his human form. Alexander couldn't turn his head to see them and they walked away. Raven didn't look back.

Octavius walked, not looking back either.

"A cat?"

"I spent the last several years as a cat. It was familiar. Besides," Raven smiled, looking at his brother-in-law, "there's just something *unsettling* about having a common housecat tell you you're going to die. They always seem to mean it when they say it without words, so they seem so credible."

Octavius smiled. "I may not be there when what happens with him happens. I just want you to know now that I approve."

Raven nodded. "We should hurry. Galadorn is still a long ways away and there's water in the way."

"There's also this mountain thing."

"Yeah, I'm not worried about that. I've got that. I can't do the same with water. There might be a boat necessary. That's why I brought you."

Octavius frowned. "You didn't bring me because it was my wife that was dying?"

Raven got a distant look, suddenly very sad. "Of course. No woman should have to die alone. Not when someone loves her. And in that case, she shouldn't have to die at all."

Octavius knew the voice of experience when he heard it and didn't press the topic. If Raven wanted to talk about it, he would. It wasn't like Galadorn was nearby.

James leaned back against the tree and folded his arms across his chest. "You have definitely gotten yourself in mess."

"Do something. Get me out of this."

The vicious looking Fae wolf growled at Alexander. James shook his head. "There's a saying amongst my people, about folks that anger Fae choosing a strange path. You, my friend, have got yourself on a strange path."

"I don't even know who that was."

"Neither do I, but he knows my mother, which is a bit unsettling."

"Why?"

"Because I don't." James held up his hand. "I thought I did, yes. But since my uncle disappeared, there have been a few discoveries. Turns out my uncle was my father. So, since I don't think he coupled with his sister, that means the woman who raised me was likely my aunt. Which means my mother is a mystery. And that very peculiar cat knows who she is and can 'summon' her. That's a very odd thing to say."

James looked at the Fae wolf. "I also think this little guy understands everything we're saying."

Alexander looked at the animal. The Fae Wolf bared its teeth. Its growl sounded like an earthquake.

"So what do we do?"

James looked north. "I can smell roasting meat from here. We must be close to Zara. I'll be back."

"Wait! You can't leave me here with this thing."

James pointed to Lauriel. "That 'thing' is a Fae Wolf. Allow me to explain something about your situation, Alexander. You have managed to alienate someone who I really respect. I've been going along to help you because my sister trusts you and believes in you. You've also done some pretty impressive things so I've given you the benefit of some hefty doubts. The people who have vouched for you carry more weight than the people who have been against you.

"Until now. That cat was a Fae Lord, or at the very least a Fae Kin. He knows who you are and what you've done. Apparently along your path, you have shot a Fae woman. You have gotten yourself *trapped* in the *ground* with strict instructions that if you die, that would be a kindness." James pointed to the north.

"In that direction is a woman who is very well connected to a place that is decidedly difficult to get into. A place *known* for its Land Worshippers. If there is *any* chance of getting you out of the hole you have very literally dug yourself into, it will be in that village. You're not going to go, and that 'thing', as you put it, is here to make sure *you* are still here when his master returns. *I'm* going to go and see if there is anyone who can and will help you."

James looked around. "I'm getting the impression that what I'm going to say next will be very difficult for you to grasp but I'm going to say it anyway. *Don't do anything stupid.* Instead, take this time to reflect upon your actions up to this point and see if you can figure out a way to stop being an idiot. If you're still here when I get back, maybe you can move forward with your life."

James shouldered his satchel and walked toward town.

"And that's how I met Drake. Raven seemed quite intent on finding Estelle. It's possible that's where they are right now. If the woman I loved was in danger of dying and someone came along who could help, I'd walk away without saying anything, if time was of the essence."

Catriona nodded. "You're right. Octavius would do anything for her. So would I." She sighed. "And I'd rather think this is the case instead of what I and Gwen originally thought."

Myrgen stood. "We should let her know too. No need to have her worry as well."

Catriona stood, looking around. "Thank you for coming here."

He nodded. "It feels different. It's just a ship now."

She smiled. "Better not let Thessius hear you say that. This is still... his home..."

He heard the catch in her throat and frowned. "You were planning on leaving it behind anyway, last I heard."

She looked away, folding her arms across her chest.

He looked away as well. "I'm sorry. That was insensitive."

"It was the reason you left before. I don't blame you for calling me out on it. However, since we last spoke, I have," she smiled, "come to my senses. I could never be with someone who could do this to the people I love."

"How long did it take you to get to that conclusion?"

"Too long. And I lost two dear friends along the way."

He patted her shoulder. "Octavius and Estelle are still your friends."

"I didn't mean Octavius."

He turned her face to his. "You never lost me."

She touched his hand. "Close enough."

"Caiptin!"

They stepped back from each other as Thessius shouted for her again.

Catriona jerked her head in the direction of the main deck. "We have some news to break to the crew."

Gwen walked over to Michael, bowing to Drake and Anika as she passed. The tournaments were going well and everyone seemed to be enjoying themselves, despite the difficult beginning of the day. Gwen remembered the first time she found out about the Ritual. She had witnessed a crime, a robbery by a foreigner from another ship. Caratia didn't have many unknown vessels and this person had lied his way onto one that had rights of passage. His job was to infiltrate the country and steal something from Ashstone, but the thief killed himself before he could be questioned.

Luckily, that didn't matter in Caratia. That time, Drake enacted the ritual while Catriona took Gwen back up to Ashstone. Seeing the Ritual when your eyes were closed and you were nowhere near the trial was far worse. She could shut out the images this time by looking away. That was not an option if one was not present. She could only hope the people who sent the Guilty were subjected to it too. Unfortunately, she had no way of knowing.

I wish I could do something like that to Alexander. But that would mean beheading Tangl.

She realized as she saw Tib smiling at her that she had spent far too much time and energy on Alexander and his faults. Catriona knew. That was all that mattered. Gwen knew Catriona wouldn't talk to Alexander alone now. He'd done too much damage.

And if I'm wrong, I'll strangle her into unconsciousness, and tell Drake. That should end this.

"How are you doing, Michael?"

"The tournaments here are very interesting. They fight with steel but they show impressive control. It still seems deadly, should someone decide to make it so."

Tib nodded. "Control is one of the primary tenets of training here in Caratia. It's emphasized from the first day. 'It's not enough to be able to hit your target. You must be able to identify it first.' That's what they teach us."

Gwen sat on the grass beside Tib and Michael. "Why would you not be able to identify your target?"

"Because sometimes things change. Someone on your side gets in the way during a melee, or maybe an animal or child wanders onto the tourney field. You always need to know how to control your attack, and have the ability to pull it back if the circumstances alter. If you commit too heavily to your blow, you aren't prepared if a problem arises."

Michael frowned. "That's fine for a tournament situation like this, but that doesn't help a warrior on a battlefield. Without committing to the blow, you end up not dealing a killing one."

"Drake says that when he was on the field of actual battle, the Land gave the power to his blows. He said that if he had made a mistake, the Land would have simply claimed that life as one it wanted. If the Land chooses to take your life, you will fall."

Michael nodded. "I remember being told that when I was a boy. The tribe said that if a person not in the hunt got killed in it, that the spirits needed that person with them. Otherwise, they would not have been in that place to be killed."

Gwen shook her head. "We don't have a saying like that amongst the Fae. Fate is not something we believe in, at least not like that."

"Why not?" Tib stretched out on the grass on his side, listening.

"Because the Fae Lords can change that. If a Fae Lord tasks you to do something or does you a favor, they can choose to extract a year and a day of service from you. Until you pay that year and a day, you won't die of natural causes. You can be hurt, that's for certain, but you won't get sick or age until you've repaid them."

Michael's eyes grew wide. "You don't age?"

Gwen shook her head. "Wouldn't do any good to try and get a year and a day of service from someone so old and frail, they could barely stand on their own. You end up staying the age you are when the debt was incurred."

"What about after you do it? Do you age all at once?"

Gwen shrugged. "I don't know. I doubt it. But depending upon how long you were alive, when you die you may turn to dust. Or it may change nothing."

Tib lay back on the grass, looking up at the light clouds. "I wonder who the longest lived person is in the world. I bet they have a lot of stories."

Gwen smiled. "I'll bet they do.

Thirty-Six

Even if you do not know the path, the Land knows where you are on it.
-The Wisdom of Stone

Myrgen and Catriona left the dry dock building. With Estelle gone, there was no need for the stone covering anymore, so she dismissed it, lowering the ship into the water on a sand covered ramp. She almost teared up again, but she shook it off. There was no point in crying anymore. If Estelle was gone, she was gone and nothing would change that. She felt heartless thinking that so soon after believing the worst, but in the end, it was better to accept this now than to fight it later.

As they passed the Church, she thought about going over to speak to the priest. Myrgen cleared his throat and she looked at him.

"The priest had no idea the monk was going to hurt Tib."

"How do you know?"

"He was horrified."

She blinked slowly, then focused her attention on the town square. "People can lie to you, Myrgen."

"Yes, but the Land would have held him there if he had been an accessory. Or we would have heard him scream when the head was burned. Right?"

She flicked her glance at him, but didn't give him the satisfaction of an actual look, despite the fact he spoke the truth. Unfortunately, he still seemed to know he was right, and smiled at her non-acknowledgement.

She wanted to be irritated at him, but she just wasn't. She was glad he was here, and was trying to respect his situation. She wasn't prying like she knew she could. He had left because she was being stubborn. Now he was back, and she wanted to take him aside and tell him he was not allowed to leave again, ever. But he had returned here against his will. She didn't want her emotions to extort him into remaining by her side when he wasn't ready.

When he was ready to be here permanently, he would let her know. Until then, she was going to respond like he was here for this celebration, but was going to leave as soon as he felt it appropriate. That's what she would want him to do, not make her feel like she had to stay to prove her love. Not like Alexander had done. One of the main reasons why she had not seen Alexander all winter was because she knew he would have talked her into abandoning her integrity so they could be a couple.

Myrgen would never do that.

They got to the square in time for the semi-finals of the tournament. One of the combatants came over to the edge of the fighting arena towards them.

"Stapana, may I speak with you?"

"Of course, Allyn. What can I do for you?"

The handsome young man took a knee before her. "I am to fight in the semi-finals but in truth, I have no lady for inspiration. Would you do me the honor of being that inspiration? I meant to ask earlier but…"

She nodded. "I understand."

Myrgen looked at the young fighter, then back at her. She saw a moment of something… not exactly jealousy… pass across his face. He saw her looking at him and took her gaze instead of avoiding it. "My lady, this gentleman seems most worthy of your attentions. And as I understand it, you have no partner for the ball tonight."

Allyn seemed to sense there was something between her and Myrgen. He started to say something but she interrupted him before he could.

"You are quite right, Your Lordship. Allyn, I would be honored to have you fight on my behalf. I shall save you a dance for this kindness."

Myrgen leaned over. "And if you win, she might save *all* of them for you."

Allyn bowed to them both. "I would never presume to steal so much of the Stâpâna's time, but perhaps a second dance would be reward enough."

She smiled at Allyn. "Then fight well. I shall be watching."

The young man stood and nodded to her. He went off to get ready for his next bout. She looked at Myrgen.

"Giving me away, are you?"

"Of course not, my Lady." He took her hand and kissed it. "You have never been mine to give."

He released her hand and bowed. Michael called out to Myrgen and he took his leave of her.

Myrgen entered the kitchen to fetch some food for the Royal family. One of the servants came over to him as he entered. "Can I help you, Sir?" The girl looked Myrgen over before realizing he was watching her. She blinked, embarrassed.

"Rose, wasn't it?" He smiled at her blush.

"Yes, sir."

"Please, call me Myrgen. You've seen my filthy hair, washed my filthy clothes, and the Stones only know what was revealed in the bath. I doubt pretenses are necessary."

Rose smiled. "True. What can I do for you?"

"The Royal Family keeps giving away their food and I wanted to see about grabbing a few things for them." He handed the girl the four baskets which had held bread, wine, meat and cheese, and fruit which were now empty.

"Right away, Si… Myrgen."

"Thank you Rose." He looked around and saw a table on the side. "May I sit?"

"Certainly." She handed the baskets off to another kitchen helper, whispering instructions as he sat back, letting out a sigh.

Myrgen had started getting a headache earlier and wanted to leave the loud town square before it split him open. He was hoping to find some willow bark to relieve the pain.

"Headache?"

"Yes, how did you…?"

"It's the Ritual. It usually strikes like this the first time. The mind fights the invasion of images. Once you get used to them, you let them wash over you and there's no after effects. You just learn to glean the knowledge." Rose opened a bottle of wine and poured some into a goblet. "Here, drink this. It will help."

He sat forward and cradled the wine in his hands. The liquid was dark, almost black, but it did not smell dry like the red wines with which he was familiar. He tasted it and found it to be sweet, like a white wine, but full bodied like a red.

"You sound like you speak from experience about the wine."

"I'm afraid so. Years ago, my father was killed in front of me by some thieves trying to steal from the metal workers guild. They broke in as he was teaching me how to smelt the gold. He splashed molten gold into the face of one who went for me and his companions killed my father for it. One slapped me as the other grabbed the gold and silver we had already refined and they ran. I tripped one and he fell, spilling the stolen metals onto the ground. The Land reclaimed them in front of their eyes and they ran in fear.

"The Stâpâna caught them as they left the guild house, cutting their legs from under them. They died in the street, their blood pooling on the rocks because the Land refused to take it. Afterwards, we needed to be sure someone in town was not responsible for the plot. We found out these men were taking the gold to someone in Myria who was taking it to Mande. He was caught and executed. You might say we don't have a good relationship with any other countries."

"You don't really need it. You have the largest, undefeated army on the continent. You don't even have to bow to Toledo because I understand your weapons and armor don't come from them."

"Well, that's not entirely true. The magic they use is given by the Land. It's placed in the ore. Caratia and Toledo have a shared border and sympathetic magics. If anyone were to attack Caratia, their metal would fail. Likewise, if Toledo was attacked, we would treat the attackers like they had assaulted Caratia directly and the army would swarm. There are reasons why the army of Caratia is undefeated."

Myrgen took another drink of his wine and he could feel the pain leaving his body. "You were right, this does help. It's different from my usual fare."

"It's unique to this country and we don't export it. It is called Caratia's Blood."

Myrgen looked at the goblet. "Fitting." He finished the wine.

Rose smiled, glancing over her shoulder at her friends. "Well, I needed to get you healed up properly for tonight's activity. The Ball is going to be very big for you. You are a hero."

"Don't quite yet know how to handle that. It doesn't feel true. I was doing my duty, just like you."

"But to us, you are a foreigner. It was not expected that you protect one of us. It's pretty important. Some will see it as an opportunity for relations with Mervolingia to become like those with Toledo."

"Well, I wouldn't want to facilitate that." He shook his head, pouring another glass. "Not after the last fiasco."

A pan dropped in another part of the kitchen and they looked over, catching a couple women watching them while they washed dishes. Rose scowled at them and they went back to minding their dishes.

"So, you mentioned earlier that the Ball was going to be important. That's means I'll need to know the dances."

She nodded. "Yes. The dances the Yorkman John Playford wrote about are popular here. We have a few pavans and basses as well, from Toledo. If you don't know them, your partner can help you get them down."

"Provided I have a good partner." He looked up at her, letting the subtle flirt tickle her cheeks.

She repaid his flirt with a blush. "I'm sure we can fix you up with someone who can help you. They'll also teach the dances before the Ball so you can get the regional differences sussed out." Her eyes snapped up to his and she got an excited look to her face. "Oh, there is one you need to know. *Korabushka.*"

"*Korabushka?*"

"Yes, it's a favorite here. Stand up."

He set his goblet down and stood as directed. She took his hand and pulled him close.

"The thing to remember about Caratian dances is that they are passionate, above all else." She stepped in closer and placed her other hand in his, then turned him to the side so that his right hand crossed behind her to her right hand by her right shoulder, and his left hand crossed his chest to hold her left hand. They were very close now. She took a step to the left, urging him as well with a small squeeze of his left hand. He followed the lead and she did it again, stomping with her right foot afterwards.

"This dance is always the opening dance. You fling your partner around like a sack of vegetables. There is spinning and clapping and it gets faster, ending with the woman sitting on the man's knee."

"I like this dance."

Rose smiled. "I think you will be quite suited for it. Just let your passion build, keeping it close to the surface but not letting it out. Do you think you can do this?" She looked into his eyes, the distance between them easy enough to close for a kiss.

He winked. "Oh yes."

She showed him the steps of the dance, where to stomp, how to spin, where to clap. "This dance can be sharked from within, so be aware."

"Sharked?" He took a three-step-turn away from her as she did likewise, memorizing the dance as he did it. *Clap.*

"Yes," Rose replied, spinning back as Myrgen did the same. "It is the term for taking over someone else's place in the dance." *Clap.* "Sometimes it removes them, sometimes it merely gives them a new partner." *Right hand to right hand, together, face to face, apart a step away from one another. Turn her under the arm to switch places with her, and drop hands throwing your partner's hand down.* Myrgen was getting the hang of this.

"Ah, we referred to it as something else in Mervolingia. We called it being Sevened." *Spin.*

"Sevened?" *Clap.*

"After the seventh commandment, 'Thou shalt not commit adultery.'" *Spin and clap.*

"Ah, interesting point of view." *Together, apart, back to the starting position.*

"It can apply to many situations, so if you've ever heard someone from Mervolingia talk about sevening or being sevened, that's what they mean." He looked down at his feet. "I think I have this. Am I doing it right?"

The girl approaching with the full baskets nodded. "Oh yes. I think you're doing fine."

"Zee!" Rose let go of Myrgen and looked at the brimming baskets. "Thank you."

Myrgen reached over. "Here, let me help with those."

Zee pulled the baskets away. "Actually, Sir, I think you should continue practicing. I can take these to the Royal Family."

"I don't know. I don't want to interrupt things here."

Rose shook her head. "It's no trouble, Myrgen, and you need the practice."

Zee nodded. "Indeed. You don't want to look foolish out there tonight."

"And we have plenty of women to help you."

Myrgen glanced at the kitchen staff around the room. "Are you sure I'm not interfering?"

The whole kitchen erupted in "not at alls" and "pshaws". He shrugged. "Okay then, who wants to teach me the next one?"

Every hand in the room went up.

Zee brought the four baskets to the family and passed them out. All three were famished and actually ate this time instead of doling out the food to bystanders. Catriona was glad to see this. Anika called her over, looking around. "Where's Myrgen?"

Zee curtsied. "Dance class, Noble Mother."

"Good. Thank you Zee. Catriona, I wanted to ask you to do something for me." She waved over a guardsman carrying a package. "We confiscated the clothes he was wearing when he got here so we could have festival clothes made for him. Tell me what you think?"

Catriona opened the parcels and pulled out the tailors' endeavors. A lightweight Caratian coat of dark blue brocade shimmered in the torchlight, the afternoon sun cantering across the stunning pattern. Shining glass buttons that matched the color and pattern of the fabric caught the eye, and the breeches of matching fabric had them as well. A shirt of lightweight silk dyed the same color completed the look. "It's perfect."

"There are boots too." She waved over another guard and showed the boots dyed the same color as the brocade. A wide leather belt with a silver buckle accented the whole look.

"Anika, this is wonderful. Thank you." She hugged her friend.

"Are you thankful enough to wear color for me tonight?"

She leaned back. "I'll see what I can do. Do we have a men's form so I can set it up in his room?"

"I'm sure something can be arranged, but I don't want you to do it. I want you to be surprised." Anika turned to the guard, nodding to the tailor who was watching the exchange with a smile. "Please let him take these to Myrgen's room and prepare a valet to assist our visitor in getting dressed when he arrives from the class."

"Right away, Noble Mother."

The tournament's final round began and Allyn came to the edge of the fighting field. "I have been vanquished, my lady. I apologize."

Catriona bowed. "You have fought well and bravely. Please, tell me which dance I shall meet you for?"

"Ah, Female Sailor, my lady, to honor you."

"Then understand that honor is given. Thank you, Allyn."

The young man took is leave and Catriona looked at her friend.

"I guess I'd better get ready, huh?"

Anika patted Catriona's hand. "I think so. Love you, dear."

"Love you too." She kissed Anika on the forehead and walked over to Gwen, Michael, and Tib. "Are you going to the dance tonight?"

Gwen stretched. "I'm not sure. I don't really have anything nice."

"I'm sure we have something you can wear." She leaned down to her friend, keeping her voice low so Anika wouldn't hear her. "By the Stones, I have something in my room you are welcome to."

Gwen looked at Michael. He looked around. "Will Myrgen be there?"

"I imagine so. After the rescue today, he'll not be allowed a moment on the benches, I suspect."

"Do you have anything that would fit me?"

Catriona raised her eyebrows. "You worried our men aren't big enough here?"

Michael looked around and nodded. "Point made, my lady."

"I'll see to it. In case you were wondering he's up at the castle. He saw that Anika and Drake's food baskets were empty."

Michael nodded and the lot of them, minus Tib, went off to the castle to bathe.

Thirty-Seven

Only the dead stay in the dark.
-The Wisdom of Stone

Catriona looked at the crimson gown hanging on the door to her wardrobe, trying to decide whether or not to wear it. The color was bold and flashy and Catriona felt it was just too much. She had a green gown on her ship but she really didn't want to go all the way to the ship to find it. Plus, she wasn't sure what kind of shape it would be in. It was the only dress of color that Catriona could bring herself to wear, and it was still too much. She had put it on and taken it off three times already. The Land wanted her in color, but had not yet been kind enough to send her the color to wear.

She turned around and faced the black coatdress that had been designed and created for this occasion specifically. It had the winged lions of Caratia embroidered in black on the cuffs and collar, and a long pin of an angel slaying a demon in bas relief holding the front closed at the knee. She wanted to wear the color, but it was simply too intense. This was safer. It was still elegant, being made of silk, like the red dress, but it was simpler, and definitely more comfortable. Catriona looked back at the other dress, then at the coat again. Suddenly, she got an idea.

She took off the black chemise she had put on when she was going to wear the coatdress, as she had three times already, and reached into the wardrobe, looking for something she hadn't seen in a while but knew would be in there. She found it inside a cloth bag designed to keep moths out of it and keep the dust off. She pulled it out and hung it up. She untied the bag and carefully took it off the hanger, exposing a black silk dress she had never worn. She hoped it still fit.

It was the gown that was made for her appointment as Stâpâna by Xannu's seamstress, but she had been unable to wear it at that time, having arrived barely in time to fight the threat facing Drake and Anika. She had been granted her position in her Captain's clothes, and had worn the same style ever since. This gown was special, and she wanted very much to wear it now. She took it off the hanger with great respect and put it on.

The top was fitted and showed her bare midriff with short sleeves and a low scoop neck. The back was low as well, but had thin strips crossing back and forth, holding the shoulders up. The skirt was separate, a long rectangle which pleated into an inner skirt. Xannu had designed it to be put on without having to fuss with the skirt, something Catriona was especially grateful for at present. Had it been an actual *sari*, she would not have been able to dance in it. The drape was designed to go over her shoulder or across her neck and fall down the back. She decided, for the sake of dancing to have it drape across the shoulder. She never got vigorous when she danced anymore and it looked more elegant. If she got too warm, she could remove it but as it was, it would make a nice entrance.

She looked at herself in the mirror. The black silk flowed like water to the floor, draping along her curves to flare slightly at the calf. Gold trim about two inches wide gave substance to the hem of the skirt, the scoop of the neck and edges of the drape. The overall effect was stunning. She picked up the gift Tib had given her, a beautiful necklace with matching earrings. The stones in them had a bit of red, obviously hoping for a bit of color this evening and she decided she couldn't disappoint him. She donned the jewelry and found it complimented the *sari* quite well, much better than she thought it would. Delicate embroidered slippers peeked from beneath the hem, flattering the entire look.

She pulled her hair back into a soft, wide braid, tucking the twisted ends into a bun beneath the braid to sit at the nape of her neck, showing off her shoulders and back. It was sleek and smooth, laying down and shining like obsidian. A lock of curls decorated each side and the special hair cream Xannu had given her provided her signature scent. Special hair sticks from Yokotama held the style in place, gold charms dangling from the ends, catching the light. Her eyes actually had makeup on them, though she had only colored her lashes and lips. Makeup did not interfere with her role as Stâpâna, but she found it did not look appropriate on her. Perhaps she was too used to going without, for the sea was unkind to vanity. Perhaps she was afraid she would look artificial. Regardless, she wanted only to enhance her own features a bit, to show this was a special occasion.

She stepped over to her sea chest and pulled out a cream that held her particular perfume and put it on her cleavage and behind her ears. She reached down and put a bit on her thighs as well, where the cream would rub off onto the inside of the dress and maintain the fragrance to keep the scent going after the exercise of the dancing would do in other perfumes. She put on her gloves and straightened her front panel, then realized the leather gloves, a staple to her everyday costume, looked inappropriate in the midst of this feminine attire. She was faced with the same choice she had faced before: Feminine versus functional. Would the Land forgive her if she chose feminine after being functional all day?

She took a deep breath and removed the gloves, then examined the whole outfit again. She was pleased with the overall appearance of the *sari*, even though it exposed far more than she usually showed. Though not uncommon for unmarried women in Yantap, it was completely foreign here and if she tried to wear this in Mervolingia, she would be stoned as a whore. Luckily, Caratia was not nearly so uptight. The silk moved like, well, silk, emphasizing even the slightest movement of body or atmosphere. It would look beautiful on the dance floor.

She was actually interested in dancing, something she had done before out of courtesy but not fully enjoyed. When she was young, she had danced all the time, but that love of dance was something she had lost after learning of Nicolai's death. Since then, she had been without a reason to dance.

Until tonight. Tonight, she was happy to do so and was looking forward to it. She walked around to see what the consequence would be to her appearance and was pleased to see the drape rippled like the sea in a breeze behind her as she moved. It would be beautiful.

She went to take a drink of Caratia's Blood, and realized it had been far too long since she had eaten when the smell overwhelmed her. The drink would have gone to her head and she wondered if the Land were trying to tell her something. *Perhaps Caratia wants me a little off kilter, a little vulnerable tonight. What do you have in mind for me, my Sovereign?*

A knock at the door heralded Anika as she poked her head in and saw what Catriona was wearing. She drew a breath and put her hand to her heart. "Catriona, that is beautiful. You're finally wearing it."

Catriona nodded, standing straight to give the best impression. "Yes. I felt it was time." She turned to face the mirror again as Anika came up behind her and put her hands on Catriona's shoulders, looking it over. "It's been in the dark for long enough."

Catriona looked at her Dûcesa. Anika was resplendent in gold and black, a tall, embroidered hat topping a violent cacophony of braids which looped and fell and flowed as she moved. The hairstyle alone must have taken two hours and explained what happened to her after Catriona went off to bathe.

"You both have." Anika kissed Catriona on the cheek. "Will you dance tonight?"

"I think I might. You will have to. Your appearance tonight is overwhelming. I have never seen you so resplendent."

Anika touched her hair and glanced in the mirror. "A lovely young woman named Lindsay offered to do it. Her own hair was longer and she had thread wrapped around it and numerous charms and talismans hanging from it. I wasn't quite ready to go to that level, but I wanted to let her ideas flourish. It took her a couple of hours. She's doing Gwen's now."

"The gentlemen will be lining up to dance with you, Anika, as always."

Anika blushed. "That may be so, but I doubt it will make an impact on Myrgen. You, on the other hand," she looked Catriona up and down. "He won't be able to take his eyes off you."

Catriona looked at the ground for a moment. "Anika, I don't know if I'm ready for you to…"

Anika took Catriona's hand and looked at her. "I won't look until instructed. Don't worry."

"Thank you."

"Do you have your sword?"

"I was going to leave it behind tonight."

"Good, I was going to tell you to do that."

Catriona moved towards the door, the dagger strapped to her thigh hidden but still comfortably present.

The feast hall was full and the noise of the merriment nigh unto deafening. Myrgen had come down with Tib and Michael, and they had been milling about awaiting the rest of the family. There were refreshments making the rounds on the shoulders of the castle squires, elaborate, savory tarts, or smoked meats with small vegetables wrapped around them. There was mulled wine over by the large fireplace and the knights would refill the goblets of any who asked. The working folk, he had learned, were not allowed to lift a finger at this event, being served by the military in thanks for their support during the rest of the year. Since this was the custom, Michael was shooed away from helping and taken by several ladies from the kitchens for refreshments. Myrgen had been most impressed by this and decided to do his part.

He stepped over to one of the knots of knights and asked, "Can I assist?"

Ûr Vilhelm recognized him and smiled. "Ah! Myrgen, was it? Indeed! Well met!" He grasped Myrgen's wrist in friendship. "What would you like to do? We have trays of food being passed around, removal of items people are finished with and dispensing of mulled wine."

Myrgen looked around. "Well, of the options, I think the wine would be the least likely to get me into trouble. Apparently, the Dûcesa had this made for me and I don't think I'd survive the night if I got it dirty."

Ûr Azir nodded, a large hat partially hiding his black hair and his large moustache partially hiding his generous smile. The feathers danced as he gave his approval. "That's good. We're actually short on folks to do this. Most want to serve the food because it gets them out amongst the populace. It leaves Vilhelm and me to do this job every time."

"Then please, allow me." Myrgen let the ladle fill slowly to avoid getting the mulling spices in the ladle and poured some in a goblet of a lady who had approached. A quick bow and a smile from all made the effort worthwhile and before he knew it, Myrgen was filling and refilling almost constantly. He could see why Vilhelm and Azir would like some help. They were working just as hard to keep up with demand.

Myrgen took advantage of a slight lull in the pouring. "So, were you gentlemen born here?"

Azir shook his head. "No. We're only here because of the festival. We're both Captains, actually. There's always a great festival in Zara around this time of year, and the Feast of Embertwist is one we can both get behind."

Myrgen nodded. "Which ships are yours?"

Vilhelm popped a cork out of a bottle of wine and poured the contents into the extra warming pot. "I captain the *Madonna Alessandra*, my wife's ship. Before that, I captained the *Arrogant*. Azir sails the *Adamant*."

"The *Arrogant?*"

"Catriona thought it was funny."

"You mean you were once crewmembers of the *Enigma?*"

Azir and Vilhelm looked at each other, then back at Myrgen. "Yes," Vilhelm answered, arching an eyebrow. "How did you know?"

"Octavius told me. You must have both repaid your life debts to the point she owed you one. Octavius thinks it's because she would be in danger of falling in love with someone to whom she owed a life debt."

"I wouldn't put it past her," Vilhelm said. The mulling pot Myrgen was using started to run low and Vilhelm opened two more bottles and emptied them carefully into the pot, directing him to one of the other two pots while this one got warm and mulled. "She's very guarded about her emotions. I don't think anyone knows what she's thinking outside of her, but Octavius is pretty insightful."

As he stood from pouring the second bottle into Myrgen's pot, he stopped suddenly. "By all the Saints in Heaven…"

Azir looked up at Vilhelm and then followed his gaze. He, too, stopped and stared. Myrgen thanked a gentleman after filling his cup, then noticed the room had gone quiet and turned to see what the attraction was. What he saw sent him into silence as well.

Catriona, Gwen, and Anika had just stepped into the doorway of the hall and were at the top of the stairs. The glow of the room and the majesty of the music heralded them in and Catriona's hair was fetched back, the light dancing off her features. She was wearing a black silk sari and the dreams Myrgen had been plagued with on the ship before Estelle broke the spell rushed back to him with the vigor of birds fleeing a bull. The silk billowed behind her, clinging to her figure and dripping down the stairs like honey as she descended. Her drape moved and sparkled, the gold accents woven into the edges giving the fabric body without weighing it down. She moved her head and a breeze from the courtyard caught it, bringing her hair across her neck and face. She moved it away and looked at Myrgen, and he dropped the ladle.

Vilhelm leaned on Myrgen's shoulder. "I agree."

Myrgen tried to speak but he found he couldn't for lack of breath.

Catriona came over to the cavaliers and knelt before them, causing Azir to lean against the hearth, clutching his chest. She stood again, holding the ladle, and handed it to Myrgen. "You dropped the lantern."

Myrgen smiled, recognizing the reference to their first kiss. "Did I? I didn't notice."

Catriona smiled at him and then bowed to Azir and Vilhelm before rippling away like a breeze on the water. Myrgen watched her go, his heart thumping in his chest as his body relaxed again. Azir and Vilhelm looked at each other and smiled. Vilhelm patted Myrgen on the shoulders. "Us too, my friend. Us too, although I don't understand the 'lantern' comment," and returned to the work of helping folks with their wine.

Azir blinked and looked at Vilhelm. "That was an actual *dress*." He looked at Myrgen. "That was an actual dress."

Myrgen, unfortunately, didn't hear a word he said. Vilhelm just laughed.

"What did you say to him?" Gwen watched Myrgen's response and the slightly smug look on Catriona's face.

"Just repeated something he said to me once," she looked back at him as he was being slapped on the back by his companions, "the first time he kissed me."

Gwen stopped in front of Catriona. The blue silk gown she had chosen had silver wolves embroidered on the sleeves and bodice. Lindsay had woven matching blue wraps in her golden blond hair with a couple of the wraps going almost to the floor. They each had tiny silver wolves cascading down them. She also wore a touch of silver and blue on her lids. She was casting quite a presence herself and Catriona loved the effect. Even Michael stopped talking to two women to watch her come into the room.

"Kissed you?"

Catriona couldn't keep the smile from her face and guided Gwen over to a corner. It took a few minutes to tell the tale, but when she finished, Gwen was flipping between wanting to hug her and wanting to punch her. In the end, the punch in the leg won out.

"You mean you let him leave the ship and travel here alone when you knew all along that Alexander wasn't for you?"

"No. I didn't realize that until, ow…" Catriona rubbed her leg. "That had better not bruise. No, not until after he had left. To be honest, not until after I saw him again here. I just couldn't think about Alexander again."

Gwen pointed to her. "Remember you said that." Then she hugged Catriona and they laughed. "I'm so happy for you."

They pushed apart and Catriona nodded to Michael. "So, what about that?"

Gwen looked around. "What?"

"Michael. I have the feeling something's not quite right there."

Gwen looked over at him. "I kind of insulted him. He hasn't really spoken to me since then, just traveling things." She sighed. "I think I really messed up."

"Can it be fixed?"

"I don't know." Gwen looked at her friend. "Can it?"

Catriona glanced at Michael, then back at Gwen. "Do you want to fix it?"

"Well, yes. Of course. He's been indispensable this whole trip. He has also been through a lot. I think I forgot that."

"Then fix it." Catriona's gaze was unwavering. She touched Gwen's shoulder. "You, more than any twenty people I know, understand the value of a true friend. You've always been one, and you know what that burden is like. You and Michael are cut from the same cloth, as if you are siblings in the spirit world. Don't let a few inappropriate words drive away that kinship."

Gwen looked at Michael and nodded. "You're right. It's time."

Catriona stepped back and watched her friend walk away.

Thirty-Eight

The eyes cannot see what the
heart can.
-The Wisdom of Stone

"Excuse me, but, do you have a moment, Michael?"

He glanced at the ladies with whom he was chatting and bowed to Gwen. "Of course, my lady. What do you need?"

She gestured to the courtyard and they stepped out into the evening. The gardens were as lovely at night as they were in the daytime. Several people were also walking or sitting in the garden and she felt like it might be a little too crowded for this talk. She moved towards the open gates and Michael followed, letting her take her time. She knew a spot just outside town, going the same way she came in.

They could hear the lilt of the dance music for blocks, and when they stepped outside the last building onto the forest road, it was finally silent. She heard the birds and insects playing a very different song and the music was more to her liking.

"I'm sorry. I remembered this place inside."

He nodded. "It's fine. Is this what you wanted to talk about?"

"Um, no, not exactly. I…" She stopped, not really sure what she had planned to say.

"Is something wrong?"

"No, no, not at all."

He leaned against a tree, arms crossed. "If you're not ready to talk, I can leave you to it. This seems like a far walk from the festivities for a chat."

She nodded. "Yes, I suppose it is. I just," she shrugged, "didn't want any interruptions."

He nodded and she gestured to the grass. "Did you want to sit?"

He looked at the ground. "Isn't that a Fae ring?"

She looked down and saw she had indeed walked right to the Fae ring she had noticed on the way into town. "Oh, um, yes." She looked up at him. "I wasn't trying to trick you or anything."

"Be that as it may, I will stand."

She sighed and started pacing a bit. "I was thinking about what happened back in the forest, when I insulted Myrgen."

He drew a breath but remained stoic and quiet.

"I wasn't trying to say he was a bad person. I just only knew him by his reputation."

He waited, and she went on.

"The whole situation in Patras was very upsetting. I left my family in Glarren so my only connections are Alan, Catriona, and Dom. I can only *imagine* what's he's going to say when I see him again. Dom's never been all that fond of me just leaving."

Michael looked away, his ire not waning.

"It's okay. He knows I'm with Catriona. I'm sure any feathers of his that get ruffled will be smoothed out just fine. And Tangl's sane again so once he knows that, he'll be good with whatever had to happen. Not that he probably knew she was going mad in the first place. I doubt he would have allowed that."

Michael rolled his eyes. "What is between you two? You seem like opposites."

"Me and Dom?" She glanced down at her hands, remembering when he proposed. "He is actually a lot like you and me."

Michael shifted, like that idea was very unpleasant.

"No, really. He just has that undying loyalty to Tangl. It's kind of what brought us together, but it's also something that keeps us apart. It's exactly like my relationship with Catriona and yours with Myrgen.

I think you and I both know that if you were about to marry someone and Myrgen said no, you wouldn't marry her. It's the same with Tangl and Dom. If I hadn't gotten her approval, he would never have proposed."

"I think you misunderstand my relationship with Myrgen." He pushed off the tree. "But then again, you already proved that." He turned and started to walk back towards town.

"Michael, wait, please."

He stopped and turned back.

"I was trying to apologize for that."

"Have you thought of using the words 'I'm sorry'?"

"I *did*. But it didn't seem to *matter*."

"Maybe if you could simply manage to leave Dominic out of it, you'd find it easier to sell it."

She looked back and forth between his eyes and the rest of his face. The outburst was surprising and she feared for a moment that he might have fallen in love with her. "Yes, I will. I'm sorry I offended you and I'm sorry I disparaged Myrgen. I can see now that I was wrong about him." She looked at him again to see if the apology was taking this time.

Michael sighed and nodded. "Yes, you were. No, their relationship didn't start out on the right foot, but you know something? They have gotten past that, and much faster than you have. You cling to your first impressions, which must be the only reason you are continuing to foster a relationship with a person like Dominic. Oh, and Tangl does not share that loyalty to Dominic anymore, so you need not fear her. When you return to Patras, he'll be all yours."

He started to leave again and Gwen shook her head confused. "Wait, what do you mean 'fear her'? I'm not afraid of her."

He rolled his eyes, and walked away.

"Dinner is done! Now, to dancing!"

Drake raised his hands and the entire room shouted in agreement. Suddenly, everyone was on their feet and the tables and benches were cleared away to another room. Those servants who wished to clean up would then be able to, while the ones who wished to dance could do so.

Within minutes, the hall was cleared, the floors were swept of debris and the musicians were setting up around the room. Myrgen wasn't certain what to do next so he watched the crowd gather.

Vilhelm and Azir flanked him. "Which one are you going to ask?"

Myrgen looked around. He saw Rose. "Perhaps her. I promised her a dance."

The Dons smiled. "Well, good luck then." They parted company with Myrgen and both went straight for the royal thrones. Azir went for Anika and Vilhelm for Catriona. The ladies accepted as Drake and Tib went in search of partners as well. Myrgen bowed before Rose. "As promised, my lady."

Rose smiled, glanced back at her friends and took Myrgen's hand. He led her to the dance floor and they assumed the beginning dance position. She said, "My lord Myrgen, I am quite honored you would choose to dance with me."

"I had indicated I would. After all, you taught me all I know about this dance. It's only proper I should dance it with you. Besides, you've seen me at my worst. If I make a mistake, I won't have to worry about sullying my reputation."

She laughed. "I'm not worried, Myrgen. You picked it up like the Stâpâna herself taught you the dance. You should be marvelous."

"Is she that good a teacher?"

"She is the one who created the dance."

Myrgen looked at Catriona who was assuming the beginning position in the center of the dance floor with Anika, Drake and Tib and their partners. Everybody in the hall of any reasonable ability to move descended upon the dance floor and made three circles, one inside the other like an archery target. Myrgen and Rose were on the second tier with the royal family in the center. The outer circle would cover less ground and seemed the perfect place for those with limited mobility or limited knowledge of the dance.

The music started and folks got prepared. Then, at precisely the same moment, everyone started on the proper beat, Myrgen included. He went through the chant in his mind and before the next set, he was on the beat and in step. The dance progressed and it got faster and faster, culminating in the final move of making the bench, sitting her down and yelling "Hey!" Everyone applauded, and Myrgen assisted Rose in rising and returning to her friends.

He bowed and looked for Vilhelm and Azir. Vilhelm had danced with Catriona and Myrgen noticed her silk drape was on and everything was in place. Apparently, she danced well enough to keep everything where she put it. He looked around the room and there were more than a few people adjusting their hair and clothing. Myrgen checked his belt and coat, but they seemed to be fine. The musicians announced the next dance and it was one Myrgen didn't recognize so he went over to Azir and Vilhelm.

The two Dons were congratulating each other on a fine coup. Myrgen asked, "Coup? Are you overthrowing the government?"

"No," Azir beamed, "we got the first dance with the royalty. Now our evening is practically our own."

Vilhelm expounded. "It is required that the *lovag,* or cavaliers in Mervolingian, dance at least one dance with the royal ladies. Otherwise, it was determined that the ladies sit the Ball out far too often. The Ducesâ insisted this not be the case and the Dûce enforces her will."

Myrgen glanced back at his partner for the first dance. "Rose told me the Stâpâna was the one who created the dance?"

Vilhelm shook his head. "A common misconception. No, it was a dance she danced when she was a young girl and she brought it here. It has begun and ended each ball since then."

Azir leaned in. "Many people think she created it, but she simply imported it. I like it though." He looked at Myrgen and Vilhelm, who both nodded in agreement.

Myrgen got a drink and watched the next dance. It was a slow, stately dance with pavan steps and scooping the air. Myrgen found his attention drawn to Catriona over and over. She moved with such grace, you'd hardly guess she had just spent two months on a ship. It seemed like a lifetime ago. He found he missed that time, when he had a chance to be alone with her occasionally. He wanted her for himself, and he shook his head as the dance ended, shaking the thought from it. He looked at his companions. "Well, I'm no *lovag,* but I will do my duty, nonetheless. Excuse me, gentlemen." He bowed and walked over to Anika, barely beating another cavalier suitor.

"Your Grace, may I have this dance?" He reached out his hand to her and she smiled and took it. Drake nodded agreement with this and Myrgen and Anika strolled to the dance floor. "I apologize in advance if I don't know this dance."

"I heard you went to a dance class today. I expect you were taught all our dances."

"Well, I suppose it does qualify as a dance class. The ladies in the kitchen took time out of their cooking to each teach me their favorite dance. It's all a jumble right now. I hope I don't embarrass them."

"Fear not, Myrgen. We requested several Mervol dances, just in case."

Myrgen smiled. "Did you?" He lifted her hand to his lips.

Anika blushed. "Certainly. How else will you find the love of your life if you do not dance?"

Myrgen's smiled dimmed a bit and he glanced down at the floor. "I wasn't dancing the first time, but it happened nonetheless."

"It sounds like it didn't end well." Her concern was palpable and he smiled, trying to get it back into his eyes.

"That is a subject for a different time, please. This is a joyous occasion. It would be inappropriate for tears to be here."

"Oh dear. Myrgen, are you married?"

"Widowed, actually. Two years now."

Anika patted his hand and he smiled, shaking off the depressing subject. He listened as the herald called out the dance and it turned out to be one Myrgen knew. He saw that Azir was finishing his own duty by dancing with Catriona this time through. "So you require your knights to dance with the royal ladies?"

"Yes. We were sitting too often during the Balls as Drake and his officers would often talk about their fighting days and military strategies. I decided to put a stop to it. This has worked out very well."

"Well, I hope they are not angry with me. I'm taking you for a dance."

Anika looked him in the eyes. "I'm sure they will find a way to survive."

The dance began and Myrgen showed his competence. He was quite familiar with this one, as it was one of the first young men were taught in Mervolingia. Anika was a good dancer, and they flirted and improvised as only two partners familiar with the dance could. At one point, the necklace with the black and gold stone on Anika slipped as if it had come undone, and she caught it deftly with her right hand as if it were intentional. She held it there and when Myrgen took her hand again, they enclosed it between them.

At first touch, the stone glowed. Myrgen could feel its warmth. Time slowed and he suddenly could see every woman in the room in vivacious detail. Every woman there was beautiful, with some trait, some quality that stood out when he looked at her. This one had a generous smile, like Azir. That one, beautiful skin despite her farm life. Another one was an exquisite mother, raising her children to be the finest members of Caratian life, children that would go on to do great, great things. Each woman glowed with a fantastic inner light, and Myrgen was astonished and humbled to be in the presence of such creatures.

He looked at Anika and saw her as the heart of all Caratia. The vitality in her body, in her features, in her spirit was most in touch with the desires of the Land. She was an entity where the heart pumped its blood into the rest of the people, and she pulsed with each beat. She smiled at him and he blinked, realizing she *had* done this on purpose. The images dimmed, leaving Myrgen with a lingering joy as the dance ended. She had shown him her place in the world and he could see the importance that role. She helped people find love and he was glad she had shown him the people through her eyes.

Thank you, Anika.

He resumed his attention on his partner and the dance resumed around him. Myrgen looked again at the Ducesâ, amazed at the world which she had just shown him. She was beautiful in shimmering candlelight, despite her age, and he smiled, impressed yet again. "Can you answer a question for me, Your Grace? I'm always struck by how incredibly beautiful women seem to be in flickering candlelight. I was wondering why they ever allowed themselves to be seen in any other light."

"Because if we never let you see us as we truly are, you would never fall in love with us."

He glanced around the room. "I don't think that's my problem."

The dance ended and he escorted Anika back to her throne. "Do you need anything, Your Grace?"

Anika looked at him. "Some water, perhaps. Dancing with you took a bit out of me." She refastened the necklace around her throat and took a deep breath.

"Instantly." He moved quickly to the area where the tables were moved and asked the servant there for a pitcher of water for Her Grace. One was produced from a cleaned and redressed table nearby, and

Myrgen saw about fifty pitchers of water had been placed there for the dancers. Myrgen smiled at the love this country had for dancing. He was going to like it here.

He returned with the pitcher and poured for Her Grace, and she squeezed his hand in gratitude. A tap on his shoulder called his attention and Viscontesâ Adria stood behind him. "You were quite adept out there, Your Honor. May I secure you for this next dance?"

He looked past her and saw several women behind her, awaiting his answer. He nodded. "Of course. How could I deny the beauty of Caratia?"

He smiled at the others as well, and in that instant, successfully insured he would not sit out a single dance all night. Each dance brought a different partner, and all walks of life joined with him on the dance floor. He met farmer's daughters and shepherdesses alongside knight's wives and female generals in the army. The head of the Seamstress Guild offered to help him with his clothing next tenday during one dance, and the next dance brought him a cobbler's daughter. Before the night was out, he had networked out all his needs, including a personal valet in the form of a younger brother of an orphaned innkeeper.

He realized how much time had slipped away when the herald called out, "And as the last dance, The 'Bushka!"

The crowd cheered again and Myrgen looked around for Catriona. He saw she was already making her way to the dance floor with a partner, and was about to be crushed, when he saw it was Drake. He looked up at Anika, who had a couple knights on intercept course and he called out in a voice he did not know he had, "Your Grace!"

The room stopped moving in the space between them and quieted quite a bit as she stood, interested in what he had in mind. Myrgen bowed. "It appears your Great Lord has abandoned you for the final dance of the evening." The solicited gasps from the crowd as Drake turned his attention to the exchange.

"You would be right, Your Honor. It appears he has a better partner in mind."

The crowd laughed as they started to catch on to what was happening. Myrgen stepped forward. "Then I think we should show him what he will be missing."

Thirty-Nine

The Land growls when it is pleased.
-The Wisdom of Stone

The crowd oohed and parted to allow Myrgen access to the Ducesâ as Catriona and Drake smiled at the challenge. She had watched him discreetly throughout the evening, hoping he would be free to ask her for a dance, but his actions of the day had done as she suspected and garnered him the most avid attention. He escorted Anika from her dais and the crowd let the more daring of their populace step into the ring with these combatants. Most of the room moved back to watch.

Myrgen and Anika lined up directly opposite Drake and Catriona and awaited the music. There was a loud clink of coins from the vicinity of the musicians, and Ûr Vilhelm spoke in a booming, heraldic voice. "My friends, I feel a challenge has been made. The visitor from Mervolingia does meet in fair combat this night with the Dûce of Caratia. As such, I have spoken to the musicians, and they are willing to make the battlefield *most* challenging! You will get one measure to get the beat, combatants. Lay on!"

Anika smiled at Myrgen and Catriona saw her tell him to get ready. Catriona scanned Vilhelm and saw what he had done. She smiled as well and whispered to Drake, "It's going to be fast." The other eight couples shifted nervously, unsure what to expect but Catriona and Drake knew this dance well. She felt quite comfortable. The music started, and Myrgen caught on to what Vilhelm meant. As she had determined, he had bribed the musicians to play the entire dance at its fastest speed. Myrgen looked at Anika and winked, then stepped and stomped.

The faster tempo made the dance even more dynamic and the dancers on the floor were tested to prove they were the finest dancers in Caratia. Heads snapped with precision, the claps were completely in time with the music and the other dancers, and the thunder from the stomping rattled the dust from the rafters. About the third round, Myrgen saw an opening and he spoke to Drake as they neared each other when they turned into the center in the three-step turn.

Drake clapped and glanced at Anika, nodding. They returned to their places, and Drake watched the women spin into the center, figuring out something. Catriona didn't have time to read him, the dance was moving too fast and it was taking all her concentration to keep her steps controlled. Catriona caught her breath, excitement firing up her blood. The dance was vibrant and she remembered why she had brought this dance here. She caught herself smiling and Drake nodded, seeing the change.

The next round, when Drake went into the center, he and Myrgen just spun towards their opponent's partner. The crowd celebrated the bold move and Myrgen made contact with Catriona for the first time that night. He flipped her around and spun her to the center with greedy excess, daring her to unleash her inner fire. She read his intentions and grinned, taking the dare. She spun to the center and suddenly switched with Anika, returning Myrgen to his original partner. The applause erupted and the other dancers were called out. The next round, Myrgen and Drake switched, but so did two other men, and the dance progressed, with more and more couples switching as the verses continued. Four passes later and everyone switched at the same time, all perfectly in step with the other couples.

The yipping of the musicians indicated there were only two more rounds to go and this time, when Myrgen switched with Drake, Catriona did not switch back to him. Instead, she pulled off her drape as she turned and threw it to an onlooker. The pins in her hair were precariously beginning to hang, and Myrgen pulled them from her hair with his left hand as he took her right hand in his. She glanced down at his hand as he did so, and her eyes flared with defiance. He held her pins in his left hand until he spun her to the center, then he passed them off to an onlooker.

The flare of her hair unfolded in glory as she spun, spiraling out, the loose braid no match for the vigor of the dance. Myrgen watched as her passion began to rage and when she turned back to him, she held a dagger in her hand that seemed to appear out of nowhere. Her heart raced as she deftly nicked the threads holding his buttons that kept his new Caratian coat closed, and some much needed air rushed over his now exposed shirt. He snarled at her and she lifted her chin as she clapped, then handed off the dagger to an onlooker. When he spun to the outside, he pulled off the coat and tossed it to Rose, freeing his arms.

They spun back together for the final move and he chose instead not to place her on his knee, but to fetch her around the waist in a sexy embrace. Their desires met at that moment and they kissed, his hand slipping into her hair as hers went around his neck. They kissed with all the passion they had been feeling for the past two months, consuming each other as the world flung itself away from them. He pulled her to him, his thumb finding that place along her jaw that caused the shudders before and being rewarded when he felt them again. She moaned with pleasure she had not let herself feel for years. She had waited far too long to feel like this again, and she wasn't about to let it go now. Her lips and her body responded to his touch like they had the first time he had kissed her and this time, she did more than drop a lantern. She dropped all facades as well.

The kiss ended as fiery as it began and Catriona dropped her head back to catch her breath as Myrgen placed his forehead on her neck, doing likewise. When they did so, the crowd, who had dropped into dead silence in shock that she would do this, began to shout in ecstasy. Their beloved Stâpâna had finally allowed her hidden passion to be seen. The spectators responded to the display as if they had long awaited this moment, and Anika and Drake came up to them, Anika distributing hugs and Drake clapping Myrgen on the back.

Anika whispered in Catriona's ear. "Do you want to know the answer?" She flicked her eyes to the Heartstone in her hand.

Catriona looked at Myrgen and smiled, shaking her head. "I've always known. I was just too afraid to admit it."

The two women hugged and Anika and Drake returned to their thrones to collect their things and retire to bed. The other dancers likewise came up and added their approval and congratulations to Myrgen and Catriona for their energy. The discussions went on for a few more minutes as the bystanders brought the discarded pins, dagger, coat, drape, and buttons back to their owners.

As the people began to filter back to their own discussions, Myrgen took Catriona's hand and kissed it, conveying his feelings for her in his eyes. *Are you sure about this?*

She gave his hand a squeeze and he decided not to let this moment pass him by. They seemed to communicate on a spiritual level, and he saw that she wanted this as well. She would not interfere this time, and he was not to hold back. He turned to Drake and Anika and nodded to them, then scooped Catriona up into his arms and carried her out of the room, followed by echoes of approval from the audience. Outside he set her down, conscious of those who saw them who did not yet know about the happenings in the ballroom. She took his arm and he escorted her to her door. He opened the door without relinquishing his hold upon her and took her in, closing the door behind them.

The instant they were out of the public eye, Catriona pushed Myrgen against the wall, pins and dagger hitting the floor beside collected buttons and clothing, and picked up where they had left off in the dance hall. Every cell in her body was crying out for him and she ran her hands inside his shirt, reveling in the feel of his skin. They kissed again, the floodgate of their third kiss finally open. Passion was allowed now. More, it was expected. He touched her face and neck, her shoulders, her bare waist, drinking in everything she gave him. He pulled the ties on the back of her top and it loosened, allowing it to come off. Her bared breasts were harvested by his lips and she threw her head back, surprised by the power of his passion.

She pulled him away from her long enough to tug his shirt off over his head, then pressed herself against his bare chest, the feel of his flesh maddening. His lips found her neck and she cried out in desire, all pretense of decorum abandoned. Boots and shoes joined the discarded piles and it was with the barest minimum of clothing that they lay down on the bed.

Myrgen pulled her leg up and found the dagger sheath. He was impressed at the fact she managed to unsheathe that dagger in front of hundreds of people and no one seemed to see it. He raised an eyebrow at it and she winked at him. He decided to leave the sheath in place. He raised her knee to give him access, and she watched the determination in his eyes couple with desire as he looked her body over. She ran her nails down his chest and he pulled her to him, undoing his breeches and exposing the rigidity within. He touched her private places and found her ready and craving his penetration. He obliged. The feel of him sinking into her caused an explosion of vocals from her and she arched her back, her hand on his hips pulling him into her. She sat up and gathered his hair in her fingers as she pulled his head forward to kiss him. He lifted her up and they seemed to fit together like it was intended from the beginning.

His first orgasm rended the air around them, and he dropped to his elbows, easing into recovery. He looked at her eyes, knowing he was hardly finished, and moved her hand to rest upon her own privates. She was puzzled and he didn't want to make her read him.

"You know your body. I don't. I don't have your gift of reading someone. Bring the pleasure to yourself between us. I want to feel your release."

She blinked, surprised and he smiled, glad that could still happen. She nodded and touched herself. She gripped his rear, moving him how she wanted him, her fingers diligently manipulating her clitoris. As her orgasm built, so did his. When she did get to the brink, she grabbed his hips with both hands, pulling him into her deep and hard. They both screamed that time, and Myrgen was grateful for the stone walls keeping their lovemaking private.

A rumble rippled through the earth around Ashstone, going out in waves. They stopped looking around as dust sifted from the ceiling. Birds launched from the garden below and Myrgen and Catriona laughed.

So much for their privacy.

"Do we need to return to the party, Stapana?"

"I believe returning to the festivities would shock and surprise everyone in town."

"Good." He kissed her again, and let that action move them back to being the only people in the world.

The ground rumbling woke Alexander. The vibrations loosened the soil around his hands and he could now close them. Not enough to free his hands yet, but he might be able to wiggle them and get them to the surface. With the soil displaced by them, he might be able to pull free. He looked at the Fae wolf to see if it also woke, but it seemed to be still sleeping. He wasn't sure he believed that.

He wiggled his fingers and felt the area around them get free. It would take a while, but he clearly wasn't going anywhere. If he wanted to get to Catriona in time to save her from herself, he needed to do something.

James walked into Zara as people started to come down from the castle. It was later than he thought it would be. What he figured would be a one hour walk at most ended up being almost three. It was probably midnight and he was surprised to see so many people on the streets. He went to an inn that was across from the docks just as a man was opening it up.

"Excuse me, sir, are you just opening?"

The man turned, his face beaming. "Yes indeed. Took some time off because of the festival. I am glad I did. I wouldn't have wanted to miss that performance. Right, Chalyse?"

The man turned to a pregnant woman who was opening the door. "No, indeed! The Stapana and that visitor! I'm so glad. They looked happy, didn't they, Eric?"

"Well, they looked *interested*, that's for certain!" Eric looked at James. "Did you need a room, my friend?"

James smiled and looked back at the woods from whence he came. Sounded like Alexander was already too late. He nodded, returning his gaze to the innkeeper and his wife.

"Yes, I believe I do."

Gwen sat down in the Fae ring, trying to figure out what just happened. He had risen to rage so suddenly, it was as if he were possessed. Why would he not accept her apology? What was he so angry about?

She thought again of him being in love with her. Would she be amenable to that? Catriona had called them *siblings in spirit*. If she read that in him, then he wasn't feeling romantic, but then again, Catriona had not read him. So maybe that *was* it.

She tried to picture kissing him, to see if there were any stirrings in her heart, but after a few minutes of trying, she opened her eyes. She just didn't feel it. Moreover, she didn't sense jealousy. She thought it was more like…

Disgust.

She felt something tickle at the back of her mind. She had seen this sort of thing before. *Where?* She looked at his back retreating around the bend into town. His walk was still upset. *Was he mad about what she said about Myrgen? Or was that covering something?* She rubbed her eyes, the trials of the last two weeks finally bearing down on her. She wanted to just lie down in the Fae Ring and sleep.

She lay back on the grass and just listened to the sound of the forest around her. She could feel her connection to the Fae returning even stronger, probably enhanced by the ring. She tried to calm her mind and let the last few weeks just drain away. She was done. She had finished her task, despite how difficult it had been.

And it *had* been difficult. Between making sure Tanglwyst didn't kill herself or them, protecting Catriona from Alexander, and just making sure Michael didn't get hurt, she had carried the load on her own, without a bit of help. It was a Fae gift she had made it that far with all that weight. No one seemed to even notice how much she had sacrificed for everyone else.

Then again, that proves I did it right, doesn't it? No one knows the burden they are, so I win.

Wow. That was incredibly arrogant, don't you think?

Gwen stared at the sky, talking to herself in her mind.

Arrogant how?

Talking like you had to carry everyone else, like it was your burden to bear. Tanglwyst got herself out of that spell, not you.

Gwen shrugged. *True, but it was my horse that died, so I'll still claim partial credit for that.*

She felt herself roll her eyes.

Okay, yeah, that was arrogant. She sighed. She had been keeping all of this to the back of her head so it wouldn't come out accidentally.

But it did come out, didn't it? To Michael.

She frowned, worry coloring her eyes and skin. *That wasn't this. It was... something else. It was almost like he was...*

She exhaled, closing her eyes. She thought about him, about what he was doing, his eyes, his body tension. He focused upon helping Tanglwyst but Gwen kept blocking his attempts because she felt like the only one who could do so. *Was he doing it because he needed the distraction? He kept trying to help but I didn't let him. I kept having him do simple things, not take care of Tangl.*

He hadn't slept much on the trip, always willing to take the night watch. Even at the inns, he was reluctant to head to bed and would be up before the women. The only times he actually slept was when there was Fae magic involved, indicating he might be vulnerable to it. He might even realize that, the way he avoided the Fae ring just now. He had not been talkative on the trip and she had not really noticed because taking care of Tanglwyst was so preoccupying. Could she have been too close to see something?

She thought again about his actions on the trip, the way he was responding. He left her to get to Myrgen, then didn't go see him. He kept shying away from human contact. She had not seen him around anyone but Tanglwyst and when they were in the first days after Patras, he had been fine with her, even laying down near her. Then, once the *geas* took hold again, he grew more distant. He seemed almost depressed.

Now that he was here, he was better, but not good yet. What was worse for Gwen was that this all looked familiar. He had seen this before in... in...

She blinked, realizing the pattern.

In someone who's been raped.

Giver opened her eyes and looked out of her cage. She had been trapped here for millennia and now, finally, she had a way to escape. Her vessel could help her. Her compassion was strong and with the

Giver's help, she had seen what Michael had endured. She was on the path. If Gwen went to Michael and helped him through this time of pain, they might couple, like he had with Tanglwyst. If they did, Giver could make sure it resulted in pregnancy. It would take all her concentration, all her focus, but it was within her power. In fact, giving life *was* her power.

All Gwen had to do was have a daughter while Giver was connected to her, and Giver could be reborn into the world. She could escape the nightmare of Heaven and return to the people. Once there, she would find her companion and help Bringer return as well. Bringer had been gone so long and Giver's sight had been so limited. She needed to be on the ground, walking the world. If she were there, she would be able to sense her friend.

Michael was a good choice, a Land Kin. A child born of these two would grant Giver the connection to the Land so that she could use it to feel where the Land had hidden the Bringer. Once they were both freed, they could break the yoke of those trapped in lies, and they could awaken all mankind. Giver had watched Heaven for too long. She knew where to strike, where it was vulnerable.

She was so close.

Bringer, hold on. I'll find you.

I'll find you.

Alistair turned to Xannu, looking away from the pillar that showed him his son.

"What was that?"

Xannu looked at him. "What?"

"I just heard a voice. It was soft, faint. 'Bringer, hold on. I will find you.'"

Xannu sat up on the bed. "Bringer?"

Alistair turned to her. "Yes. Bringer."

She shook her head. "Bringer of what?"

He tilted his head, disbelief scarring his features. "You are a terrible liar."

"No, I'm actually a very good one." She lowered her eyes, holding his gaze. "You have not yet realized you were never supposed to be here."

He watched her as she slipped back across the bed and got off on the other side. "Who is Bringer?"

"I don't think I want to tell you that."

"But you know."

She scraped her teeth across her lip.

He smiled. Xannu had been humble for far too long. He had known her for a while now. Here, in this place he knew she represented balance, and now, he played on that.

"Come on. I'm trapped here. There's no chance I can actually interfere with your plans."

It worked.

"No one knows. That's the trouble. The Death Bringer has not been seen in centuries. The last time she walked this world, your friends cast her beloved into the darkness along with the Last Child. As a result, she had been lost to us."

"Who is 'us'?"

"Heaven, the Land, the Fae, Karma. We have all searched for her over the decades, but she is lost."

"Why?"

"Because only one can remind her of who she is, and he cannot reincarnate. Your people saw to that."

Alistair thought, his mind racing through the final actions of the Soulless War. The First Dûcesa and her Stapan, Slade, fought the armies of empty monsters, protecting the Tower of Persephone while Alistair and Gloriana had maintained their test subject in ice, away from all the others. Calpurnia and her beloved, Merrick, used their understanding of the arcane and searched for a way to lock them up.

He remembered the Archangel Michael wrestling the Shadow of Mephistopheles into a holy stone, which was later wielded by a Templar knight to destroy the monsters that escaped York. The Shadow was what allowed the Soulless to move so freely, and without it being contained, the world was doomed. Michael left Heaven forever to be trapped in the stone, his battle literally eternal.

He remembered making the bells from blessed ore, holy bells that rang, trapping the Unsouled wherever their tones reached. The carpenters of Persephone used plans created by a dwarven engineer named Artemis, the last of his people. He designed the towers that held the bells, allowing them to be portable and ring out for miles. The armies of York rang them throughout the battlefield, stopping the progress of the Unsouled, whose touch consumed the soul in a living thing in less than a minute.

And the soil, trod upon by St. Clara as she paced her home village crying for her children, arrested their movements, corralling them. Raven had gathered every grain, for it was the only thing that could stop the Last Child. The Fae Lord Embertwist had trapped the monsters in York by tricking the roads closed, and the Dûcesa had raised the cliffs on the border to stop animals, birds, and insects from fleeing after they were infected. They destroyed all the Unsouled until they had the Last Child and a handful of Unsouled in one final place. Raven had spread the soil in an unbroken line around them.

Calpurnia and Merrick brought the spell, the combatants surrounding the threat to the world. Unfortunately, there was only one casting of the spell and it would likely kill the Fae Lord. Regardless, Calpurnia had cast the spell and opened the pocket dimension that would hold the Last Child and all his remaining minions.

A great wind drew him and all the others into the dimension and he fought it, clawing at the bystanders. The Dûcesa was too close and she started to be pulled towards the dimension. Slade grabbed her and moved her away, but the Last Child touched him on his way by. Slade released the Dûcesa before he fell to the sickness, dropping his Granite Sword of State, and allowed himself to be drawn into the void.

As the Dûcesa screamed his name, Calpurnia had drawn the dimension closed, Slade inside as one of them.

"Slade…" Alistair looked at Xannu. "He was her anchor here."

"After she died, she sank into the ground, remember?"

He nodded. "Yes, but she came again after a few days, stepping out of the field where she died. Raven recognized her. She looked like a child of the previous Dûcesa and someone from that area of York. But that woman died a day later. Raven, unfortunately, told her who she was and the memories that flooded into her killed her."

"And as a result, he didn't do that the next time, did he?"

Alistair shook his head. "No. He told her nothing and let her lead her people like a normal person."

"Well, when that one died, the Bringer disappeared. No one has seen her since, and trust me, Heaven keeps looking. Heaven always kept an eye on her, ever since it turned out she was here."

He frowned at her. "What do you mean, 'turned out she was here'?"

Xannu stretched her arms to the sides, sighing in relief. "Ahhh,.. That feels much better. Sorry, my balance has been restored. I no longer need to answer you." She put her hands on her hips. "You can be so irritating."

Alistair nodded. "Yes, but I'm just as charming."

"True."

"You said I wasn't supposed to be here. Why am I?"

She sat on the bed, her eyes earnest and caring again. "Because you were going to go somewhere, and one of those options was that pocket dimension. I brought you to this one instead."

Alistair bowed. "Thank you, my friend."

Alistair went to one of the decanters and poured them glasses of sweet wine. Although he was polite and changed the subject, he was very worried. If he could have ended up in that place, that meant one of those things could find a way out.

And if even one got out, everyone died.

Fourty

There is truth in dreams.
-The Wisdom of Stone

"By the *Stones!*" Myrgen laid back, the sweat from their coupling gleaming on his shoulders. Catriona collapsed upon him, smiling. He let his breathing calm a bit before he tried to speak, not wanting sleep to overtake him just yet. He furrowed his brow, thinking. "So, what exactly does that mean?"

"What?" Catriona's hair spread out across his shoulders, which was wonderful, but he knew it would not be long before it was too warm. *Until then, though...*

"'By the Stones.' What stones?"

Catriona shifted, rolling off him, relieving the concern he had of asking her to move later. *Her ability to anticipate is amazing. Would that I could do the same for her.*

"I'm not sure. There's this ancient tale about a woman who protected her lover and avenged his death when a bunch of superstitious villagers tried to kill her. They said when she came, she brought Death, so they tried to destroy her thinking they could stop Death. I think they got her guardian instead and she summoned the stones of the Land to destroy them."

"So, our people swear by these stones?"

"The proper oath is 'By the blooded stones', indicating the killing justified by the Land. It means you are seeing an extreme circumstance." She ran her finger along his skin. "I just prefer to swear in Caratian."

"I have heard you use those terms. I must say, Caratian sounds pretty abrasive when it needs to."

"It can also sound very kind and loving. *Kikotu* means safe harbor." Her eyes got glossy and sad. "I'm sorry. I shouldn't have mentioned that. It's what Alexander called me."

He stroked her hand. "I would rather know that so I didn't accidentally call you the same thing."

She arched an eyebrow. "Does that sound like something you'd call me?"

"Well, no. But why risk it?" He looked at their hands as the entwined. "I didn't know he spoke Caratian."

"He doesn't. He learned a few words but I spoke fluent Mervol so we only talked in his language."

He frowned, thinking. "What language am I speaking in now? I'm not sure I can tell."

She laughed and slapped him on the stomach. He flinched, calling out in mock agony. They tumbled around in battle until they ended up kissing, not really committed to the fight. She looked into his eyes, enjoying the feel of him so close.

"I'm so glad you are here."

"I almost wasn't. But if I ever see Raven again, I'll certainly owe him a favor." He kissed her and they settled into each other's arms. He looked at the ceiling, red glowing veins running through every stone. "Raven said there were about sixty Ducesas? That number seems high."

"Sixty? That would mean we went through one every five years."

"That's what *I* thought too, I figured his math *had* to be off. So that would mean Anika was the sixth or seventh?"

"Yes, though the First Dûcesa lived a long time. Hers was a deep tale, and ended in sadness. It was the sacrifice the Land required though."

"Sacrifice?"

"The Land required her to sacrifice something very important to her. Since she had no children, no husband or lover and no money or land, the Land told her it would extract a price suitable in the future. They swore for her to fulfill this promise and she became the First Ducesâ.

"This was just the beginning, however. She still needed to conquer the people of Caratia in order to unite them. She went forth and fought the chieftains of every tribe in Caratia, every champion, using the power of the Land to defeat them all. She never killed them, but explained that she needed their strength to unite the people against attackers and to forge a nation. The tribes were barely sustained by their hunting and gathering, and she used the power the Land had given her to create fertile land for the crops to take. Then she left, telling the people she would be in a tower by the sea when they were ready to find her.

"She came here, put up a grand tent and waited. Soon, as harvests were better than ever and people were fed, they came to this place to see her. When the first snows of winter threatened on the horizon, she turned to the rock face and raised her hands, calling forth from the living rock a place to shelter these people for the winter. And thus Ashstone was born, exactly as it is right now. The veins in the rock were heated with lava so the rocks were always warm, keeping it just like this. The courtyard was fertile and produced food throughout the winter."

Myrgen leaned on his elbow, facing her. "That's why the gates are always opened in the morning. To feed anyone who wants to eat."

"Yes, it is from those first days. Nearly every tradition we have stems from those first days. The gates were created to keep out predators while herd animals were tended inside. The rooms around the keep were used by those who came and eventually, people moved from the keep to build houses of their own. Most of the people who serve the Dûce and Ducesâ are descended from those first people who spent the winter here. They spilt blood upon their stone floors, claiming them for their own."

"Does the Land require blood?" Myrgen wondered if losing Boots was part of his sacrifice to the Land.

"No. It requires something of value to you. For some people, the connection by blood is very important. Those who serve here have

345

chosen to serve through their blood. With each new generation, they renew their choice."

"So it's not something their children are locked into?"

"No. The First Ducesâ made a law that said no one could speak for another when it came to life choices. We choose our own paths, no matter what. She believed no one should be defined by the accident of their birth. That's why the Trials were created. It emphasized not only commitment because the candidates are offering their lives to the Land, live or die, but it emphasized the personal connection to the Land for each candidate. This is a personal choice, not one your parents made."

Myrgen closed his eyes, exhaling. He thought of the curse of royal birth in Mervolingia. Alexander had not wanted this burden, yet he had been required to take it, and it had destroyed him. At least Myrgen was choosing this path. "Have you ever seen a Trial?"

Catriona shifted. "You mean the Trials of Succession?" She shook her head. "No. Drake was already Dûce when I met him. It's only been seven years and he took this on a while ago."

"When did you become Stâpâna?"

"About three years ago. After I left Tib with Anika and Drake while I was being hunted by Giovanni and his men, I went in search of a way to bring him down. While following a lead, I ended up in Myria, south of here, and saved a family from an attack. At that time, the Land let me know."

"How?"

"I had bought a sword and when I used that sword to defend those people, it turned out the stone in the pommel was that of the Stâpan, or the Stâpâna in my case."

"Wasn't there already a Stâpan? Thomas?"

Catriona shook her head, reaching for the water she had set by the bed. "No, he had stepped down earlier that year. Riding injury."

"And the Land knew it." He raised his eyebrows and exhaled. "I guess I shouldn't be surprised. It knows everything that happens upon its surface. It heard my oath break in Patras, and my prayers in the woods outside Portabella."

He stroked her shoulder, trying not to sleep. Touching her now seemed intrinsic, required by the laws of nature and he was happy to oblige. He suddenly had everything he wanted and he wanted to revel in it for now. All too soon, it would be over.

"It doesn't have to be."

He looked at Catriona, who was watching him. "Huh?"

"Over. It doesn't have to be."

He looked into those glittering emerald eyes of hers and realized what she meant. "You mean step away from the Trials and let them pass me by, don't you?" He shook his head. "Would you do that? The Trials are happening for you as well."

"I've thought about it. Honestly, how could I not? To know that to stand means to lose you, and to definitely lose Drake and Anika. I thought, maybe, if I didn't stand, if no one stood but them, they would remain."

"But they can't, can they? If they could, the Trials wouldn't be starting."

She took a deep breath, like she was tempering the metal of her heart. "No. I don't know what's wrong, but I know they won't be here when the Sigils go dark."

"So you are thinking about stepping away from the Trials?"

She nodded, but only barely, like she was ashamed. "I just don't think I'm meant for this role."

"If you don't believe you are, then you aren't."

She looked down and pushed off of him. He grabbed her wrist and drew her eyes back to him. "That wasn't a judgment, Catriona. If you decide not to participate, then that is a relief. If you doubt yourself going into the Final Trial, you'll die. I couldn't bear the thought of losing you, especially not now." He raised her hand to his lips, drinking in her scent and she blinked slowly, waiting. "As for the other subject, I don't feel as though I can just let them pass me by. I have been graciously accepted by this place and it has given me so very much." He stroked her hair by her face.

She kissed his palm, her momentary prickliness forgotten. "I understand. I had the same dilemma when I was chosen as Stâpâna. I knew I could return the stone and refuse the position but I didn't. I *wanted* this connection to this place. Moreover, it wanted one with me. It was very hard to deny such a feeling of worthiness."

"I, for one, am grateful that you made that choice. It was that position that allowed you to rescue me from my prison, both times."

She smiled. "I just need to watch you closer, to avoid letting you get into that kind of trouble."

He grabbed her waist and rolled her onto her back. "Oh, I have other kinds of trouble I plan on getting into."

She smiled and let him kiss her.

Alexander felt the soil give way around his arm, and then the entire area he had been working with collapsed, seizing his entire body again. His hand was pinned closed and he couldn't move it so much as a shudder. His chest was being squeezed now and he feared suffocating. He wanted to scream, desperation causing him to lose hope. He closed his eyes, exhausted.

He felt the amulet on the edge of his vision, his consciousness. He knew it was there. All he had to do was call for it.

He opened his eyes. He could do it. He couldn't go all the way to Zara, having never been there, but he could go right over there. He could see that far. He closed his eyes and summoned the amulet into his hand.

The instant he felt the gold in his palm, suddenly, the ground shifted around him. The soil touching him dissolved away like water dropped in spun sugar. It shrank back abandoning him. Lauriel looked up with a yelp, sniffing. He got to his feet, growling like a horrible nightmare. Alexander looked at the Fae wolf from the expanding pit and shook the amulet at the animal. It fled through the woods in a dead run.

Good riddance.

He put the amulet in his pocket and climbed out of the pit. The sky was starting to lose its midnight blackness and he could tell which horizon was going to show the sunrise. He needed to get to her. He was out of time.

Myrgen stepped out of the alleyway into the darkness and knew precisely where he was. It was Patras, St. Michael's Day night. The sound of screaming and metal clashing with bone and rock filled the night. He had left Tanglwyst at the cathedral and now he was on the streets, running towards his own family. He saw the shadows of two men behind him and he knew they were there to kill him. He had no idea why. This had never been revealed to him in all the years, all the

nights where he had experienced this dream. It was common enough to be almost nightly and he had never had a reprieve from it. Tonight, of all nights, he wished that the happiness of being with Catriona would have dispelled the evil, if only until dawn, but it appeared this was not the case.

A terrible storm thundered around him, rain and lightning crashing to the ground in equal amounts. He looked through the rain and saw a battle raging on the Enigma. It was different than the previous dreams. Patras had no real docks, only barges that navigated the shallow river. Catriona's ship could never moor here. Perhaps he was wrong, and this wasn't the nightmare he knew. A hand on his shoulder turned his attention to his right and Octavius nodded to the mayhem. Myrgen nodded in response and the two men ran towards the fighting. Fists and belaying pins, chains and swords all met, the blood from the conflict staining the decks and pouring with the rain into the hold.

Myrgen felled an attacker and then looked around to see he and Octavius had vanquished their foes and the crew of the ship began the process of clearing the decks of the dead. He looked ashore and saw movement in a tavern, a tavern he recognized all too well. He thought he saw his wife and son pass before a window and he left the deck to the crew. He heard a scream and a gurgle as he opened the door, then the thud of a body hitting the floor.

The room was bathed in blood, arterial spray dripping down the walls and windows, mirroring the weather. His son's mother, his mother and father, even his sister and Catriona were lying sprawled where they had eventually fallen. Everyone inside had been tortured to death for hours from the looks of the corpses, yet he knew he was just here minutes ago. The two men who were behind him at the beginning of the dream were standing in the middle of the carnage over the body of his son, viscera and gore dripping from their blades. Myrgen turned and Octavius was beside him again.

"Hey, I've got this one." The First Mate strode into the tavern and engaged one of the men. Like every time, every night, Octavius felled his opponent but died in the process. Myrgen watched the undertaking with the horror of knowing the outcome, the futility of the effort. He waited, expecting to awaken as he always had. He most often awoke when his son was slain, seconded by the sight of his son's mother. Over

the summer, Octavius had been inserted into a role previously held by a faceless biped.

But this time, he did not awaken and he knew he was going to see this one through to the end. He entered the tavern with revulsion and fear and the second killer grabbed him, dragging him into the gore-filled room. He forced Myrgen to his knees, the blood of his loved ones splashing as he did so, soaking through the wet canvas of his pants.

"It's your turn to die, Myrgen, and there's nothing you can do about it."

The killer pulled a pistol from his belt and put it to the back of Myrgen's head. Myrgen looked around the room and realized something for the first time since the massacre: The killer was mistaken. He straightened up and inhaled.

"No, you're wrong. It's true that there's nothing I can do to stop it, but you're wrong that it's my turn to die."

The killer pulled the trigger on the wheel lock pistol and Myrgen heard a click as the gun failed to fire. The killer primed it again and fired with the same result. He tossed the gun aside.

"I'm done. You pass."

Myrgen turned to see his assailant and recognized Alistair. Alistair released him and stepped back, motioning for the door. Myrgen rose and walked over, but as he touched the door, Alistair's parting words gave him pause.

"She still loves you, and we'll tell her what happened."

Myrgen stood, the blood from the room running down his shins inside his pants, and opened the door to find the storm gone and the sun shining. He stepped into the light and woke up.

Michael opened his eyes with a start, his heart racing. He looked around the room he had been given at Ashstone, checking the shadows for Dominic.

He sighed, breathing out the nightmare. He threw back the covers and sat up on the edge of the bed, trying to decide where to go if he did get up. He had returned to the kitchen after leaving Gwen but had been shooed away. As a result, he knew of nowhere to go. He got up and walked over to the window looking onto the harbor. The moon lit the water and ships, and a few lights still flickered in the buildings below. The party had ended here, but some still continued in town. He wanted to go to them, but feared they would somehow know what had happened to him.

He felt broken.

Across the sea, he could almost make out a faint line of land. *Nubia.* For the second time in as many days, he found himself thinking of home. He had been gone so long, he knew it would be foreign to him. He was no longer a part of that world. The Mandians had stolen his home, his dignity, and now, even his soul. Would they only be happy once he was dead?

He looked below at the courtyard. He was high, about thirty feet. If he were to open this window now, he could throw himself from it. He'd die when he hit the ground. He opened the window and leaned on the sill, feeling the sea air on his face and filling his lungs. This should be a glorious feeling, but all he could think was how it would feel to end this shame. He couldn't tell Myrgen. He hoped Tanglwyst would keep his secret from her brother.

He felt his hand get wet and realized he was crying. Tiny scars of cold marred his face until he wiped them away. He couldn't leave Myrgen, not yet. Soon.

Soon.

He picked up a pair of loose pants he had been given to wear from the bath room earlier. He put them on and pulled the good shirt over his chest. His traveling clothes were in the laundry but there were no boots his size, so he had cleaned and shined his own for the party. They looked almost new. He put them on and left his room.

The courtyard was blooming night flowers and the scent of jasmine dominated the area. It was protected from the winds that bore the sea scents to his window, containing the scent in the gardens. He sat on one of the benches and looked up at the sky. He tried to configure the stars like he had learned on the *Enigma* but as he had only been there a short time before Myrgen arrived, he only knew of the Compass Star and the way to find it.

He wondered if Gwen had returned or if she was still in the Fae ring. With nothing better to do, he got up and left the courtyard. He walked down the road past the quieting tavern where he met Brain, only a few folks still shouting over board games within. He listened to the thunk of his boots on the stones, his attention on the way ahead so he could see if Gwen had stayed or returned to civilization. He didn't really care either way. It was a distraction, something to keep him busy until exhaustion drove away the dreams.

He saw the Fae ring ahead and Gwen kneeling in the center. A faint glow surrounded her and she seemed to be speaking, though her eyes were closed. He went forward with caution, aware only now he had no weapon should trouble arise. Not that he had ever needed one. He balled his fists and crept up to the scene.

Gwen was whispering in the circle and he stepped closer to try and hear what she was saying. He thought for a second she said his name, then suddenly, everything got dim. She looked at him, her eyes almost white instead of blue. He fell to a knee and felt a chill, like a snowy breeze was cutting through the clearing. Her hair tinked in the light wind, like a chime on a porch.

He fell forward, his head in the circle and turned over to look up at the stars. She touched his head, stroking his hair.

Be at peace, warrior. Release the pain that haunts your dreams.

He looked at her, the aura making her hair shimmer like it was brushed with moonlight. "...what..."

It was all he could get out before he fell asleep.

Fourty-One

Blood will tell.
-The Wisdom of Stone

Myrgen opened his eyes to the bright room. Catriona lay sleeping beside him, her dark hair splayed across her pillow. He kissed her shoulder, his gratitude present on his lips. The dream was over and he felt, for the first time since the nightmare had begun, that it would not return again. He was done with this one, and it was due to this woman who possessed his heart.

He rose, being careful not to awaken his lover. He donned his shirt and pants from the night before and left Catriona sleeping. The day was bright and the air sweet with the fragrance of the sea and growing things. He could smell breakfast cooking and hear the clang and clatter of shops opening and a tinker pushing his cart down the cobblestone roads. It was good to be alive here, and he was beyond grateful for his good fortune. Although he had never officially gone through the naming ceremony, he knew his place in the world.

Myrgen walked around the corridors to his own room to get dressed. He needed to use the privy and didn't want to use the one in her room. They were still too new in their relationship for such base acts of nature to be done in each other's company. He found the privy and relieved himself then went to his chambers. He saw the guards getting ready for the day, changing watches. Soon they would open the gates and folks would start filing in for breakfast. He went to his room, humming Korabushka to himself. The servants had been in sometime during the night or morning to tidy up and he had fresh water in the pitcher and new soap in the dish beside it. He took a moment to get cleaned up and looked in the closet for his traveling clothes.

It looked like they had been replaced with hunting garb and another set of nice stuff. He pulled out the hunting gear and pulled it on. During the Ball, Drake had mentioned going hunting at some point. Hopefully he'd get the chance to see this hunting lodge where Drake met Anika. He brushed his hair back into a tail and tied it with a long leather sheath that laced closed. His teeth cleaned and tongue scraped and a clove to banish morning breath got him ready for the day.

He met up with Drake in the corridor. He, too, was dressed for a hunt and he carried a stone great bow with him, a powerful item that seemed to compliment him quite well but just had to be heavy as a horse. "Hail, Myrgen!"

"Hail, Your Grace!"

Drake waved his hand, dismissing the title. "When we are here, we are family. Titles are as inappropriate here as in the throes of passion."

"I definitely wouldn't use a title in that circumstance. That's where I do my praying."

Drake smiled, gesturing for them to walk. "Your companion, she is good?"

Myrgen glanced down the corridor to her door and nodded, a little embarrassed by the discussion. "Yes, she is sleeping."

"That was quite a bold move you did last night. It could have gone horribly awry."

Myrgen smiled at him and looked at the brightening sky. "I don't get the feeling the State of Caratia would have tolerated bumbling at that particular moment. She might have seen it as treason."

Drake nodded, his full hair bouncing with the action. "She would have indeed. You don't want her angry at you."

They stepped into the full sunlight and Drake took him over to the wall where they could look out over the city. The view was impressive. Tops of buildings glittered in the morning light and Myrgen saw the Enigma floating in the harbor. Drake leaned on the wall, the bow shining like marble in the sun.

"That is a fine bow," Myrgen nodded to the weapon.

Drake unslung it and handed it to Myrgen. "This is the Granite Bow. It is an artifact of this country."

Myrgen took the bow and arched an eyebrow at Drake as the weight drew his arm down. Drake's massive arms had made the bow appear light. "Is this thing really made of granite?"

"As far as I know."

Myrgen realized it felt the same as the sword the Land had given him and he wondered briefly if they were the same weapon, just different for each person. Regardless, the bow looked impossible.

"And it is your connection to the Land that enables you to pull it?"

"Yes, I'm convinced of it. I could never pull this bow otherwise. It's made of bloody stone."

Myrgen leaned against the crenellations and smiled. "This country seems almost alive. It has a very real connection to its people. I've never seen the like. In Mervolingia, this would be heresy. Only the Churches are allowed to be worshiped."

"I've never understood the point of view of those churches. I've seen people invoke the saints to gain assistance, but it seems there are saints for everything, every profession. That makes them servants of the people, which I support. People support the Land, the Land supports the people. This is a good arrangement. The Church seems to want people to worship only in the way they want, in the language they want, as if to control the populace. This is not a good arrangement."

Myrgen shrugged. "The things that get done in the name of Heaven are often atrocities. If I must believe in Heaven, then I fear, if it really is the source of these divine initiatives, that I cannot endorse its Judgment. For the sake of my own soul, I surmise that the Saints are either ignorant of what people are ascribing to their will, or flat out evil. Either way, it ruins the myth for me."

Myrgen looked the bow over and did the only thing he could do as an archer and a man enduring the Trials of Succession. He put his fingers on the string to give it a try.

Drake handed him an arrow. "Here, aim for that tree over there." He pointed into the forest to a tree that was separated from the others. Myrgen looked skeptical. Drake nudged his chin and Myrgen sighed, nocking the arrow and pulling the bow.

The string and bow acted like they were made of stone, completely unyielding. He looked at Drake, who patted him on the shoulder. "At least you didn't hurt yourself!"

"Thank the Stones for little favors."

Michael opened his eyes and looked around. His neck was stiff and his back felt like it had been at an odd angle for hours. He shifted and Gwen moved underneath him. He was on his side, his head on her leg and she groaned as he stirred. He sat up, his muscles popping from the effort.

Gwen opened her eyes where she had apparently fallen asleep. She was still kneeling and when she started moving, her groaning turned to a sharp yip that startled him.

"Aaah! OW! Cramp! Crampcrampcrampcrampcramp!"

She shook her legs and he pulled them carefully out from under her. "Which one?"

"Leftleftleftleft!"

He lifted her leg to his shoulder and then pushed her toes towards her shin, applying slow and steady pressure. She hissed her breath through her teeth as the pain subsided, then he switched legs to do the same with the right. "Did that work?"

She flopped back on the ground, arms to the side. "Yes, thank you."

He put her feet on the ground and sat back, stretching to avoid cramps himself. "How long were we out here?"

Gwen looked up at the sky and saw the morning light on the bay. "Looks like all night."

"When did I get here?"

"After midnight. How do you feel?"

He blinked, surveying. "Good. Rested."

She smiled. "Rested? Really?"

He let her smile infect him. "Yes. *Yes.* Really."

"I take it that is unusual?"

He nodded. "Yes. Of late." He stood and reached out his hand to her to help her up. She took it and got to her feet. "Did you do something?"

She smiled and looked at the dents in the grass where they had been. "I might have." She put her free hand on his shoulder. "Don't be mad. You just were… suffering."

He smiled and kissed her hand. "Yes, I was."

"Is it gone?" Her face was pensive, like she had done things before that hadn't gone quite as planned.

He nodded, grinning. "Yes, yes it has. Thank you." He released her and went to the tree nearby. He rubbed his back against it like a bear, scratching an itch. Gwen laughed as he sighed in relief.

They turned towards a sound that echoed from the street and he offered his arm to her. "To Ashstone?"

She took it and nodded. "To Ashstone."

The pair left the slightly crumpled Fae ring and moved on towards breakfast.

Alexander stumbled into town, tired and filthy. He looked around as the town doors started opening. On the hill before him was a castle and he set his sights on that building. If she wasn't there, they would know where she was. He glanced into the harbor on his way by and saw the *Enigma* floating there, looking unharmed.

Good. There will be no reason for her to refuse me.

His relief was stolen by distraction as he saw an Augustinian church on his left. He smiled. This would mean they could marry today when he found and claimed her. Myrgen would not get another chance to steal her away. He moved with purpose up through the town, not really caring much for the locals. He paused for a moment when he smelled sausage cooking at an inn.

He dismissed the urges of his stomach in his determination until he felt a hand on his shoulder. He turned to see James behind him.

"You got out."

Alexander growled. "No thanks to you."

"Whoa. Hey, you need to calm down. You're angry and that will *not* go over well with anyone you speak to. Come, let's eat first."

"I don't *want* to *eat*. I want to *claim my wife.*"

"Yes, and if you don't want her to run you through for your arrogance, then you will sit, and eat, and possible even get cleaned up." James guided him into the tavern and sat him at a table. There was already some bread and eggs on it and James sat at the partially finished plate. He waved over more food and drink for Alexander.

"Now, how did you get out of that pit?"

"Diligence. I wiggled my fingers until they got to the surface. There was also an earthquake, which loosened everything."

"And that Fae wolf just let this happen?"

"It was asleep. By the time it woke up, I was out. It ran off."

"It slept through an earthquake?"

"No, but it wasn't bothered by it."

James looked closely at Alexander but the food arrived, distracting him from whatever he was looking for. Alexander ate quickly, not wanting to waste much more time. A couple of sailors came in and Alexander recognized them as being from the *Enigma*. They sat at the bar, laughing.

"Hey Eric! Well met."

"Ambrois! Sebastian! Well met indeed!" The innkeeper hugged the sailors. "What can I get you today?"

"Breakfast sounds good."

"Indeed. So, I saw you at the Naming but not at the ball."

"Yes, we had some repairs to get done. Since the Captain took her out of dry dock, we've been getting it ready."

"You going to set sail soon?"

One of the men shrugged. Alexander thought it was Sebastian. "Tough to say. There's talk she may be settling down, letting the *Enigma* sail without her."

"Ah, you mean she might be staying with that Mervol fella up at the castle?"

Alexander slowed his chewing, swallowing and listening. James looked at him over his tankard.

"Myrgen, ya mean? Dunno about that."

Eric leaned back, nodding. "You didn't see that kiss they had."

Both sailors choked on their ales. Alexander gripped the table, his nails etching marks into the wood. He looked at James. The young Glarren man set his tankard down.

"Alexander, wait."

Alexander refused to listen. James had stalled him, and now he was too late. He stood, knocking his chair over. "You knew. You knew this had happened."

"I was going to tell you about it, once you got some food in you."

"*Why?* So I could *throw it up?*"

"Is something wrong over there?"

Alexander looked at the innkeeper, then stormed out of the building. He heard Eric calling out and James responding but he didn't care about any of that. Myrgen would pay for this with his life and Catriona would as well. He was almost to the castle when James ran up to him.

"James?"

Alexander and James turned to see Gwen and Michael walking up to the castle, arm in arm. Alexander felt betrayed a second time.

"*Alexander.*" Her fear was powerful in her voice, then she sounded almost outraged. "When did you get here?"

"Where's Tanglwyst?" At that moment, he wanted her in his hands his fingers around her throat. He would kill her in front of Myrgen, right before he killed her brother.

"She didn't come." Gwen folded her arms across her chest. "She's free of you, Alexander. You don't control anyone anymore."

James put his hand on Alexander's shoulder. "We need to leave. This isn't what you thought it would be."

Alexander threw it off. "*Catriona!*" He walked into the courtyard. He would not be denied this confrontation.

Tib saw Myrgen and Drake on the wall and climbed the steps to join them. Myrgen nodded to the prince. "Good morning, Tib."

Tib smiled. He was glad Myrgen wasn't having trouble with his name. It meant he really was a Caratian. "Good morning, Myrgen. Good morning, Noble Father."

"Good morning. Have you seen Anika today?"

"She's probably in the kitchen. She likes to cook breakfast. Have you seen my mother, Myrgen? Everyone says you two left together last night."

Myrgen blushed and Drake leaned on the ramparts, whistling. "Um, yes, she's sleeping still. We were up kind of late. Praying."

Drake laughed, and it sounded a bit like he hurt himself doing so. "I'm going to see my wife." He started down the stairs.

Myrgen leaned the Granite Bow towards Drake. "Did you want this?"

"What am I going to do with it in the kitchen?" Drake smiled and walked into the courtyard. He nodded towards one of the hallways on the second floor.

A moment later, Catriona came out of it, dressed in a very pretty blue coat. Tib looked at Myrgen.

"Isn't that your coat from last night?"

Myrgen's eyes grew wide, but lit up like the sun at seeing Tib's mother. He was glad. She also looked happy. "Momma!"

She looked at the wall and waved to them. Myrgen sighed and started to walk down the stairs. Suddenly a bellow ripped through the courtyard.

"Catriona!"

Tib's heart went cold as he saw Alexander, looking like he'd been pulled through a very dirty knothole, enter Ashstone. Gwen and Michael were near him, talking to a Glarren man. All three followed Alexander in.

Myrgen put his hand out behind him. "Tib, you stay here."

"What is *he* doing here? How did he get here?"

"I'm not sure. Michael mentioned he was trying to get here."

"Why?"

"To take your mother back to Patras."

Tib panicked. *"No. He can't.* She's with you now."

Myrgen looked over his shoulder at him. "I'm pretty sure she'll make that clear, if she wants that known, son."

Catriona walked down the steps from the balcony. "Alexander. I had heard you were on your way here."

The coat on her looked very elegant, even if it was a little big. She lifted the front to walk and Tib worried it wasn't something she could fight in. She never wore things like that.

"Then I would imagine you would be better prepared for me." Alexander looked over her clothing. "It's not enough that you whore around with a traitor, but do you have to flaunt it as well?"

Catriona bristled. Tib realized it wasn't going to matter that she wasn't in her fighting clothes. Alexander was another foul comment away from eating ashtones.

She blinked slowly, not rising to the comment. Gwen got between them.

"How *dare* you, you *monster?* You have no right to walk into these walls and disparage *anyone!* She knows what you did to Tanglwyst."

"It's hardly worse than what *she* did." Alexander's tone was steady, unflinching at the assault Gwen was unleashing.

Catriona put her hand on Gwen's shoulder. Michael came over to Gwen and at Catriona's direction, stepped back with her. The Glarren man came over to Alexander.

"Your Majesty, this is neither the time nor place for this discussion. Let's let these fine people at least get dressed and we'll come back in an hour?" The young man got a hopeful look on his face and Gwen seethed less.

Catriona blinked again, slowly, and nodded. She turned to leave and the young man pulled at Alexander. The king refused to move, shaking off the tug but it looked like the young man was going to prevail. Then a shout came from the gate.

"James!"

Everyone looked at the newcomer and Tib saw a tall, bald man in a long, tattered black coat come into the courtyard. The Glarren man turned at the sound of his name and then everything went crazy.

Myrgen's heart stopped as he saw the Shadowalker enter his new home. He pushed Tib back and down and shouted to Catriona. She looked up at him, rushing down the stairs, then at the man who had just entered the gates. Alexander turned and saw the man and panic coated his features like paint.

"Duncan, get out of here!" He turned to James. "Get him out of here now!"

James looked confused but Alexander turned back to Catriona. She looked at Myrgen and he pointed the nocked arrow at Duncan, pulling back on the stone bow. The string gave, the bow drew. He realized he was going to have to choose his target. He only had one shot.

Alexander turned back to Catriona, shaking his head. "Look, you belong with me. You *love me.* You've just forgotten that right now. So I'm going to remind you. I'm taking you home."

Alexander flicked his wrist and Myrgen saw something gold fall into his hand.

It was an amulet.

Black tendrils climbed up his arm and he reached out for Catriona. Duncan shouted out and ran for Alexander. He grabbed onto the man, pulling him back from her just as she dodged Alexander's grasp. James backed away from the king as he saw the shadows curl up his arm and then looked at Gwen. Michael went to Catriona and stepped between her and Alexander, blocking another attempt to teleport away with her.

Blood dripped from Myrgen's fingers down the bowstring.

Tib screamed. "Don't let him take her, Myrgen!"

He needed no other prompting. This was the day Alexander died.

He let the arrow fly towards Alexander's chest. Gwen looked at Myrgen and saw the arrow fly. She looked at Tib and stepped in front of the arrow, taking it full in her throat. The arrow went through her and stabbed into Alexander's shoulder. As her blood sprayed on him, the king's horror took over.

James propelled himself towards Alexander and fell to his knees. She looked at him, reaching out for his hand. James looked at the king and yelled at him to save her. Alexander grabbed Duncan's arm and the three of them disappeared in a flash of shadow and sulfur.

Fourty-Two

Friends come and go, but
enemies accumulate.
-The Wisdom of Stone

"Where did they go?" Myrgen ran over to the place where, moments before, three people had been in dire tableau. Michael looked around, as frantic as Catriona. Tib ran up and hugged her and Myrgen put his hand on her shoulder. Her face had a few flecks of blood from Gwen.

Catriona felt the ground. "I can't find them. Alexander isn't… and neither is the other one… and Gwen…" Her eyes were blank, wet. She was in shock.

"The church." James looked up from the blood soaking into the stones of the Keep.

Myrgen looked at James.

"Why?"

Catriona gasped. "Does it matter?"

Michael didn't wait another moment, and neither did James. They both ran out the gates.

Nothing more needed to be said. James took off, accompanied by the guards. He pointed to Myrgen as he ran. "Stay here. Protect her. He may return."

Myrgen knelt beside Catriona. He wanted to ask if she was hurt, but stopped himself. Of course she wasn't.

"What do you need?"

"Why did she do that? Why did she protect him? She *hated* him at the end."

"It was my fault."

Myrgen and Catriona looked at Tib. Myrgen put his hand on Tib's shoulder. "No, it isn't, Tib."

Tib's tears were brutal in their flow. *"It is.* She did it to protect *me."* He looked at Catriona. "I am Alexander's heir to the Mervol throne. If he dies, I have to go back." He looked at Myrgen. "I told her and she stopped you from killing him."

Catriona hugged him to her and Myrgen held them both to him.

James ran down the street separating the city from the harbor. The Church. It made sense. Maybe he thought he saw her move or saw her breathe. Alexander would take her to the only place he could heal her.

By any means necessary.

The church came into view and he saw Alexander on the ground outside. Duncan was crouching behind him, covering his eyes with his hands. Alexander was holding Gwen and crying. He looked up when James and Michael approached.

"It won't let me in." He looked at the Church doorway, and James saw the trail of blood that started at the door and ended in the street under Alexander's knees. "I tried to take her but," he looked down at the arrow, "this thing... it isn't of the Church..."

James looked down at Gwen's body. Her eyes were black and oozing down her cheek. A strange smell was coming off her, like decay from an animal left to rot by a poacher. Her blood wasn't even red anymore. It was the brown of days dry. This blood was running off the stones like it was bleeding onto glass. The soil wouldn't even take it.

James closed his eyes. "Put her down, please."

Alexander set her aside and started to stand but James kicked him in the head. Alexander went sprawling across the stones of the street towards the Church.

"You diuchaidh... You took her through the Shadows." James ran his hands through his hair. "Look what you *did* to her, you self-serving *maggot! I'll kill you for this!"* He kicked Alexander again.

Michael knelt beside Gwen's body but it folded into itself, like it was dissolving. He tried to touch her and jerked his hand back as her blood burned him. He turned his gaze to Alexander and started to stand.

Duncan put his hand on Alexander's wounded arm. "Let's get out of here. There's nothing more you can do. Give me the amulet you used."

James caught his breath and tried to look again at her body but couldn't. He turned again to take out his anger on Alexander and saw the sadistic gleam in Duncan's ink-soiled eyes. He touched the amulet and they disappeared.

Appendices

Appendix A: Characters of the Saintlands

Alan Moriarity: Catriona's son. After his Naming Ceremony, Victor Tiberius Morganosa

Alexander Angloume (ANG-loo-may): King of Mervolingia, Alexander succeeded the Throne after Charles. Alexander is also the Duke of Anjou, the family lands of the Angloume house.

Anika Heartholder: Dûcesa of Caratia and adopted mother of Catriona.

Antoinette: Cook in the mornings at the Patras Royal Palace.

Alistair MacGlarren: In service to Gloriana, the Midwinter Queen, Alistair is also the bloodline heir to the throne of York. The original Black Sparrow, he retired from this position after succeeding in learning about Tanglwyst's pirate operations. He stopped when Catriona, his former lover, found out. Alistair is also the father of James and Gwen. Since his death at the hands of Duncan McVryce, he has been serving Karma in the afterlife.

Anika Zapolya- Dûcesa of Caratia. Holder of the Hearstone.

Archbishop Alonzo de Patrone: Archbishop of Patras.

Artemisia: Mythical name of the Moon and mother of the Sea Goddess Calista.

Black Sparrow: Notorious pirate who attacked the Tanglwyst Trading Company. Taken out by Catriona Moriarity.

Bringer- An entity of Power that has been missing for centuries. Counterpart to Giver.

Catriona Moriarity (CAT-tree-OH-nah MORE-ee-AR-it-tee): Stâpâna of Caratia. The Stâpâna is the Protector of the Land's People in the country of Caratia, the second highest rank in the country. The Stâpâna is chosen through a secret ritual known only to those in Caratia. Lover of Myrgen.

Charles Maxamillian IX: Former King of Mervolingia, ruler and instigator of the St. Michael's Day Massacre.

Dominic D'Medici (DOM-uh-nik dee MED-ee-chee): Fiancé of Gwen. As Acting Chancellor of Mervolingia, he is in charge of all funding and expenses for the entire kingdom.

Don- A general title of noble station. In Augustinian countries, it means Lord.

Drake Zapolya: Dûce of Caratia. The ruler of Caratia can be either male or female and is chosen directly by the Land through a ritual involving several trials and finally culminating in a ceremony in the town square of Zara.

Duncan McVryce: A notable member of the Back Streets of Patras, Duncan has played a role in several events involving members of the Royal family, the Augustinian church and Tanglwyst's interests.

The *Enigma*- Catriona's ship, it houses a Fae spirit named Estelle, that is the daughter of Corrigan, the Midsummer King. Estelle is wife to Octavius.

Entivia "Boots" Malatesta- Horse in the Stable of Assassins owned by Giovanni Sangiardo.

Father Benjamin: A priest in service to Marco Giovanni, he was killed helping Catriona escape her captivity in the breeding pans of the Giovanni estate.

Giver- An entity of power being held captive in Heaven. Counterpart to Bringer.

Gomez de Santander: Head of Alexander's personal guard, Gomez began as a guard at the Giovanni estate.

Gweneviere "Gwen" Douglas (GWEN-eh-veer DUG-lus): Handmaiden of Catriona, Gwen has the distinction of being her most trusted companion. Daughter of Alistair and Gloriana, twin of James.

King Henry II: Father of Francois I, Charles, Alexander and Margaret, husband of Catherine, Deceased.

James Douglas- Captain of the
Lawrence of Cleves- Keeper of the Watch on the *Enigma.*

Marco Giovanni: Mandian Count and head of the Apolodorus family, Giovanni almost married his cousin to secure a large financial conglomerate but murdered his son and then committed suicide the tenday before his wedding, leaving the Apolodorus fortune to his oldest child. Father of Dominic.

Michael - Myrgen's Nubian Slave. A very large man who is fiercely loyal to Myrgen.

Morgan Wolf - Viscount in St. Marguerite, and Myrgen and Tanglwyst's brother.

Myrgen "the Grey" de Sablonierres (MUR-gun dee SAB-yon-air): Former Chancellor to Mervolingia, he was accused of the regicide of King Charles. Wandering the world in search of his path, he is Catriona's lover.

Nicolai Moriarity - Husband of Catriona Moriarity and father of Tib. A guard in the Patras Palace. Dead by poison.

Nigel - King Charles's Castellan before Myrgen.

Nina Richeleau- Gardin of the Royal Palace at Patras, she is Gomez' second in command.

Octavius - First mate of the *Enigma* under Captain Catriona Moriarity, husband to Estelle.

Pope Gregory - Head of the Augustinian Church.

Princess Isabelle - A Mandian Princess of marrying age

Princess Marie-Elizabeth - The daughter of Elizabeth and Charles.

Queen Elizabeth of Krakte - Queen of Mervolingia, married to Charles Maximilian IX. Mother of Marie-Elizabeth. A school friend of Tanglwyst's along with Adriana Capaletti

Queen-Mother Catherine D'Medici - Mother of Charles and Alexander. Married to Henry II.

Sebastian- Bo'sun on the *Enigma.*

Tanglwyst de Holloway (TANG-gul-wist dee HALL-oh-way): Owner of the Tanglwyst Trading Company and Catriona's secret partner. Sister of Myrgen and Morgan Wolf.

Thessius- Glarren member of Catriona's crew on the *Enigma.* Former First Mate to Ramerez on the *Crimson Veil.* Quartermaster on the *Enigma.*

Tristram Wulfschlager - Captain of the *Righteous*, one of Catriona's ships.

Urien Atredes - Husband of Tanglwyst de Holloway, a Latian Merchant who owns The Atredes Trading Company, which along with the Tanglwyst Trading Company controls 73% of the Mervol - Mandian trade.

Ûr- Caratian form of noble address

Wilgefortis- The wife of Raven Grasshair, she was also the Baroness of Conterbury in York and the Seneschale of Persephone during the Soulless War.

William- Navigator on the *Enigma*

Appendix B: The Augustinian Calendar

The world of the Saintlands has four seasons, and those are the purview of the Fae Lords. Embertwist Apocraphix, the Vernal Monarch, rules over spring, Corrigan Starshadow, the Midsummer King, rules summer, Calpurnia Allegheri, the Autumnal Sovereign, reigns over fall and Gloriana Talnig, the Midwinter Queen, rules winter.

The combat these lords, the Church originally invoked the Archangels against them. These were sufficient but as Heaven gave the Church the Saints, these former humans were invoked in addition, adding to the strength of the protections against Fae trickery. The saints were originally celebrated upon the day of their ascension and delivery by Heaven into the Rolls.

However, 300 years ago, the Church, in the aftermath of a great war, decided to write down a formal calendar, honoring saints for their purviews instead of their date of ascension. This was to battle non-church beliefs, unify the masses and establish lines of Church control.

Pope Richard I told the cardinals to which he assigned this task to begin the year prior to the apex of Gloriana's control, so as to get ahead of the rise of her power. The Cardinals discussed it and Cardinal Cosimo of Pardua offered up Genevieve, invoked against disasters, to start the year. Richard approved and the calendar was begun.

Genevary became the first month and the months were divided into 31 day sets with 10 day tenday. In the center of the month, the 16th, is the Devotional Day, where all work stops for a day to pray and invoke the saints of the month. This strengthened the divinity in the realm, repelling anything not Heaven related. Although the new calendar reorganized the role of Saints during the year, many days are still known by the saint who ascended upon that day, though the Archangel's days were established during the Augustinian Calendar.

Months

1st: Named after Saint Genevieve, Genevary 16 honors Sebald, Martin of Tours, Raphael the Archangel. Genevieve is invoked against disasters, which abound in the Saintlands during the winter. Sebald once burned icicles in a poor woman's home to proDûce heat, Martin of Tours cut his cloak in half to give to a naked beggar, and Raphael brings the heat of the sun and dawn to battle freezing cold.

2nd: Named after Saint Vitus, Vitusary 16 honors Medard, Catald, and Barbara. Vitus is invoked against storms, but is also the Patron saint of dancers so balls abound in Vitusary. Medard is invoked against bad weather because he sheltered the beautiful queen Angelica, granddaughter of Saint Marie Angelica, when she fled the intrigues of Mervol court during a storm. Medard gave his own tent so she would be safe and dry, so an eagle sheltered him from the weather, creating an umbrella for him as he rested. Catald cured the ill and is invoked against plagues, which often abound from bad weather and Barbara was saved when lightning struck her attackers during a siege.

3rd: Named after Saint Florien, Florias 16 honors Vincent, Jude, & John of Nepomuk (bridges & flooding). Florien is invoked against floods, a common problem in the Saintlands the third month. Saint Vincent Ferrer is the patron saint of builders, often put to work during this time, Jude helps the hopeless and John of Nepomuk strengthens bridges during floods to save the towns.

4th: Named after Saint Elmo, Elmos 16 invokes Fiacre (gardeners), Phocas (market gardeners), & Uriel the Archangel. Elmos starts the sailing season, so Saint Elmo, patron saint of sailors marks this month. Fiacre and Phocas bring the first harvests from winter, began indoors or in warmer climes to feed the masses while Uriel protects the people from the lies and trickery of thieves.

5th: Named after Saint Walburga, Walpurgisnacht 16 invokes Valentine, Rose of Lima, & Theodore of Sykon (reconciling the unhappily married). Walpurgisnacht 1 allows the young and amorous to pursue each other unhindered and as such, this month marks the beginnings of many marriages. Valentine honors true love, Rose of

Lima honors florists and flower growers and Theodore, known for his counseling skills, reconciles the unhappily married, reminding them of the way they felt their first month of marriage.

6th: Named after Saint Wilgefortis, Vilgfort 16 honors Felicity (women wanting sons), Monica (wives), & Marie Angelica (nun who married). Felicity is invoked by women wanting sons, usually royals, due to her miracle of delivering sons whenever she was a woman's midwife. Monica honors wives as she was Heaven's example of a perfect wife and Marie Angelica was a nun who married for the sake of the world. A vision held that Marie Angelica would have a daughter who would alter the church and though she was a nun, she was persuaded to leave her vows to fulfill this vision. Her daughter, Tanglwyst Angelica, inherited a powerful shipping company which was destined for the hands of a corrupt Church. Her sacrifice honors all women who must abandon their own dreams for the sake of a greater good.

7th: Named after Saint Maurice, Maur 16 honors Elizabeth (war), Clara (savior in the Soulless War) and Michael the Archangel. This is the season of war, and thus, the people invoke Saint Maurice to keep their soldiers safe while away from home while Elizabeth is invoked to find peaceful resolutions to wars. Clara was a woman whose role in the Soulless War enabled the plague to be destroyed through the spreading of soil she had walked upon, preventing the plague from crossing it. Michael fought the creatures of Hell to preserve the faithful during the great wars.

8th: Named after Saint Francis, Franco 16 honors Hubert (hunters), Andrew, & Sebastian. Saint Francis honors all animals and those who tend them. Hubert honors the hunters, Andrew the fishermen and Sebastian protects archers.

9th: Named after Saint Thomas Aquinas, Aquin 16 honors Ivo, Augustine, and Albert. The season of scholarly pursuits, Aquin honors those who devote themselves to study. Ivo honors lawyers, Augustine honors theologians and his ideals of Heaven are the basis for the Augustinian Church, and Albert honors scientists and herbalists.

10th: Named after Saint Benedict, Benedine 16 honors Gabriel the Archangel, Giles, & Margaret. As this is a time of darkness descending upon the land and things turning cold, people were often creating tales of ghosts and fear. Those who had died in the wars of the summer or in the professions of the year were often "seen" wandering the desolate places during this month. To counter these tales of fancy, the church brought in their strongest saints against fear and superstition. Saint Benedict fought his greatest fear, being homeless, and opened his home as a shelter. As such, he is their patron saint. Giles protects against night terrors and Margaret defends against those being attacked by devils, enabling their escape. Gabriel the Archangel heralds Heaven's will, driving away doubt and fear.

11th: Named after Saint Ferdinand, Ferdin 16 honors All Saints (Fer 1), Eloi & Anne. To celebrate the survival of the month of fear, All Saints Day was noted as the first Church holiday. It also honors those responsible for the greatest achievements of humanity: Ferdinand for Engineers, Eloi for jewelry and metal smithing and Anne for pregnancy.

12th: Named after Saint Brigit, Brig 16 honors Cosmas & Damian, Raymond, and Roch. A most notable saint, Brigit was one of the first saints ascended to Heaven after giving her life to heal others, and her blood created a fountain by which those who were ill or damaged could be restored. This fountain is in the center of the Papal Palace in the Papal City. Cosmos and Damian are conjoined twins who became doctors, Raymond honors midwives and Roch is invoked against epidemics.

Weekdays

Day 1: Honorasday: named from Honoratus, for bakers.

Day 2: Bernaday: Named after Saint Bernadette, shepherds.

Day 3: Rufinasday: Named after Saint Rufina, potters.

Day 4: Simproniday: Named after Four Crowned Martyrs, stonemasons.

Day 5: Julianusday: Named after Saint Julian, boatmen.

Day 6: Vincentsday: Named after Saint Vincent Ferrer, builders.

Day 7: Wencesday: Named after Saint Wenceslas, brewers.

Day 8: Genesday: Named after Saint Genesius, Actors & Comedians.

Day 9: Columbasday: Named after Saint Columba, poets.

Day 10: Dismasday: Named after Saint Dismas, undertakers.

Appendix C: Religions

Augustinian (AHG-us-TIN-ee-uhn)

The Augustinians believe God made the world and made Heaven. God set up the ability for Man to ascend to Heaven body and soul by doing good works. If a human is good enough and helps enough people, they can become a Saint. Each Saint in the Augustinian Rolls was once a human and their name appears in the Heavenly Roster when they ascend. The Heavenly Roster is a book kept in the Papal City on the Official Altar in the center of the Cathedral under constant guard.

In the 1300s, the Church stopped acknowledging new names in the Roster after The War of the Soulless which they blamed upon the heathen religions. The reason cited for this denial was the War made it difficult to believe all the reports of ascended Saints. At the time, it was unknown by the populace about the Heavenly Roster but after the declaration and an investigation by nobles outside the church, this information was revealed to the public. Regardless, once the Pope responsible passed away and the scandal was uncovered, the new Pope acknowledged the updated Rolls and the new Saints were canonized.

The main Tenant of Faith in the Augustinian religion is the Saints are the world's connection to Heaven. It is only by praying to the Saints that one can communicate with Heaven. It is against the Laws of the Church to pray directly to God, bypassing his appointed representatives, to make requests, though one can offer praise unto Heaven without invoking a particular Saint. However, if one prays to a particular saint for guidance or assistance and they receive it, it is against the laws of the Church to not acknowledge the Saint who answered the prayer.

Emilianite (uh-MEEL-ee-uhn-ITE)

After the War of the Soulless and the Scandal of the Unacknowledged Saints, a group of followers broke away from the Church. Citing corruption in the dictations of the papacy, it was determined that apparently the Church could communicate directly to Heaven without the help of the Saints since they refused to acknowledge the Saints received in the Rolls. They called these Saints "the Abandoned Children" and called themselves Emilianites, after Emilio, the patron Saint of abandoned children.

The Emilianites believe that man cannot be trusted with the will or intent of Heaven through a conduit, for that can be hidden or destroyed. Instead, they believe man can be more assured of correct information if he prays directly to Heaven. If Heaven wants the Emilianites to pray to a Saint, they will communicate that Saint's name to all the Faithful. Until that happens, the Emilianites will pray directly to Heaven. Since the Scandal of the Unacknowledged, no Emilianite has ever noted a Saint's name being given to them. As such, they continue to offer prayers only to Heaven.

Land Worship

The Maker split in two, creating the Heavens and the Land. Both are sentient and great entities unto themselves. Heaven holds the Well of Souls and deals with all things ethereal such as dreams and thoughts, ideas and concepts. The Land deals with all things physical, be it body, plant or liquid. If it can be held, it is the purview of the Land.

When the body dies, the Land takes it into itself and dissolves the flesh, leaving the soul. The soul is filtered and cleansed of the sins of its life and when all the sin is gone, the soul that is left is returned to the Well of Souls. The Land interacts with the people on a daily basis, feeding them, clothing them, healing them. They trust the Land and count on its gifts for life.

Calista's Call

Oceanus, Father of Waters, was alone and lonely. He wandered across the world without drive or direction. Sometimes, to relieve his boredom, he would slice through a mountain or sink an island he made but in the end, he was aimless and alone. Then, one night, he heard a stirring song. It beckoned him from across the Land and he fell upon a beach, kneeling before the singer. A beautiful maiden of silver hair and glowing pale skin sat naked on the beach, her voice filling the night. He crept up behind her and she saw him and screamed, then grabbed her clothes and fled to the sky.

Every night, he went to the beach to fall upon the shore, begging her to return. He brought her gifts from the sea and faraway lands, creatures and stones, wood and plants. Eventually she peeked from behind the curtain of night and slowly emerged, a little more each night, until she fell in love with Oceanus and they made love upon the beach. They created a daughter of rich blue skin like her father and glowing white hair like her mother. They called her Calista and the salt from their tears of joy at the sight of her soaked her, making her touch turn water into salt water.

Calista watches the sea and keeps her secrets and those of her followers. She is a fickle goddess though, and prone to fits of fury that can seem unprovoked. When she is happy or dealing with honorable people, her hair is the white of sea foam. Mermaids gather the honored dead and if a sailor is a good follower, Calista recognizes them and grants them the ability to live underwater as merfolk in her cities. Her dolphins and sea mammals guide ships through treacherous areas and are always signs of her pleasure.

But she has her primal side as well and when dealing with the dishonorable, she sends her teeth to rend them. Her hair turns bloody red and her sharks and sirens call the evildoers to their destruction. If there is an argument in ship at sea and sharks arrive on the scene, it means someone in the fight is lying. If a criminal is sentenced to death at seas, the sharks will take him, but if the criminal is remorseful, they take him to the depths where he becomes a Marked One and serves Calista for as long as they breathed air. Sirens call the unjust to the sharks' maws so if one hears a siren's call, the heavier the sins on their soul, the harder it is to resist them.

If a body is rendered with fire at death, Calista will know them not and shall cast their spirit out of her mouth to walk the earth forever.

The Ancient Ones

Sovereignus was a good king. He loved Magic so much, that he mated with her, and fathered the Fae. The Fae were everywhere. They were the merfolk in the sea and the harpies in the air. They were the pixies and dryads in the trees and the white-furred talking animals in the snows. All the magical creatures, great and small, frolicked in the love of their mother and father. The Fae loved humans and played with them, guiding them to good places and punishing the lazy or wicked with their games and tricks.

But then a sickness came, one that threatened all the magical creatures. Dark men captured the Fae, torturing them to find the sources of Elemental magic. Sovereignus roared and rode to war against these dark men and felled them. In the battle, he was mortally wounded and returned home to die. He gave to his four eldest his power, divided as to their gifts.

To his youngest son Embertwist Apocraphix, he gave the powers of Spring. The Vernal Monarch is the quintessential thief and like a thief, it comes in the night, stealing the cold of winter and revealing the living things beneath her skirt. To his oldest son, Corrigan Starshadow, he gave the powers of Summer. As the Midsummer King, his paladin nature marches forthright towards the good and just.

To his oldest daughter, Calpurnia Allegheri, he gave the powers of Autumn. Calpurnia so resembled his beloved Magic, she channels the gifts of change and harvest during her reign as the Autumnal Sovereign. To his youngest daughter, Corrigan's twin, he gave the power of Winter. Gloriana Talnig, the Midwinter Queen, uses the cold to stop disease and preserve and heal, but also to punish the wicked and delay the unjust. The children split and went to different parts of the world to preserve their realms from the followers of the Dark Men, but each season, they return to Sovereignlumin, the great Tower That Watches All to transfer the power of the seasons.

Karma

Karma is all about balance. For each act, there is an equal and opposite reaction in a person's life. As they get closer to the end of their life thread, they can find themselves bound by the threads they have thrown. Negative acts cause sticky threads, positive acts throw stabilizing threads. If a soul has cast more sticky threads than stabilizing, they can be caught up in the negative and it will strangle them. Thus are many of the symbolic gods of Karma multi-limbed creatures.

The Primordial Egg

The Primordial Egg twitched and cracked and from the shell, four Dragons emerged. They opened their mouths and breathed forth the world. The Earth Dragon formed land and grass, ore and metal, wood and dale. The Water Dragon formed oceans and rivers, lakes and streams, snow and ice. The Fire Dragon breathed the sun and stars to warm the world. And the Air Dragon gave life and the moon. As all things came from magic, all creatures upon the world were magical, and all things communicated with one another in the combined tongue of the elements.

But then, a threat loomed on the face of all and it tried to conquer the magic in the world. It's flashing sword and violent means crushed all but its own belief, slaying the dragons in the world. The Elemental Dragons Rose against it, but to destroy the threat meant to destroy all they loved as well. Instead, they seized their followers and sealed them away in special places. The Earth Dragon hid the giants and Dwarves in the mountains. The Fire Dragon hid her faithful in the ash and lava. The Water Dragon took her children and gave them the ability to breathe water. And the Air Dragon took his children to the sky, to the place between life and death.

At first they spoke aloud to one another, but monsters found their hiding places, so the Dragons broke the world and spoke only in secret languages so none could find their whereabouts. The Earth Dragon spoke through entrails and omens, the Water Dragon through storms. Fire claimed its own hypnotic power and Air spoke through the dead. Together, they all keep the legends and the magic safe, making certain that only those who wish to keep magic in the world can find them.

Fang and Claw

The practice of having an animal choose to join with a person's soul to guide them is standard practice in the followers of Fang and Claw. They also believe in the consuming a part of the animal allows for that animal's superior quality to enter the consumer.

As a rite of passage, warriors of the tribes will hunt a dangerous animal with which to partner. Shaman may not be led by a dangerous animal, but by a wise one such as Snake or Owl. And those who become the Seers find themselves in the company of spiders.

Appendix D: Countries

Caratia (CUH-ray-SHEE-uh)
Capital City: Zara
Native tongue: Caratian (CUH-ray-SHEE-uhn)
Dominant Religion: Land Worship

Glarren (GLARE-uhn)
Capital City: Kilmory (kill-MORE-ee)
Native tongue: Glarren
Dominant Religion: The Ancient Ones

Krakte (KRAHK-tuh)
Capital City: Austra
Native tongue: Krakten
Dominant Religion: Augustinian, Emilianite, the Ancient Ones

Latia (LAH-tee-uh)
Capital City: Cheryb (SHARE-eeb)
Native tongue: Latian (LAH-tee-uhn)
Dominant Religion: Calista's Call

Mande (MAHND)
Capital City:
Other Cities: Pardua, Floren, Roma
Native tongue: Mandian (MAHN-dee-uhn)
Dominant Religion: Augustinian

Mervolingia (MER-vole-LIN-jee-uh)
Capital City: Patras
Other Cities: Rouen (ROO-en), St. Giles, St. Andrew, St. Marguerite
Native tongue: Mervol (MER-vol)
Dominant Religion: Augustinian, Emilianite

Nubia (NOO-bee-uh)

Capital City: Leeus Brul (lee-OOS bruul)
Native Tongue: Fangspek
Dominant Religion: Fang and Claw

The Papal City (PAY-puhl)
Capital City: None
Native tongue: Mervol
Dominant Religion: Augustinian Church Seat

Toledo (toe-LEED-dough)
Capital City: Tuscan
Native tongue: Toledan
Dominant Religion: Land Worship

York (YORK)
Capital City: Landen
Other cities: Canterbury, Kent, Oxford, Cambridge
Native Tongue: Yorkish
Dominant Religion: Emilianite

Yndia (YIN-dee-uh)
Capital City: Yantap (YAN-tap)
Native tongue: Yndian
Dominant Religion: Karma

Yokotama (YO-ko-TAH-mah)
Capital City: Kūki doragon
Native Tongue: Yokotaman
Dominant Religion: Dance of the Air Dragons

About the Author

    Tonya Adolfson has been a member of the Society for Creative Anachronism since 1988 and has met thousands of people with very interesting personas. Many of these people have made it into these books and she is grateful to them for enriching her life.

    Tonya lives in Boise, Idaho with her husband, two children, two housemates, four cats and two dogs and yet, strangely, the house is actually pretty clean.